"It's my son's future, Daniel," Beth said quietly.

"So that weighs against me selling the store." She paused, seeming to consider her decision. "If it were just my concern, I'd turn the offer down."

Daniel nodded. That was only right. "Take your time, Beth. Talk to anyone you want. I'm not in any hurry. Whatever you decide, I won't argue."

"Denke." Relief flooded her face. "I don't want to be at odds with you. No more misunderstandings between us—it's much better to speak honestly, *yah*?"

Daniel immediately thought of his promise—of the thing he should tell her but couldn't. No. He corrected himself even as he had the thought. It wasn't he who should tell Beth. She seemed to take his agreement for granted, so he didn't have to speak.

An image of the life he really wanted arose in Daniel's mind—a picture of himself and Beth together, with Benjy growing up and working beside him. But given his secret, that now seemed very far away, if not impossible…

A lifetime spent in rural Pennsylvania and her Pennsylvania Dutch heritage led **Marta Perry** to write about the Plain People, who add so much richness to her home state. Marta has seen over seventy of her books published, with over seven million books in print. She and her husband live in a beautiful central Pennsylvania valley noted for its farms and orchards. When she's not writing, she's reading, traveling, baking or enjoying her six beautiful grandchildren.

With over seventy books published and millions in print, **Lenora Worth** writes award-winning romance and romantic suspense. Three of her books finaled in the ACFW Carol Awards, and her Love Inspired Suspense novel *Body of Evidence* became a *New York Times* bestseller. Her novella in *Mistletoe Kisses* made her a *USA TODAY* bestselling author. Lenora goes on adventures with her retired husband, Don, and enjoys reading, baking and shopping…especially shoe shopping.

MARTA PERRY

The Amish Widow's Heart

&

New York Times Bestselling Author

LENORA WORTH

Seeking Refuge

LOVE INSPIRED

INSPIRATIONAL ROMANCE

LOVE INSPIRED®

INSPIRATIONAL ROMANCE

PLEASE RECYCLE · THIS PRODUCT IS RECYCLABLE

Recycling programs
for this product may
not exist in your area.

ISBN-13: 978-1-335-41888-3

The Amish Widow's Heart and Seeking Refuge

Copyright © 2021 by Harlequin Books S.A.

The Amish Widow's Heart
First published in 2020. This edition published in 2021.
Copyright © 2020 by Martha P. Johnson

Seeking Refuge
First published in 2020. This edition published in 2021.
Copyright © 2020 by Lenora H. Nazworth

This edition published by arrangement with Harlequin Books S.A.

For questions and comments about the quality of this book, please contact us
at CustomerService@Harlequin.com.

Harlequin Enterprises ULC
22 Adelaide St. West, 40th Floor
Toronto, Ontario M5H 4E3, Canada
www.LoveInspired.com

Printed in U.S.A.

CONTENTS

THE AMISH WIDOW'S HEART

Marta Perry

This story is dedicated, as always,
to the love of my life, my husband, Brian.

With all lowliness and meekness, with
longsuffering, forbearing one another in love;
Endeavouring to keep the unity of the Spirit
in the bond of peace.
—*Ephesians* 4:2–3

Chapter One

Bethany Esch looked at her husband's black jackets, hanging from the wooden pegs on the bedroom wall, and her heart failed her. She took a hasty step backward, bumping into the large box her cousin Lydia was carrying, and fought the panic that filled her.

Lydia dropped the box onto the double bed, catching Bethany's arm when she would have fled from the room, her lively face sobering when she saw Bethany's expression.

"Beth?" Lydia shook her arm lightly. "Komm now. It's time we got busy."

"No, I can't. It's too soon."

Lydia knew her so well. Why didn't she see that Bethany couldn't get rid of James's clothes? Not yet.

"It's been over a month." Lydia hugged her as if to soften the words, but nothing could really ease them. James was gone.

"I know it's hard, but you'll feel better once it's done, and James's things will be a blessing to someone else."

The tears that came so easily filled Beth's eyes. "It doesn't feel like a month. It feels like yesterday."

She lived it again—the township police officer coming to the door late in the evening, his face somber, his voice halting as he described the accident: the Englisch driver going too fast on the narrow road, young and careless, unable to stop when he saw the buggy light.

"I know." Lydia's hand stroked her back in a comforting gesture. "The accident was such a shock. That makes it much worse. But..."

Beth wiped tears away with her fingers. Lydia was right, she supposed. James's death would be easier to face once she didn't have constant reminders. Easier for Benjy, too, and that was the force that strengthened her spine. At four, Benjy didn't understand, but he was beginning to accept the fact that Daadi wouldn't be coming home anymore.

She could hear him now, giggling at something her niece Janie had said. Fourteen and the child of Beth's oldest brother, Janie had been a treasure over the past month, showing up often to watch Benjy or take him to play with her little brothers and sister.

"Yah, okay." She straightened, trying to find a smile. "You're right. I certain sure can't let Benjamin see me falling apart."

"Gut." Lydia gave a brisk nod of approval. "The sooner we start, the sooner we're done. You hand things to me, and I'll fold and pack."

Taking the first jacket from its hook was the hardest. This was the jacket James wore for worship, and she'd always thought he looked so handsome in it, his fair hair even lighter against the black wool. She forced herself to hand it on quickly, resisting the urge to press it against her face.

Somehow, once she'd done the first one, the action

became easier. She was helped along by Lydia's constant flow of chatter, talking about the latest news running through the Amish grapevine of Lost Creek—who was harvesting a big crop of celery, hinting at a wedding soon, how her daad's vegetable stand was doing now that fall was coming on, who had missed worship last Sunday and why. Lydia, with her lively personality and ready laugh, was a good antidote to pain.

"Did I tell you I have a letter from Miriam?" she said now. "She actually got it out quickly this time. I've already added my share, so you can do yours and put it in the mail."

"I'll try," she said, although writing a newsy letter felt like an impossible chore just now.

Miriam Stoltzfus, the third of their trio of cousins, had moved out to Ohio to stay with an aunt and uncle several months ago, and they both missed her. Their round-robin letters weren't a good substitute for seeing her.

The three of them had been closer than sisters since they were babies sleeping on their mammis' laps during worship, born within weeks of each other. Better than sisters, maybe, because they didn't have the rivalry some sisters did: Lydia, lively and mischievous; Miriam, quick and daring; and her, always trying to keep the other two out of trouble.

"You know what Grossmammi would say," Lydia said. "Don't try, just do it."

Beth actually did smile over that—Lydia had caught their grandmother's attitude perfectly. Grossmammi never shrank from any task, no matter how difficult. She had shrunk with age, and her memory might be a little misty, but nothing could quench her spirit. Would Beth ever reach that calm acceptance of what came?

With the hanging clothes packed away, Beth turned to the bureau. It was easier, she found, if she picked things up without concentrating too much on what they were and just passed them on to Lydia. The very act of doing something positive seemed to be lifting her spirits, making her pay attention to what was going on around her.

Family and church members had been in and out constantly for the past month, taking over so much that there'd been little she had to do. And Daniel, James's partner in the general store, had taken care of everything there. She was better for something to do.

At some point she had to talk to Daniel and make some decisions about the store, but not yet.

She reached for the last few items in the drawer, her fingers touching something that wasn't cloth. Paper crinkled under her fingers.

Curious, she pulled it out of the drawer to look at. A half sheet of paper, torn off and folded. Frowning, she flipped it open, read the few words it contained and felt her heart freeze.

Beth stared at the penciled words, trying to comprehend, but her brain felt as chilled as her heart. She forced herself to concentrate, reading the words as slowly as if they were in a language she barely knew.

I have to see you one more time. Meet me tomorrow night at the usual place. Please. Don't fail me.

There was no signature, only a penciled heart shape. No name. No date. But the meaning was clear, wasn't it?

"Beth? What's wrong? Tell me." Lydia's arms came around her, and she sounded almost frightened. Beth knew she must look terrible. As terrible as she felt.

"I can't." She stammered the words out and thrust the paper toward Lydia, glad to have it out of her hand. She clung to a faint hope that Lydia would see something different in the words…something that wouldn't shatter her heart and grind it to dust.

Lydia gasped, and then she was silent, probably trying to take it in as Beth had done.

"Maybe…" Lydia was hesitant, her blue eyes dark and troubled. "Maybe it doesn't mean what it seems to."

She didn't sound as if she believed that any more than Beth did.

"What else could it mean?" Anger and pain broke through the ice that encased her. "Someone…some woman…was meeting James on the sly. The usual place—what else could that mean?"

"Maybe…" Lydia faltered, clearly trying to think of some explanation that wouldn't hurt as much. "Well, maybe it was just someone who had a crush on James. He was attractive, and he could be charming, but it didn't mean anything. You were the one he loved."

She clung to the words. That was true enough, she supposed. James's charm had been what had drawn her to him, back when they were teenagers. With his laughing eyes and his enticing smile, he'd had all the girls in a tizzy at one time or another. But he'd chosen her. He'd married her, promising to be faithful.

Something in her hardened against the pain and grief that threatened to envelop her. He'd promised to be faithful in front of God and the church.

"He was meeting this woman, whoever she was," she

said firmly. She couldn't ignore the obvious. "That's not an old note—the pencil marks are still dark. Besides, I cleaned everything in this drawer not that long ago."

Her mind started to work again, remembering when that had been. Her gaze met Lydia's. "That was no more than a week before the accident. That note wasn't in the drawer then."

Lydia didn't speak. Most likely she couldn't think of another explanation, any more than Beth could. James had been seeing another woman just before he died. It was incredible. Impossible. But it had happened.

"That night," Beth murmured, almost speaking to herself. "He said he'd be working late in the store. What was he doing out on Owl Hollow Road? I never even thought about that...never questioned it."

"You think it was the night the note refers to?" Lydia understood her quickly. "But you can't be sure of that. And you can't go around asking people." She sounded horrified at the thought.

"No, I can't go around asking." Pain forced the words out as she realized what this would mean for her. "I can only go on wearing black and pretending. No one must ever know, especially not Benjy."

No matter what she felt, she couldn't damage Benjy's memory of his daadi. No matter how much it cost her.

But there was one thing she could do. She could find out if Daniel knew where James had gone the night he was supposed to be working at the store. Daniel was James's best friend as well as his partner. If anyone knew James's secret, it was Daniel.

Daniel Miller turned from restocking the canned goods shelf to check the time. The plain round clock on the back wall of the store showed nearly four. Since they closed at five, business should be quiet for the next hour. Time for him to make the visit he'd been putting off for weeks—a visit to Bethany, James's widow.

He still couldn't get used to that word. *Widow.* They were too young to be experiencing this—it was for old people. If it affected him that way, how much harder must Beth be finding it?

Shaking off the question, he rounded the end of the shelves and approached the cash register, where Anna Fisher was taking advantage of their lack of customers to clean the glass-fronted cabinet.

"Anna?"

She glanced up, her round, youthful face responding. "Yah? Something you want me to do, Daniel?"

"Just keep an eye on things for me. I have to run an errand." He smiled, nodding toward the battery section, where his nephew Timothy was replacing batteries in their proper bins. "And you might take a look at those shelves when Timothy finishes. Just in case."

Anna nodded. Fourteen-year-old Timothy had been helping out for only a couple of weeks. They'd needed an extra pair of hands once James was gone.

Timothy was eager, but not always accurate. Still, Anna was responsible, not flighty like most sixteen-year-old girls, and she'd been working in the store for over a year.

"I'll manage everything. Don't worry." She was obviously pleased at being left in charge, but a trace of apprehension showed. "You'll be back to close up, yah?"

"For sure. No worries."

He headed for the door, pausing a moment outside to admire, as always, the General Store sign. They had a good location—he and James had decided the lot between their two properties at the end of Main Street would be just right for the business that was just a dream six years ago.

They'd surmounted plenty of obstacles on the way to making the dream a reality. He'd just never thought he'd be carrying on alone, without James. Pain clenched his heart. James had been his best friend since they'd entered first grade at Creekside Amish School together.

Funny, when he stopped to think about it, that they had linked up so quickly. He was one of seven, growing up on the ninety-acre farm that spread out from the road to the ridge that overlooked the village of Lost Creek. He sometimes felt lost in the midst of siblings, and it had been startling to realize that James's life was so different from his, even though they were part of the same church district.

James's mother was a widow, and James her only child. They lived right in town, and at six, James had known little of the farm life that was so routine for Daniel. But still, they'd been best friends, and when James married Bethany and they bought her great-uncle's holding and orchard, they became neighbors, as well.

The lane at the side of the store led back to Beth's property. Daniel strode along, noticing the signs of autumn beginning to show in the yellowing fields and the bright plumes of the sumac bushes. The leaves hadn't begun to turn yet, and the weather held sunny and warm, but the children were back in school and autumn was on the way. He could see the glint of red here and there in the apple orchard that covered the lower slopes beyond the farmhouse where Beth and little Benjamin now lived alone.

As usual, he felt a twinge at the thought of Beth. How would she manage without James? And just as important, what would she want to do about her share of the store?

He had his own ideas about that, that was for sure. He'd been Beth's friend even longer than he'd known James, since she'd spent a lot of time at her great-uncle's place. In fact, if she hadn't caught James's eye when she did, he might have been the one…

Well, there was no point in letting his thoughts stray in that direction. His task now was to do his best for Beth and her son.

As he neared the house, he caught sight of Benjy in the backyard, tossing a ball back and forth with Janie Stoltzfus, Beth's niece. Instead of heading for the back door, he veered to join them.

"Looks like a gut game. Can I play, too?"

"Catch the ball, Daniel," Benjy shouted, obviously pleased to have the game enlarged. With his silky straight blond hair and his round, chubby face, he still looked a little like the baby he'd been such a short time ago.

Would he have to grow up faster now that his daadi was gone? And at four, how much did Benjy actually realize about death? Daniel didn't have any answers, but he knew that Beth would do her best to protect him. And he would, as well. He owed it to his friend.

Benjy tossed the ball short of Daniel, and he had to sprint forward to catch it.

"Benjy's getting better all the time," Janie said, laughter in her eyes.

Nodding, Daniel sent a soft underhand toss in Benjy's direction. He put it right on target, and Benjy's gratified surprise at catching it made him smile.

"I got it. Did you see, Janie? I caught it."

"Yah, gut job," Janie responded. "Now throw it to me."

Benjy raised the ball to throw, dropped it and went scrambling after it. Daniel took advantage of the moment. "Is your aunt Bethany inside? I need to see her."

"Yah. She was in the kitchen when we came out. Do you want me to go see?"

"That's all right. I'll find her." With a wave, he headed for the house. He tapped lightly on the screen door and went into the mudroom, then on into the kitchen, calling out as he did.

Beth answered, sounding normal, but when she turned from the stove and Daniel saw her face, he was shocked. During the visiting and the funeral after James's death, she'd seemed frozen, hardly aware of her surroundings. Now the ice that had encased her was gone, and he could read her loss too easily.

The gentleness had disappeared from her usually serene oval face, and her skin seemed shrunk against the bones, making her green eyes huge and tragic. Even her light brown hair had lost the curl she tried to suppress, straining back to the white kapp she wore.

He gathered his wits together and struggled to sound normal. "There's a ball game going on in the backyard. Don't you want to join it?"

Beth managed a smile at that, but it was a pitiful attempt. "Not just now. Can I do something for you, Daniel?"

"That's my question. You know I'm here to help with

anything you want." He pulled out a chair from the kitchen table. "Can we sit down for a bit?"

After a moment's hesitation, she nodded, coming to sit in the chair he'd pulled out while he took the one facing it. "How…how is everything at the store?"

There was nothing of interest in her voice. In fact, it seemed that all her attention was turned inward to something that obsessed her to the exclusion of everything else.

"Doing fine." His voice sounded unnatural to him. "In fact, we need to talk about the store. I…" He stopped, shaking his head. "What's wrong, Beth? We're old friends, ain't so? You can talk to me."

A flash of something that might have been anger crossed her face and as quickly disappeared.

"Nothing." Her voice was tart. She pressed her lips together for a moment before continuing. "I'm sorry. You were saying, about the store?"

"Yah." He'd like to press the matter, because it seemed clear to him that even more was wrong than grief, but something told him it wouldn't be welcomed. She was only a couple of feet away across the width of the table, but it might as well be miles.

"I wanted you to know that I've brought my nephew Timothy in to help out, now that James…" He stopped and started again. "We needed a little extra help. Anna's a gut worker, but she's young and needs direction."

He took a breath, deciding he was going in the wrong direction. He didn't want to pile problems on Beth, only keep her up-to-date on the store that was her livelihood.

"Anyway, I thought you'd want to know what was going on. Business is gut, and naturally your share remains the same." He hesitated before going on with what he'd rehearsed saying.

"I thought you might want to be a little more involved now, since it's your business, too. You could come in a few hours now and then, maybe. Or look over the books, if you want."

She'd paid attention for a moment, but now he knew he'd lost her. She'd turned inward again, back to whatever it was that obsessed her. James's death? Tragic as that was, he sensed there was something more going on.

He'd thought to assure her that the store was under control and possibly to interest her in taking a more active role. But that seemed to be the last thing on her mind.

"Beth." He said her name gently, and after a moment her eyes focused on him. "It's all right. I'll keep on with the store the way I have been. I can see you don't want to talk about it now."

She nodded, putting one hand up to her forehead. "Not now," she echoed. "We'll talk later, yah?"

"Later." He stood, disappointed in himself that he hadn't found a way to help her. "Anything I can do, you know I will. I'll see you later, then."

But when he moved toward the door, Beth seemed to come back from wherever she'd been. "Daniel."

He turned, eager to do something—anything—she needed.

"There's something I need to ask you." She hesitated, as if trying to arrange her thoughts, and he waited.

"That last night...the night of the accident." She stopped, obviously struggling, but before he could say anything, she went on. "James said he was going to the store to do inventory."

Now it was Daniel's turn to collect his thoughts. Half-afraid of where she was going, he nodded. "Yah, that's right."

Beth had stood when he did, but now she leaned against the table, her hands planted on the top as if for support. She had always been slim as a young girl, despite having a child, but now she was almost gaunt.

"What took him away from the store? Why was he out on that road where the accident…"

She couldn't finish it, and he had a moment to compose himself. He should have realized that at some point she'd ask that question. He should have prepared an answer. Did she suspect… No, that was impossible.

Well, he couldn't lie to her, so maybe it was just as well he hadn't known where James had gone that night. "I'm sorry, Beth, but I don't know. We'd finished up, and he went outside ahead of me. I saw he had the buggy, but he was already driving out before I had a chance to say anything."

That was the exact truth. What he'd thought…feared, even…he would keep to himself.

"You don't know?" Her gaze was fixed on his face, her eyes enormous.

"I'm sorry." He sought for some possibility. "We'd been talking about adding a few more crafts to the store. Maybe he was going to talk to someone about it."

It sounded feeble, even to him. Why would James be doing that at eight o'clock in the evening?

But to his relief, Beth seemed satisfied. She nodded. Then, without a word, she turned back to the stove.

There was nothing more to say. He slipped out quietly.

It was all right, he assured himself. It had been a natural enough question for Beth to ask, once she'd gotten over the initial shock. There was no reason to think she suspected James of anything wrong.

He'd need to keep it that way. His loyalty to his friend, his deep longing to protect Beth and Benjy... everything combined to insist that whatever his suspicions, they should never be spoken.

By the time Mamm and Grossmammi arrived to take Janie home, Beth had managed to convince herself that she was calm. Unhappily, she was aware that her composure was like a thin sheet of ice, ready to shatter at the slightest breath. She forced a smile and went outside to greet her mother and grandmother. Grossmammi was already chatting with Janie and Benjy, which probably meant that she was having one of her good days, living in the present instead of the past.

"It's gut to see you, Grossmammi." She reached for the line to clip the harness to the hitching rail, but Janie got to it first. Benjy, very intent, helped her to latch it.

Her mother slid down, not waiting for a helping hand, and landed lightly on her feet. With her rosy cheeks and bright blue eyes, she didn't look like the mother of five.

They both reached up to help Grossmammi down. She pressed her cheek against Beth's for a moment, but her attention was on her great-grandchildren.

"My, you two look as if you've been having a fine time. What have you been doing?"

"We played ball. Daniel did, too. And we gathered the eggs," Benjy said. "I found three."

"Gut job." Grossmammi patted his cheek. "How many did Janie find?"

It was apparent that number was beyond him, so Janie helped him out, whispering the number in his ear.

"Eight," he said proudly.

"We'll have scrambled eggs for breakfast, ain't so?" Bethany was pleased that she was able to sound almost normal. She glanced from her grandmother to her mother with a question in her face, but Mammi could only shrug, probably meaning it was hard to tell how long her grandmother would stay grounded.

Mammi lifted a basket down from under the buggy seat. "Who wants a whoopie pie?"

"Me, me!" Benjy bounced up and down, and Janie looked as if she would as well, if not for remembering that she was fourteen now.

"Let's go in and fetch a napkin, and then you two can have yours out on the porch while Mammi gets us grown-ups a cup of coffee."

Beth put an arm around her grandmother as they walked into the house together with Mammi following. It took only a few minutes to settle the kinder with juice and whoopie pies. Then the adults gathered at the table with their treat.

Grossmammi watched as she nibbled at the edge of hers. "Better eat it," she said. "You've lost too much weight in the past month."

"Yah." She couldn't deny it, since the bodice of her dress hung loose on her. "I don't have much appetite."

"Natural enough," Mammi said. "But you must try. Take a real bite now."

Beth obeyed, inhaling the scent of chocolate and savoring the sweet, creamy filling. To her surprise, it actually went down without sticking in her throat.

Grossmammi watched her with satisfaction, her face

alert. Mammi had noticed the alertness, too, because she relaxed a bit.

Her grandmother focused on Beth's face. "Now, tell us what has you upset today."

Beth narrowly escaped biting her tongue. How did Grossmammi know? Still, when she was alert, there was no getting away from her.

"Nothing," Beth said, hoping she sounded convincing. "I'm not upset."

"Ach, Bethany, tell that to someone who doesn't know you like we do." Her mother joined in. "Komm now, tell us. Benjy said that Daniel Miller had been here. Did that upset you?"

"No, no, of course not. He just wanted to let me know about how things are at the store." She hesitated. "Well, and talk about the future, but I... I wasn't ready to do that. He might have waited."

Mammi clucked her tongue. "That's natural enough for him, ain't so? After all, you are his partner now. He'll want to know how things are going to change."

"I suppose so." She felt a flicker of resentment. She'd expected Mammi to be on her side. Not that there were any sides to it. She'd have to focus on business soon. Just not today. "Well, I can stop by the store sometime soon, but I don't know much about running it. James always said I had enough to do with the orchard and the garden and Benjy to look after."

"Yah, that's so." Mammi still studied her face. "You're sure there's nothing I can help with?"

First Daniel and now Mammi wanting to help. But they couldn't, even if she told them, and she didn't intend to do that.

"Nothing," she said firmly.

Mammi rose. "I won't tease you to tell me anything you'd rather not. Just remember we're here, and there are lots of people who love you and want to help."

Grossmammi reached out to touch Beth's cheek. Her grandmother had experienced loss, she knew, and Grossmammi's expression was tinged with sorrow as she looked at Beth. "And God is always ready to listen, ain't so?"

Beth managed a nod, tears stinging her eyes. She wasn't sure she even wanted to pray about this burden. Not now. Now she needed to be alone long enough to figure out how this had happened to her.

Chapter Two

Beth still had her grandmother's words in her mind a few days later when she and Benjy walked up to the orchard together. Grossmammi's advice was good, but Beth's prayers seemed to bounce around until she wasn't sure whether she was talking to the Lord or to herself. She prayed for acceptance, and in the next breath she was railing at James for his deception or wondering how she'd failed that he had turned away from her.

"Look, Mammi, look!" Benjy tugged her along, pointing. "Look at the red apples. Is it time to pick them?"

"Some of them." She steered him away from the McIntosh. They wouldn't be ready for a few more weeks. "Look at that tree. Those apples are called Honeycrisp. Some of them are ready to pick."

Running ahead, Benjy threw his arms around the tree in a hug. He looked up into the branches, standing on tiptoe to reach a ripe apple. "Can I pick it? Can I, Mammi?"

"Yah, for sure. Let me show you how." She closed her hand over his small one. "Twist it just a little while you pull gently. Like this."

The apple came away in Benjy's hand, and he held it up with a delighted smile. "I did it."

Her heart swelled with love. "You did. See if you can reach some other ripe ones. I'll hold that one." She picked up the corners of her apron to form a makeshift basket.

Benjy darted off in search of others he could reach, and she picked a few more, inhaling the rich apple scent. It seemed to carry with it a score of memories—her little brothers vying to see how many they could pick, and Daniel, always kind, boosting the smaller ones up to reach.

Funny, that the orchard didn't carry memories of James. He hadn't been part of that early childhood, when Daniel as a near neighbor had naturally been there to help her uncle with the picking. James, living with his widowed mother in the center of town, had had no place there. Even after they bought Onkel Isaac's place, James had left the orchard to her.

So preoccupied was she with memories that she didn't notice the figure coming toward them until Benjy's shout.

"Grossdaadi!" He hurtled through the grass, his chubby legs churning, and bolted into her father's arms. Daadi lifted him over his head, then gave him a hug and set him down.

"Komm, schnell. See all the apples I picked. They're called Honey…" He looked at his mother.

"Honeycrisp," she prompted. "Because they're sweet like honey and crisp when you bite into them." She polished one against her apron and handed it to him. "Try it."

Grinning, he bit into it, rewarded by a spurt of juice

that dribbled down his chin. "Yummy." The word was muffled by apple, and she and Daad exchanged a smile.

When Benjy ran off to find some more to pick, her father gestured to the rough-hewn bench Onkel Isaac had built long ago. "Komm. Sit."

Once they were settled, he glanced around the orchard. "A gut crop of the Honeycrisps this year. You can sell some at the store, ain't so?"

Beth tensed at the mention of the store, conscious of the fact that she still hadn't had that talk with Daniel. "Did Mammi talk to you about me?"

He patted her hand. "You can't keep folks who love you from talking about you. You wouldn't want to, now would you?"

"I guess not," she admitted. "I suppose you think I ought to make some decisions about the store, too."

Her father paused for a moment, as if considering the matter. "You want some time, for sure. But maybe you're not seeing it from Daniel's point of view. With James gone, you own his share of the store. It's natural that Daniel would be anxious about your plans."

"I guess. But I don't have any plans, not yet." If she could be alone in her grief and betrayal...

"Sometimes I think Daniel is married to that store." Daad's craggy face softened in a smile. "It's natural, ain't so? He doesn't have a wife and kinder, and his father's farm will go to his brother. He's a hard worker. Always has been."

Was he making a contrast with James? She couldn't tell. "James did a gut job with the store," she said, feeling compelled to defend him, despite what she'd learned.

"Ach, yah, I'm not saying he didn't. All the more reason why Daniel wants to know what your plans are."

Daadi studied her face, maybe looking for a sign that she agreed. Then he glanced at the apples again.

"I'll send some of the family over tomorrow to help you do a first picking of apples. Then, if you want to sell them…" He waited, looking at her.

"Yah, all right." There was no getting out of it. "The Honeycrisp should be eaten when they're ready, since they aren't such gut keepers. We'll give some to the family." She forced herself to smile. "And I'll talk to Daniel about selling them."

"Gut." Daadi squeezed her hand, and that was as good as praise. "I can stay with Benjy while you go and see him. We'll go ahead and pick a basket for you to take to him."

She hadn't meant now, and she suspected Daad knew it. Still, if she must do it, it was better done now. And the same held true about making decisions for the future.

Daniel glanced up from the low shelf he was arranging at the sound of the bell and started to rise. He stopped for an instant before completing the movement. It wasn't his imagination. It was Beth.

He headed for her, relieved to think she was doing better. She must be, since she was here. Another step brought him close enough to chase that idea away. If anything, Beth looked even worse than she had the day he'd stopped by to see her. Strain had drawn her skin tautly against the bones of her face, and her cheeks seemed hollow. It was like seeing her when she was very old, and he could hardly keep from exclaiming at the sight.

For a moment he couldn't speak. Realizing that every customer in the store seemed similarly affected, he forced himself to say her name. "Beth, wilkom. I'm wonderful glad you came by today."

With a quick movement, Beth thrust the basket she carried at him. "Honeycrisp apples," she said, as if that was an explanation for her presence.

He saw the movement of her neck when she swallowed, and then she went on.

"We're going to do the first picking of the early apples tomorrow. Do you want a few baskets to sell? If you think anyone will want them, I mean."

"I'm certain folks will—"

An Englisch customer moved closer to peer at the basket. "Honeycrisp, did you say? I can hardly ever find them. I'll stop by on Friday morning. Hold a peck for me, will you?"

"Yah, I'll be glad to, Mrs. Warren."

"Good." She darted a curious glance at Beth before moving on to look at the bread case.

"There's your answer, ain't so?" Daniel smiled. "If you need any more help to pick, I can send my nephew over."

"Denke, but my daad is coming with some of the young ones."

"Your daad will get the job done fast. I remember what he was like when we all helped your onkel to do it. He's not one to take excuses."

She actually tried to smile at that. "He's still the same. He's watching Benjy right now so I could come over."

"Whether you wanted to or not," he finished for her.

"You did say we needed to talk about the store, ain't so?"

He touched her arm lightly and gestured. "Let's go to the back room. There should be coffee on." He raised his voice. "Anna?"

Anna Fisher, their sixteen-year-old clerk, sidled in from the storeroom and stopped. Shy, he supposed, at the sight of the new widow. Like everyone, she'd been shocked by James's death.

"Take charge for a few minutes. We'll be in the back, talking."

She nodded, moving behind the counter without wasting a word. He'd been doubtful at first that someone so shy would be successful as a clerk, but she'd surprised him. He was thankful for her now, with James no longer here to help.

Leading the way, he took Beth to the room that served as a combination office and break room. Sure enough, there was coffee staying warm on the small gas stove. While he got out cups and spoons, his mind worked busily, trying to figure out the best approach to this conversation. If he had his way, Beth would come in as a partner, and together they'd keep the store going as it was. But that might not be Beth's idea of a future.

He turned to the table, sitting down across from her as he put the coffee mugs in place. "How are you, Bethy?" The childhood nickname had come up without his thinking about it, but it actually made her face lighten a little.

"All right, I guess." But then her expression closed down again, negating her words. It made him want to grasp her hand, the way he'd have done when they were children and something had frightened her.

But he couldn't, of course. They were grown-ups now, and Beth was the widow of his best friend. He would help her in any way he could while still respecting her position.

Daniel cleared his throat, trying to find the way forward. "I... I hoped you might have made some decision about the store."

"Daadi said something about that, too." Beth ran her hand across her forehead, as if brushing away cobwebs. "I'm being stupid, I guess. James never talked about business with me. I don't even know how I stand and whether I have enough to support my son."

The thread of what might be anger in her voice startled him. He'd never heard her say anything critical about James. He must be mistaken. Beth had always adored James.

He'd have to assure her as best he could. "You needn't worry about supporting Benjy. You own half the business now, and we're doing pretty well. And you own the house and the orchard free and clear, ain't so?"

She nodded, her expression easing. "Yah, you're right. Onkel Isaac made it easy for us to buy. He was wonderful gut to me."

"Your uncle was a fine man, and a gut neighbor, as well." Little Beth had been his favorite among his many nieces and nephews, so it wasn't surprising that he'd wanted to protect her. "You want to stay where you are, then?"

"Yah, for sure. I never thought of anything else." She glanced up at him, a question in her green eyes. "As for the store...well, what else can we do but carry on as we are?"

It was tempting just to agree, but Beth ought to consider her options before she came to a decision.

"You do have other choices. If we go ahead as we are, we might have to hire another helper. Or you could come in and help. Even a few hours a week might be enough." He took a breath. "Or you might want to sell your share of the store."

There, it was out. If she did want to sell, he'd have no choice but to make the best of it.

"Sell?" She'd obviously never considered it. "Do you mean you want to buy my share?"

"No." Daniel couldn't get the word out fast enough, and it startled him. He hadn't realized he felt so strongly about it. "I mean, I'm afraid I couldn't afford it, not yet, anyway. But even if I could…" He struggled to articulate what he felt about the store.

"James and I took a risk when we started this place, but it's paid off. We liked working together. I guess now I'd like to think of Benjy growing up and becoming my partner, working beside me." He seemed to see the boy grown up, with his mother's sweetness and loving heart as well as his father's laughter and charm. "The store is his legacy from his father, ain't so?"

At his words, an expression he couldn't begin to interpret crossed Beth's face. He'd known her most of their lives, but he'd never seen her look like that before.

It was gone again, leaving him feeling disturbed without knowing why. "What do you think?"

Beth was silent for a moment, her gaze seeming fixed on something he couldn't see. Then she let out a long breath. "For now, I'd like to go on the way we are. But maybe that's not fair to you. James isn't here to do his share of the work, so we can't take his share of the profits. It wouldn't be right."

He hadn't expected that, and maybe he should have. Beth, for all her softness, had a strong sense of what was right.

"We can work that out," he said. "Like I said, we could hire someone else. Or you might want to spend some time helping out, ain't so?"

He could see how that idea shook her, could anticipate the instant refusal coming.

"I… I can't. I've never done anything like that. And anyway, I can't leave Benjy."

Again, he had that longing to reach out and take her hand. "Not full-time, no. But why don't you come in for a few hours a day? You can bring Benjy with you. He'd enjoy it."

"I don't know…"

He sensed her considering it and pressed his advantage. "It makes sense, Beth. You ought to see the operation for yourself. Maybe look over the books and get a little understanding of how it works. It's part yours now, yah?"

She rose, and he stood up with her. It looked as if she'd leave without a decision, but then she nodded. "I can't promise more, but I'll come in one day. Not tomorrow, but soon."

He'd have to be content with that for now. But he for sure wanted to know what was behind her reluctance.

The next afternoon Beth stood in the driveway, waving as her father's horse-drawn wagon reached the main road and turned in at the store. The apple-picking had been enjoyed by all the young cousins. She'd been expecting someone to fall out of a tree, but Daad had kept a stern eye on his grandchildren, so there'd been no horseplay.

Each of them had taken a small basket home with them. They'd stopped at the store to deliver ten peck baskets of apples. There'd be more in a few days, but she'd wait to see how the first ones sold. She didn't want to burden Daniel with anything he couldn't sell.

She was starting toward the back door when she saw a buggy turn into the drive. Company for her? She gave her skirt a quick shake, hoping she didn't have any leaves or twigs caught in her clothes. Then she recognized Lydia, so she smiled and waved, walking to the driveway to meet her cousin.

"How nice. I'm having lots of company today." She fastened the line to the hitching post. "Wilkom, Lydia."

Lydia gave her a quick hug and stood back for a moment, scanning her face. She gave an approving nod. "You look better today. Gut!"

"Always better for seeing you." They linked arms as they walked into the house. "Tea or coffee?" She usually preferred tea in the afternoon, but sometimes Lydia liked coffee. "I have a pot I made for Daad."

"Coffee, then." She took the chair she usually sat in for their afternoon break. "I saw your daad at the store. Looked as if they were unloading apples."

"Yah, we did the first picking of the early apples. I'll put some in a basket for you to take home. Tell your mamm they're Honeycrisp."

"I'll do that. Denke." She took the mug of coffee Beth handed her. "All right, tell me. Why *are* you looking better today?"

Beth shrugged, taking her seat. "I'm not sure. Just

being busier helps, I guess. The apple-picking today, and yesterday I went to the store to talk to Daniel." She frowned a little at the thought of what she'd promised. "What about you? Have you been working a lot?"

Lydia nodded, making a face. "Waitressing at the coffee shop isn't a very challenging job. Sometimes I wish the regulars would order something different, just for a change."

"Why should they? You have the same thing every day for breakfast at home, don't you?"

"That's different. I have whatever Mamm cooks. If I had my way, I'd fix something different every day."

Beth couldn't help but smile. Lydia always claimed to long for something different, but she went on in the usual Amish routine all the same.

"Laughing at me?" Lydia said. "Ach, I deserve it. I should be ashamed to complain. Never mind that, anyway. Tell me what Daniel wanted."

Now it was her turn to grimace. "Everyone keeps pushing me to make some decisions about the store, and I can't think of anything but...well, you know."

"Yah, I know." Lydia reached across the table to clasp her hand. "Did anything new come to light?"

"No. I asked Daniel where James was going that last night, but he didn't know."

"You think he was meeting that woman, whoever she was? It might not be that at all."

"Then what was he doing out on Owl Hollow Road?"

Lydia didn't have an answer to that. After a moment she countered with another question. "What exactly did Daniel say?"

She rubbed the tense muscles in the back of her neck. "He said they'd been working on something in the store, and when they were about finished, James went out first. I guess he thought James was just going home."

"So James didn't say anything to him."

Was there doubt in Lydia's voice? She couldn't be sure. But Daniel wouldn't lie to her. "If he'd known where James was going, he'd have told me." She clenched her teaspoon so hard her fingers stung. "Now I'm supposed to take over our share of the store, and I don't know a thing about it."

Lydia glanced down at the liquid in her mug, as if mulling something over. "I was always a little surprised that you didn't help out in the store sometimes, especially once Benjy wasn't a baby anymore."

"That's the way James wanted it. He said I had enough to do with Benjy, the house, the garden and the orchard. I never questioned it."

She'd grown so used to the fact that she'd never really wondered about it. Plenty of women with families helped out in the family business.

"It would be easier now if you had been more involved, but I don't suppose James envisioned a time when he wouldn't be there." Lydia glanced at her, as if to be sure her words hadn't hurt.

"Yah, it would be. I don't believe James ever considered the need. After all, his mother never did work outside the home, and she just had the one child and the little house in town."

Lydia's dimples showed at the mention of Beth's mother-in-law. "It's certain sure Sarah Esch never thought of anything on her own. I've never seen a woman so...so passive in my life."

Beth had to suppress a smile. "Sarah is like a soft, fluffy pillow you can push into any shape." Fearing that sounded critical, she hurried on. "But she's a wonderful, sweet mother-in-law."

"I guess." She hesitated. "Pillows are all very well to rest on, but they don't help you get anything done. And she always doted on James. Spoiled him, some folks say."

"He was all she had." Beth felt compelled to defend her mother-in-law, but it was true that Sarah's fluttering over James and then over Benjy drove her wild sometimes. "She's another person who can never know the truth."

"I guess not. But I just wish you didn't have to carry this burden all alone."

"I have you," Beth said softly. "Denke."

Lydia wiped her eyes and then chuckled. "We'd best find something else to talk about before we're both crying. So what are you going to do about the store now?"

"Daniel has this idea that I should start going in for a few hours a day. That way at least I can learn something about the business, but—"

"But what? It sounds like a gut idea to me," Lydia said. "Unless you're thinking to sell your share?"

"Daniel said something about the store being Benjy's legacy from his father, and it's true. If I sell, we'd have the money, but money isn't everything. Benjy wouldn't have the store."

"You don't have to decide right away, do you? Why not try Daniel's suggestion?" Lydia was practical, as always. "Maybe you'll find a way to be a real partner in the business."

The very thought sent a shiver through her. "I don't know that I can."

"Why not?" Lydia's voice was brisk. "You're smart,

and you're a hard worker. And you don't want to turn into a fluffy pillow, ain't so?"

Halfway between laughing and crying, Beth threw a napkin at her. "All right. Don't be so bossy. I'll try. I'll go in and see what it's like, but that's all."

"Tomorrow," Lydia said firmly.

Beth wished she had another napkin to throw. "Tomorrow. I promise."

She just hoped she wouldn't regret it.

Chapter Three

For Beth, the walk down the driveway to the store the next day went too quickly. She'd agreed to spend the morning learning about the store, but that didn't mean she wanted to become part of it. Maybe she and Daniel could figure out some other way...

"Hurry up, Mammi." Benjy, in a rush as always, tugged at her hand. "I want to see what we're going to do at the store."

"I told you, remember? I must learn how the store works. And you have your jigsaw puzzle to work on and your farm animals to play with."

"Can't I help? Please?" He looked up at her, his bright blue eyes, so like his father's, pleading.

She had to guard against the temptation to give in when he looked at her that way. "You'll have plenty of time to work when you're older. Komm, let's go in."

Despite her words, she was the one who hesitated as they neared the glass door at the front of the cinder block building. She remembered the good-natured arguments between James and Daniel when they planned the store. Daniel had been cautious, thinking it should be smaller, but James had laughed at him, saying he should have more confidence in their success. In the end, James had prevailed, as he so often did.

But he'd been proved right, hadn't he? The store was a success. Grasping Benjy firmly by the hand, she pushed the door and stepped inside.

Daniel came forward immediately, smiling in welcome. "Ach, Beth, wilkom. And you, Benjy." He gestured, and the other two people in the store came forward. "You remember Anna Fisher, don't you? She's been working for us for about a year."

The teenager gave Beth a quick glance before lowering her eyes again. Given how shy Anna was, it wondered Beth that she could wait on customers, but from what James had said about her, Anna was a conscientious worker.

"It's gut to see you again, Anna. I understand the store couldn't get along without you."

A flush brightened the girl's pale cheeks. "Denke," she murmured.

Poor child. Everyone knew what a disagreeable person Hiram Fisher was, and Beth didn't imagine he was any better with his daughter. No wonder the girl looked as if she'd wilt at a sharp word.

Thinking Anna would relax once the attention was off her, Beth turned to the third person, who waited next to Daniel.

"This is one of your nephews, ain't so? Timothy, right?"

The boy grinned, his blue eyes dancing. He must be about fourteen or fifteen to be out of school, but he looked younger with that mischievous grin and the freckles that dotted his nose.

"Yah, Timothy, that's me."

"My brother Seth's oldest," Daniel added. "He's been helping us out since…for the last few weeks."

Since James died, he meant. She'd have to convince them that they didn't need to fear mentioning him, even if it was difficult.

"That's wonderful gut of you, Timothy."

"Denke." And then, as if it burst out of him, he added, "I really like it. Maybe I'll have a business of my own one day."

Daniel reached out to ruffle his hair, smiling. "You're a far distance from that just now, young Timothy. You have some stocking to do, ain't so?"

Nothing seemed to disturb Timothy's grin. "Bossy," he muttered, and drifted off. Anna took advantage of the opportunity to slip away as quietly as a mouse.

Benjy tugged at Beth's skirt. "Everybody is working, Mammi. I want to work, too."

"Not today." She handed him the bag containing his toys. "We'll find a place to set up your puzzle."

He took the bag but obviously had something else to say. "Grossdaadi said that one day part of the store would be mine. I should help."

"Not today, I said." She was aware of Daniel listening and suspected he was disapproving.

Benjy got his mulish look, but before he could say anything, Daniel intervened.

"Komm, let's find a table where you can work your puzzle." He held out his hand to Benjy. "Maybe you can help me set the table up, all right?"

One thing she could say for Benjy—he was easily distracted. He trotted along after Daniel, and she had time to breathe for a moment.

What would Daniel think of her, being so sharp with her son? She could hardly tell him why being in the place so associated with James had set her nerves on edge. Was it here that James's involvement with the woman started? It seemed likely.

But when Daniel returned after he and Benjy had set up a folding table and Benjy had dumped out the puzzle pieces, he didn't appear to be thinking any such thing.

"Since you haven't been here much, why don't we start off with a walk around, just to remind you where everything is?"

Beth nodded, and together they checked out the small break room, where the coffeepot steamed, and took a look in the storeroom, which stretched across the back of the building. Timothy was there, loading what looked like heavy boxes of canned goods onto a cart. He glanced up with a grin before turning back to the boxes.

"We have a pretty fast turnover most of the time, so we try to stay ahead of what's going to be needed," Daniel explained, gesturing toward the marked cartons. "It's been a big help having Timothy here. In fact…" He stopped, as if reconsidering what he was going to say.

Before she could ask, he'd moved on. "Here's the office. All the book work is done here. If you want to go over the books, I'll be glad to show you where everything is."

She had a quick vision of James sitting at the desk, his hair ruffled as he struggled with figures. "Not right now," she said. Then, unable to resist prodding the pain of picturing him, she added, "Did James do the record keeping?"

Daniel chuckled. "Not James. He didn't like jobs that required sitting still. He enjoyed interacting with the customers and the suppliers, so he took care of that side of things."

"It was kind of you to let him do the job he liked." But with his outgoing personality, James had probably done it well.

Daniel shrugged. "James was used to getting his way."

She gave him a sharp look, but it was apparent that wasn't meant as an insult. It was simply the truth. James did usually get his way, and things seemed to turn out as he wanted.

When they got back to the store proper, several customers had come in. Anna was busy in the baked goods section, leaving no one at the checkout counter. Beth expected Daniel to head there, but instead he gave her a hopeful look.

"Would you mind running the checkout counter for a bit? A fresh produce order should be coming in, and I need to talk with the driver. There's an adding machine on the counter, and the price should be marked on everything."

"I guess I could do that." She felt shy taking it on, but surely it couldn't be that hard. If she kept busy, maybe she'd stop picturing James everywhere she turned.

The gratitude in Daniel's face chided her. She had given little thought, enmeshed in her own misery, for how this affected Daniel and the business.

"I'll shout if I need help, yah?"

Daniel's smile lit his normally serious face, making her think of how James had teased him, saying it made him look like an old man. Pushing the thought away, she hurried to the counter.

The first couple of checkouts were easy. The customers were from her own church district, so all of them had already had opportunities to express their condolences. They still all commented on how good it was to see her out of the house, but she could handle that.

Several people commented on the Honeycrisp apples, knowing that they'd have come from her orchard. She was a little surprised at the lift that gave her. The fruits of the orchard were her products, maybe that was why.

By taking a few steps, she could see around the nearest counter to where Benjy sat. He'd been working on his puzzle, but soon he had given that up, and he seemed to be putting his miniature farm animals into and out of a barn improvised from a box.

When she turned back to the counter, she recognized Ellen Schultz heading toward her, wearing an expression composed of sorrow and curiosity mixed. Beth braced herself. Ellen belonged to the sister church district, which shared the same bishop, so this was her opportunity to express condolences.

"Ach, Beth, I didn't think to see you in the store. Poor thing." Ellen grasped her hand, and ready tears welled in the woman's eyes. "I'm that sorry for your loss. James is safe with God, but you are left to carry on, ain't so?"

Clearly the woman didn't expect an answer. That was just as well, since Beth didn't have one. Would James be with the Lord, despite the pain and betrayal he'd left behind? She hadn't considered it, and she didn't want to.

"Denke, Ellen. You're so kind."

As she added up Ellen's bill and collected the money, she let the flow of commiserations go in one ear and out the other. How long, she wondered, would it take for people to stop thinking of her as "poor Beth"?

With a few more expressions of sympathy, Ellen car-

ried her packages out the door. Beth took a deep breath,
relieved that no one else was headed to the counter at
the moment. She'd just check on Benjy…

She moved the few steps that let her see the table.
The table was there all right, with Benjy's puzzle scattered on top of it and the farm animals in their barn.
But Benjy wasn't there. Panic gripped her heart. Benjy
was gone.

Daniel was carrying a carton of lettuce through the
storeroom when Beth rushed through the door, her face
white and her eyes filled with panic. Shoving the carton
onto the nearest table, he raced toward her.

"Beth, what's wrong? What happened?"

"Benjy! I can't find Benjy." She stared frantically
around the storeroom. "Benjy! Are you in here?"

"Easy, slow down." He clasped her arm to keep her
from rushing off. "He can't have gone far. Are you sure
he isn't in the store?"

"He's gone. I just turned away for a few minutes
to check out a customer, and when I looked again, he
wasn't there." Her voice shook on the words.

"He probably got bored and went to look around,
that's all. Komm, you can't help by panicking. I'll help
you look."

Beth shot him an angry glance, but then she sucked
in a breath and nodded.

They separated to move quickly through the storeroom, although Daniel felt reasonably sure the boy
couldn't have gotten in. The latch on the storeroom
door was too high for Benjy to reach, he'd think.

They met back at the door. "He must be in the store,"

he said, trying to keep any doubt out of his voice. For sure Benjy would be there. Where else could he be?

"Just stay calm," he said, holding the door for her. "There's nowhere else he could have gone."

Her eyes widened, as if what he'd said had frightened her. "The door. What if he slipped outside? It's so close to the road—" She didn't finish, just darted toward the front door.

Daniel let her go, knowing there was no sense in trying to stop her. She was frightened, and that wasn't surprising. Only a month ago she'd buried her husband, and the responsibility for their child must weigh heavily on her. The best thing he could do was to look for Benjy himself in the most likely places. He started through the aisles.

And sure enough, the most likely place it was. Benjy stood behind a stack of boxes, peering around them at Timothy, who was unloading cans of vegetables.

Safe enough. And natural, too, that the boy would be looking for some activity after sitting so long. Any smart, active four-year-old would want to be part of things.

Leaving them without speaking, Daniel headed for the front door. Through the glass door he could see Beth looking up and down the road for any glimpse of her son. The anguish on her face ripped at his heart.

He covered the remaining space to the door in a few swift strides, shoved it open and reached her. "It's all right. He's fine. He's inside."

Beth's green eyes, dark with worry, searched his face and saw the confidence there. She let out a long breath. "Thank the gut Lord. Where is he?" She started toward the door, as if to rush in and scoop him up.

He clasped her wrist to stop her, feeling it pound against his palm. "Wait, Beth. Calm down. Benjy doesn't think he's missing. You don't want to scare him, ain't so?"

For an instant he thought she'd flare up at him, but then she seemed to struggle for control. She took a deep breath, and then another.

"You're right. I guess I overreacted. When he wasn't where I expected him to be, it just seemed to wash me off my feet."

"I know. With everything…with losing James…it's natural you'd be off balance."

She nodded. Letting out another long breath, she managed a slight smile. "All right. I can behave now. Let's go in."

They walked back toward the canned goods, and he could almost feel the tension in her making her long to grab Benjy and fuss over him. He was tempted to repeat his warning, but if she resented it, he'd have done more harm than good.

When they reached the last row of shelves, Beth stood quietly, just watching the two boys. Relieved, he stood behind her and looked over her shoulder.

Benjy stood next to Timothy, who was kneeling on the floor, transferring cans from the boxes to the shelves. "…each kind of vegetable has its own place," Timothy was explaining. "See, I look at the picture on the can and then at the cans on the shelf. This one is corn, so where do you think it goes?"

His small face serious, Benjy studied the shelves. "There!" he said, triumph in his voice. He pointed to the right place, and Timothy, grinning, put the can in its spot.

"Gut." Benjy hesitated. "Can I put some on the shelves? I could help you."

Now it was Timothy's turn to hesitate. "If your mammi says it's okay." He nodded toward them. "Why don't you ask her?"

Benjy spun around, seeing them for the first time. "Can I, Mammi? Can I help Timothy?"

The last of Beth's tension seemed gone. "If Timothy is willing to show you, that's fine. But mind, if he has to do something else, you don't pester him. All right?"

Benjy's smile was like sunshine breaking through the clouds. "I won't, Mammi. I'll do just what Timothy says."

"Gut." Beth turned, coming face-to-face with Daniel. He stepped back. He was pleased to see her smiling as they walked away.

"I hadn't thought of that," she murmured. "That's how we learned, yah? By standing next to someone, learning and then trying it ourselves."

"That's it, for sure. Remember when your onkel taught us how to pick the apples? He was a patient man, letting a bunch of kids like us loose in his orchard."

"I remember." Her face eased into a smile. "Denke, Daniel. I'm glad I brought Benjy."

By the next afternoon, Beth regretted she'd said those words. Benjy seemed determined to turn their visit to the store into a regular routine. He was dismayed to find they weren't heading out first thing the following morning. After his third complaint, Beth knelt beside him.

"I know you like going to the store, and we'll do it again. But not today," she added, before he could burst into speech. "This afternoon the cousins are coming to pick apples again, remember? We have to be here."

Benjy wasn't one to be discouraged at a single obstacle. "But this morning—"

"This morning I have my regular work to do so I can be free for the apple-picking. And you're going to clean up your bedroom."

The firmness in her voice must have told him argument was useless. He headed toward the stairs, his steps dragging. Suppressing a smile, she turned back to the breakfast dishes.

Benjy was a good boy. He liked to get his own way, but what four-year-old didn't? If he had a little brother or sister, he'd have learned to be more flexible, she supposed. Now…well, now she couldn't see that it would ever happen. She'd have to take extra care not to spoil him.

Despite Benjy's enthusiasm for the store, she couldn't help wondering how long it would last if she committed to working a regular schedule. She could have someone watch him, but she hated the idea of leaving her little one with someone else.

But how else could she do her share of the work? The business belonged to her and Daniel now, and it wasn't fair to him if she didn't contribute something to the store. The issue swirled around and around in her mind, making her dizzy with indecision. She felt a wave of anger toward James for dying and leaving her in this predicament, and an instant later she fell to her knees, praying for forgiveness.

"Mammi?" Benjy's voice penetrated her misery. "What's wrong? Did you fall down?"

The tremor in his voice brought her back to her

senses. She pressed her palms against the braided rug in front of the sink.

"No, no, I'm fine. I thought I dropped a pin, that's all." She rose. "All finished upstairs?" At his nod, she went on. "Let's go out and check for eggs, then."

Benjy was easily distracted, but her conscience continued to trouble her for the next few hours. Anger might be a natural response, but for the faithful, it was one to be conquered. Whatever wrong James had done, it was vanished in God's forgiveness now.

Beth had just cleared up from lunch when she heard the rattle of the wagon coming down the drive.

"Mammi, they're here!" Benjy had been perched on the back porch steps, watching eagerly for any sign of his cousins.

"I'm coming." She hurried out to welcome them, surprised to see Daniel sitting in the back of the wagon next to her brother Eli and several of her nieces and nephews.

"Wilkom. I can see we'll get a lot of picking done this afternoon with all this help."

"Hop on," Daad said. "We'll take the wagon up to the orchard so we can load easily."

"You go ahead. I'll fetch the baskets."

Even as she was speaking, Daniel slid down and lifted Benjy into the wagon. "I'll give you a hand," he said.

"Denke, but shouldn't you be at the store this afternoon?"

"I thought it would be gut for Anna to be left in charge for a bit. Besides, the sooner we get the apples picked, the faster we'll sell them. I've had folks asking for them."

Giving in, she led the way to the shed where she'd

stored the baskets. He bent to pick up a stack of them, and she followed suit, wondering if he were trying to make her feel good about the apples. But it was true that the first few baskets they'd taken in had sold quickly.

Beth half expected him to bring up the idea of her coming to work at the store on a regular basis, but he didn't, just chatting easily about the orchard and reminding her of other days of apple-picking.

When they reached the early apple trees, Daniel dropped his stack of baskets and began to hand them out.

Daad grabbed one. "Let's get started. Eli, you and Daniel might bring the stepladder. I don't want these young ones climbing too high."

"Ach, we can do it, Grossdaadi." Eli's twelve-year-old, Joshua, was brimming with confidence, and she hoped Benjy wasn't going to emulate him.

"The last time you climbed too high and Daadi had to get the ladder to bring you down," Janie said, flattening him as only an older sister could.

"That was years ago," he protested.

Eli and Daniel, coming from the shed with the stepladder, overheard some of it, and Eli frowned at both of them. "No fussing, you two. And, Joshua, you listen to Aunt Beth. They are her trees, ain't so?"

Joshua grinned, unrepentant. "Yah, I will."

"That one's as full of mischief as his daadi was," Daniel commented, seizing a basket. "I remember Eli clowning around when we were picking once and breaking a branch. Your onkel laid into him something fierce."

Before Beth could answer, Benjy tugged at her skirt. "Mammi, where's my basket? I have to pick."

"Right here," Daniel said quickly. "You and I are partners, ain't so?"

"Yah!" Benjy's face lit up, and he grabbed the basket. "Hurry, before they pick all the apples."

"We can't let that happen." His eyes laughing, Daniel winked at Beth and went off with her son.

Beth stood where she was for a moment, not sure how she felt about letting Benjy go off with someone else. *Foolish*, she scolded herself. *You can trust Daniel, and you don't want to tie Benjy to your apron strings.*

Grabbing a basket, she headed for the tree where young Janie was picking.

"The apples are wonderful gut," Janie said, putting her foot in the crotch of the tree and moving higher. She'd hung a smaller basket around her waist so that she didn't have to climb up and down and was picking with quick, deft motions.

"Yah, they are. It's the best crop of Honeycrisp we've had in several years. They're choosy about the weather." She seemed to hear her uncle's voice echoing in her head. "That's what Onkel Isaac always said."

Janie nodded. "You'll be able to sell a lot in the store." She hesitated, looking as if she wanted to say something more.

Beth smiled at her, thinking how dear this sweet niece was to her. "Did you want to ask me something, Janie?"

Smiling back, she ducked her head. "I was just thinking… Daadi said you maybe would be working in the store more. If you are, I could watch Benjy for you, couldn't I?"

Every member of her family seemed to think they knew what she ought to do. Or what she planned to, which was more than she did. Still, this was the obvious answer to one of her concerns.

"I don't know yet what I'm going to do," she said carefully. "But if I do work at the store, I think that would be a fine idea."

Janie's eyes danced, probably at the idea of having an actual job. "I'd like that. Anytime you need me."

Putting a couple of apples in her basket, Beth stretched her back. When she looked across the orchard, she could see Daniel holding Benjy up to pick some apples high over his head.

Benjy showed no fear, she realized. He trusted Daniel just as he trusted his family. He wasn't afraid of the future.

The thought struck her. Was that what was behind her reluctance to take her place as Daniel's partner? Fear?

There was no need for fear. Wariness, maybe. She didn't think she could ever trust a man in the way she'd trusted James—blindly sure that she knew him. But it wasn't that holding her paralyzed.

She felt as if she were poised on a stone in a rushing creek, longing to stay in the familiar place, but knowing she couldn't. Knowing it had already crumbled under her feet.

It was time to move forward. Everyone, it seemed, knew that but her.

Beth set her basket down. "I'll be back in a minute, Janie."

Without waiting for a response, she headed toward Daniel. When he spotted her, he lowered Benjy to the ground, watching her warily.

Did he think she was going to protest his boosting Benjy up in the tree?

"Are you two getting lots of apples?"

Benjy beamed at the question. "Look, Mammi. Me and Daniel picked half a basket already."

Beth touched his soft cheek. "We always put the other person first, remember?"

He ducked his head. "Daniel and me."

Daniel's mouth twitched at that, and she had to suppress a smile. At the moment she was teaching the Amish way, not grammar.

"Better," she said. She looked up at Daniel. "I just wanted to ask. Which is best for the business—for me to work mornings or afternoons?"

He understood, and his face lit much as Benjy's had. "Either is gut. Denke, Beth. I'm glad."

She took a deep breath and tried to settle the qualms she felt. She'd committed herself now, and she'd have to go through with it.

Chapter Four

Beth held Benjy's hand as they walked out the driveway early the next morning. She tried not to smile at his solemn expression as he trotted along beside her, very conscious of his black suit and white shirt. The serious nature of his Sunday clothing always made him just a little more eager to appear grown up, not that any clothing could do that. The sweet curve of his neck and his rosy cheeks still reminded her of babyhood.

She couldn't say that she took much pleasure from her widow's black clothing. Not that she was prideful about her appearance—that would be wrong. But black seemed to draw all the color from her face, making her look older than her years. Or maybe it was the grief and pain that had this effect.

They reached the road and fell in with the other families from along their road. Worship this morning was at Sam and Miriam Shuler's barn, no more than a half mile away. Had it been much farther she'd have waited for Mamm and Daad to pick her up in the family carriage. They had offered to stop for her today, but she relished the quiet walk. It gave time for reflection, something generally missing from her busy life.

The fields on either side of the road had begun to show a glimpse of gold as the weather cooled down. This morning was a bit brisk, but the sun promised a warm afternoon.

"Today is the first Sunday of preparing for fall Communion." She spoke softly to Benjy, wondering whether to warn him that the service might go longer than usual. "We all want to prepare our hearts for Communion."

He considered that for a moment. Did he remember the conversation they'd had prior to spring Communion? Whether he did or not, it was good to reinforce the teaching. The burden of her son's training in Amish ways was solely hers now.

"What should I do?" he said finally.

"We settle our hearts on the Lord, and we forgive anyone against whom we have been angry." She had more to say, but the words dried up on her tongue.

Anger and forgiveness. She had been angry, and try as she might to lose that anger, it flared up again and again. Her heart cramped. If she had not reached forgiveness of James and of the woman who had ruined her happiness, she wouldn't be able to take Communion. What would that say to her son, as well as the rest of the community?

Please, Lord. She tried to find the words to forgive, but each time she tried, her heart rebelled. *Please, Lord, show me how to forgive. Please.*

Grossmammi had reminded her to talk to God, that He would be listening. But right now she felt as if she prayed into emptiness.

They'd reached the farm road, and it was a short walk

to the barn. Those who had already arrived were gathering outside. Benjy spotted his grandparents, tugged his hand free and hurried to them, trying not to run.

By the time Beth reached her parents and grandmother, Benjy was talking a mile a minute to his grandfather. She could only be glad he was doing it in a soft voice.

Her grandmother smiled at her expression. "He's trying," she murmured. "Best to let him get it out before he goes in to worship."

"I know. Three hours is a long time for such a chatterbox to keep quiet."

"Ach, let him be," her mother said indulgently. "I love to hear him talk. He's so bright and happy it gives us joy to hear him."

"You can be the one to keep him quiet during the service, then," she teased. "He's certain sure not like me when I was his age."

Unfortunately, the words just reminded her that Benjy took after his father in that respect. She said a panicked prayer that that was the only way he resembled James.

She had to stop thinking this way. It would soon be time to go into the barn. It might be only a barn, but when the community was gathered together, the Lord was there. She couldn't carry angry thoughts with her.

The business of finding her place in the line of young married woman distracted her attention. There were welcoming smiles, and more than one person clasped her hand briefly in passing. She exchanged smiles with Lydia, still in the group of unmarried women. Her gaze was caught by Daniel, who gave her the solemn nod that was appropriate to worship, and then her line passed into the barn.

Settling Benjy next to her on the backless bench, she considered getting something out of the small bag of toys and snacks she'd brought, but at the moment he was looking around happily, so she left it.

There, in the silence, she prepared her heart for worship, knowing already that today's service would be focused on Nicodemus and new life in Christ. The worship year followed its traditional pattern. In two weeks it would be Council Meeting Sunday, with its emphasis on giving and receiving forgiveness. And the worship after that would be Communion. It wasn't much time, it seemed, to find her way to forgiveness.

The lead singer sounded the first wavering note of a hymn, and worship had begun.

When the final hymn had been sung and the final prayer said, the quiet atmosphere of worship gave way to the bustle of preparing for lunch. Several women—the hostess, her daughters, her sisters and close friends—hurried toward the kitchen to begin carrying food out. Meanwhile the men and older boys started transforming the benches into the tables that would be used for their meal together.

"Mammi, can I go find my cousins?" Benjy wiggled with pleasure at no longer being still.

"Put your toys back in the bag first, and then you may." She held it open while he hurriedly dropped his small horse and buggy in place.

He scurried off and she followed more slowly, intent on finding Lydia. Lydia seemed to have the same thought in mind, because she was there in a moment, putting her arm around Beth's waist as if they were ten again.

"All right?" she asked, keeping her voice low. "I thought the first Sunday after..." She let that trail off, glancing around.

"Yah. It was difficult, but I'm fine."

Lydia's scrutiny said she doubted it. The barn was emptying out, and they walked slowly toward the door together.

"The thing is..." It would be a relief to unburden herself to Lydia, but she was ashamed of some of the thoughts she'd had during worship.

"What?" Lydia pinched her. "Komm on, I know there's something. Spill it. I'm hungry."

That made her smile, as Lydia had known it would. "Are you ten or twenty-four? Hungry sounds like Benjy. He's probably pestering his grossmammi for a snack right now."

"I intend to pester you until I get an answer, and I can pester a lot better than Benjy. Tell me. Have you found out something?"

Her nerves jumped at the thought. "No, not really. But when I looked over at you during the second sermon, I realized I was seeing all the unmarried women of the community sitting on the same bench. It made me wonder..." She stumbled to a halt.

"You wonder if it was one of them." Lydia's blue eyes grew somber. "Yah, I have to say I've been thinking that, too. But it doesn't have to be, you know. It could just as easily be someone from a nearby community. Or a married woman. Or even an Englischer. Working in the store, he had to meet plenty of them."

"I've thought of that. It's getting so every woman I

look at makes me wonder. *Was it you? Are you the one who stole James from me?"*

Lydia's eyes flashed. "James had something to do with it, too, ain't so?"

"I know, I know. I'm not saying he didn't. But the thing is, I know I have to forgive them if I'm ever going to stop going around in circles. And how can I forgive her when I don't know who it was?"

Lydia looked troubled. "Ach, Beth, surely it is best not to know. Not to picture the two of them together."

"I still picture them," Beth blurted out. "I just can't see her face."

Lydia gave her a quick hug. "Let it go, Beth. It's a terrible bad thing, but you have to get past it."

Not even Lydia understood, it seemed. She spoke with sudden clarity. "I can't do that. I have to know. I have to know who the woman was. I have to."

Leaning against the fence, Daniel joined in the talk after worship about Sam's new pair of draft horses— Percherons, they were, and a fine-looking pair with strongly muscled bodies.

"Sam says he got a gut deal on the pair of them. He went clear down to Lancaster County for them." Daniel's older brother Seth, who was taking over the dairy farm from Daad, stood beside him. As if they knew they were being admired, the massive animals raised their heads to gaze back at them.

"Sam's got his heart's desire, I guess," Daad said, eyes twinkling. "Everyone knows he's been trying to convince Miriam for a couple of years now."

The group of men chuckled, and someone moved

the talk on to the price soybeans were bringing and the possibility of planting a few more acres in the spring.

Daniel could almost list the topics of conversation from memory. Every other Sunday the men gathered after worship to exchange talk of farming, lumber, dairying and the work of the coming month. He'd guess that the women were doing the same thing, only their subjects would be babies, fabric, the best place to buy children's shoes and who would host the next quilting bee.

Those frequent conversations seemed to make up the patchwork of Amish life, creating the dense, tight fabric that meant being Amish. His gaze roamed the farmyard—the children playing, the teenage girls watching the babies, the women either carrying food or clustered in small groups, heads together.

He glimpsed Beth in a clutch of young married women, the people she had the most in common with, he supposed. But even as he watched, she slipped out of the group, her black dress contrasting with the blues and dark greens the other women wore.

Did she feel uncomfortable with them now that she was a widow? Maybe so, because she went quickly to her mother and grandmother, maybe taking refuge in the family circle.

He pulled his attention back to the group, and just in time, because Elijah Schmidt mentioned his name.

"...hear tell that Beth Esch is working at the store now. That right?"

Something in him resented the question—in fact, any mention of her by someone who was fairly new to the district and couldn't claim to have known her since childhood.

"Yah," he said, hoping the short answer would deter the man.

Elijah didn't seem to get the message. He shook his head, frowning. "Hope she's not thinking she can take her husband's place in the partnership. That sort of work would never do for a young woman like her."

Annoyance rumbled inside him, but before he could speak, his daad chipped in. "It's not like Daniel will have her unloading trucks. That's what young Timothy is there for."

Seth grinned. "If Daniel can get a day's work out of the boy, that's enough to make me happy. He'll never make a farmer, that's certain sure."

"You have other sons," Daad said. "It's never wise to set a youngster's hand to the wrong plow."

Several other fathers nodded in agreement. Usually in every Amish family there'd be one destined to be a farmer. Seth's second boy showed every sign of being the one, even though he was just ten. At least they'd gotten Elijah off the subject of Beth.

But it seemed Daniel was wrong, because Elijah brought it up again almost immediately. "Now, what the widow ought to do is sell her share in the business. I wouldn't mind owning half a thriving business like that myself. What do you suppose it's worth?"

Daniel couldn't control himself any longer, but before he could find the words to say what he thought, Seth broke in, his face suddenly solemn. His deacon's face, the children called it.

"The Sabbath is not the time, and this isn't the place for talking business." His tone was so severe Daniel almost didn't recognize it.

In any event, it seemed to abash Elijah. Muttering

something that might have been an apology, he turned away just as the lunch bell rang. Everyone started moving to where the long tables were ready with the usual after-worship lunch.

Daniel fell into step with his brother and father. "Denke," he murmured. "It seems it takes a deacon's word to shut Elijah's mouth."

Seth grinned and nudged him. "Thought I'd best intervene before you said something you might regret. It's fortunate for him that he didn't say that around one of Beth's brothers or he'd have gotten the wrong side of the tongue for his trouble."

"Yah." Daniel figured it best to agree, although he didn't think he'd regret anything he might have said to the man. "You have to extend wilkom to a newcomer, but Elijah doesn't seem to fit in very well. I just hope he doesn't say anything to Beth. It would upset her."

Seth nodded his agreement. "How is Beth getting along? Mary Ann says she's going to take a meal over sometime this week and ask if there's anything we can do to help with the orchard."

"It's early yet, but she seems to want to do her share with the store. She's planning to work a few hours each day to start."

Daad frowned a bit, his thick, graying eyebrows seeming to bristle. "You'd best make sure she doesn't do too much. It takes time to heal from a loss like hers."

"I know. I'll keep an eye on her." He saw the white, strained expression Beth sometimes wore. "Seems to me it's doing her gut to get out of the house and talk to people."

"You'll know, I expect. You two were always close

when you were small. In fact, your mamm and I thought that the two of you would make a match of it."

The only safe thing Daniel could do was nod, but Daad's casual comment sent his thoughts spiraling back to his teens—to the evening at a singing when he'd quite suddenly stopped thinking of Beth as a tomboy friend and seen her as a young woman. And known he loved her.

Strange, that it was that same evening when James began looking at Beth in a new way, too. James, who charmed every girl, hadn't yet tried his charm on Beth, but he was abruptly sure she was the girl he wanted. Beth, like every other girl, fell victim to his easy, laughing smile.

He'd stepped away. What else could he do, when James was his best friend? God was wise in not letting anyone know the future. James had brought Beth to grief in the end. Still, she'd never had to learn anything negative about him while he was still with her.

Did that make it any better? He wasn't sure.

By Tuesday morning, Beth was beginning to get used to her new routine, and Benjy had fallen into it as if it were normal. They arrived before the store opened, and once she had Benjy settled with something to do, she helped set up for the day.

Benjy seemed happy enough to play in a corner Daniel had set up for him with room for a few toys, books and games, so she hadn't yet called on her niece to babysit. She should do that soon, so that Benjy could spend more time outdoors while the nice weather lasted. Janie would jump at the chance, she knew.

She started toward the checkout counter and then

paused, noticing Anna doing the same. Anna was still so shy and reserved around her, and she didn't want to make the girl think she was taking over her job.

Daniel appeared next to her, so she didn't have to make a decision. "I asked Anna to take the checkout first this morning so we could spend some time on how the storeroom is arranged and stocked, if that's okay with you."

"For sure. I thought we should be venturing into there soon. Just let me tell Benjy where I'll be." She detoured around the end of a counter to where Benjy was creating what was probably a barn from some blocks. "I'm going in the storeroom to work for a little while."

"Can I come, too?" he asked, before she could even finish what she was going to say.

"Not this time. I'll show you what I've learned later. If you need any help, Anna is at the counter. You can ask her, yah?" She'd noticed that Anna wasn't nearly as shy with Benjy as she was with adults.

He pouted a little but then went back to his blocks without a word. She would talk to Janie later today, she resolved. Benjy would be better for a break.

"Okay?" Daniel raised his eyebrows as they walked to the back of the store.

She nodded. "Daniel, I was wondering…does Anna think I'm taking over her job?"

"No, not that I know of, but maybe I haven't been noticing. Has she said something to make you think so?"

"She hasn't said anything at all…well, very little. I know she's rather shy, and I haven't wanted to push her. But I'm not that scary, am I?"

He chuckled. "Not that I've ever noticed. Except for

the time one of my brothers put your doll up in the apple tree. You were plenty scary over that, as I remember."

She couldn't help smiling. "I was plenty mad. And I never knew for sure who it was. Are you trying to convince me it wasn't you?"

"I shouldn't have said that—the boys all had a pact not to give each other away." He pushed open the door to the storeroom.

Still smiling, Beth walked in. Talking about those happy times was like taking a little rest from today's worries and griefs.

"Anyway, about Anna..." Daniel took a clipboard from a nail on the wall as he spoke. "I'd guess she's not sure how to talk to someone who has so recently lost a spouse." He gave her a sidelong glance, as if to be sure he wasn't causing her pain by mentioning it.

"Please." She reached out impulsively to Daniel. "Please just talk normally about James. The worst thing is to have people trying to avoid saying his name." No matter what she knew about him, James had been her husband and the father of her son. Grief was expected and normal.

As for the thing that wasn't normal—well, she had to find her own way of dealing with it.

Seeming reassured, Daniel gestured to the clipboards on the wall. "This is the main thing I wanted to show you. Each company or person who delivers merchandise has a sheet of their own. It's easier to keep track of that way. This one is for Larks Suppliers. They provide crackers, cookies, packaged chips...that kind of thing, and they usually come about twice a month. When you check them in—"

"Me?"

She glanced up in time to see a slightly guilty look on his face. "Sorry. I guess I should have mentioned that first. I have to make a trip out to the lumberyard to pick up some supplies. Do you mind doing the check-in if Larks comes before I get back?"

Beth pushed down a moment of doubt. Of course, she could do this. It was part of running the store, after all.

"No, I don't mind. As long as you don't mind if I make a mistake."

"I'm not afraid of that happening." His tone was light, his eyes amused.

Daniel's face didn't give much away, but when you knew him, you realized that his eyes told you everything you needed to know. If she had to have a partner, she was fortunate that it was an old friend like Daniel.

Chapter Five

Daniel went off to the lumberyard, and they were on their own. Beth felt confident of her abilities right up to the moment when she heard the buzzer that announced someone at the loading dock. Then her pulse jumped, and her voice went dry.

Silly, she told herself, and marched back to the storeroom. She paused, momentarily forgetting how the loading dock worked, but then she spotted the pulley running along the right side. The pulley system made it easy to open the large doors at the dock, and once she'd done that successfully, her confidence began to return.

The Englisch driver gave her a cheerful wave and, as he drew closer, a curious look. He probably realized she was someone new.

"Good day. Just let me get the clipboard, and I'll check in the order." She tried to sound as if she did it every day, but suspected she'd failed.

"Right you are." He swung himself up to the back of the truck like a young man, although he had to be in his forties at least, with thinning hair partially hidden by a ball cap and the beginnings of a paunch. His brightly colored T-shirt stretched across it.

Hurrying back to the opposite wall, she seized the Larks clipboard, quickly scanning the form. Simple enough, she thought. All she had to do was list the items delivered and the number of them.

The driver was already unloading, so she hurried to find the contents on the outside of the cartons. Filling in the name was easy, since she was familiar with most of the products. The amount baffled her until she realized it was the number of cartons, not the individual bags.

The driver's curiosity got the better of him as he stacked cartons of crackers. "You're new here, right?"

Beth nodded. "I started last week." There was no reason to get into details with the man. "You have a nice day for your deliveries." The sun had burned off the early morning fog that was so typical in the fall.

"Sure is. Let's see now." He stood back, checking his own list to compare it with what he'd brought. "Sure you don't want another case of those sea salt chips? They're selling fast."

"Just what's on the list." Beth softened the refusal with a smile. She certainly wouldn't venture to order something on her own, not yet.

He shrugged, holding out a receipt for her signature. "Nice seeing you. You're a lot prettier than the guy who usually helped me. James, his name is. He off today?"

Her stomach cramped. She should have realized the drivers would be familiar with James. And she certain sure shouldn't have let herself be jolted just by his name.

"He's not with us anymore." There, that was all she need say.

The driver nodded, swinging himself up to his seat. He

leaned out for a final word. "Not surprised he got the ax. Probably chased out of town by a jealous husband, right?"

He slammed his door and drove off, leaving her standing frozen.

How long she'd have stood there completely numb, she didn't know. She was shaken into movement by the sound of footsteps behind her. Trying to hold herself together, she turned, not quite looking at Timothy.

"I'll get that." He reached past her to close the door. "That was Tom Ellis, yah? Did he talk your ear off?"

"N-not quite." She gestured toward the boxes, shielding her expression with the clipboard. "These are all checked in. Do you know what to do with them now?"

"Yah, sure. I'll do that as long as you take care of the paperwork. Onkel Daniel doesn't trust me with that since I marked down a dozen packages instead of a dozen cases."

He didn't seem very upset, lifting several boxes in his arms. He looked at her quickly, and then his gaze moved away just as fast. "Everything okay?"

Beth pulled herself together. "Yah, sure. I'll just go…" She let that trail off. What she wanted to do was to be alone someplace where she could cry and yell if she wanted to. She couldn't do that, but maybe she could find some privacy.

Walking quickly back into the store, she paused. She wanted to hurry into the office and shut the door, but she'd better check on Benjy and see if Anna needed her first.

Before she reached them, Anna raised her hand to catch Beth's attention. She hurried to the counter, where Anna was loading baked goods into a bag for a young and pretty Englisch woman.

"Will you… Would you mind taking my place for a

few minutes?" She raised her eyes long enough to indicate the restroom.

"Yah, of course." What else could she say? She slid behind the counter and put the last few items into the woman's bag. She had the usual things the Englisch looked for when they came here—the fresh fruit and vegetables along with the baked pastries and homemade soups.

"There you are." She forced herself to smile at the woman. What she wanted to do was to ask the questions that pounded in her mind. *Did my husband flirt with you? Did he arrange to meet you somewhere?*

Before she could do something so foolish, Benjy came trotting around the corner. "Timothy says I can help him put out the crackers and cookies. Can I, Mammi?"

His smile sent enough warmth through her to slightly thaw her frozen heart. "Yah, but you must do what Timothy tells you."

"I will." He was turning already to race back to Timothy.

Another customer moved to the counter—the sort of person who fussed about everything. Were the squash really fresh? Didn't she have any better spinach? Why didn't they have any bananas?

It took all the patience she could find to deal with her when what she wanted was to throw something. She stepped back with relief when Anna returned.

"Denke, Anna." She spun and hurried to the office before anyone could stop her.

Safely inside, she closed the door and leaned back against it. She could hardly lock it without raising the questions she wanted to avoid, but at least she was alone for the moment.

Burying her face in her hands, Beth stumbled toward the desk. Now that she could cry, the need for tears had left her. She stared, dry-eyed, at the calendar on the far wall, trying to think.

She should not have been so shocked by the driver's comment. Wasn't it what she'd been thinking herself… that James hadn't saved his charm for her? He'd been exercising it on other women so openly that even strangers noticed it.

If strangers saw it enough to make jokes about it, what were the Leit saying? Her heart sank. The members of her own church family must have been talking about it.

A rational thought stopped her before she could go too far down that road. It could not have been so obvious, could it? If so, the ministers or the bishop would have spoken to James. At least, no matter how humiliating it was, it hadn't reached that level.

Anger surged through her again. Was that all she had left to be thankful for? That James hadn't exposed them to the church's discipline with his behavior?

The door behind her rattled. She spun around and then wished she hadn't. Daniel stood there, and his expression made it clear he saw that something was wrong.

Daniel was aghast at the look on Beth's face. What on earth could have happened in the short time he'd been gone? Two quick strides took him to her.

"Ach, Beth. Don't look that way. Whatever happened, it will be all right."

He shouldn't have asked her to take care of the delivery. It was too soon to expect her to jump right into the running of the store. What was wrong with him?

She shook her head, her eyes brimming with tears she obviously tried to hold back.

"It doesn't matter if there's a problem with the delivery. We'll straighten it out in no time."

He was trying to comfort her, but the anger in her face told him he was on the wrong track.

"Delivery! Do you think I'm so stupid I can't do something so simple?" She raised the clipboard, shoving it at him. "There, you see?"

"Yah, of course you can." Whatever he said was wrong, clearly. But what had happened to get her into such a state in a short time?

But that quickly the brief flash of spirit was gone, replaced by a pain he could almost feel. "Please, tell me."

Beth looked away from him, biting her lip. "He… the driver…"

"Tom Ellis? What did he do to upset you?" It was hard to imagine Tom getting out of line with her.

"He asked where James was. I just said he wasn't here any longer. And then he said—" She stopped, swallowing hard. "He said somebody's husband must have chased him out of town."

So that was it. Had Beth really been so oblivious to James's flirting? Apparently so. Now he had to smooth this over as best he could.

"Ach, Beth, you can't get upset at anything Tom says. He didn't realize James had passed away, and he always has to tease. He didn't mean anything."

Her head came up, eyes flashing. "I'm not a baby, Daniel. Don't treat me like one. The man meant something by saying that, and I want to know what it was."

Daniel's mind swung wildly through the possibilities. He couldn't lie to her, but he couldn't bear to hurt her more than she was already hurting.

There was nothing for it but the truth, spoken as gently as possible.

"Maybe Tom had the wrong impression of James. After all, he only saw him for a few minutes each time he came by. You know what James was like. With such a lively personality, he couldn't help but chat with every customer. They enjoyed it."

"I guess they did," she said, her voice somber and a little husky from holding back tears. "We both know James was a charmer, ain't so? Was he flirting with some of the Englisch customers?"

He had to answer when she looked at him that way, as if trusting him for the truth. "You could call it that, but he wouldn't do anything out of line. You know that."

"Do I?" She seemed to wilt. "I'm not sure what I know anymore. And you… Would you be trying to cover up for your oldest friend?"

"Beth…" He took her hands in his, unable to suppress the need to comfort her. "James wasn't my oldest friend. You are. No matter that we were friends and partners, I wouldn't lie to you for him."

He wasn't lying. His suspicion wasn't a fact, and he couldn't speak of it to her.

She was very close, and when she looked up at him, he could see the darkness in the green eyes that were usually as clear as glass. If he'd given her more pain…

She put her hands up to her face, and he knew she was crying silently. His heart twisted. He put his arm around her, patting her shoulder.

Daniel's conscience pricked him. He didn't just want to comfort Beth. He wanted…

No. He couldn't let himself feel this way for his friend's wife. But he couldn't seem to control it, and he couldn't push her away when she needed comfort so badly.

Beth must have been hit by the same thought. He could feel it in the way she stiffened. She took a step away from him. She wiped her eyes with her fingers, hiding her face from him.

"Beth…" He struggled to find words.

"I'm sorry. I didn't mean to…to make you uncomfortable. I'm sorry," she said again.

"It's nothing." He tried to sound normal. "Everybody needs to let their feelings out sometime. We'll forget it, yah?"

She forced a smile through the tears. "Yah. Denke." She hurried away, heading back to the restroom to repair the trace of tears, he supposed.

And he was left wondering what he should do. If he spoke of his suspicions to Beth, it wasn't only a question of betraying his friend. He would hurt Beth even more than she'd already been hurt.

But if he kept quiet, and then she found out… There were no good answers.

Beth found she was still brooding on the incident when she was doing the dishes after supper. It was foolish to dwell on such a small thing as leaning on a friend, but all the determination in the world couldn't seem to wipe it from her mind.

She had needed comfort in the wake of what she'd heard from the driver. She'd have turned to anyone who happened to offer sympathy, to Lydia or Grossmammi, but of course it hadn't been. She'd put Daniel in an awkward position. Still, trying to apologize would only make it worse, wouldn't it?

The sound of a buggy coming up the lane did succeed in chasing the thoughts away. She leaned across the sink to peer out the window. It was Lydia, with Beth's niece Janie sitting beside her. She hadn't expected anyone tonight, but already Benjy was clattering down the steps, eager for company.

"Look, Mammi, it's Janie. Maybe she came to play with me."

"Maybe." Wiping her hands on a tea towel, she followed him to the door. "Lydia is there, too. Be sure you greet each of them."

She didn't have to worry about that, as Benjy hurtled himself first at Janie and then at Lydia, beaming with pleasure. Did that outgoing personality of his come from his father? A chill touched her. It was a wonderful trait, as long as it didn't lead him too far. Like James.

"It's wonderful gut to see both of you. But what—"

"There, I told you she'd forgotten," Lydia said. "You did, didn't you?"

Beth stared blankly, and Lydia laughed.

"It's the night our rumspringa gang is getting together at Esther Mueller's house, remember? Well, never mind. We'll be in plenty of time, and Janie is here to stay with Benjy."

"Yaay!" Benjy didn't hesitate to express his joy. He grabbed his cousin's hand. "Komm. We'll play a game, ain't so?"

Janie nodded, and they scurried toward the living room before Beth could object.

"I did forget." She turned back to Lydia. "Honestly, I think I'd rather not go. I've had a long day, and…"

"And you need to get out of the house and talk to some friends. If there's anything our gang can do, it's talk."

"But I really don't want to." She'd have to be firm, or Lydia would have her in the buggy before she knew it.

"But you really need to," Lydia countered. "Don't bother to tell me you weren't brooding, because I can see it in your face." She linked her arm with Beth's. "Is that the face you want your son to look at tonight? Komm, schnell."

Lydia's analysis was too accurate, and Beth stopped resisting. "All right, I'll go. But I warn you, I'm not going to be the life of the party."

"That's okay, so long as you're there." Lydia hustled her out to the buggy.

The sun was lingering at the top of the ridge, turning the valley a golden hue that looked like autumn. The chill in the air reinforced that thought. She'd always loved fall better than any season, but this year it threatened to be a melancholy time.

The buggy turned onto the main road and headed away from town toward the Mueller farm. Lydia swung to study her face. "Komm now. You may as well tell me."

"Tell you what?" She tried to sound as if she didn't know what Lydia was talking about, but it sounded hollow even to herself.

Lydia's gaze grew skeptical. Beth, unable to ignore that look, shrugged. "All right. If you must know, I heard something that upset me today at the store." She hesitated, wanting to tell it without getting into what had happened with Daniel.

"One of the drivers, an Englischer, asked where James was. And when I said he wasn't here any longer, he…" She seemed to run out of breath. "He said that some husband must have chased him out of town." She got it out in one breath.

Lydia didn't speak, but her hand clasped Beth's, and sympathy flowed from her in waves. "I'm sorry. He didn't know who you were. When he finds out, he'll feel like a monster."

"There's no reason he should ever find out," she said quickly. "I don't want to embarrass him. But it makes me think…" Her fingers tightened on Lydia's hand. "That's what everyone is saying, ain't so? Everyone knows what James was like."

"Not everyone." Lydia was trying to soften it, but that didn't help.

"Everyone who knows him." She had to accept it. "So they're all either feeling sorry for me or laughing at me. Which is it?"

"Ach, don't be so foolish," Lydia scolded. "Most people just recognized James's outgoing personality. As long as you didn't seem upset about it, no one else would take it that way."

"Obviously that driver did." Beth shook her head impatiently. "It doesn't matter, not for me. But Benjy— what if Benjy heard something like that about his father?" She tried to imagine dealing with that, trying to explain it to a four-year-old, but couldn't.

Lydia was silent as the buggy negotiated the turn into Mueller's lane. "He's not old enough," she said finally. "If he heard something, he wouldn't understand it, would he?"

"I guess not," she admitted. "Not now. But someday."

"I know you want to protect him." Lydia patted her arm. "But when the day comes that he asks you about it…well, by then it should be easier."

Somehow Beth couldn't imagine the time when it would be easier, but she knew Lydia was trying to help, and she was thankful.

Chapter Six

Lydia's buggy stopped at the back door, where Esther's husband and their oldest boy stood waiting to take the horse and buggy. He greeted them with a grin.

"Are you two ready for a night of talking? I don't know how you can find so much to say to each other, that's certain sure."

"The same way you men find so much to say after worship or when you go to the hardware store," Lydia replied, never at a loss for words, as usual.

Beth, not so talkative, just smiled, following her.

But at the door, Beth hesitated, doubts assailing her. Was this really a good idea? Was it too soon to come back? She gave her black skirt a shake to fluff out the wrinkles. She wanted nothing so much as to be normal this evening, talking and reminiscing with her childhood friends. The black dress marked her out as different.

She couldn't retreat now, so she walked into the kitchen, where several of the gang were helping themselves to coffee. "Go on into the living room," Esther said, making shooing motions with her hands. "I'll bring dessert in when it's ready." She caught sight of Beth then and came toward her, wiping her hands on her apron.

"Ach, Beth, I'm wonderful glad you came. Lydia said she'd bring you, but I…"

"You thought I'd resist," Beth said, embracing her. "You know it's no use resisting when Lydia's decided you should do something."

"She's like a horse within sight of the barn." Esther grinned as she hugged her. "Get your coffee and head on into the other room. I don't know why everyone always wants to linger in the kitchen."

"Because it smells so gut," Beth replied, feeling more relaxed every moment.

"Because we like to get in your way," Lydia added.

Picking up their cups, they followed the sound of talk toward the front of the farmhouse.

Beth gave a quick look around. It seemed they were all present. There had been twenty girls in their original group, and every one of them had stayed here in the area. Except for her cousin Miriam, and Miriam was in Ohio helping her sister with a new baby and visiting her aunt and uncle there. She'd surely be home soon.

Beth found a seat next to Ella Esch. Beyond Ella was her twin, Della. The two of them had married the Esch brothers, second cousins of James, and now lived in two cottages on the Esch family's dairy farm. It wasn't all that unusual for two sisters to marry two brothers, but it certain sure added to the confusion, especially with such a common name as Esch.

Ella clasped her hand warmly. "We're wonderful glad you came. Since the accident—" She stopped, flushing a little, and then blurted out, "I told my Davey

I didn't want him going out on that lonely road at night. I don't want to lose him."

No sooner had the words gotten out than Della started scolding, quickly echoed by everyone who was close enough to hear. Ella flushed bright red up to her hair and hid her face.

Beth sat perfectly still for a moment. That was it, and she hadn't realized it. The awkwardness with them wasn't just because she was a widow now. It was because they feared if it happened to her, it could happen to them.

"It's all right..." she began, only to be drowned out by Della's scolding.

"You are the most tactless person in the world." She looked as if she'd like to shake her twin the way she'd done when they were six. "Apologize to Beth."

"I'm sorry." Ella raised a tearstained face, and Beth reached out with a handkerchief to blot the tears away.

"It's all right, really." She gave Ella a quick hug. "I understand. And it's gut to remind our loved ones to be careful." She kept her voice calm and light, even though she was still shaking a little inside.

Still, she was just as glad it had happened. Poor Ella. Her habit of saying exactly what she was thinking had gotten her into trouble in school more times than they could count. But this time the fault, if that was what it was, had helped Beth understand what other women were feeling when they looked at her.

"None of us has changed, yah?" Beth looked around the circle of faces. She wanted to go on, wanted to say that the black clothing didn't change who she was inside, but she hesitated, afraid they wouldn't understand.

But her words had banished the awkward moment,

and when Esther began forcing pieces of peach pie on them, they were quickly back to normal.

"What's happening with your cousin Miriam, Beth? We thought she'd be back with us by this month."

"She intended to come back by the time her sister's boppli was six weeks old, but the older children got some kind of a bug, and they've been sick one after another. So of course Miriam felt she had to stay."

Esther's eyes twinkled. "I thought maybe she'd met a wonderful nice man and was courting."

"Not unless she's keeping it a secret from us," Lydia said. "She'd better not be keeping secrets from her favorite cousins." She smiled at Beth, and it seemed the smile carried assurance. *You're doing fine, yah?*

The talk drifted to children, as it often did—the way little girls grew out of their clothes while the boys wore out of them, the need for a couple of new swings at the schoolyard, and the challenge of keeping the little ones from catching everything the older ones got.

"How is your little Benjy doing, Beth?" Della leaned toward her.

"He's doing fine. My niece Janie is with him now. She's willing to watch him while I'm at the store if I need her, although he seems happy enough at the store. I thought he might feel shy, but he enjoys it."

"Just like his daadi, then," Ella said. "James was always smiling in the store."

Beth froze for a moment, trying to hold a meaningless smile on her face. Was she imagining it, or had the other women frozen, too?

She looked down at the cup she still held before setting it carefully on the table next to her. All of them would have seen James at the store. Probably most of them had talked to him when she wasn't around.

How many of them had watched James flirting with other women? Had they been pitying her all this time?

Maybe it was worse. Maybe one of them had been the woman who'd written that note.

She was back in the trap, running around and around, searching for the truth. Wondering if she would ever know. Or if she could find peace without it.

Daniel glanced at the clock when he saw Beth and Benjy coming the next morning. They were about ten minutes later than usual, not that it mattered. He was happy to have her come whenever she could make it. Every day that passed seemed to make her more a part of the business.

"I'm sorry we're late." She glanced at the clock as he had. "I don't know why we couldn't get moving this morning."

"You're one of the bosses," he said lightly. "You can come whenever you want." His gaze fell on Benjy just as the boy gave a huge yawn and rubbed his eyes. Daniel chuckled. "I think I see why."

Beth's lips trembled on the verge of a smile. "It's not entirely his fault. I got together with my rumspringa gang last night, so Janie came to stay with him. And he always manages to get one more game or story out of his cousin Janie before she puts him to bed."

Benjy seemed to realize they were talking about him. "Cousin Janie likes to play games and tell stories," he protested.

"I know. I do, too. But bedtime is important."

"Especially when you're getting up to go to work in

the morning," Daniel added, winking at Benjy to show that he was joking.

Benjy twinkled back, looking marginally more awake. "I should see what Timothy is doing," he said, and darted off toward the back of the store.

"Speaking of Janie, she's going to watch him a couple of mornings a week, so that Benjy won't be here every day." She glanced at him, as if wanting to see his reaction.

"We love having him here," Daniel protested, concerned about what was behind this decision. She wasn't regretting the idea of staying involved with the store, was she? His dismay at that was probably obvious to her.

She smiled, shaking her head. "You're very kind, but I think it's best if he has a break sometimes. And Janie's eager to have a job, so it works out all around."

He couldn't very well argue, but… "We'll miss Benjy when he isn't here. Timothy likes having somebody younger around." He grinned. "He's used to having young ones around. But sometimes I think he'd rather be an only one."

Beth chuckled, her eyes twinkling. "Isn't that always the case? I think being in the middle is best."

His heart warmed at seeing her looking so much like her old self. "Me, too. There's always plenty of room to distribute blame when somebody's in trouble. Whoever's oldest usually gets held responsible."

Her smile faded, and her face became thoughtful. "We don't know what it's like to be an only child, do we?"

She was thinking about James, he felt sure. He hesitated, leaning against the counter while he tried to make up his mind what to say.

"James seemed happy to be an only child," he commented finally.

"Yah." Trouble still darkened her eyes.

Clearly, he hadn't helped. "I used to think…"

"What?" Beth studied his face, as if trying to read more than he'd said.

"I kind of envied him. He didn't have chores to do, living in town like he did. My daad never ran out of jobs for us to do if he caught us wasting time." He smiled, remembering. "And his mamm didn't say no nearly as much as my mamm did."

"I don't suppose she did." Beth seemed to focus on her mother-in-law, and she wasn't smiling.

That didn't surprise him. Sarah Esch had always been one to fuss over a person, and as a mother-in-law, she'd fuss twice as much, he'd imagine. Beth wasn't one to like that.

Beth seemed to shake off thoughts of her mother-in-law. "I should get to work. I'll finish updating the inventory of canned goods I started."

He nodded, watching her go. There had been moments when the conversation had been as comfortable and relaxed as ever, but then he started feeling he hadn't been very helpful. There was something behind her troubled look, and he wasn't sure what it was. The truck driver's comments? Or something else?

His musing was interrupted by Benjy tugging at his pants. "Are we going to fix that step? You said I could help." Benjy fixed his wide-eyed gaze on Daniel.

The boy was not only smart and talkative. He was also determined.

"Yah, sure." It had to be done, so it might as well be now. "Komm, we'll get the tools."

Benjy skipped along beside him as they walked to the back door. "I like fixing things," he said. "Don't you?"

Daniel smiled at his enthusiasm. "Yah, I do. Especially when I have someone like you to help."

"Gut."

Once they'd reached the rickety step, he squatted down to examine it, amused when Benjy mimicked his motion, balancing on his heels and putting his elbows on his knees.

"See how the step is working away on this one side? This nail is loose, ain't so?"

Benjy wiggled it with a small finger. "Yah. We'll put a new one in, won't we?"

"We will," he agreed. "You hold the hammer while I get the nails out."

Benjy grasped the hammer with both hands, his small face intent and proud.

Daniel's heart warmed at the sight. Here, at least, was a way he could help.

To Beth's surprise, she and Benjy found her mother waiting on the back porch for them when they went home. Benjy rushed forward for a hug, and Beth wasn't far behind him.

"Ach, this is a nice surprise." She relished the feel of her mother's arms around her. "Will you stay for lunch?"

Mammi smiled, her blue eyes twinkling as she held up the basket she'd parked on the floor. "Better. I brought a picnic for the three of us."

Benjy was already bouncing with pleasure, and he tried to take the basket, but Beth forestalled him. "We'll need something to sit on, yah? You bring the rag rugs we keep in the back closet."

He darted off, and Mammi chuckled. "That boy has more energy than the two of us put together."

"Easily." She picked up the basket. "This is a nice idea. I was just thinking that I hadn't seen you since Sunday."

Her mother linked arms with her as Benjy hurried out, his arms loaded with the rugs. "It's time for a talk, ain't so?"

"What's in the basket, Grossmammi?" Benjy stretched himself on tiptoe for a moment, trying to see in, but a striped tea towel hid the contents.

"We'll see when we get to the picnic spot," she said, smiling so sweetly at him that Beth's heart warmed. "You remember where we went last time?"

Benjy nodded vigorously. "Up there." He pointed toward the orchard. "I'll put out the rugs."

The sight of him trying to carry the rugs and run at the same time had Beth smiling. No matter how many grandchildren she had, her mother had time and love for each one.

"I want to hear all about working at the store, but I guess we'd best feed this hungry boy first."

Mammi helped Benjy spread out the rugs. Sitting down, she took the basket and started lifting out food, putting it on the tea towel.

"Sandwiches with church spread." Benjy's eyes widened at his favorite—the spread of peanut butter and marshmallow cream that was so popular with the young ones. He looked as if he'd say more, but his mouth was quickly plugged with the sticky mixture.

Beth was glad to see that her mother had included

meat and cheese sandwiches. She'd outgrown her love
for church spread before she was out of her teens. Finding a spot on a rug, she relaxed, taking in the scent of
apples that filled the air with its reminder of harvest.
If she'd been blindfolded and brought here, she'd have
known where she was without looking. No other place
could smell quite this way.

Mammi began telling Benjy a story as they ate, and
Beth leaned back on her elbows, enjoying the warm
fall afternoon. Off to the right from where they sat,
she could see Daniel's family farm, with his mamm
out in the backyard hanging up clothes. To the left lay
her parents' farm, but the curve of the hill hid most of
the house. Daadi was in the pasture next to the road,
mending fence before any of the cows took a notion to
go looking for greener grass.

The curve of the road bounded the property, and
the store sat there, almost directly in front of her. With
the ridge behind her, nearly everything she could see
was her place in the world, and Benjy's. That was as it
should be. Even fatherless, Benjy would grow up surrounded on all sides by people who loved him.

Benjy leaned across his rug to hug his grandmother.
"Denke. That was a wonderful gut picnic."

She squeezed him back, smiling, and turned back
to Beth as Benjy skipped off through the windfall apples. "It's hard to resist that little one. He has his daadi's charm." She paused for a moment. "But he has your
heart for other people, too. He'll be all right."

"I'm not worried about that," Beth said quickly, sensitive on that subject.

"Komm, Beth." Her mother patted her hand. "That

quality in James caused you sorrow sometimes, ain't so?"

She couldn't speak, because Mammi's words were too close to the bone.

Her mother didn't seem to expect an answer, going on. "I was worried from the first time I saw you were interested in him. He could smile and make a woman feel that she was important to him. But I thought he spread it around too much."

"Why didn't you say anything to me then?" She studied her mother's face, looking for an answer.

Mammi smiled a little sadly. "You were in love. You wouldn't have listened. Besides, I thought once you were married, maybe he'd save his charm for you. All I could do was pray that it was so."

Beth averted her gaze to study the pattern of faded colors in the rug. How had she not known that her mother had those reservations about her marriage? She began to think she had been blind when it came to James.

"So now all you can do is to forgive him if he hurt you." She reached out to touch Beth's chin, tilting it to see her eyes. "Have you been able to do that?"

Her mother didn't know how much she had to forgive, or how far James had strayed. And Beth couldn't tell her.

"I try, but it still bothers me some." It bothered her a lot, but surely it would get better soon.

"I knew there was something you weren't saying."

"How could I?" She desperately wanted this conversation over before she said something she shouldn't. "I can't talk about James's faults, especially now that he's gone."

"My poor Beth." Mammi patted her hand. "Peace will come, in God's own time."

"Until then…"

"Until then, you must pray to be able to forgive. And you must do and say what you would if you really had forgiven."

She was silent, wrestling with it. "That sounds like you want me to pretend."

"It's not pretending," her mother said. "It's trusting the gut Lord to give you what you've asked. Will you try to do that?"

Beth brushed back a strand of hair pulled loose by the wind. Her fingers touched her kapp, with its constant reminder to pray.

"Yah," she said finally. "I'll try."

Chapter Seven

Janie arrived early the next morning, obviously looking forward to her new job. Benjy was delighted to see her, but not so delighted to learn that he wasn't going to the store this morning.

"But, Mammi, I'm a big help at the store."

Beth pulled her sweater on against the chill of the fall morning, hoping to make the parting short and sweet. "Of course you are. But we'll get along without you for one day. And besides, Janie wants to play with you. Maybe she'll even take you for a hike."

"Sure I will." Janie responded quickly. "Meantime, why don't we go and gather eggs? Do you know where the egg basket is?"

"Yah." He gave her a sidelong glance. "But the big rooster…"

They both knew that Benjy was a little scared of the rooster, who had a habit of lunging at intruders to his kingdom.

"Tell you what," Janie said. "We'll take the broom, and if he tries anything, we'll give him a gut swat. Okay?"

Benjy considered a moment, and Beth edged toward the door.

"Yah, okay." Benjy grabbed Janie's hand. "Bye, Mammi."

Relieved, she gave him a quick hug and slipped off, half expecting a call after her. But apparently Janie had things under control, and a glance over her shoulder told Beth they were off toward the chicken coop, carrying the broom and the basket between them.

Setting off down the lane alone felt odd. Since Benjy's birth, there had been few times that they'd been separated. Maybe this would be good for him. In two years, he'd be off to school, hard as it was to believe.

As for her—well, she was going to her job, and she felt a certain satisfaction in that fact. At first, she hadn't been able to imagine doing this, and she still remembered the fear she'd felt at Daniel's suggestion.

Smiling, she waved a bumblebee away from her face and watched it dive toward the asters along the fence. Working at the store had been even scarier than the belligerent rooster. Now she looked forward to it.

When Beth reached the front of the store, she paused for a moment, glancing at the displays in the two big windows. Would a person call them displays? Stacks of various canned goods didn't seem to her to be an attractive advertisement for the store.

How would Daniel react if she suggested doing something different? She could think of half a dozen things that would make the window more attractive.

Daniel had been fine with her helping around the store, but he might feel she hadn't been there long enough to change things. Still, her newfound confidence might be great enough to try. She began thinking about how to bring it up.

As soon as she entered, she spotted Daniel, his face clouded, striding toward her.

"I'm glad you're here," he said abruptly.

"I'm not late, am I?" She glanced at the clock to see she was right on time.

"No, not at all." He chased away the frown. "Sorry. I just heard that Anna is going to be late today, and I've got a shipment arriving in a couple of minutes and a couple other things to do in the back. But now you're here, you'll be able to mind the store."

Beth could sense that he was still concerned, and she made a guess. "Is there some problem with Anna?"

He gave her a rueful smile. "Just the usual one. Her father. Every once in a while, Hiram starts in on her about respecting your father and mother and how she should be doing more at home. I guess this was a bad morning—she stopped at the convenience store at the other end of town to call."

Beth's ready compassion went out to the girl. "That's foolish. After all, she's already working a full day here."

"And taking her paycheck home to her parents," he added.

She shook her head, praying she'd never be that sort of parent. "It's one thing to be strict about the Ordnung and another to be downright nasty. My parents managed, even with my brothers, to insist on right behavior without being so..."

"Nasty," he finished for her. "You had the right word to begin with. We were fortunate in our parents, ain't so?"

Beth nodded. "Yah, we were. They set a gut example, and they were firm but never unfair."

The buzzer went just then, announcing the delivery truck, and Beth hurried behind the counter. "You go on. I'll take care of things out here."

He flashed her the smile that crinkled his eyes. "I know you will."

Beth found herself dwelling on Daniel's words as he headed back to the storeroom. It sounded as if he found her a help. She didn't kid herself that she could do everything that James had done in the partnership, but she liked knowing Daniel appreciated her efforts. It might be easier than she'd thought to bring up changing the window displays.

The Englisch woman who'd been browsing at the far end of the store came toward the counter with a full shopping basket.

"Ready to check out?" Beth smiled at her, admiring the way her turquoise scarf contrasted with the dark red of her hair. Not many Amish had red hair, and if they did, it was usually a light carroty color. This red was as rich and dark as the sorrel gelding Daad had once owned.

"I suppose so." The woman looked at her questioningly. "You're new, aren't you?"

"I've only been working here for a short time." Beth weighed the bag of apples the woman had picked out, tempted to tell her that they'd come from her own trees. "Did you find everything you were looking for?"

A frown creased the woman's smooth skin. "Not quite. I was hoping you might have a few quilted table runners in the craft section, but it's looking pretty bare right now."

In an instant, Daniel's voice slid into her mind, saying that maybe James had been going to visit some crafters the night he died. Her fingers shook, and she grasped the carton of eggs with both hands.

"Is something wrong?" The woman was looking at her strangely.

"No, not at all. My husband used to handle the craft section before he…before he passed away. We'll probably be getting some more things in soon, if you'd like to come back."

"I'm sorry." The woman looked horrified for a moment. "I didn't realize. It was your husband who had that buggy accident, then."

Beth nodded. She shouldn't have said anything, but it had been surprised out of her. And now that it was done, she couldn't help noticing that the woman was even more upset than she was.

It wasn't her fault. She couldn't have known that her words would have an effect on Beth.

"It's all right to mention him." Beth produced a smile, but her mind was working busily behind it. The woman was attractive—very much so—and not a lot older than Beth, although it was always hard to tell age in an Englisch woman.

She'd already told herself that the woman James had been seeing might have been an Englisch woman. He met all kinds of people in the store. Could this be the one?

She looked down to bag the woman's produce, glad she had an excuse not to look at her. She could hardly go around accusing other women of being involved with her husband.

She ought to say something. The customer would find it odd. But before she could speak, the woman had thrust the money at her and had seized her bags and gone.

* * *

Daniel had just finished unloading when Anna scurried in, averting her gaze in a way that said she didn't want to talk. Frustrated, he shook his head. Not that he wanted to interfere with Hiram Fisher's family, but Anna was a good, hardworking youngster and he hated to see her so upset.

He considered following her, trying to get her to talk, but she went straight to the counter to relieve Beth, and he gave it up, a little relieved. If anyone could get her to talk, Beth would do a better job than he ever could.

He saw them exchange a few words. Beth gave her a gentle pat on the shoulder, but Anna seemed to flinch away. As he'd feared, Anna was determined to keep her troubles to herself.

A few minutes later, Beth joined him in the back of the store. She cast a concerned look at Anna. "Someone should talk to Hiram."

"I doubt it would do much good."

When anger flashed in her eyes, he shook his head.

"I know. I'd like to fix it, too. But I fear anything we might say to Hiram would make things worse."

The anger faded. "You're right, I suppose. At least she's here much of the time, instead of constantly under his eye."

"I never thought of the store as a haven, but you might be right." He kept his voice deliberately light. Beth had enough to deal with on her own without fretting over someone else.

He was rewarded with a hint of a smile. "Speaking of the store," she began, then seemed unsure how to continue.

"Yah?"

"Have you ever thought…well, of doing a sort of display in the windows?" Beth's voice faltered a little, as if fearing he'd be insulted.

Well, he wasn't—he was delighted. Beth was showing enough interest in the business to want changes. That meant she'd begun to consider it hers.

"I never thought of it." That was true enough. "It's a fine idea, but I wouldn't know where to begin. Do you have any ideas?"

"Actually, I have thought of a few things that would make it look brighter and more appealing. And maybe highlight some of the autumn fruits and vegetables."

"That sounds great." He'd have said that in any event, just to see her smile. "Why don't you take it on?"

Beth's green eyes lit with enthusiasm. She looked as if he'd given her a present. "I'd like that fine. Are you sure you don't mind?" Again that hint of apprehension in her voice made him want to chase it away.

"Mind? It's a great idea. Where should we start? You tell me what to do, and I'll carry things for you."

Apparently, that convinced her. She went to the window so quickly he had to hurry to catch up.

"I just thought of it this morning, so I don't have it all planned out yet. But I was thinking since autumn is coming on, we could arrange things that remind folks of that. A few pumpkins and cornstalks, maybe."

The pleasure in her face was enough to convince him to do whatever necessary to keep it there. "I'll bring the cornstalks in tomorrow. There are some dry ones in the lower field that haven't been cut. And what about maybe a pail or basket with winter squash and such?"

"Yah, gut. That way I can switch them out every day

or so." She grasped a case of canned beans and started to pull it out of the window.

"Whoa. I'll move cases. You just say where." He reached past her to take the box, his hands brushing hers and sending a little flush of warmth up his arms. He pulled the box away quickly.

"I'm not that helpless." Her face lit with amusement. "Don't you remember how we used to load baskets of apples? I could do as many as you."

"I don't know about that." He climbed into the window, relieved to see that Timothy, whose job it was, had kept it clean. "But you weren't bad for a girl."

As they cleared out the window, preparing it for the transformation, Beth seemed happier than she had in a long time. Maybe it was partly the excitement of a new project combined with some easy chatter about old times. Reminiscing, even when she mentioned James now and then, came easily, and he encouraged it, searching his memory for happy times they'd shared.

With the last cardboard box removed, Beth looked around the space with satisfaction. "Gut. I have some of those old crates that my onkel used—they'd be just right to set things on."

"I remember them. Didn't we take some in to school for a spring program?" he asked, remembering. "And James jumped on one and broke it. I thought the teacher would be angry, but she didn't say a word." He shook his head. "He was the teacher's pet, ain't so?"

He glanced at Beth, but he didn't see the answering amusement he expected. "Yah." Beth's lips tightened. "James could always charm any woman."

If it helped, he'd slap himself for saying such a foolish thing. Clearly Beth hadn't forgotten the careless words the driver had spoken. And what must he do but say something that reminded her.

Above all else, he had to avoid letting her sense his own suspicions. "That was Teacher Emma, I'm afraid. She liked the boys better than the girls, I always thought." It was a foolish comment, he supposed, but he had to say something.

Her face tightened, and he knew she wasn't soothed.

"Did you notice the woman I was helping when you went to do the unloading?" Her tone was abrupt.

"I… I guess so. Red-haired, wasn't she? That's Mrs. Philmont. She comes in pretty often for fresh produce. Why?"

Beth didn't meet his eyes. "She seemed a little odd when she realized who I was. I thought…well, maybe she was someone James liked to flirt with." She shook her head quickly. "Never mind. I'm sorry I said it. I can't go around wondering about every woman who comes into the store."

Daniel didn't know what to say. He'd give anything to be able to say that James never looked at another woman, but she'd know that wasn't true. James had always looked. Even when they were teenagers…

He tried to stop that line of thought, but it wouldn't be stopped. James had only had to look at a girl to melt her heart. Even Beth, the girl his best friend cared for.

The fault was his, not James's. If he'd spoken up sooner… But he hadn't, and he'd lost his chance with Beth. It had been too late for him a long time ago.

Beth found herself mulling over that conversation with Daniel as she clamped the food mill onto the kitchen table that evening. Lydia would be there any minute, and they were going to can a batch of apple-sauce with some of the McIntosh apples she'd picked. With Benjy visiting his grandmother, they'd be able to have a good talk.

Would she or wouldn't she tell Lydia about Daniel? There wasn't that much to tell, she assured herself… just the fact that she'd spoken more frankly with Daniel about James than she'd done with anyone else, even her mother.

She couldn't tell her parents. It would hurt them too much. And Lydia had found out just by being there.

But Daniel knew at least part of the problem because she'd turned to him in her pain, and he'd been there, comforting and sure. The kind of good friend who came along a few times in a lifetime.

She wondered at the amount of trust she'd shown in him, but she couldn't go back and undo it.

The sound of hoofbeats in the lane told her Lydia was there, and her heart lifted. She'd enjoy their time together, she decided, and not worry about what she should say and what she should keep quiet.

The inevitable chatter erupted as soon as Lydia reached the house. She came into the kitchen like a whirlwind, dumping down a box of canning jars, tossing her heavy sweater onto the hook and hugging Beth.

"I thought I wasn't going to get out of the house. My sister stopped by, for a minute, she said, but she wouldn't stop talking. And I wanted to get on with the dishes, but Mamm would think that was rude."

"It's all right. We have plenty of time. Is your sister okay? Which one?"

"Doris, of course. Who else would be complaining?" She grabbed a knife and started cleaning apples.

"There's always something—if it's not the baby teething, it's the twins catching colds and her mother-in-law saying she should give them cod liver oil. It's enough to discourage you from getting married."

"You don't mean that," she said, thinking how popular Lydia had always been. Still, she'd never seemed to get serious about anyone.

"Maybe. Maybe not. I wish Miriam were home again," Lydia said, pausing in processing apples through the food mill. "It seems like forever since all three of us were together."

Beth nodded, picturing the youngest of the three cousins. Miriam's lively nature added spice to the time the three of them spent together.

"Soon, I hope," she said. "Her mamm mentioned that as soon as the last of the kinder got well, she'll head for home."

"We'd better wish none of those kinder catches another cold, or she'll be stuck there forever," Lydia grumbled.

Beth, knowing a bit more about the trials of having a sick youngster in the house, just shrugged. Lydia would learn when she had young ones of her own.

"Did I tell you who I saw in the store this week?" she asked, deciding to change the subject. "Aaron King came in with his bride." The King brothers were distant cousins, and everyone had been so pleased when Aaron came back where he belonged after too long in the Englisch world.

"How did they look?" Lydia gave her a mischievous look. "What do you think? Is Sally expecting yet?"

"What would your mother think?" she scolded. "An

unmarried girl like you speculating on whether some-one is pregnant?"

Lydia chuckled. "She'd think it was a sign I should be getting married myself. Come on, tell me."

"Don't you dare say I told you, but I think so. She has that glow a woman gets. And with her sister-in-law expecting soon, too, they'll have a happy time."

"A busy time, anyway." Lydia began filling jars with the still-warm sauce. She glanced at Beth. "Are you longing to be back washing diapers and getting up in the night?"

Beth shrugged. "No point in thinking about it, is there? That part of life is over for me." The words sent a sharp pain to her heart. She tried not to think of it, but she did long for more babies. Grieving for James meant grieving for those babies who wouldn't be born.

"Nonsense," Lydia said sharply. "I suppose it's too soon now, but one day you'll marry again. It's the nat-ural thing to do. Benjy needs a father, and you deserve to have a family to love."

She was shaking her head before Lydia finished speaking. "I can't. You of all people should realize that. How could I trust someone enough to marry again?"

"Ach, Beth, don't say that." Lydia left the apple-sauce to put her arm around Beth's waist in a quick hug. "James was the way he was, but every man isn't like that. There are plenty of gut, reliable men around. Daniel, for instance."

Beth pulled free of the hug. "Don't, Lydia. Daniel is a friend, but I couldn't feel that way about him."

Lydia didn't say anything for a moment, but Beth could feel Lydia's gaze on her, studying her. She seemed

to be making up her mind what to say, but Beth knew
better than to think she'd given up.

"I don't see why," she said finally. "Daniel has been
your friend since childhood, and now he's your partner. Working together in the store, it's natural that you
should grow even closer. Benjy likes him, doesn't he?"

She thought about Benjy's intent gaze following everything Daniel did when they worked together on some
project around the store.

"Daniel's good with him," she admitted. "Benjy does
like him, but that's not enough for marriage."

"You don't want Benjy to be an only child, like James
was, do you?"

That stung, but she knew Lydia didn't mean to be
unkind. "James's mother spoiled him, I suppose. But I
won't do that." She wouldn't, would she? What if she
was a little too protective at times? That was better than
letting Benjy get hurt.

"Yah, she did. And other people did, too, I'm thinking." Lydia didn't seem inclined to give up on the subject. "Just because he could be such a charmer…" She
hesitated, and then went on. "Well, I'm just saying that
it would be gut for Benjy if you remarried. Give him
another man to look up to. And you couldn't find a better man than Daniel, I'd say."

"Well, you've said it, but you don't have to keep repeating it." If that sounded tart, Beth couldn't help it.

"All right, I'll let it go for now," Lydia said. "But at
least Daniel has helped you get out and do things. Look
how pleased you were just at seeing Aaron and Sally.
Being Daniel's partner is good for you."

Beth raised her eyebrows. "I thought you were letting
it go," she reminded her. "I grant you everything you've

said about Daniel. He's a fine, trustworthy man, but I'm still thinking I don't want to marry again."

Lydia began to protest, but Beth raised a hand to stop her. "If I change my mind about that, you'll be the first to know. In the meantime, just leave it, Lydia. Please."

"Sorry." Lydia grimaced. "I guess I got carried away. I just want you to be happy."

"I know." Beth's voice gentled. Lydia wanted what was best for her, but she didn't even know herself what that best was.

Daniel was the best of partners, and as Lydia pointed out, he was a good friend. He might not be exciting and charming like James was, but he was reliable and steadfast. She was blessed to have him in her life, but that didn't mean either of them were thinking about marriage.

And as for her instinct to confide in him…well, that didn't mean anything more serious, did it?

Chapter Eight

The rest of the week passed peacefully enough, with Benjy getting used to staying with Janie several days. He also went to James's mother for one morning and confided that it wasn't as much fun as staying with Janie.

Beth talked to him about the importance of appreciating what people did for him, although she couldn't help understanding. His grandmother loved him very much, but since she lived in a small house in town, there wasn't much for a little boy to do there.

The extra time allowed Beth to finish her decorations of the store windows without having Benjy want to climb into the windows, too. Now, standing back and looking at the finished product, she felt a sense of satisfaction, as well as feeling more a part of the business than she ever had.

"Beth..."

She turned to find Anna standing behind her, looking as hesitant as she always did. Beth's heart went out to her.

"Yah, Anna. Do you want me for something?"

"Nothing... I mean, I thought you could double-check yesterday's receipts for me before you go."

"For sure, though I think you're better at addition and subtraction than I am, ain't so?"

She accompanied Anna back to the counter, wondering a little that Anna had consulted her rather than Daniel. The receipts were always checked by two people, but this was the first time Anna had asked her. Was it a sign that she was getting used to Beth?

She couldn't help thinking that it would be good for Anna to have another woman to talk with, though she didn't suppose she could give any very useful advice.

Together they bent over the page. "We got so busy just before closing that I was in a rush." Anna gave her an apologetic glance.

"It's all right. We know it's important that you get home on time or your father will worry." Though *worry* probably wasn't the right word.

"Denke," Anna murmured. "I... I don't want to disappoint Daniel. He and...and James were so kind to me."

Poor child, she didn't seem to have much kindness in her life. Still, just the fact that she was working in the store made it more likely she'd find someone to love. Preferably a young man strong enough to stand up to her father, she amended.

"You're a big help," she said. "James often said what a gut worker you are." That was stretching the truth a bit, but she felt sure he'd said it at least once or twice.

"He did?" Her face lit. "Denke."

As Anna turned quickly back to the accounts, Beth decided that was all the progress she'd be able to make today. Still, it was good to get that far with someone as shy as Anna.

"There, absolutely right," she said a few minutes later. She glanced at the clock. "I had best get those few groceries I wanted and be off home before it starts to rain." The clouds had been darkening for the past hour.

Anna hurried to pick up the bags she'd left behind the counter, and Beth took them in her arms. Her pantry was well stocked, but there was always something she needed, even so.

Daniel hadn't come back from deliveries yet, but she was comfortable leaving Anna in charge. If the threatening rain came, business would be quiet, anyway.

She made her way out the back door, only to find that the rain had arrived. She stood for a moment, debating. She wouldn't melt if she got a little wet, but the groceries might not fare so well.

Just as she decided to leave them until tomorrow, Daniel's buggy came around the store. He pulled up by the steps.

"You need a ride home, ain't so? Let me take those." He jumped down and relieved her of the grocery bags.

A surge of pleasure went through her at the sight of his smile and the sound of his voice. Because she didn't want to walk in the rain, she assured herself.

"It's been looking like it'll rain all day, and if I'd left a few minutes earlier, I'd have missed it."

"Or you'd have been halfway home and gotten soaked." Daniel extended a strong hand to help her up to the seat, and she smiled her thanks.

"Well, you were right on time to save me," she said lightly. "You finished the deliveries?"

"Yah, all done. Joshua Miller is sinking, so his

daughter said. I passed the bishop going in as I came out."

"Ach, I'm so sorry for her. She'll miss him." It wouldn't be appropriate to feel sorry for Joshua. He'd had a long life, and when the Lord took him, it would be a relief from pain and a joy to him.

Daniel nodded. "Emma will miss him, despite the difficult time she's had taking care of him. Death wipes out the trouble folks have caused, I guess."

She couldn't help wincing. "Not always."

He swung to face her, drawing up the horse. "Ach, Beth, I'm sorry. That was thoughtless. But no matter what James might have done or what I suspected—"

Daniel came to an abrupt stop, and she saw the guilt wash over his face. Saw it and in an instant feared she knew what had caused it.

"What do you mean? Suspected what? You know, don't you? James was carrying on with someone, and you knew."

"No, no, I didn't." He reached for her hand, but she pulled it away.

"Don't tell me lies." Anger carried her on so strong a wind that she couldn't think straight. "Tell me. What do you know? Who was the woman?"

"Beth, stop. It's not like that. I don't know anything, not for sure. I just thought that there was something…" He shook his head, as if angry at himself. "Look, it wondered me. Sometimes he left early—drove off without telling me where he was going."

The anger faded slowly, and she tried to hang on to it. It was better to be angry than to let the pain have free rein. She'd known, hadn't she? The note had told her so. But Daniel…

"You lied to me." The anger surged back. "I trusted you. I believed you when you said it was just James's way to chat with all the women."

"I didn't lie. I didn't really know anything. I might have suspected, but I couldn't condemn a friend based only on suspicion."

"I thought I was your friend." She threw the words at him and swung around. All she could think was to get out of the buggy, to walk away and never have to look at Daniel again.

He grabbed her wrist, holding it firmly. "What are you doing? You can't get out in the rain."

"I'd rather get soaked than talk to you any longer."

His face paled, but he picked up the lines with his left hand and set the horse moving. "I won't say anything. You'll be home in an instant."

It would take an undignified tussle to get out here. She closed her hands over the edge of the seat, staring straight ahead. If he said another thing…

But Daniel was true to his word this time. He stopped the buggy at her porch. She jumped down before he could move to help her, snatched her bags and fled into the house.

Somehow Daniel managed to keep his face normal during the afternoon, although he saw Anna give him a wondering look a time or two. Timothy noticed nothing, of course. He was as oblivious of other people's feelings as most teenage boys, but at the moment, Daniel was just as glad. At least Anna wouldn't say anything, no matter how much she might wonder.

He might be able to hide his feelings from other people, but not from himself. How could he have been so careless? He should have known that Beth was too sharp and knew him too well to let any slip get by her. He'd doomed any chance he might have had with Beth, and he'd put the future of the store in jeopardy. That didn't mean anywhere near as much as the fact that he'd hurt Beth and let her down.

The ironic part of it was that he still didn't know anything for sure about James. Had he been involved with another woman? He wanted to reject that idea— wanted to be ashamed that he even suspected it. But he couldn't. Maybe he knew, in some deep, unacknowledged part of his soul, that James could have done it. Whether he did or not…

Now that he thought back over what he'd said and what Beth had said, he started to wonder. How had Beth jumped to the conclusion so quickly? Surely that foolish comment by the trucker hadn't been enough to make her think that.

It didn't really matter how it had all happened. He had to do something. He had to talk to Beth, to beg her forgiveness and to pray she had it in her heart to forgive. No matter what she said to him, he deserved it.

He stayed on at the store after closing, busying himself with one chore after another. There was no sense in trying to have a conversation with Beth until she'd put Benjy to bed.

Finally it seemed late enough to make that likely. The gentle glow of autumn was fading into dusk as he walked quickly down the lane. He tried to form an opening sentence in his mind, but everything he thought of seemed too feeble to convince anyone.

It wasn't until Daniel neared the house that it occurred to him that Beth might have visitors. He couldn't say any of the things he needed to say with others there. Beth might not let him say them if she were alone, either. Practically the last words she'd spoken to him commanded him not to speak to her.

His effort to come up with a good opening line was unsuccessful, but at least there was no sign of anyone else as he approached the kitchen door. He hesitated a moment, breathed a silent prayer and knocked.

From beyond the door came the sound of footsteps. He saw the knob start to turn and then stop.

"Who is it?" Beth was either being cautious or else she suspected it was he.

"Beth, please let me in. I must speak with you. You have to hear my explanation."

"No. I don't." The words were implacable, but he didn't hear her move away, and that gave him a whisper of hope.

"No, you don't have to," he agreed. Demanding wasn't the way to do this. "But I'm praying you'll let me say how wrong I was and how sorry I am."

Nothing but silence came from the other side of the door. The cold of despair settled into him. She would never forgive him.

The knob rattled. Slowly the door opened. Beth stood in the opening, her face pale and rigid. Then she stepped back wordlessly to let him in.

The house was silent. Benjy must be in bed, or he'd come rushing to see who was there.

Beth closed the door and folded her arms as if she were cold. "A few minutes. That's all."

He nodded. "Please, try to believe I was trying to do my best for you and Benjy." Seeing a retort forming in her expression, he hurried on. "I didn't know. I still don't know, not for sure. I'd started to be suspicious, that's all. I didn't want to believe it."

She didn't speak, but she gave a slight nod, and he felt encouraged. She must know what that was like. How did you believe that a person you cared deeply about could commit such a wrong?

She still didn't speak, and he knew he'd have to explain more fully.

"James…well, James always had a way with him. All the women liked him. Not just young women, but little girls and old women, too. I was used to it. I never suspected…"

He let that trail off. Maybe if he'd noticed, if he'd taken it more seriously, he could have headed it off before James did something wrong.

"Maybe a month or two before his accident, I noticed he started leaving earlier. Or he'd come in to do inventory in the evening and make an excuse to leave after an hour."

Now for the hardest part. "It wondered me. I didn't want to think it. It was like a betrayal of my friend. But finally I couldn't hold it back. I had to speak. I told him my suspicions."

Beth didn't move, but her fingers dug into her arms hard enough to leave marks. He thought she was trying to shield herself from what she feared was coming.

"At first he tried to laugh it off."

Beth finally moved, maybe wanting to postpone the inevitable. She took a few steps and grasped the back of a kitchen chair.

"That last night…" His throat tightened, and the words came out hoarsely. "I tried again. I let him know

I didn't believe him. He got angry. He stamped out. A few hours later I heard about the accident."

Beth sagged as if her bones had turned to water. Galvanized, he caught her before she could fall and lowered her into the chair. Why hadn't he realized… he shouldn't have told her that way. But she wouldn't settle for anything else.

He bent over her. "Just sit here. I'll get you water." Not waiting for a response, he grabbed a glass and splashed water into it, sloshing some onto the floor as he took it to her.

She tried to hold the glass, but her hands shook. He clasped it in his and raised it to her lips. She gulped it down as if thirsty, but then in a moment she pushed it away, straightening in the chair.

"Enough," she murmured. "I'm all right. Sorry."

"My fault." He sank into the chair next to her. "Beth, please understand. James was gone, and you didn't seem to suspect anything. How could I tell you then? It would have hurt you to no purpose. I wanted to protect you and Benjy. If I was wrong, I'm sorry."

She shook her head slowly. "I understand. But I'd rather have the truth."

They sat silently. Daniel felt empty. He'd told her everything he knew. He couldn't do more.

After a bit, his mind started to work. He went back over everything they'd said to each other about James, and he saw something he'd wondered about.

He straightened, staring at Beth. "You suspected, didn't you? Not just because of what the driver said about James. You already thought something was wrong, didn't you?"

Beth looked at him, her green eyes darkening as if night was falling.

"Yah. I did." Beth seemed to come to a decision. "Wait here."

She walked to the hallway, and he heard her light footsteps going up the stairs. He stood where he was, wondering what was coming and how he could deal with it. He owed something to James as his friend, but even more to Beth, who was hurting so much.

It took Beth only a few moments to retrieve the note from its hiding place in her bedroom. She hesitated, holding it by the edges. She disliked even the feel of it against her fingers.

Perhaps if she'd burned it the day she'd discovered it, she'd have been able to forget, but it had been impossible. At first, she'd tortured herself by reading it over and over, trying to tease some meaning or identity from it.

Since she'd become so involved in the store, the power of that piece of paper had lessened. She hadn't looked at it in days, and she didn't want to see it now. And most particularly she didn't want to show it to Daniel.

There was no getting out of it now. She'd given too much away to keep it a secret now. Besides, she owed him the truth. He'd been open with her.

It couldn't have been easy for Daniel to tell her about that last conversation he'd had with James. She'd had no trouble recognizing the guilt and pain in his eyes when he'd spoken. After all, she'd felt the same herself—regretting every sharp word or thought of their marriage.

Refusing to let herself delay any longer, she marched back downstairs and into the kitchen. Dropping the note in front of him, she slipped back into the chair she'd vacated.

"I found this about a month after James died." She struggled for a second and then blurted out the rest of it. "Lydia had come over to help me get his clothes ready to give away." She felt again the aversion she'd felt that day. "I didn't want to, but she pushed me into it. I found the note in his drawer of the chest upstairs."

Daniel had read it by this time, and his forehead was knotted into a frown. "You're thinking it referred to that last night, but it might have been something old—some girl who had a crush on him."

He was trying to find an alternate explanation, just as Lydia had at first. She shook her head.

"No. I'd been in that drawer just a couple of days earlier. And look at it. It's not old."

Given his own suspicions, Daniel seemed to be having difficulty accepting the proof. Beth could almost see his internal struggle, and the moment in which he accepted it.

Daniel nodded slowly, his jaw hardening. "Yah. You're right."

He looked at her, studying her face so intently that she seemed to feel the touch on her skin. "This shows us what the woman felt about James. But not what James felt about her."

"It doesn't excuse him." Her voice was tart.

"No, it doesn't." Daniel folded the paper so that the words were hidden. He held it up between his fingers. "What are you going to do with this?"

"I don't know." She wavered, unsure.

"Wouldn't it be best to destroy it? You wouldn't want Benjy ever to see it."

"No, but…" She reached out and took it from him. "I'll burn it. But not now. I'm not ready yet."

Resentment rose in her. Daniel had said very little, but she knew he thought the note was better destroyed. Did he think her jealous or vengeful for hanging on to it? Maybe he did, and maybe he was right. She just knew she wasn't ready.

Daniel seemed to recognize the depth of her feeling. He put his hand over hers, and she felt compassion and understanding flow through the touch, finding its way to her heart. He wanted to protect her, much as she wanted to protect Benjy.

For the first time in too long, healing began, very slowly, to make its way through her. Gratitude welled in her heart. Without volition, her hand turned in his until they were palm to palm, clasped snugly. Beth didn't try to figure out what it meant. She just sat still, accepting.

Chapter Nine

"I'm going with you this morning, Mammi, ain't so?" Benjy was eager to firm up his plans for the day as he hopped down from his seat at the breakfast table.

"That's right." Beth hesitated, wondering if she was doing the right thing by taking him to work with her. Was it better than leaving him with Janie or worse? There didn't seem to be any guidelines that fit her situation, making her feel guilty either way.

"You like going to the store, don't you?" she asked.

"Yah, for sure." He gave a little hop that said he was eager to get started. "Daniel said I could help him today."

Beth felt an interior tremor at the mention of Daniel. The memory of what had happened between them the previous night was too fresh. She still hadn't managed to decide how she felt about it.

"What are you going to do?" It was cowardly to avoid saying his name. She'd best get herself together before they left for the store.

"Make a new shelf in the office. That's what Daniel said. He said we could make it in a jiffy."

She'd noticed her son was prone to quote Daniel several times a day now. "That will be wonderful gut. We need more space."

Benjy stopped his energetic hopping and stood still, seeming deep in thought. "Daniel's gut at making things." He paused, then looked up at her, his blue eyes wondering. "Was Daadi gut at making things?"

Beth's breath caught. She'd warned herself that one day Benjy would start asking questions about his daadi. She just hadn't expected it now. Should she simply answer, or did he need more assurance about his father?

"Daadi didn't make a lot of things at the store," she said carefully. "Daniel did that, and Daadi was gut at other things, like taking care of the customers. That's why they were partners…they each did something the other didn't."

She waited, watching his small face. Did he need more than that?

But she couldn't read any doubts in his eyes. He nodded as if satisfied and skipped toward the hall. "Hurry and get ready, Mammi. We need to get to work."

That startled a laugh from her. Where had he picked up that phrase? Well, it was true enough.

"As soon as I finish the breakfast dishes, we'll go. Did you make your bed yet?"

"I will." He darted off, and his feet thudded on the stairs.

Beth shook her head. One small boy could certainly make a lot of noise. And ask a lot of questions.

She wasn't sure how she felt about his growing closeness to Daniel. But it was natural, she supposed. In the past week, he had spent more time with Daniel than with his grandfather or his uncles. And there was never a need to worry when he was with Daniel.

Her thoughts slipped back to the previous night. She'd been so determined to hold on to her anger with him, but she hadn't been able to. She had understood him too well for that. He'd been torn by his long friendship with James fighting against his growing suspicions.

She would have been as well, if she hadn't found out in such a devastating way. The note had left no room for doubt.

The note. Daniel obviously thought it best destroyed at once. And he'd been right about the dangers of anyone else seeing it. If Benjy ever learned about his father's failing, it shouldn't be that way.

Or any way at all, if she could manage it. Lydia and Daniel were the only ones who knew, except for her. And the unknown woman.

Maybe Daniel had been right. There was no reason to keep it, and every reason to destroy it. Quickly, before she could change her mind, Beth retrieved the note from the drawer where she'd hidden it after Daniel left. Striking a match, she held it over the sink and lit the edge of the paper.

It burned quickly, the words disappearing into the flame, then the whole paper crumbling into ash. She turned on the faucet and washed the ash down the drain.

There. It was done. She wouldn't torment herself with it again. It was time to start looking toward the future, not the past.

Benjy galloped down the stairs and into the kitchen and stopped to sniff. "It smells like burning, Mammi."

"I guess it does." She kept her face away from him

as she took her sweater from the hook and pulled it on. "It was just a little bit of trash. Komm, let's go to work."

The lane was still damp after yesterday's rain, and rain had brought down a fresh drift of leaves, as it always did. The season was moving on quickly, and it would soon be time for cider-making if she intended to do it this year.

That was one of the few orchard chores James had enjoyed, probably because they always had a group of people there to help and it always turned into a work frolic. Everyone brought something to share for supper, and they all had to try the fresh golden cider.

Beth struggled with the idea for a few minutes but then glanced at Benjy. He'd love it, even if he didn't remember it from last year.

She should mention it to Mamm and Daad, and together they'd pick a date. She couldn't stop doing it just because it reminded her of James.

A burst of wind swept them along with some bright yellow leaves, and they hurried into the store, laughing a little. "We beat the wind here," Benjy crowed, and trotted toward the back, where she could spot Daniel opening a carton.

Instead of heading in that direction, she paused at the counter to exchange greetings with Anna, who was smiling as she watched Benjy.

"I tell him not to run indoors, but it doesn't seem to stick," she said.

She scanned Anna's face with the usual concern, but she actually looked better this morning. She didn't have the pallor she sometimes did. Maybe things were better at home. Beth said a quick prayer that it was so.

"Ach, no one cares that he runs here," Anna said. "We all love him."

It was the most personal thing Anna had ever said to her, and Beth's heart warmed. If she could grow closer to the girl, she might be able to help her.

"That's gut of you to say. But we all have to learn manners, ain't so? The trouble is that he usually makes me laugh just about the time I should be correcting him."

Anna was still watching Benjy. "He looks just like his daadi." Her words came out in a whisper, as if she were talking to herself, and then she seemed to hear what she'd said. She flushed, tears welling in her eyes. "I'm sorry. I shouldn't have said…"

"It's all right. It's gut for Benjy if people talk normally about his father." She reached out, thinking to comfort the girl with a pat on the shoulder, but Anna winced away.

"I… I should go and help Timothy." She scurried off.

Beth moved behind the counter. The poor girl had embarrassed herself, thinking she'd said the wrong thing. She remembered that stage where she'd wavered between being a child and a grown woman. It wasn't easy for anyone.

Daniel eyed Beth cautiously while he welcomed Benjy, pleased that the lad immediately started helping him unpack the carton. Beth seemed occupied with Anna, and as far as he could tell, she hadn't looked in his direction at all.

Was she angry with him about last night? He'd thought they'd parted with forgiveness on both sides, but maybe she'd regretted letting him comfort her. Or she might think he'd gone too far in saying she should get rid of that note. It wasn't his business to advise her to do something she didn't want to do.

The note had shocked him, and he could easily imagine the impact it had made on her, fresh from mourning her husband's death. A flicker of anger went through him. James should have had better sense. He'd been wrong to be seeing another woman, but if he'd been determined to sin, he might at least have destroyed that note and saved Beth a great deal of pain.

He'd been mad at James a number of times when they were young. That was only natural—kids fought and made up again, sometimes resorting to a shove or two. Still, he'd never felt as disappointed or as angry as he did now. How could anyone fortunate enough to have won Beth for his wife even look at anyone else?

Benjy tugged at his sleeve, and he realized the boy had been asking him something.

"Aren't we going to build the shelf today? I told Mammi, and she said that was gut." He tilted his face, obviously considering something. "Maybe she really needs it."

"I'm sure it will make her happy if we build it," he said gravely. "Let's break down this box and put it in the storeroom, and then we can get started."

Benjy, like any boy, enjoyed jumping on the box to flatten it. Even though it was now taller than he was, he carried it to the storeroom, talking all the time.

"I told Mammi that you were gut at making things. She said that Daadi was gut at other things."

"That's true." He held the storeroom door while Benjy slid the box through. "That's why we were partners."

"That's what Mammi said." Benjy beamed with satisfaction. He carried the box over to the right stack.

It was high enough that Benjy couldn't reach the top, so Daniel lifted him. The boy felt ridiculously light, and a wave of affection surged through him. He'd always been fond of Benjy, but since he'd been coming to the store, Daniel's feelings had grown deeper. If he could help it, Benjy wouldn't miss any of the care he needed. After all, there were some things only a man could teach a boy.

"Gut job," he said, setting Benjy down.

Benjy stood for a moment, eyeing the stack of cardboard. "Are you going to have a big fire with the boxes?"

He shook his head. "We keep them here, and anyone who needs boxes to pack things in can come and take as many as they want."

"Mammi was burning some trash this morning," Benjy volunteered. "She did it in the sink. I thought she should burn it outside."

"It must have been something very small." Something the size of a piece of folded paper.

Benjy didn't seem inclined to talk about it. "Are we going to build the shelf now?" He looked up at Daniel, his eyes filled with eagerness. "I want to learn how, so I can help."

"We'll get the tools and start, okay?" His mind wasn't on carpentry. Instead, he'd focused on the fact Benjy had innocently let slip.

Maybe he shouldn't have listened, but how could he help it? And had Beth been burning that note this morning?

He glanced across the width of the store to where Beth was helping a customer pick out a pumpkin. She was smiling, looking perfectly normal. In fact, she might be looking a little more at ease than she had in a long time.

If she had burned that note, he could only be thankful. No doubt he should have kept his opinions to himself. Still, she'd shown it to him. She wouldn't have done that if she hadn't wanted to hear what he had to say.

Daniel's stomach still turned queasy at the thought of it. Even if the note was gone now, the words were engraved on his mind. And, he didn't doubt, on Beth's, as well.

He'd thought it would be far better for Beth if she could forget about knowing who was going to meet James that last night. She'd have to forgive, no matter who it was, but that wouldn't be easy. *Forgive if you would be forgiven.* The Lord hadn't left any room for evasion in the words. He, too, had to forgive. James had hurt him, too, although not in the grievous way he'd caused pain for Beth.

She hadn't looked at him, he told himself as he and Benjy headed into the office with the toolbox. That didn't mean anything. She might not have noticed him. But he'd like to find out what she was thinking.

With the materials already gathered for adding the shelf, it wasn't going to take long. The challenge was to find something Benjy could do.

But Benjy was easy to please. Standing on a chair, watching intently, he grinned as they finished screwing in the second bracket.

"We did it," he exclaimed, so happy that Daniel had to grin back at him.

"We still have to put the shelf on," he cautioned. "Shall we try it?"

Benjy nodded. He seemed to hold his breath until the shelf was fixed into place. "There!" He paused. "If I learn a lot, will I be a gut partner, like Daadi?"

He hadn't expected the question, and it struck him right in the heart. "I think you'll be a very gut partner one day. Let's go tell your mammi."

Grinning, Benjy bolted across the office and on toward his mother. Daniel followed more slowly. Did he dare to bring up what Benjy had said? Probably not, but he longed to know.

Beth greeted him with a smile. "I understand you and your helper finished the new shelf."

"That we did. Is Benjy going to show it to you?"

"That's why he's pulling on my hand." She glanced at her son. "Just wait a minute," she told Benjy. "I have something to say to Daniel. You go ahead, and I'll be there in a minute."

Benjy let go and scooted off at his usual trot, and Beth looked at Daniel. "Denke, Daniel. I'm sure it takes longer when he helps, but he does love it."

He shrugged. "It's nothing." He'd do far more for Beth and her son if he could.

Beth hesitated a moment, glancing away as if she didn't want to meet his eyes. "I wanted to say… I took your advice. It's gone."

Unable to help himself, he clasped her hand for a second. "I'm glad."

Beth looked fleetingly into his face and then hurried after her son.

Standing there, seeming to feel the warmth of her hand still in his, Daniel faced the truth. He loved Beth. It might never come to anything but friendship, but he loved her.

* * *

Benjy was skipping alongside Beth as they headed for home later, making her feel she'd like to skip, as well. She seemed inexpressibly lighter, and she had no idea why.

She swung Benjy's hand, loving the way his fingers tightened on hers and the sweet expression in his soft, round face as he looked up at her.

"What makes you want to skip?" she asked.

His forehead crinkled as he considered the question. He took another skipping step, and then his forehead cleared and his eyes lit. "I know. Because I feel happy, and when I skip, I get more happy."

Laughter bubbled up in her. "Gut. I'm glad you feel happy. I'll have to try that—maybe it will make me happier, too."

"Aren't you happy, Mammi?" With a quick change, his face turned serious.

"For sure I am." She scooped him into her arms for a hug. "Because I have you, and you make me happy all the time."

"Even when I'm naughty?"

"Even then," she assured him. And she knew just as suddenly why she felt so much freer. She'd resolved to turn away from the past and focus on their future—hers and Benjy's. No doubt she'd falter sometimes, but at least she was looking in the right direction.

Benjy tugged at her hand. "Skip with me."

Laughter bubbled up in her, and together they began to skip toward the house. Benjy had been right. Skipping did make her feel happier.

They were laughing and breathless when they reached the porch. Trying to catch her breath, Beth glanced at the door and found her mother-in-law looking back at her.

Sarah's expression sobered her instantly. It said she didn't approve—whether of the laughter or the skipping, Beth wasn't sure.

She forced herself to smile. "Look, Benjy. Here's your grossmammi come to see us."

Benjy scurried to hug his grandmother, and Sarah's disapproval transformed into a look of indulgent affection and pride. She pushed open the screen door and bent for a hug.

"Ach, there's my sweet boy. I'm sehr glad to see you."

When the hug went on a little too long for Benjy, he started to wiggle. Going to the rescue, Beth grasped the door to usher them inside.

"Sarah, this is such a nice surprise. If I'd known you were coming today, we could have come home a little earlier from the store."

"I didn't know myself." Sarah smoothed Benjy's silky-soft hair down where it tended to curl at the sides. "Myra Miller had to pick something up at her brother's place, so I said I'd ride along. I thought I could get some apples from you."

"For sure," Beth said, thankful she'd cleaned the kitchen up before they'd left. "Will you have lunch with us?"

"Better not." Sarah glanced at the clock. "We'd best get the apples so I'm ready when Myra comes back."

Myra, as Beth well knew, was Sarah's closest friend. Also a widow, she lived less than a block away from the cottage where James had grown up. An unstoppable talker, Myra was, and Beth had sometimes wondered how the two of them heard the other when they talked simultaneously.

Lifting a basket from a hook in the mudroom, Beth handed it to Benjy. "Let's pick them now. Would you like McIntosh or Red Delicious?"

"McIntosh, please. Then I'll make apple dumplings for when Benjy comes to visit me tomorrow. And maybe one or two of the Delicious."

Benjy was already scurrying out the door with the basket. "I'll get them," he called.

"Now, you wait until we get there before you start picking," Sarah said, hurrying after him.

"It's all right. He knows which ones to pick." Beth fell into step with her.

"But he might get hurt." Sarah gave her a look that suggested she was a negligent mother.

"I'm sure he'll be fine." After all, Sarah had lost her only son. She was bound to be feeling overly worried about her only grandson.

They walked in silence for another few steps, but Beth sensed Sarah had more to say.

Sure enough, Sarah emitted a sigh. "You know I'm not one to interfere," she began, "but I really have to caution you." She shook her head. "When I saw you running and laughing down the lane…don't you realize anyone might have seen you? And in your black dress, too."

Beth didn't know whether she felt more annoyed or more guilty, and she tried to compose herself before replying. "I'm sorry, Sarah. Perhaps it did seem frivolous, but Benjy was in such a happy mood that I wanted to encourage him." She tried to say more, but her throat seemed tied up in knots.

She certainly couldn't say anything about her own feeling of relief. Sarah wouldn't understand without knowing of James's failing, and she was determined that Sarah never would. That was the best thing she could do to protect her mother-in-law, and she'd keep that secret no matter what.

A glance at Sarah told her that she was near to tears. "Yah, for sure Benjy comes first. I just wouldn't want anyone to think you weren't properly mourning my son. It's important what others think of you. It reflects on James."

All Beth could do was nod and keep silent. There didn't seem to be any appropriate response that was also truthful.

"Well, let's forget it," Sarah said. "I'm sure you'll think again another time."

Sarah's attention was diverted by the sight of Benjy perched in the crotch of the biggest McIntosh tree, and she rushed toward him, uttering cautions and insisting he hang on until she could lift him down.

Benjy assumed his mulish expression, knowing that he was allowed to climb that high alone. In a moment he'd be telling his grandmother so. Murmuring a silent prayer for patience, Beth went in pursuit of Sarah, preparing to intercede and knowing it wouldn't be welcomed by her mother-in-law.

A memory popped to the front of her mind—Daniel's firm, quiet voice countering her objections to letting Benjy help that first day at the store. He'd been right, and she knew that now, but she doubted Sarah would ever admit to being overprotective, either toward Benjy or toward James.

Chapter Ten

The next afternoon Beth and Benjy walked down the street toward Sarah's cottage. Sarah would be looking forward to his arrival. She glanced down at Benjy. For some reason, he seemed to be dragging his feet.

Familiar doubts nagged at her. Should she have left him with Janie this morning, knowing he'd be going to his grandmother's this afternoon? He was only four. Maybe all of the changes in his life were too much. Maybe he needed her with him more, not less.

As if he felt her gaze, Benjy looked up at her, his straw hat slipping on his soft corn-silk hair. Smiling, she straightened it.

He shook his head, obviously not caring if his hat was crooked. "What are you going to do this afternoon, Mammi?"

"I'm going to stop and see your other grossmammi. And *my* grossmammi, too."

Benjy puzzled over that for a moment and grinned when he got it. "I have an extra grossmammi, ain't so?"

"You do. We have lots of family around us."

"Yah. It's nice," he said. Then a cloud came over his

face. "I wish I could go with you. It's more fun at the farm, especially if my cousins are there."

She could understand his feelings, but she couldn't let him have favorites among his grandmothers. "Your cousins are at school now, remember? And even if they weren't, you have to remember that different people live differently. When you're a guest, your job is to fit in."

Benjy nodded, but he still looked mopey. Even while she debated about whether she should say something more, he looked up with the smile that was so like James's.

"I'll behave, Mammi. And Grossmammi made me apple dumplings."

Apparently, the way to Benjy's heart was through his stomach. As long as he was good, she'd take it. Time enough for him to learn to be a gracious guest for the sake of kindness.

Sarah was waiting, opening the door as they went up the short walk to the cottage that had been her and James's home since before her husband died. As always, it looked spotless and tidy, the small patch of grass trimmed and the chrysanthemums along the porch tied to stakes so they wouldn't sprawl.

"Benjy!" Sarah held out open arms for a hug. "Komm in. I'm happy to see you." She glanced over his head at Beth. "I'll bring him home by suppertime, yah?"

Beth nodded. "Denke. Have fun, Benjy. I'll see you later."

He waved, seeming already lured by the scent of apple dumplings, and she chased the guilt away firmly. Benjy was all right. And she was doing the best she could with each new day.

It was a short walk back to the lane that curved behind her place to the farm where she'd grown up. The fields stretched back toward the ridges and along the flat area that bordered the lane—golden now in the autumn sunlight. A wordless prayer of thanks for the beauty of this land seemed to flow from her heart. She was blessed to live here, surrounded by family and dear friends on every side.

Her steps quickened as she neared the kitchen door of the farmhouse. The sound of women's voices floated out, accompanied by the smell of baking. Her mother and grandmother had already started the cookies for Grossmammi's quilting frolic the next day.

They were so engrossed in talk that they apparently didn't hear her approach. She opened the door, smiling in anticipation.

"You must not need my help with the cookies. It smells as if they're almost done."

Her mother rushed to hug her, closely followed by Grossmammi, brushing flour from her hands and transferring it to her apron. With their arms tight around her, Beth felt like a little girl again, seeking sympathy from the most important women in her life.

Wait…sympathy? She would have said she didn't need it, but she realized in an instant how much she longed to tell them everything—James's betrayal, her doubts, her fear that she was to blame for his wandering.

But she couldn't. Two people already knew, and every other person in on a secret made it more likely that something would slip. Her need to protect Benjy must be stronger than her yearning for their sympathy.

"We saved shortbread cookies to do with you," Mammi said. "We've already made the snickerdoodles and brownies."

Beth went to the sink to wash her hands. "Grossmammi, you must expect a lot of hungry women at the quilting frolic."

Her grandmother chuckled, her rosy cheeks crinkling. "Quilting is hard work. It needs a lot of fueling. Besides, everyone will be able to take some cookies home."

Obviously Grossmammi was having a good day. She hoped that would be true the next day as well, although her fellow quilters were old friends who understood.

"You can take yours today," Mammi said, handing her a bowl for the shortbread cookies. "After you do your share."

Beth set to work on the familiar recipe. Every family seemed to have its special recipe that had been handed down from generation to generation. Her family's was the rich, buttery recipe for shortbread cookies, and the thought of them made her mouth water.

Even though they'd seen each other a couple of days before, there seemed to be plenty to say. Family chatter kept them occupied until the shortbread was in the oven, when Mammi declared it was time to take a break for tea and cookies. Beth grabbed the kettle, laughingly arguing over who would fix the tea.

Grossmammi drew her to a chair. "Tell us how everything is going at the store. Do you like it? Where is Benjy today?"

"With Sarah this afternoon." She started with the last question first. "She dropped by for some apples yesterday." She paused, remembering how difficult it had been to deal with Sarah's determination to keep Benjy from doing just about everything.

"And?" Her mother had heard the unspoken thought, it seemed. "Was something wrong?"

"Not really. I was just afraid Benjy might talk back to her because she was so protective—not wanting him to climb or run or even reach for the apples."

"Did he?" Mamm asked.

"No," she admitted. "But it made me nervous the whole time. I tried to explain that those were things he normally did, but she's so cautious."

"She always was." Grossmammi took a sip of her tea. "She spoiled James with all her fussing over him, and she'll do the same with Benjy if you're not careful."

Beth glanced at her mother. Grossmammi was becoming more outspoken the older she became. What she said might be true, but Beth had to be tactful with Sarah, especially since James was gone.

"Now, Mammi," her mother said. "Beth will handle it all right. And a little fussing won't hurt the boy."

Beth held her breath, fearing an argument, but Grossmammi just shrugged. "I just don't want Benjy to be too much like his father."

Beth sought frantically for another topic of conversation. It almost sounded as if Grossmammi knew, but she couldn't.

Mammi stepped in. "How is it going at the store? Does Benjy enjoy going there or is it too much for such a little one?"

"It's definitely not too much for him." Relieved, she smiled at her mother with thankfulness. "You should see him going from one person to another trying to help. And they're all so good with him. Especially Daniel." She pictured Daniel's large hands guiding Benjy's as they worked together.

"Ach, Benjy is such a sweet boy. Of course they're gut with him." Mammi beamed with pride over her grandson.

"And Daniel is a gut man," Grossmammi added. She was still for a moment, her gaze seeming to drift to the past. "There was a time when I thought he'd be just right for our Beth." She smiled. "Maybe it's not too late, yah?"

Beth's mother drew in a shocked breath. "Mammi! It's much too early for Beth to be thinking of that."

Grossmammi chuckled. "Nothing wrong with thinking," she said, twinkling at Beth.

Shaking her head, Beth busied herself with her tea, hoping the cup would hide the fact that she might be blushing.

By the time Beth reached home, she had convinced herself that she had shown no reaction at all to her grandmother's comment about Daniel. He was a friend, and that was all.

Besides, after what had happened with James, she wasn't at all sure that she could trust anyone enough to marry again. Even if she did grow to feel more confident about her own judgment, Benjy might resent the idea of someone taking his father's place. And as her mother had said, it was much too soon to be thinking about that at all.

Benjy should be back before too long, and she suspected his grandmother would have given him several treats during the afternoon. A light supper would suit them both, and she had several quarts of the beef vegetable soup she'd made back in the spring. With only herself and a young child to feed, it had become increasingly tempting to skip making a heavy meal for supper.

She'd have time to feed the chickens before Sarah and Benjy arrived, so she headed into the mudroom to mix up the mash for the hens. But she'd barely gotten started when she heard a buggy coming up the drive.

Leaving the pail on the counter, Beth headed for the door. Sarah must be bringing Benjy back early. Maybe an active four-year-old was a bit much for her.

She stepped out onto the back porch, but the horse and buggy weren't familiar. When it drew nearer, she recognized Elijah Schmidt from the church. She knew him, of course, but he and his family were newcomers and lived on the opposite side of town, where he ran a couple of small businesses—a harness shop that his oldest son managed and a fabric store that was his wife's favorite project.

There didn't seem to be any reason for him to be calling on her, but she went forward with a welcoming smile.

"Elijah, wilkom. What can I do for you?" She stopped at the bottom of the steps. She didn't intend to ask him in. That seemed unsuitable when she was alone here.

"How are you, Beth? And your young one?" Elijah heaved his considerable bulk down from the buggy seat. He wasn't fat, she scolded herself. Just…large.

"We're fine, denke, Elijah. And your family?" She spoke the expected words, still wondering what had brought him here.

"Fine, fine." He didn't seem to be thinking of them. "I guess you're wondering what brought me here."

She was, but it didn't seem polite to say so. "Anyone

of the Leit is always wilkom here. Everyone has been so kind since James's passing."

"A sad thing," he said. "In a way, you might say that's what brought me here. It's about the store."

Beth looked at him blankly. She supposed his family sometimes shopped at the store. Most of the community did, but she didn't recall seeing them.

"Your share of the store, I should say." He propped one foot on the step, the movement making him closer to her than she liked.

"I've been thinking that it must be difficult for you, having your husband's funds tied up in the business. Probably doesn't leave you and your boy much to get along with."

She stiffened, feeling the urge to say that wasn't his business. "You needn't be concerned about us. We're doing fine."

A faint look of irritation crossed his face. "You've got your family, of course, but they're busy with their own farms. So it seemed to me you might be glad of someone to buy out your share."

The comment startled her, coming out of the blue. It had always been a possibility, but she had settled in so well at the store that she hadn't thought of it at all.

"I don't think…"

He didn't let her finish. "I'd be prepared to make you a generous offer for your share of the business, cash in hand. Then you wouldn't have to worry about business at all."

The sum he named sounded like a great deal. Still, she had no idea what the store was actually worth.

She collected her thoughts. "That's generous of you, Elijah. But I don't think…"

Elijah seemed determined not to let her finish. "You'll want to talk it over with your daad, that's for sure. An inexperienced young woman like yourself wouldn't know what's fair."

Beth's impulse was to turn him down immediately, but maybe she ought to consider it. She'd been determined from the beginning that whatever she did had to be what was best for her son.

"I'm afraid I couldn't make any sudden decision. If I should want to talk about it, I'll be in touch."

Elijah's heavy eyebrows came down in a frown. "If you want. It's a fair offer. Anyone will tell you that. And if you don't decide soon…well, I might not be interested. I'm looking to invest in another business, and I'm considering a couple of things besides the store." He leaned toward her. "I'll be glad to talk to your father anytime. An inexperienced young woman like you ought to leave the business to the men."

That was the second time he'd called her inexperienced and young, and she discovered it annoyed her. James had never said it in so many words, but she realized now that had been his attitude each time she'd suggested helping with the store.

In fact, he'd kept her in ignorance of the store's running, so that she hadn't been prepared when she had to take over his share. If not for Daniel's help…

She stopped that train of thought. She should consider Schmidt's offer carefully. But she wouldn't let anyone pressure her into a decision.

"I'll have to take that chance," she said, putting as much firmness as she could into her voice. "If I want to talk to you about it, I'll let you know."

It was more or less what she'd already said, and she

wondered if he'd accept it this time. Beth could see him debating whether to push his argument or not.

At last he nodded. "Fine. I just hope I won't have to let you down."

Deciding there was nothing more to be said, Beth retreated up the steps to the porch, watching him clamber back into the buggy, turn and drive off. Her thoughts lingered on the amount of money he'd offered. It had sounded like a fortune to her, but money wasn't everything. Benjy's future was what mattered.

Daniel locked the front door of the store and stood for a moment, admiring the windows. Beth had been right about how they'd looked. Her design, with the fall colors, fall fruits and fall vegetables, made him smile when he glanced at it. Other folks had commented favorably, as well.

Did Beth know that? He didn't think he'd ever mentioned it, and he should have. Beth needed the confidence that came with doing her job well. He'd seen the look of doubt that came too often to her eyes. She still wasn't sure she was pulling her weight in the business, and he had a responsibility to see that she didn't give it up in discouragement. She had something to offer—the display proved it.

He wasn't sure why neither he nor James had ever thought about putting up a display—maybe because they'd never found it necessary to advertise. Their customers were mostly Amish who came to them because they carried the things they needed at reasonable prices. At least, he supposed that was why.

Recent years had seen an increase in Englisch customers, especially for baked goods and homemade soups. They seemed to have the feeling that those kinds of Amish goods were better. More natural, one of their customers had told him. Funny, when he thought about how the Amish teens were crazy for frozen pizza.

He stepped off the porch, feeling a little restless. Cooped up in the store all day—that was what he'd been. He ought to take a good tramp through the woods, or better yet, find out if Daad or Seth needed any help.

"Daniel!"

Before Daniel could move, a small figure came rushing toward him and grabbed him by the legs. He bent, surprised by Benjy's enthusiastic greeting, and patted his back.

"Benjy. What are you doing out here by yourself?"

Benjy was convulsed in giggles at his question. "I'm not by myself. Grossmammi is with me."

Daniel smiled at Sarah over his head. "So I see. What have you two been doing?"

"Having a busy afternoon," Sarah said, her gaze on her grandson a little perplexed.

Was she looking at Benjy and seeing his father at that age? He certainly resembled James, although the closer they became, the more he saw of Beth in her son.

"Grossmammi had apple dumplings," Benjy volunteered. "But it's time to go home now." He tugged at Daniel's hand.

Benjy sounded a little too eager for his afternoon to be at an end, and Daniel glanced at Sarah, hoping she hadn't noticed. But Sarah just looked tired, as if an active four-year-old had worn her out.

He made a sudden decision. "I have to speak to Beth about some more apples for the store. How about if I save you the walk and take Benjy the rest of the way home?"

Sarah looked relieved. "Denke." She held out her arms to Benjy. "Give me a hug now, Benjy. I'll see you soon, yah?"

Nodding, Benjy hugged her quickly before grabbing Daniel's hand again. "Denke, Grossmammi. Thank you for having me." He ran the words together, his thoughts obviously jumping ahead.

Sarah nodded, turning to walk back the way she'd come, and Benjy gave a few more hops.

"I have the wiggles," he announced. "I had to sit too much at Grossmammi's house."

"I guess you'd better run, then." He released Benjy's hand. "Go ahead. I'll be right behind."

He watched Benjy race down the lane, shaking his head a little. He'd hate to see Benjy favoring one grandparent over another, but it was only natural at his age to prefer all the things he could do on the farm. Still, Beth had a firm hand where her son's behavior was concerned.

After racing in circles a few times like a hunting dog just off the leash, Benjy trotted back to him and together they covered the rest of the distance to the house.

Benjy galloped up the steps to the porch and on into the house, letting the door bang so that it popped open again. Following him, Daniel closed the door, making sure it latched before going after him into the kitchen, where he could hear Beth's voice.

"But where is your grossmammi?" she was asking.

"I ran into them outside the store. I told Sarah I'd bring him the rest of the way." He probably shouldn't have come right into the house without asking. Things that had been normal when James was alive needed thought now.

But Beth seemed to take his presence for granted. "Poor Sarah. Was she tired out?"

"I'm afraid so." He grinned, glancing at Benjy. "Little folks are a bit much when you're not used to them."

"Were you polite, Benjamin?" She fixed him with a firm stare.

"I was," Benjy protested. "I told you I'd be gut, but there's nothing to do at Grossmammi's house."

"Well, I have something for you to do. Take out the bucket of chicken food from the mudroom. I'll have your supper ready when you get back."

Benjy rushed out, leaving Daniel alone with Beth and too aware of the fact to be comfortable.

"I'd better go so you can get your meal on." He was heading out even as he spoke.

Her light footsteps sounded as she came after him. "There was something—"

Beth grasped his arm to stop him, and as quickly as that, she seemed to forget what was in her mind. Daniel understood, because the same thing had struck him in that moment. He turned slowly, impelled by the pressure of her hand against his arm.

He'd felt it before—this compelling attraction—and fought it. But this time Beth felt it, too. He could tell by the way her lips parted and her eyes darkened.

With a wrench that seemed to tear at his heart, Daniel pulled away and hurried out.

Chapter Eleven

"**M**ammi, someone's coming." Benjy thundered down from the bathroom, where Beth had sent him after a look at his supposedly washed hands.

Stepping to the window, Beth saw Lydia's buggy pass the window and pull up at the hitching rail. "It's Lydia," she said, but Benjy had already raced past her, and she could hear his voice chattering away, not giving Lydia a chance to speak.

"Enough," she said, following him to the porch and putting a gentle hand on his cheek. "Let Lydia get a word in."

Grinning, Lydia gave hugs, first to Benjy and then to Beth. "Remember how excited you were when he started to talk?" she teased, making Beth smile.

"I like to talk," Benjy said. "Today I went to Gross-mammi's house, and I talked to her."

"I'll bet she liked that." Lydia put an arm around his shoulders and let him lead her into the house. Beth skirted them, hurrying to stir the soup before it could stick.

"Stay for supper?" she asked with a glance at Lydia.

"Sounds gut." Lydia promptly took another plate and bowl from the cabinet, making herself at home as always. "I was hoping for soup. I had to work the supper shift because a couple of the girls were out sick. At least, they said they were sick, but I heard a rumor there was a dance over in Boonsboro tonight."

"Englisch girls, I trust," she said, amused at Lydia's accounts of her work at the diner.

"Yah, for sure."

"What's a dance?" Benjy asked.

Before Lydia could get tangled in explanations, Beth steered him toward his seat. "Climb up there, now. I'm ready to serve. No talking until after the blessing," she added, seeing him ready to repeat his question. Normally she would take the opportunity to explain the differences between the Leit and the Englisch world, but Benjy was a little young for this one, she decided.

Once the silent blessing had concluded, Benjy was too occupied spooning soup into his mouth to continue the questioning. Lydia raised her eyebrows in a question. "Which Grossmammi?"

"Sarah," she said. "I was over at my mamm's helping get ready for Grossmammi's quilting frolic."

"Your grossmammi never slows down, does she?" Lydia's smile was affectionate.

"I have three grossmammis," Benjy volunteered, obviously remembering their conversation.

Under cover of his chatter, Beth could let her mind stray to those moments with Daniel. Awkward moments, she thought, except that it hadn't really felt awkward. Instead, it had felt familiar and comfortable.

She'd reached out to Daniel as her childhood friend, but in the instant they'd touched, he had turned into someone else entirely, and she didn't know what to do about it.

Beth was more than usually grateful for Lydia's visit. With their chatter and laughter, it had been possible to put Daniel out of her mind, at least for a short while.

After supper, she played a game with Benjy and then read to him from his favorite book. It was a relaxed evening, and gradually the stress over her reaction to Daniel subsided.

Surely it was just a momentary thing—an impulsive reaction born of loneliness and gratitude. There was nothing to worry about.

Once Benjy had gone to bed and they settled at the table, Lydia gave her a measuring look. "What's wrong? Are you fretting about that note again?"

"Note?" Her mind was blank. "Oh, no, not exactly. In fact, I burned it."

"That's gut, ain't so?" Lydia stirred her cup of tea absently, her gaze on Beth's face.

"I guess so." She grimaced. "I haven't forgotten it. But at least I don't think about it all the time." Especially now, when she had something new to worry her.

"I'm glad to hear it. That means you're looking ahead instead of brooding about the past."

"Sometimes I think whatever I do, I'll feel guilty. I don't want to forget James, but when I remember what he did, I feel like he wasn't really the person I married at all."

"I can see that," Lydia said slowly. "I think so, anyway. I guess I'd feel the same."

"I hope you never have to." Since she had married James, she'd wished that Lydia might find someone to share her life with. Now...well, she didn't know.

Lydia's smooth forehead wrinkled in thought. "Did you ever think that maybe James didn't have it in him to love somebody deeply? Maybe he was just…well, all on the surface. You know what I mean," she said, growing frustrated with her inability to explain. "Some people are just deeper than others. Like your daad. Or Daniel."

The mention of Daniel jolted her back to the memory she'd been holding at bay. She tried, unsuccessfully, to shove it away again.

Could she tell Lydia? The answer came without thought. No, she couldn't. She and Lydia had shared so many things, but this…

No, she'd have to deal with this herself. She had to learn how to handle her own rebellious impulses. And if she couldn't—well, she had the answer right at hand. If she couldn't handle this, her only choice might be to sell so she could stay away from Daniel.

The following morning, Daniel was still trying to convince himself that yesterday had never really happened. Discovering he'd just dropped the onions in the bin that held sweet potatoes, he fished them back out and told himself sternly to concentrate on what he was doing.

Two minutes later, he was thinking about Beth again. Should he try to talk with Beth about it? Apologize? But she was the one who'd touched him.

His memory sent him right back to that moment—to the feel of her hand on his arm, to the sense that a current flowed between them each time they touched, to the instant that her green eyes had darkened and he'd known that she felt what he did.

Was he sure? Maybe it had been wishful thinking

on his part. If she hadn't felt anything, trying to talk about it would just be embarrassing for both of them.

And even if what he thought had happened had been real, it might still be best to pretend. If they could each hold on to their composure, their partnership would be able to go on without hindrance.

Daniel's argument with himself ended abruptly when the bell on the door jingled. Looking down the row of shelves, he saw Benjy and Beth come in, with Benjy chattering away to his mother. Benjy spotted him and came running, so Daniel set the basket of onions aside and went to meet him.

"Whoa, slow down." He felt obligated to correct him about running in the store, even though it warmed his heart to see Benjy so eager.

"No running in the store," Beth reminded her son. She managed to focus on Benjy without apparently seeing Daniel, so she may have decided to ignore the incident, too.

"But I have to tell Daniel," Benjy said, grabbing his hand. "We're going to have a cider-pressing on Saturday, and everyone is coming. Grossmammi, and grossdaadi, and my onkels and aunts and cousins and everyone. You'll come, won't you? Please?"

He looked at Beth, trying to read her reaction in her face. Would she rather he made some excuse?

"Yah, do come." She seemed to hold on to normal manner with an effort. "Everyone is coming and bringing something for supper, so we'll have a fine time. You can all take some cider home with you, like always."

Her words reminded him of other years, other cider-pressings, when he'd helped with the press while James greeted everyone. He had a moment's doubt, but probably it was right for Beth to carry on the yearly tradition. She couldn't cancel everything that was a reminder of James, and the apples would need to be processed.

He nodded. "I'll come as soon as I can get away and help with the press, if you want."

"Gut. I thought I'd ask Timothy, too. And Anna."

"Let's hurry and tell them," Benjy said. "I think they'll be happy."

He thought a sense of relief crossed Beth's face as she let her son tug her away. She probably was relieved to end her conversation with him. The less they were together, the easier it would be to let the memory of yesterday fade into nothing.

A few minutes later he heard laughter from the other side of the store, which he guessed was Benjy talking to Timothy about the cider-pressing. He'd go, for sure. Timothy was always up for anything new.

Anna he wasn't so sure about. He'd noticed Beth's efforts to make friends with the girl, as well as Anna's lack of response. Anna could use a friend like Beth—someone young enough to remember those teen years and mature enough to steer Anna in the right direction. But with Anna's painful shyness, it would take time and patience, he thought.

The bell over the door rang, and Elijah Schmidt came in. A glance told him that no one was at the checkout counter. If Beth was talking with Anna, there was no point in interrupting them. He'd take it if Elijah showed signs of wanting to check out.

Elijah didn't move toward the register. In fact, he didn't appear to be shopping at all. He just wandered down the aisles, looking but not picking anything up.

Daniel watched him, curious, for a few minutes. Then, giving in to his curiosity, he walked over to him.

"Elijah, gut to see you. Can I help you?"

Elijah gave him what seemed to be an appraising look. "Denke, but I'm not buying today. Wanted a look around, just in case."

Daniel stared at him blankly. "In case of what?"

"Didn't Beth tell you? I figured she probably told her partner everything."

Irritation made Daniel's voice sharpen. "I don't know what you mean." And he certain sure wasn't going to discuss Beth with him.

"I stopped by to see her yesterday. Been thinking about it for a time, but I didn't want to be too soon after her husband's death." He leaned against the shelf behind him, knocking over several boxes of corn bread mix. "I made an offer for James's share of the store. If it goes the way I want, I'll be your new partner. What do you think of that?"

Daniel schooled his face to express nothing of what he felt. If he'd made a list of all the people he didn't want to work with, Elijah would have been on it. Everyone knew he cut every corner that wasn't illegal in his various businesses.

He couldn't just stand here. He had to say something. "I think you'd better wait until Beth gives you an answer before you make any decision."

"We'll see." Elijah shrugged and then turned and walked off.

For a few seconds, Daniel stood with his stomach churning. Thinking about it did no good at all. He had to talk to Beth.

Just about the time he reached the storeroom, Anna

hurried out. Avoiding his gaze, she murmured something about taking the checkout and skittered off.

Beth emerged from the storeroom, her troubled gaze fixed on Anna. "I don't understand Anna, I'm afraid. I thought she'd like to come to the cider-pressing. She doesn't get much fun, poor girl. But she looked terrified at the idea."

He shook his head, dismissing Anna for the moment, and gestured toward the office. "We need to talk. About Elijah Schmidt."

By the time the office door closed behind them, Beth had gone from being blindsided by Daniel's words to being annoyed at his high-handed attitude. She didn't answer to him. She was his co-owner, not his employee.

"What's going on?"

It was practically a demand, and Beth's back stiffened. And how on earth could he know about Elijah's visit already? "What are you talking about?"

"Elijah Schmidt was here already this morning, looking around like he owned the place." Daniel's eyebrows were a dark slash across his face. "He said he's made you an offer for your share of the business."

"Did he say I'd accepted it?" she snapped. "If you'll calm down a bit, I'll tell you exactly what happened."

Daniel seemed to hear her. His chest heaved as he took a couple of deeps breaths. By the time he met her eyes again, his anger had been tempered by embarrassment.

"I'm sorry." He bit off the words and then took another breath, clearly fighting his temper. "Please tell me. Are you thinking of selling?"

Beth put up a hand, not willing to answer that question right now. "Elijah Schmidt stopped by the house yesterday afternoon. He said he wanted to talk business." She grimaced. "I think he really wanted to talk to my father, since he seemed to feel women can't possibly understand business. But that was the gist of it. He wants another business, and he's had his eye on this one. He made me an offer for my share."

"How much?" he said sharply, and then shook his head. "Sorry." He was trying not to antagonize her, she thought. "If you don't mind telling me, at least I could see if it's reasonable."

Her anger faded at Daniel's effort. The store meant the world to him. It was only natural that he'd be upset, but she couldn't let herself be influenced by that. Benjy's future was at stake with her decision. She named the amount.

Daniel considered. "It's not an awful figure, but it's worth more, in my opinion. Do you really want to sell?"

That was an impossible question. There were so many different things involved—Benjy's future, the question of a fair offer, Daniel's opinion of someone who might be his partner. And most of all, the fact that if she needed to see less of him, this was the only way of doing it.

"Not exactly." She picked her words carefully. "It would make things easier, in a way, but that's not what's important. I have to consider Benjy first."

"Wouldn't it be best for Benjy to have a successful business to step into?"

"Maybe. But he's too young to make that decision right now. I have to do it for him, and it's hard."

Her voice wavered on the last word as she thought

of the weight of responsibility on her, and she could see him wince.

"Are you seriously considering it?" His voice had roughened, whether at the thought of Elijah Schmidt as his partner or at the loss of her and Benjy, she didn't know. But even if it hurt him, she had to give an honest answer.

She cleared her throat before she could say anything. She had a longing to speak openly. To say that being around him was too difficult. But that would mean admitting that she was attracted to him, and she couldn't do that.

"I have to think about it. And talk to my daad about it, despite not wanting to oblige Elijah. You understand, don't you?"

The muscles in Daniel's neck worked, but he nodded. "Yah. I understand." He hesitated. "You'd best tell your daad that he can look at the books anytime he wants."

"Denke, Daniel."

If this went on much longer, she was going to be in tears. Shaking her head, she made her way blindly toward the door. Daniel grasped the handle and opened it for her. She could feel his gaze on her as she went out, but he didn't speak. She could only be grateful.

Chapter Twelve

Daniel had suggested that Beth stay home from the store on Saturday, telling her that she had plenty to do with the cider-pressing that day. He knew that was true, but he also knew they'd been uncomfortable around each other for the last couple of days since he'd found out about the offer from Elijah.

He realized he was clenching his fists and deliberately relaxed them. He'd also been standing and staring into the meat case. He shook himself with a command to get busy and stop thinking about Beth. He could do the one but not the other.

The possibility she'd decide to sell out, combined with struggling about his feelings for her—

Again he stopped what he was doing, this time feeling as if he'd been hit in the stomach. How stupid could he be? The very fact of their attraction could be giving Beth the impetus to sell. Now that he saw it, he couldn't believe it had taken him this long.

"Onkel Daniel." Timothy sounded as if it were not the first time he'd spoken. "Onkel Daniel, are you all right?"

"Yah, for sure." His face probably looked as if he'd seen a ghost. "What do you need?"

Instead of speaking up, Timothy stared down at his feet. "Well, I wondered… You see, I was talking to Janie, and she said she'd be at Beth's all day helping get ready for the cider-pressing." He came to a halt, and Daniel had the unique experience of seeing his self-confident nephew turning bright red.

"And?" he prompted, trying to disguise his amusement.

"Well, we're not too busy this afternoon, and I thought Janie… I mean Beth and Janie, might use my help. If I could leave early."

Daniel made a point of looking around the store, taking note of the fact that, as usual, Saturday afternoon was a slack time. In the morning they'd been busy, but not now.

"All right, you can leave now. Just make sure you're helping, not distracting…someone."

Timothy grinned, over his embarrassment. "Denke, Onkel Daniel. I'll help." With a light step, he headed for the door.

Fortunate Timothy, not wondering if it was all right to care for someone.

As for him…was there any way to relieve Beth's need to avoid him? Or was he completely wrong about the whole thing? He'd like to ease any fear she felt without offending her, and if he tried to say he didn't feel that way about her, he'd be lying.

The afternoon wore on without any answer coming to him. He'd almost rather have more work than he could handle than to have the clock crawling along at a snail's pace.

Finally it was near enough closing that he thought he could start getting ready for the closed day tomorrow. There was always a little extra to do in preparing for the Sabbath. That way he could get on his way to Beth's promptly.

Daniel walked toward the rear of the store and stopped, arrested by a noise coming from behind the shelves in the far corner. It almost sounded as if someone were crying.

Anna, he thought. It must be. He stood undecided for a moment, having the usual male reaction to coping with someone's tears. But if Anna needed help, he had a duty to give it.

Rounding the end of the shelf unit, he saw that he'd been right. Anna was crumpled into a heap on the step they used to reach the top shelf, trying to muffle her sobs with her apron.

He squatted down next to her. "I'm so sorry you're upset. Do you want to go on home? I can get the buggy out and have you there in no time."

Anna shook her head vigorously at that, choking on a sob to say she'd rather stay here. Giving a regretful thought toward the cider-pressing, Daniel sat down next to her.

"Is it your father? If you want me to talk to him…"

Another head shake, even stronger. "It's not Daadi. But when he hears what I did…" That trailed off into a wail, and her flow of tears seemed inexhaustible.

Daniel sucked in a breath, trying to think of the comforting things his mother had said to him when everything was wrong. "Do you… Do you want to tell me about it?" He asked the question, hoping the answer was no. "If so, I promise not to tell anyone."

Her sobs lessened. "You promise?"

"Yah, for sure." What kind of trouble could a kid like Anna get into? It probably wasn't nearly as bad as she thought.

"I thought… I thought I'd die when I knew. I wish I'd died." Her voice rose, and he feared this was something way beyond his ability to cope with.

"If you'd rather talk to a woman, I could fetch Beth—"

"No, no. Not Beth. She can't know." She looked at Daniel, her face blotchy and tearstained, her eyes red. "You don't understand. It was me. I was the one James was coming to the night he died."

Daniel rocked back on his heels, nearly toppling over. Not Anna. Not a poor kid who already had more than her share of troubles. Anger soared. If he had James in front of him right now, all the faith in the world wouldn't keep him from striking out.

He forced himself to focus on Anna. "I think you'd better tell me all of it." He said the words as kindly as he could, given all the grief that had resulted from James's action.

"It wasn't…it wasn't all that bad. I mean, all we did was talk. James was so kind." Her eyes seemed to glow with the memory. "He just kissed me. Twice. That was all. He made me feel like I…like I was worth something."

"Anna, you are worth something. You're a good, kind, hardworking girl, no matter what anyone says." And James had taken advantage of that, bolstering up his ego by persuading Anna into an action that would bring her under the discipline of the church.

"I'm not. I'm wicked." The tears welled again.

Daniel had never felt quite as useless in his life. But one thing he did know. "You have to tell Beth. You know that, don't you?"

Her sobs grew shrill, probably hysterical, not that he knew what that was like. Praying no one would come into the store, he spoke softly, trying to reason with her.

It was no use. Somehow, he'd known it wouldn't be. Anna seemed incapable of facing Beth. He'd promised not to tell, so his hands were tied. How this would ever come right, he couldn't imagine.

Beth paused on the back porch to check the progress of her cider-pressing. So many people had come early to help that she couldn't believe how easily it had all come together. Daad had helped her set up the cider press, her oldest brother, Eli, had organized a team for picking the apples, and others in the family took care of washing and cutting the apples.

By now, the actual pressing had started, with everyone vying to be the one who turned the crank to crush the apples. Benjy and various cousins watched with fascination as the round metal plate was pushed down on the apples. Golden liquid began to flow into the bucket beneath the press.

Beth felt someone behind her and turned to find her grandmother.

"That's Isaac's press," she said, and Beth wondered if Grossmammi was looking at the present or the past.

"Yah, it is. He gave it to me when he sold us the property."

Grossmammi looked confused for just a second before making a mental adjustment. "It must be fifty years old. More, most likely. I remember the cider he used to make. Best in the county."

Beth nodded. "He always said it was the apples he mixed that made the difference. This year we're using a mix of Red Delicious for the sweetness and McIntosh for the tartness."

"I… I don't remember what Eli used." Her faded blue eyes clouded with confusion.

"I think he especially liked the McIntosh from that one tree. Remember? He always said they were best for cider, didn't he?"

Grossmammi's eyes cleared, and she touched Beth's cheek lightly. "Ach, I'm getting a bit forgetful. You're a gut child, putting up with my wandering."

"I'd rather listen to you wandering than most folks' babbling." She pressed her cheek against Grossmammi's, a little more withered now than it had been even a year ago. Sometimes it seemed the old got smaller and smaller and lighter and lighter until they were ready to slip right up to Heaven.

Tears stung her eyes for a moment, and she blinked them away. Since James's death, she'd found that tears came quicker about most anything.

Grossmammi's hand closed over hers. "Just look at it." Her gaze seemed to sweep the scene, from one group of workers to another, from the golden stubble in the fields to the golden leaves carpeting the ground and the red glow of the oaks on the ridges. "It's beautiful. And it's home."

"Yah, it is." Peace flowed through Beth, wiping away for the moment the worries and indecision of her situation. They'd be waiting to spring out at her, she supposed, but she'd cling to the peace of this moment as long as she could.

Mammi came out of the kitchen and joined them. "What are you two doing?"

Beth and her grandmother exchanged a smiling glance. Grossmammi always said that Beth's mother couldn't see anyone idle without giving them a job to do, to which Mammi would answer that anyone who'd raised five children would do the same.

"Just remembering," Beth said. "Do you need some help, Mammi?"

Her mother shook her head. "Everything's ready for supper whenever you want to take a break. Just say when. Is everyone here now?"

Beth didn't need to look to see that Daniel wasn't here. Nor was Anna, though she didn't really expect Anna. She'd been firm in refusing the invitation.

But Daniel…she'd expected him to be here by now. She was ashamed to admit that she'd been watching for him. He might have been held up at the store, she supposed. And anyway, what difference did it make?

She looked down the lane for the twentieth time in the past hour. This time she spotted Daniel's sturdy figure coming toward them at an easy pace.

Her heart lifted despite her effort to tamp down her feelings. "Here comes Daniel. I think he's the last. But we'd better keep them working for now. You know how hard it is to get folks moving again after a gut meal."

When Daniel reached the group, he headed for the press, greeting the men who'd begun to gather around it. That was what she expected, she told herself. There was no need for him to greet her, after all.

Just then Timothy hauled a protesting Benjy up the

steps to her. "I don't want to," he was arguing vehemently.

"Ask your mammi," Timothy said, unmoved. "If she says it's all right, then it is. But I know what happens with my little brothers if they drink that much fresh cider."

"How much?" Resigned to a bellyache, she detached her young son from Timothy's grasp.

Timothy grinned. "Six cups that I saw, but there might have been more."

"Will said he could drink ten cups of cider," Benjy said indignantly. "And I said I could drink more than he could, and he said I couldn't."

Timothy shook his head, used to dealing with his young brothers. "I'd better collect Will before Daadi hears."

"Send him into the house for some crackers," Beth said. "Maybe that will absorb some of the cider. Denke, Timothy. I should have been watching for that."

With a firm hand she guided her son into the kitchen. "Didn't I tell you not to drink more than two cups?"

"But it was gut…" Benjy said, but he stopped, apparently realizing that his mother wouldn't be moved.

In a few minutes Beth had her son and young Will at the table with some crackers in front of them. "There," she said. "Eat all of those, even if you don't want it. I told you not to drink more because too much fresh cider will make your tummy hurt."

Her mother, who'd come in with them, sliced off a couple of pieces from the loaf on the counter and added them to the boys' plates. "Bread will help, too. You want to be able to eat some of that fried chicken I brought, don't you?"

Both of the boys nodded vigorously and applied themselves to eating. Mammi chuckled and glanced at Beth. "You go on and do what you need to do. I'll keep track of these two."

Hoping Timothy had caught the boys in time, Beth went out, wondering why little boys got twice as many bad ideas when they were together as when they were alone.

No sooner had she reached the bottom of the stairs than she found Daniel blocking her way. He hastily stepped back. "Sorry. I was just coming to look for you. Your daad wants to know if there are any more jugs for the cider. Looks like he'll need about two more to finish up this pressing."

There was no reason for her to feel awkward around Daniel, she reminded herself. He was the one who'd been unreasonable about Elijah Schmidt.

"I washed them all and put them in the pantry." Gesturing him to follow her, she went back inside. "I'll show you."

She led him into the shelf-lined pantry, filled with canned foods. One section of shelves she used for canning jars and other containers, and on the floor she'd set the extra jugs. "Here you are." She hesitated. "I'm glad you came. I was afraid…"

Daniel had bent to grasp the glass containers, but he straightened at that, the movement bringing him close to her. "I was delayed, or I'd have been here earlier. I wanted to say how sorry I am for the way I acted about Elijah Schmidt. I jumped to conclusions."

Beth glanced down, not sure she wanted to meet his steady gaze. "It wasn't your fault. I did intend to tell you about the offer. I just…well, I was trying to find the right way to do it."

Neither of them said anything for a moment. Was he hoping she'd say she'd already refused the offer? She couldn't do that, not when she didn't know her own mind.

Apparently deciding she wasn't going to say any more, Daniel bent and picked up two of the jugs. "It's all right," he said, his voice colorless, and walked out with the jugs.

Beth stood looking after him, frustrated with him and with herself. It was all very well to resolve to move forward, but how could she when her emotions were such a tangled mess?

Worship was at her friend Esther's house on Sunday, so once Beth had turned her horse and buggy over to one of the boys taking care of them, she sent Benjy to join his grandparents and headed for the kitchen to see if she could help.

Esther, looking rather frazzled, was directing a kitchen crew consisting of her sisters along with the twins Ella and Della. Lydia must have come in just ahead of her, because she was already asking if she could help.

"I'll help, as well," Beth said, bumping her elbow against Lydia's.

She grinned and added, "Yah, both of us."

Esther looked at the clock and then at the workstations in her kitchen much as Beth had surveyed the cider-making crews the previous day. "Denke, but I think we're all right now. If you'll help with serving or cleanup…"

"Right, we'll be here," Lydia said, after a glance at Beth for her approval. She caught hold of Beth's arm as they went out, stopping her when they were far enough from the various groups not to be heard.

"What's wrong?" Her grasp tightened.

Beth, taken by surprise, could only stare. "Does it show?"

"Probably not to everyone," Lydia said. "But you ought to know you can't hide things from me."

Beth glanced around to ensure that no one was nearby. Even so, she wouldn't discuss her confused feelings over Daniel, not here. "Elijah Schmidt stopped by the house a couple days ago. He offered to buy my share of the store."

Lydia's eyebrows shot up. "That's a shock. I wouldn't have thought he had ambitions to be a grocer."

Beth hadn't thought of that, but now that Lydia had mentioned it, she realized that it surprised her, as well. "I don't know that he does," she said slowly. "But he does seem…well, proud…of his businesses. And he offered me what seemed like quite a lot for it."

"Are you going to accept?" Lydia seemed to be keeping her face deliberately blank.

"You don't need to worry. I'm not asking you to tell me what to do. I'd just like to talk it over." And something even more troubling to her peace of mind. "Can you come over after work? Maybe tomorrow?" Seeing her mother looking at her, she began moving.

"Definitely tomorrow," Lydia said. "We'd best get in line, or your mother is going to blame me for detaining you. She always did think I talked too much. And she was probably right."

Smiling, Beth squeezed her hand, relieved at just the

thought of talking this over with a good friend. Lydia was the only one who knew enough to give her an unbiased opinion.

When she reached her family, Daad gave her a frowning look.

"They're not ready to go in yet," she pointed out, feeling as guilty as she would have in similar circumstances when she was a child. In some things, her parents didn't think she'd grown up.

"Just don't want you to be late." He didn't smile, but his eyes began to twinkle. "Your mamm and I remember how you girls always did talk."

"That's what friends are for," she said. "Where is Benjy?"

"With your brother. He and Will want to sit together."

Beth raised her eyebrows. "I hope he realizes what he's in for. Those two boys together are five times as mischievous as they are one at a time."

"They're a pair of snickelfritzes, all right," Daad said indulgently. "But Eli can handle them."

Things were changing, Beth realized as she hurried to her place in the line. Not that long ago, Benjy had clung to her at the very suggestion of sitting apart from her. Now he'd trotted off without even asking her. Her little boy was growing up.

Before she could decide how that made her feel, the line began to move, and they were entering the pole barn for worship. Even as she sat down and the unmarried girls filed into the benches in front of her, she realized that Anna was missing. A quick glance showed her that the rest of the family was there. She hoped Anna wasn't sick, both for her sake and because it was sometimes difficult to get along without her.

At the end of the three-hour service, she and Lydia scurried out to join the women who were serving. But Daad must have left quickly as well, because he caught up with her before she could reach the kitchen.

"A word with you," he said. At his look, Lydia moved away.

"I'll get started," she said. "Don't hurry."

"What's wrong, Daad?" His expression told her this was more serious than being late to get into line.

"There's talk going around," he said bluntly. "Talk that Elijah Schmidt is buying your share of the store."

Beth saw red. "That man—I'd like to tell him just what I think. But not on the Sabbath," she added. Hurriedly.

"So it's not true?" Daad touched her arm and leaned a little closer, as if hinting that she shouldn't lose control.

"It's true he made an offer to buy my share." She tried to arrange her thoughts. "It was that day I'd been baking with Mammi and Grossmammi. He stopped by when I got home. I certain sure didn't say that I would. I haven't even decided if I want to sell."

Her father's face seemed to relax. "I thought you wouldn't do that without telling us."

"I certain sure wouldn't," she said, a little indignant. "I want to have a talk with you about it. Soon. I want to do what's best for Benjy."

"It's not right for Elijah to go around acting as if you'd decided." Daad frowned. "I don't understand why he'd do that."

She thought she did, and she didn't like it. "I think he's trying to push me into selling."

"Then he's being foolish," Daad said. "No one can do that."

She was surprised at the implied compliment. "That doesn't mean I don't want your opinion."

"I'll look into it for you, if you want," he said. "But your mamm and I know the decision has to be yours." He patted her hand. "You're recovering now. Getting more like yourself after the shock. We trust you to make the right choices."

"Really?" She raised her eyebrows questioningly.

He chuckled. "If I tried to tell you what to do, you'd think I was interfering, ain't so?"

Beth squeezed his arm. "You are a very gut father. Do you know that?"

"I had gut material to work with," he replied.

"Denke, Daadi." Her heart warmed.

"One thing," Daad said, cautioning. "You'll talk to Daniel about it, ain't so? After all, he and James built that business together."

She nodded, hearing the truth of his words. The little they'd spoken about it could hardly be called an actual conversation. She had to do that, no matter how uncomfortable it was.

Chapter Thirteen

Daniel finished his lunch in a hurry and made his way to the other side of the barn, where he hoped to find some peace. Everyone was talking about Elijah Schmidt buying Beth's share of the store as if it was a done deal.

What if it was? Or would be? This was an eventuality he and James had never considered when they'd made up the simple agreement between them. Maybe they should have.

Well, they hadn't, so he and Beth would have to figure it out. He wanted what was best for her and Benjy, but they might have different opinions as to what that best was.

"Daniel?"

He swung around at the sound of the voice he'd recognize anywhere. Beth stood a few feet away from him.

A quick glance told him no one else was in sight, though he could hear the hum of voices from the other side of the barn.

"How did you find me?" He felt as if he'd been thinking of her so much it was like sending out signals to her. But that was just silly.

"What did you always do when you were upset?" She moved a bit closer, resting her hand on the fence railing. "Run away and hide, that's what. Since your buggy was still there, I knew you hadn't gone home, so I just looked for a likely hiding place."

"I could have been in the barn loft," he said lightly, trying to hide the stress of Elijah's offer.

She just shook her head, looking out across the field toward the road that would soon be filled with buggies. He could lean back against the fence and study her without being seen.

Beth looked different this morning, and he tried to figure out how. And why. Ever since James's death she'd been a shadow of herself, worn out by trying to cope with his death as well as the knowledge of his betrayal.

Now she'd become more definite—like watching the fog lift from the valley, allowing the colors to come out again. Beth was finding her way back to herself, and he was thankful.

"Elijah has been talking again," she said. "I told Daad the only reason I could see is that he hopes to push me into agreeing."

"Is it working?" he asked, trying not to let his feelings show.

"It's more likely to have the opposite effect." Her voice was tart in a way he hadn't heard for a time. "I have to keep reminding myself that I should consider what's best for everyone, especially Benjy. His future is the most important thing."

He couldn't argue with that, even if he wanted to.

"Daad reminded me that we haven't actually talked it over yet—you and I, I mean."

"My fault," he said, knowing it was true. "I over-reacted. I'm—"

"You already said you're sorry," Beth said. "It's all right. Now tell me what you really think about it."

Daniel frowned, staring down at his hands grasping the top rail of the fence. "I can't really be fair, I think. James always talked about how Benjy would come into the business with us as he grew. I got so used to thinking that way that I can't picture anything else."

"Yah, I know." Beth's voice was soft, remembering. "One day that could happen, but in the meantime…well, I worry that I can't pull my own weight when it comes to running the store."

"Don't think that," he said quickly. He could hardly tell her that he lived in anticipation of the next time she was in the store. "You're doing a fine job. Nobody expects you to replace James, but you have your own things that you do well. We're doing all right the way we are."

"Denke, Daniel. But even if that's so, and you're not just trying to make me feel useful, I have to consider other things."

"Like the money you'd get from selling," he finished for her. "It seems like a lot, but money runs out eventually. And then Benjy wouldn't have a business to inherit."

"That's true, but it's not what I was thinking about."

He looked at her, surprised by the remark, to find her smiling at him.

"What I wanted to know was how it would work out for you, having Elijah as your partner."

"Elijah." He let out a long breath, trying to think what he should say. Truthfully, he hated the idea of working with the man, but he didn't want to put Beth on the spot.

Before he found the right words, she added, "What you really think, please. What you would say if he weren't part of the church family."

He was surprised into a smile. "That makes it even harder, yah? I can't say I'd enjoy having him as a partner. James and I always had the same picture of what the store was going to be—that we'd give value to our customers and deal with them fairly and kindly. Like delivering things without charge to those folks who can't get out."

"You don't think Elijah would go along with that vision?"

He hated to speak negatively of a member of the Leit, but he couldn't be less than honest with Beth. "Based on how he runs the businesses he has, no."

"Neither do I," she said. "So that weighs against selling." She paused, seeming to consider her decision. "If it were just my concern, I'd turn him down, but I have to remember that it's Benjy's future."

He nodded. That was only right. "Take your time. Talk to anyone you want. I'm not in any hurry. Whatever you decide, I won't argue."

"Denke." Relief flooded her face. "I don't want to be at odds with you. No more misunderstandings between us—it's much better to speak honestly, yah?"

He immediately thought of his promise—of the thing he should tell her but couldn't. No. He corrected himself even as he had the thought. It wasn't he who should tell Beth. It was Anna. That poor girl would never be whole until she'd confessed to the person she'd hurt.

Beth seemed to take his agreement for granted, so he didn't have to speak.

An image of the life he really wanted arose in his

mind—a picture of himself and Beth together, with Benjy growing up and working beside him. It seemed very far away.

Church Sundays usually meant having supper with family, but Beth had begged off for once. After having been occupied with the cider-making the previous day, she was more than ready for a little quiet, and she thought Benjy could use some downtime, too. Even his boundless energy should get a rest once in a while.

"How about this one, Mammi?" Benjy, helping her pick some vegetables in the garden for supper, parted the leaves of a butternut squash plant to show one. "Should I pick it?"

She stepped over a row of fading tomato plants to look closer. "I think it needs to get a bit bigger," she said, knowing that Benjy liked picking better than any other part of gardening. "See if you can find a pepper ready, and we'll have it in salad."

Benjy grimaced, salad was not his favorite dish, but he went obediently to the pepper plants.

Beth stared absently at the tomato plants, thinking about everything that had happened that morning. Daad, despite his determination not to make decisions for her, had agreed to look into the offer for her. He would be fair, and he'd be able to find out more about Elijah's reputation as a businessman than she would.

Most men would have jumped at the chance to have a full-time partner instead of an inexperienced woman with a child only able to work part-time. But Daniel clearly didn't want to work with Elijah, although his determination to do the best for his old friend's family would govern his reactions. If she decided to accept Elijah's offer, he'd deal with it.

She was fortunate to have a friend like Daniel. She firmly kept her thoughts away from any suggestion that he might, one day, be more than a friend.

Movement caught her eye, and Beth realized that a buggy was coming down the lane. To her surprise, it was Sarah, James's mother.

"Benjy, look who's coming."

"Grossmammi!" Benjy shouted, jumping over several rows and knocking down the remains of one tomato plant in his rush to greet a visitor.

By the time Beth reached them, Benjy had helped tie up the buggy horse and hugged his grandmother. Beth was just in time to hear what he said.

"Did you bring me a treat?"

"Benjy!" Aghast, Beth didn't know what to say. "Never, never, ask someone for a treat. That is very rude."

Benjy's eyes filled with tears at the sharpness in her tone. She longed to apologize, knowing her reaction was at least partly because it was her mother-in-law. But she couldn't do that. Benjy had to learn what was acceptable and what wasn't.

She bent over him, intent on explaining. "Sometimes people bring you a little present and sometimes they don't, but we should never expect it. Then it's a nice surprise when it happens. Understand?"

He blinked away the tears and nodded. "Yah, Mammi. I'm sorry, Grossmammi."

Beth wasn't sure what Sarah would say, but she just smiled and nodded.

Relieved, Beth straightened. "We're so glad to see you. Will you stay for supper with us?"

Sarah hesitated. "Not if it's inconvenient. I just thought I'd like to talk a bit."

Beth caught the sideways flicker of her eyes toward Benjy and realized she meant in private.

"For sure. We were just getting some vegetables for supper. Benjy, will you bring one of the small baskets and pick a few things for Grossmammi to take home?"

He nodded vigorously and dashed off to the shed for a basket.

"I'm sorry," Beth began, not sure how to apologize for correcting Benjy in front of her.

But Sarah spoke at the same time. "I'm sorry," she said. "I'm afraid I've given Benjy too many treats. I know that's not good for him."

She hadn't expected an admission from her mother-in-law, and she didn't know how to handle it. "Well, I... I've noticed he doesn't eat his meals properly if he's had too many treats." She'd have called it junk food, but that would probably insult Sarah, who always had a stash of candy bars in her pantry.

"You're right, I know. It's a bad habit of mine." Sarah paused for a moment, apparently thinking of something she wanted to say. "I was thinking..."

"What is it, Sarah?" Beth gestured toward the back porch. "Let's sit down and talk."

Sarah nodded, following her to the porch swing, where they settled to watch Benjy searching through the garden with his basket.

Sarah cleared her throat. "It was so nice of you to let me have Benjy every Wednesday afternoon." She sounded so reluctant that Beth couldn't guess what was coming.

"But I was thinking that there's not much for an active little boy to do at my house."

Beth had the horrified idea that he'd broken something his grandmother valued. "If he broke something—"

"No, no." Sarah actually smiled. "He's fine. I just wanted to say that maybe he'd enjoy it more if I came over here instead of having him come to my place. My friend Alice was saying…you know Alice King…that lively little boys need to be outside playing or helping, not sitting in the house coloring pictures." She smiled ruefully. "Alice has twelve grandchildren, so she knows."

Beth nodded, relaxing. She'd half expected there was a criticism coming, but it seemed not.

"I think that would be very nice. And I could work in the afternoon or do my shopping without worrying about Benjy."

Sarah relaxed, as well. "That's gut. I want to be helpful." She watched Benjy, choosing a tomato for her. "I've been thinking so much about…about James."

Her voice shook a little, and Beth clasped her hand.

"I'm afraid I spoiled James a bit when he was little. Being the only one. But I don't want to make the same mistake with Benjy."

It was almost as if she were apologizing to Beth about James, and she wasn't quite sure what to say.

Finally, when the silence grew too long, she patted Sarah's hand. "Denke, Sarah. We'll work together on that, yah?"

Sarah smiled. "We will."

"Maybe sometimes Alice could come over with you and bring one of her grandchildren. It would be nice for Benjy to have someone to play with."

"Yah, that's a gut idea," Sarah said. "It's not right for

Benjy to be an only child." She stopped for a breath. "I just wanted you to know that if the time comes that you want to marry again, I'd be happy for you."

That took Beth's breath away. She wouldn't have expected that from Sarah, and she couldn't help but wonder if Sarah might have heard rumors about James's flirting.

She chose her words carefully. "I don't see that happening anytime soon, but even if it should, you would always be Benjy's grossmammi."

Maybe it was good that Benjy came hurrying toward them, the basket bouncing against his legs. Anything else said between them would probably result in tears.

She patted Sarah's hand and stood up to rescue the basket. "Denke," she said softly, meaning it with all her heart. Sarah had just given her a gift, and she wouldn't forget it.

Beth arrived at the store ready to work Monday morning, leaving Benjy with her niece Janie. It was a sunny, brisk morning, and she'd heard them planning to rake leaves. In her experience, jumping in the piles they made would probably leave the yard looking about the same as it had been, but it would keep them busy and happy.

To her surprise, Timothy was running the checkout, something he didn't usually do. She spotted Daniel back at the meat counter helping a customer, but there was no sign of Anna.

Removing her sweater, she hurried to the counter. "Do you need me to take over for you? Where's Anna?"

He shook his head and shrugged his shoulders at the same time. "I don't know. She just didn't show up this morning, so Onkel Daniel trusted me with the check-out." He grinned, obviously pleased at what he probably thought was a promotion.

"I'll go and see where he wants me to work."

Timothy's customer asked him something just then, so not waiting for an answer, she went back to where Daniel was wrapping a chuck roast for one of the Stoltzfus cousins. Emma smiled, asked her how she was, and then took her package and went off without waiting for an answer. Used to her ways, Beth just smiled and looked at Daniel.

"I understand we're shorthanded today. Have you heard anything about Anna?"

Stripping off the gloves he'd worn to cut the beef, Daniel shook his head. "Not a word from her. No one has called, but then Hiram probably wouldn't."

"No, I suppose not." Anna's father was extremely conservative and boasted that he'd never used a telephone. "She wasn't at worship yesterday."

"Maybe she's sick." Daniel looked more concerned than she'd have expected. "I'd think they could have sent a message."

"I should have asked her mother about it after worship, but I was busy." She'd been busy talking to him, in fact. She'd thought they'd cleared the air between them, but Daniel seemed restrained this morning.

After the way Elijah had behaved, talking as if a deal was settled between them, she felt a strong urge to tell Daniel that she had no intention of selling out to Elijah. Despite the difficulties that had arisen between her and Daniel, she really wanted to keep things exactly as they were.

She almost spoke, but she was deterred by the fact

that she'd asked Daad to look into Elijah's offer. She shouldn't decide without listening to him.

Daniel still seemed withdrawn, or maybe he was just worrying about Anna and how to run the store short-handed on what was usually a busy day.

"What do you want me to do?"

Daniel was quiet for a moment, his forehead knotted in thought. Or worry. Finally he looked at her.

"If you don't mind, I'd like it if you could go over to the Fishers' place and check on Anna."

"Go there," she repeated. "But don't you need me here? I'm sure we'd have heard if there were something seriously wrong with Anna."

"We can handle things here." His face set stubbornly. "I'd go myself, but a woman is much more likely to get answers."

In the face of his obvious concern, there was nothing she could do but agree.

"All right. I'll go this afternoon if Janie can stay with Benjy."

Daniel was already shaking his head. "Look, I can't explain, but I think something's wrong. Anna…" He stopped, and then he started again. "She hasn't been herself recently. You're the right person to do it, Beth."

There was an odd but compelling emphasis in his voice that Beth found contagious. Anna had been odd— almost in tears when Beth invited her to the cider-press-ing.

"All right. I'll go back to the house and get the mare harnessed. I'll be back as soon as I can."

Now that she'd decided, Beth found she was hurrying down the lane. Common sense told her that this was an unnecessary trip, but the more she thought about Anna's behavior, the odder it was.

Benjy came running when he saw her. "Mammi, are you going to help us rake leaves?"

She looked over his head to Janie and shook her head. "I'm afraid not. I have to get Daisy harnessed up and do an errand. You do a gut job with Janie, yah?"

He pouted a bit, but before he could say anything, Janie had caught his hands and swung him around. "Let's see who makes the biggest pile of leaves."

Beth hurried on to the small barn. It was a matter of minutes to hitch Daisy to the small buggy, and she was on her way. She'd picked up the sense of urgency from Daniel, so she let Daisy trot out quickly. The mare was eager to move on such a brisk morning, so they were through town and on their way to the Fisher farm without problems.

Once Beth had left town behind, she started wondering what kind of reception she'd get. Daniel had been right in saying that she'd have a better chance at getting in than him. Etta Fisher knew her fairly well, although they weren't close friends. Etta's husband didn't seem to encourage her to share in the quiltings and work frolics that the other women did.

All she could do, it seemed to her, was to be honest. She was concerned because Anna didn't come to work today and had missed worship. If there was anything she could do...

As she turned into the lane to the Fisher place, she pulled up Daisy to focus on a prayer that her words would be guided and that she'd be able to help Anna. She'd like to pray that Hiram wouldn't be home, but that didn't seem quite right.

She drew up at the hitching rail outside the run-down farmhouse. Hiram must feel it would be prideful to paint his house and outbuildings. Climbing down, she took a deep breath and knocked on the door. Nothing showed at any of the windows, and for a moment she thought no one was home.

Then she heard slow footsteps coming to the door. It swung open. Etta stared at her for a moment.

Summoning up her courage, she said, "I've come to see Anna. We were worried when she didn't come—"

Etta interrupted her by seizing her by the arm and pulling her in. She looked down the road and then shut the door. "Hiram is at the sawmill." She said the words as if it explained her actions.

Beth tried to focus. "Is Anna all right? I should have asked you about her when I saw she wasn't in church."

Etta shook her head. "She wouldn't go. She won't do anything. She just sits in her room and cries."

"I… I'm so sorry. If there's anything I can do, I'm happy to." What could be wrong with the child? A few dark possibilities crept into her mind and were chased out again.

"Denke, Beth." Etta clutched her arm. "Maybe she'll come out for you." Her face worked as she tried to control herself. "I'm at my wit's end."

Fearing she wasn't up to this mission, Beth followed Anna's mother up the dark stairs to the upper hall that was equally dark. Etta gestured toward a door.

"That's Anna's room. If you can get her to talk…" Her eyes filled with tears. "Please, Beth. Please try."

Chapter Fourteen

Taking a deep breath, Beth tapped at the door. "Anna? It's Beth. May I come in?"

A muffled sob was the only answer.

Etta reached around her to turn the knob. The door swung open and Etta practically pushed her into the room.

Anna was curled up in a ball on the bed. She glanced up and then promptly hid her face.

But that look was enough for Beth. Anna's face was pale and drawn, as if she hadn't been eating, and her skin was blotchy from crying. Red-rimmed eyes had glanced briefly at Beth before Anna clamped them shut as if she couldn't bear to see.

Beth's heart cramped at the sight. The poor girl—whatever had happened, she desperately needed to have someone on her side. She probably wasn't the answer Anna needed, but she had to try.

Sinking down on the bed next to Anna, Beth put her arms around the girl, ignoring Anna's wince into herself. "Hush now, Anna. It's going to be all right. You don't need to worry. I'm here."

They were the simple phrases she used with Benjy—probably the very ones her mother had used with her. They might not make a lot of sense, especially since she didn't know what was wrong, but they soothed. So often in recent months she'd longed to feel someone's arms around her and to hear someone whisper that it was all right.

She kept on patting Anna's back, repeating the soothing words over and over. Gradually the hysterical weeping lessened. Beth wrapped her arms more closely around her. "It's all right. Just tell me what's happened."

Another strangled sob sounded. "I'm sorry," Anna whispered, seeming unable to make any louder noise. "I'm sorry, Beth. I'm so sorry."

Beth began to be exasperated. If Anna couldn't tell her anything, how could she help her?

"Komm now, Anna. Tell me what's wrong. Can you sit up here beside me and talk?"

Anna nodded, so Beth helped her to sit up. There, that was a step in the right direction.

"That's better. It's going to be all right. Just tell me what's wrong."

Anna tried to speak, but her voice broke on a sob. "I never wanted you to know. I never wanted anyone to know. He said no one would ever know."

He. The word set up a faint train of thought, misty and unclear, but frightening.

"Everyone will hate me." Anna's voice was stronger.

Beth sensed it would all come out now, and fear gripped her. It wasn't too late. She could run away, pretend she didn't know…

But she couldn't. There was no sense in hiding from the truth.

"It was you, wasn't it? You were the one who wrote to James." The words weren't an accusation. They were a statement of fact.

"You know?" Anna raised horrified eyes to her. "How did you know? He said no one would ever know."

Oh, James, how could you? Anna is a sixteen-year-old child. What were you thinking?

But she knew the answer to that, didn't she? He hadn't been thinking. He'd been scattering his careless charm over anyone female, and this time it had exploded in his face.

"I found a note in James's drawer. It was probably the last one you wrote—about meeting you in the usual place." She ought to feel rage, but instead all she felt was grief, both for Anna and for herself. "What was the usual place?"

Anna mopped her eyes, but she avoided looking at Beth. "That…that old schoolhouse. Down on Owl Hollow Road. We…we thought no one would see us there. But that night he didn't come, and I had to go home." A sob interrupted her. "The next day I heard…"

Anna didn't want to finish that thought, and neither did Beth.

Another sob burst from Anna. "I was just so unhappy. And when he smiled at me, it made me feel better."

"So you started meeting in secret." She couldn't help the edge to her words.

"You don't think—" Anna's eyes opened wide. "It was never anything. Just talking, and sometimes he gave me a hug. He kissed me two times." She put her hand on her cheek, as if cherishing it. "But it was wrong, and now you'll hate me. Everyone will know, and I'll be under the bann, and Daadi will be so angry…"

"Hush, hush a minute." Everyone would know. Anna would be hurt, but she wasn't the only one.

Everyone would talk, and she'd know they were talking about her, pitying her. Sarah would find out about the son she adored. How could she even survive that? And worst of all, Benjy would know. He wouldn't understand, not now, but he'd be aware that his daadi had done something shameful. Someday he'd understand, and that would be even worse.

In all her initial need to know who the woman was, she'd never considered how that would come about and what damage it would do. If only she could see another way…

She studied Anna, who had lapsed back into misery again. Anna would never be able to keep quiet about it. She had confessed because she couldn't go on, and her conscience would force her to complete the act and confess to the church.

Beth rubbed her forehead, feeling a band tighten around it as she tried to see a way out. Maybe…maybe there was a way to do the least harm possible.

"Anna, listen to me. Can you keep quiet about this a little longer now that you've told me?"

"But I have to confess, and then the whole church will know. And Daadi will be so angry…"

For an instant she wanted to shake the girl and shake Hiram Fisher, as well.

"I know. Just another day, to give me time to think this out. That's not too much, is it?"

She couldn't see any hope in Anna's face, but at least she didn't look quite so miserable.

"I'll try, if you say so."

"Gut." She didn't have a plan, and she certain sure hadn't dealt with her own feelings, but she saw a glimmer of hope. "Now, listen. I want to tell your mother that you're feeling better, and you're going to come to work tomorrow, all right?"

Anna seemed to shrink. "How could I? Everyone would be looking at me."

"You can work in the storeroom, if you want. Just do this for me, and I'll try to help you. All right?"

She sniffled a little, but then she nodded. "Denke, Beth. Daniel said I should tell you the truth, and he was right. I'll do whatever you say."

Daniel. So Daniel had known, and he hadn't told her.

Beth pushed that into the back of her mind to be dealt with later. She had enough to handle right now.

"Now you go and wash your face and freshen up. I'm going to talk to your mother, but I'll see you tomorrow at the store." She hesitated, fearing Anna would slump back into despair the instant she was gone. "Anna, I forgive you. And I'm sure God forgives you. It's going to be all right."

"I don't... I don't deserve that."

"Never mind that. Just do as I say. It will be all right."

She hoped. At the moment all she wanted was to be alone so that she could think all of this out. The important thing now was to handle it in a way that would hurt as few people as possible. She would deal with her own pain later.

The day seemed to drag by after Beth left, despite how busy they were. Daniel longed for Beth's return and dreaded it at the same time.

If she succeeded in seeing Anna, she probably knew the truth about Anna and James by now. And she'd also know that Anna had told him and that he'd kept silent.

It had been the right thing to do, hadn't it? It was far better for Anna to confess to the person she'd wronged. Beth would be more likely to believe and forgive if she heard it from Anna.

Where did that leave him? Beth, with her tender heart, would most likely forgive Anna, but it was less likely that she'd forgive him. He might very well have lost her forever.

The Monday morning press of customers had eased off abruptly, and the store was silent except for Timothy dragging a carton across the floor. Daniel planted his hands on the counter and leaned on them, head down, pain dragging at him. He didn't see a good outcome from this for anyone, and he feared he'd be a good long while forgiving James for leaving such a mess to be cleaned up.

Daniel jerked out of his painful thoughts at the sound of footsteps behind him. Beth had come in the back door, and a glance through the side window told him that her horse and buggy were parked at the hitching rail.

He forced himself to meet her eyes, afraid of what he'd see there. He didn't find the anger he'd expected, not now at least. Beth seemed distracted, as if she were trying to figure something out.

Unable to stand the silence, he spoke. "Were you able to see her?"

Beth focused on him. "I saw her. She was shut up in her room weeping, but I finally got her talking. So far her parents don't know anything, and I convinced her not to say anything about it until I'd had a chance to decide how to handle this."

"Do you think you can rely on that?" Anna didn't strike him as someone who'd be able to keep a secret. Still, she'd done it this long.

"I don't know." She rubbed her forehead, her face pale against the black brim of the bonnet she'd worn for the drive. "I hope so. I told Etta that it was a misunderstanding. That she'd made a mistake, and she thought we were blaming her, but we're not."

She caught his look, and her eyes snapped. "I didn't lie," she said. "With that father of hers, it will be better if this isn't generally known."

Daniel frowned, feeling his head begin to hurt just as much as hers probably did. "I don't see how you're going to manage that. Anna won't be able to forgive herself until she's made it right, and that means confessing."

Beth's anger seemed to spark. "And what will happen if she confesses before the church? Everyone will know, and a lot of people will be hurt. Think of Sarah, learning that about her son. She's already at the point that she'll never stop grieving. I can't do that to her. And think of Benjy."

"And you." Daniel added the words in a soft voice. "Do you think I don't realize that? You'll be hurt twice over by what James did."

Should he have laid the blame so firmly on James? He couldn't help believing that James was the most culpable. He was a grown man, and Anna was just an impressionable child, longing to idolize anyone who was kind to her.

Beth seemed to shrug that off. "I'm wondering what would happen if I went to see the bishop with Anna.

After all, they didn't…commit adultery." She struggled with the word, and he saw her wince with pain. "Maybe he'd agree to a private confession and penalty."

He considered. What she said was true, in a way. This wouldn't, he thought, rise to the level of a kneeling confession in front of the whole Leit. With the bishop's agreement, she might be able to minimize the backlash hurting innocent people.

"Can you really do that, Beth? Can you go to the bishop and listen to the story all over again?"

She shrugged. "It's the least I can do, don't you think? She's hardly more than a child. James…well, James should have known better."

That was putting it mildly, he thought. "Do you want me to go with you and Anna?"

Her anger flashed again. "Why would you do that? Because Anna confessed to you, and you didn't tell me?"

He met her eyes steadily. "You're angry with me."

"Don't I have a reason? You could have told me this. I trusted you."

"Yah, I could have told you. But I thought it would be better for Anna if she confessed to you herself. That's why I pushed you into going over there today."

He saw her absorb his reasoning, but he didn't see any indication that she agreed with it.

After a moment, Beth shook her head irritably. "Anna is coming in to work tomorrow. I thought she should be out of the house. I'll try to talk to Bishop Thomas before that to find out when he can see us."

He nodded. There didn't seem to be any answer to make. Beth was facing a painful situation, and she wouldn't let him help her. He'd forfeited that right.

There was no hope left for them, but that didn't change his feelings. He would love her forever.

Beth went home, feeling as if she'd like to get into bed and sleep for the next twenty-four hours. It couldn't be done. She had a son to take care of, and she must contact the bishop and set up a time to see him tomorrow.

That was easier said than done. She'd have to call and leave a message on the bishop's answering machine and hope he'd check it sometime soon. And she'd have to put enough urgency into her voice so that he'd see them tomorrow. She didn't think Anna could contain herself any longer than that.

As she neared the house, Benjy came running toward her. "Mammi, Mammi! You should see the big pile of leaves we made."

Beth hugged him, holding him close a bit longer than usual and inhaling the sweet little boy scent. When he wiggled to be free, she let him go reluctantly.

"Show me your leaf pile."

He looked confused for a minute, glancing around as if he thought to see it right next to him.

Janie giggled, and he started to giggle, too.

"We jumped in it too many times, didn't we, Benjy?" Janie caught his hand and swung it back and forth. "But it was lots and lots of fun."

"Yah, it was." He seemed satisfied. "We could make another one."

Beth touched his cheek lightly. "I have to make a phone call first. And maybe we should get something to eat."

"Grossdaadi is going to pick me up," Janie said. "He

wanted me to tell you that he'd like to talk to you for a few minutes."

She nodded. He must have looked into the possibility of selling. She'd about decided to forget it, but she'd been so tied up today that she'd have to rethink the whole question.

Benjy tugged on Janie's hand. "Doesn't Grossdaadi want to talk to me?"

"I'm sure he does," she said, smiling. "Let's go fix a snack while Mammi is making her phone call."

In a few minutes, Beth was walking back from the phone shanty. If she'd sounded as desperate as she felt, Bishop Thomas would probably want to see her immediately.

When she got in the house, she realized it was well past lunchtime and she hadn't even noticed it. Janie caught her dismayed look at the clock and shook her head, smiling.

"It's all right. Benjy and I had our lunch already. We'll have some cider and cookies now. Can I fix something for you?"

"I'm not hungry," she said quickly, afraid she wouldn't succeed if she tried to eat something now. "I'll wait and see if your grandfather wants something."

Janie seemed to be studying her, catching on to the fact that she wasn't as usual. She'd always been a sensitive child, concerned for others, and now she'd added a maturity to it that was very attractive.

She was only a year younger than Anna. The comparison made her stomach turn over.

"So sorry I was late getting back today. I hope it didn't mess up any plans." She managed a smile.

"No, nothing at all." Janie glanced to the window.

"Ach, here's Grossdaadi." She gulped down the rest of her cider. "Let's go say hi."

Benjy bolted from his seat. "I want to tie up the horse." The screen door slammed behind him.

Beth forced herself to her feet, feeling about a hundred years old. But before she could get outside, her father had come in. He caught her in a hug.

"Sit down, sit down. You look tired."

"I guess I am, a little. Do you want coffee?" She turned to the stove, but he shook his head.

"I'll have some cider. Sit down."

Taking it as an order, she sank into the chair. Daadi poured a glass for each of them.

"How did you convince Benjy not to come in with you?" she asked.

"I said he could help Janie drive the buggy up and down the lane. Don't worry about them. Janie is a good, responsible girl."

"Yah, she is. I was just thinking that." She hesitated. "You wanted to talk to me?"

Daad gave a brisk nod and brushed his hand against his full, brownish-red beard. "I looked into this business of Elijah wanting to buy into the store." He hesitated. "I don't want to speak ill of someone in the church, but I think you'd do better to look for someone else if you want to sell. He has a reputation for cutting corners and not treating his employees very well. What does Daniel think?"

Daniel's name was like a sensitive spot on her skin. She tried to collect herself. "He wants me to do whatever is best for me and Benjy. But he did make it clear that he'd hate to be partners with Elijah."

"And what about you? Do you want to sell?"

Beth thought of everything that had happened in the past weeks. She'd enjoyed working in the store, and it had given her a sense of accomplishment. Her feelings for Daniel had grown, to be honest with herself. But she wasn't sure any longer. Could she go on working with him every day? She certainly couldn't decide when she didn't know what was going to happen with Anna and the bishop.

"I don't know." She struggled for words, but before she could find any, Daad had given a brisk nod.

"Well, then, you shouldn't decide. And that's a gut way to turn Elijah down. If you do decide later, you should take your time and look at all the possibilities."

It made the most sense of anything she'd been thinking. "Denke, Daadi. I think that's what is best, too."

"That's settled, then. Do you want me to speak to Elijah for you?"

She'd love to say yes, but that probably wasn't befitting a grown woman who was partner in a business. "No, I'll take care of it. Denke."

"Gut." He stood up. "Now I will take Janie and Benjy home with me for supper, and we'll bring him back at bedtime. In the meanwhile, you have a nice rest."

She followed him, protesting. "You don't need to do that."

"We want to," he said, watching as Benjy drove the buggy back to them with Janie's hands hovering over his on the lines. "Rest now. You don't have to do everything yourself."

No, she didn't. And she was truly blessed to have such a loving family to help her.

Chapter Fifteen

Beth had thought to be at work early the next day, but by the time she'd seen Benjy off to her brother Eli's house to spend the day, she had to hurry down the lane to the store. She didn't know what her family knew or guessed, but without any questions or advice, they had rallied around.

When Daadi had brought Benjy back at supper time, he'd also brought a meal, still warm and ready to be put on the table. And with it he'd brought an invitation for Benjy to spend the day with his cousins. She had nearly cried with gratitude.

If you don't know what else to do for someone in time of trouble, you can pray and take food. That's never the wrong thing to do.

Her mother's oft-repeated advice made her smile, despite the fact that she'd assumed this day would include nothing to smile about. Her very practical mother had it right. The warm supper had comforted her, and with Benjy off having fun with his cousins today, she didn't need to fear that he'd hear something he shouldn't.

Beth shivered a little, wrapping her sweater more

tightly around her. The morning breeze was colder, sweeping along the lane and stripping leaves from the trees. Autumn seemed to be passing faster than ever, or was it just that she was a year older?

And a year wiser? She thought back over the events of recent months, unsure as to whether *wiser* was the right word. Certainly she'd had her eyes opened, but it was too soon to know if she'd learned something.

Going in the back entrance, she listened for voices. The only one she heard was that of Timothy, irrepressible as always, teasing Daniel about something.

What if Anna didn't come? The bishop had responded to her call, suggesting she and Anna come between ten and twelve this morning. If he'd been curious as to what brought the two of them to seek his advice, he hadn't betrayed it in his voice.

If Anna didn't show up… Well, she didn't know what she ought to do. Shaking off the question, she hung up her sweater and bonnet and told herself to stop borrowing trouble. She had enough worries without jumping ahead to create more. Anna was probably here already, wondering where she was.

Smoothing her apron down, Beth marched from the office to the store, uttering an inarticulate prayer and hardly knowing what to pray for.

She sent a quick searching glance around the store, but she didn't find Anna. Her gaze caught Daniel's, and he shook his head at her obvious query.

Beth felt flattened and her worries came back in force. If Anna had lost her nerve, Beth would have to think of some explanation for the bishop. If she'd told her parents, she supposed that Hiram would try to exact the full penalty of the church, and the whole ugly story would become public.

With a word to Timothy, Daniel came over to her. "She hasn't come in yet, and I haven't heard from her. Have you heard anything?"

Beth shook her head. She tried to remember to treat him coolly, but she was too worried, and Daniel was the only one she could talk to.

"Not since yesterday. We can see Bishop Tom this morning between ten and twelve. If she doesn't show up, I'm not sure what to do."

Daniel touched her hand lightly—a barely felt brush of a leaf. "Try not to worry. She may well be here before then. If not, we'll figure out what to do."

She ought to resent his effort to include himself, but she couldn't help being relieved to feel she wasn't alone. "Denke." She kept her voice low, seeing Timothy approaching.

"You want me to put the Open sign up, Onkel Daniel?" His gaze slipped from one to the other of them, obviously wondering, but at least not asking what was going on.

"Yah, go ahead. Then you can take the checkout."

Timothy made a slight grimace at his uncle's directions, but he didn't say anything. When he walked off to unlock the door, Beth gave Daniel a questioning glance.

"What does he have against checking customers out?"

Daniel attempted to smile. "I think it gives less time to talk to any girls who happen to come in. What his mother would say, I don't know."

"I can certainly take it. Having something to occupy my mind will help."

"Are you sure you wouldn't rather work in the office? You can update the orders. If… When Anna shows up, I'll send her in."

Actually, that did sound better. It might be difficult to talk to customers when her mind was skittering from one thing to another like a water bug on a pond.

"All right." She hesitated, feeling as if there were something else she should say but not finding the words. Finally, she gave him a meaningless smile and hurried off to the office.

Closing the office door behind her, Beth let out a long breath. Daniel had been right. She needed four walls around her, protecting her from any curious glances.

If Anna didn't come… She slammed the question down. She'd cope with that if and when it happened. Right now, she was better off concentrating on facts and figures.

She'd made her way through one column of figures and started another when the office door creaked. Anna crept in, wrapping a shawl around her and sliding along the wall as if to remain invisible.

Beth hadn't realized how much she'd feared that Anna wouldn't show up. Relief made her feel weak for a moment.

"I'm glad you're here, Anna. Are you all right?"

Anna nodded, but her face was so sallow she looked as if she wanted to disappear into the woodwork. "The bishop?"

Beth stood. "He'll see us this morning. We should leave in about forty-five minutes." She rounded the desk and took Anna's arm. "We'll have coffee before we go. That will make you feel better."

It could hardly make her worse. At the moment she looked as if she'd pass out at an unkind word.

Putting her arm around the girl, she led her next door to the break room. Guiding her to a chair, she pushed Anna into it and started making the coffee.

This might be a little easier if they talked, but she couldn't find anything to say. The main thing between them loomed like an enormous barricade that might collapse on them at a careless word.

She'd have to find a way to talk before they reached Bishop Tom, or they'd sit there staring at each other.

Beth and Anna arrived at Bishop Thomas Braun's wheelwright workshop, with Beth relieved to see that no other buggies were pulled up in the lane. Bishop Tom's services were in demand, since wheelwrights were few and far between. She remembered her grandmother telling her once that some folks were dismayed when the lot fell on Thomas Braun, calling him to the ministry. Some had feared he wouldn't be able to do both jobs.

Somehow, like every Amish person called by God, he'd taken care of the community's spiritual needs as well as their buggies. Now that he was bishop, he had in his charge not only their church but also the adjoining one. He'd never failed to be there when his people needed him.

Swinging herself down from her buggy, Beth murmured a silent prayer that both she and Anna would be able to explain this tangled story in a way he'd understand.

When she rounded the buggy, she found that Anna was still sitting on the seat. Her head was bent, and she seemed frozen in the spot.

Beth reached up to touch her arm, fearing she'd have to push and pull the girl into the bishop's presence. "Komm now, Anna. It's time."

Anna looked at her, her eyes wide with fright and her lips trembling. She gave Beth the impression she was unable to speak.

"I know," she said softly. "But it must be done, no matter how hard it is. For either of us."

Maybe the reminder that Beth was hurting as well got through to her. With Beth's help, Anna climbed down. Grasping her arm, Beth propelled her into the long metal building.

Bishop Thomas rose from kneeling beside the wheel of a family buggy and came toward them.

"I am glad you're here," he said, his voice grave as befitted the occasion. "Komm. We'll go into my room."

The room proved to be a small frame shed attached to the workshop, containing a desk, a shelf of books and several chairs. Following his gesture, Beth led Anna to a seat and sat down next to her, feeling as apprehensive as if waiting for a scolding from Mamm for some childish mischief. But there was nothing childish about this.

"Now we can talk. No one will disturb us." He looked from one to the other, his blue eyes keen and kind.

With his long beard, grown gray in his service to his people, he'd always reminded Beth of an Old Testament prophet—one of the stern but forgiving ones.

Beth realized that Anna was frozen again. Apparently, she'd have to go first. Maybe that was the best thing—she could unravel the story as it had occurred to her.

"I'm afraid it's a long story." She glanced uncertainly at Anna. "I'll have to start at the beginning."

He nodded. "Take as long as you need."

A deep breath seemed to give her the courage she needed. "It started when Lydia, my cousin, and I were getting James's clothes ready to give away. I hadn't touched anything until about a month after his passing."

She stopped for breath. At least she'd started. There was no turning back now. "In a drawer under his clothing, I found a note. It was obviously from a woman, and it pleaded with James to meet her at the usual place."

Bishop Tom's eyes twitched at that, and he glanced toward Anna.

"At first I didn't know what to think. I was angry and hurt, and I kept thinking I must find out who it was." She paused, trying to think how to put it. "I was hurt and angry with both of them. I couldn't think of anything else. But I kept trying to pray about it, and as time went on, I knew I couldn't keep living in the past. It wasn't gut for me or for Benjy. Then this week, I found out." She looked at Anna. "She confessed to me, and she asked for my forgiveness."

She came to a stop, not knowing what else to say. It was Anna's turn now.

Bishop Tom looked from her to Anna, who seemed to shrink under his gaze. "Anna?"

Her face twisted as she struggled to speak. "I was the one. I didn't mean to do anything wrong. I was so unhappy, and James was kind. He was always smiling, and when he smiled at me, I felt better."

"So you met with him. Did you sneak out to do this?"

Anna sniffled and nodded.

"How many times?"

Was he counting up Anna's sins? Maybe they had to

admit each wrong in order to be forgiven. How many sins did *she* have on her conscience?

"F-four," Anna whispered. "At that old schoolhouse on Owl Hollow Road."

He was still for a moment. When he spoke, his voice was grave. "I must ask you, Anna. How far did this relationship with James go?"

Anna was crying now, tears flowing freely, and Beth felt her eyes sting with tears.

"We just talked mostly," she whispered. "Sometimes he hugged me. Twice he…he kissed me." The whisper had gone almost to silence.

When she looked at the bishop again, Beth had the sense that he'd aged in the past few minutes. It was as if he'd taken their wrongs upon himself.

"And that's all?"

Anna nodded, sobbing.

"Do you wish to confess your sins and be restored to a right relationship with God and His people?"

"Yah." Her voice was choked with sobs, but she seemed to sense that she had to say this aloud.

Bishop Thomas turned his gaze to her, and Beth felt as if he could see right through her.

"Beth, have you forgiven Anna for the wrong she has done to you?"

"Yah." She couldn't say it fast enough. How could she blame that miserable child for what had happened? It was James who would be difficult to forgive.

"Have you forgiven James for breaking his wedding vows?" He seemed to read her mind.

"I am trying." She wiped away tears. "I say I forgive him, but I have to do it again." She looked at him. "But I am trying."

He nodded, as if satisfied. "Do you wish to confess whatever lack of forgiveness is still in your heart and be restored to a right relationship with God?"

"Yah." She wiped the tears again. "I do."

He glanced from one to the other. "Please kneel and confess."

Anna was almost on her knees already, but she sank the rest of the way. Beth, slipping to her knees, watched Anna warily, half-afraid she would pass out.

But she began, managing in a shaking voice to confess her wrongs and ask for forgiveness.

Then it was Beth's turn. Confessing her initial anger was easy enough, as was declaring her forgiveness of Anna. The challenge was asking with a whole heart to be able to forgive James.

When it was done and forgiveness proclaimed, a cleansing warmth swept through her. It was in the past, forgiven. No one else ever needed to know. She turned to Anna, and in a moment they were in each other's arms, weeping but rejoicing.

Daniel had managed to spend most of the day within sight of the windows, watching for any sign of Beth's buggy. Finally, at midafternoon, it came in view, but she didn't stop at the store. She drove straight down the lane toward her own house.

He fought down his disappointment. He'd expected that at least she'd tell him what had happened. Maybe she felt he'd forfeited any right to feel concern for her.

Since she was alone, he'd guess she'd taken Anna on home. How would that have gone? If Anna had to tell her parents the whole story, that would have been an unpleasant time, to say the least. For the Fisher family, for sure, but for Beth, as well.

He rubbed the back of his neck, feeling the taut muscles react painfully to the touch. He told himself he'd done the right thing for both Beth and Anna, but that was small comfort given Beth's feelings.

When Timothy left, Daniel locked the front door and pulled down the shades. On any ordinary day, he'd check out and then go home, where Mamm and his sister-in-law would have supper ready. Today he'd choke if he tried to eat.

They wouldn't worry if he didn't show up. They'd just put something back for him, assuming something had detained him at the store. He was detained, all right, but not in the way they'd think. And there was always something to do here.

Daniel was checking inventory in the storeroom when he heard the rattle of the front doorknob. If it was a belated customer wanting him to open up, he or she would have to do without.

Before he could argue with himself about it, he heard another sound—a key turning in the lock and the door opening. Beth? His heart jumped into his throat, and his fingers slid from the shelf.

Cautious, half-afraid of how she'd look and what she'd say, he opened the door a few inches and stood watching her.

Beth wasn't looking in his direction. Did she think the store was empty? She walked slowly back through the store, pausing to look from one thing to another, reaching out to touch a shelf or straighten a carton.

It was almost as if she were saying goodbye, and his heart sank. He could hardly expect anything else. If she thought he'd deceived her, she wouldn't want to work with him any longer.

She turned slightly, and he got a better look at her face. It was pale and drained, and yet she didn't look shaken. She looked at peace, as if she'd accepted whatever happened with the bishop as God's will.

He must have made some sound, because Beth glanced toward the back of the store and saw him. He held his breath, wondering if he'd know what she was thinking when she spoke.

"Daniel. I thought you'd left."

He shook his head. "I couldn't. Not when I was worrying about what happened to you. Did Bishop Thomas agree with the way you wanted to handle it?"

For a moment, she looked as if she didn't know what he was talking about. Then she seemed to realize. "Yah. Well, actually, I never had a chance to ask it. He listened to both of us, and he was so kind, so understanding." Her face relaxed in a half smile. "Once Bishop Thomas took over, I guess I realized that it was foolish to try to tell him what to do."

That was good, he guessed. He'd never had to confess anything of that sort, but he thought a great deal of the bishop's wisdom and his knowledge of his people.

"What about Anna?" He moved a little closer to her, alert for any sign that she found it intrusive.

"I was afraid once or twice that she'd pass out. But other than that, she was all right. She held herself together and told the whole story, just the way she'd told it to me."

"Gut." He began to relax a little. If the truth was out to the bishop, surely there was not much to worry about. "I'm glad. I was afraid she'd fall to pieces and not be able to tell him."

Her old smile lit her face. "Me, too. I've never been so glad. I didn't have to try and explain it."

Daniel was so relieved to see the old Beth again that he wanted to laugh. "No public confession?"

Beth shook her head. "Bishop Thomas listened to her confession and announced her forgiveness. And then he asked me to confess."

"Wh-what did you have to confess? You were the injured party."

"He asked if I had forgiven Anna. And then he asked if I'd forgiven James."

"That would be harder."

"Yah. I could only say I was trying. And I'd keep on trying." Her voice shook a little. "Sometimes I think I have, and then it jumps back up again."

She was struggling, and he longed to help her but didn't know how. "That is natural, isn't it? When someone has hurt you so badly?"

Beth nodded, giving him a look of gratitude, her eyes filled with tears, so that they looked more than ever like two green lakes. He couldn't help it—he took both her hands in his. She didn't pull away.

"I think I understand James better now," she said. "Or maybe I see him more clearly. He had faults and weaknesses like we all do, but he wasn't a bad person."

Daniel thought of his friend as a boy, as a teenager and then as the man he'd become. He'd been self-centered at times, spoiled, maybe, but Daniel couldn't regret their friendship.

"Yah, you're right."

"For a time, I thought that I could never trust anyone

again." She went on, her voice as soft as if she spoke to herself. "But that was so foolish. There were people I already trusted, even when I told myself that. People like Daad and Mamm. And you."

He was sure he'd heard only what he'd wished. But she was looking at him, her eyes clear and untroubled. He felt her pulse beating against his hands, and he knew that what he'd always wanted was within reach.

It was too soon, of course. They both knew that. But he had to speak. Even if they had to wait, it would be worth it.

He moved his fingers caressingly on the soft skin on the inside of her wrists. "Once, a long time ago, I realized that it was you I wanted, but I let James edge me out of the picture. I won't do that again."

A smile trembled on her lips as she lifted her face to his. "No. Please don't do that again."

Carefully he drew her closer, until she rested against him and their lips met once, very lightly. "I love you, Beth. When it's time, I want to marry you. To be Benjy's father and maybe the father of other kinder with you. And I will cherish you all my life."

They stood close together, hands clasped, and he knew that out of the shattered remains of marriage and friendship had come a love that was stronger—one that would last a lifetime in obedience to God.

* * * * *

SEEKING REFUGE

Lenora Worth

Dedicated to all the silent women out there
holding pain inside their hearts.

Seek the Lord, and his strength:
seek his face evermore.
—*Psalm* 105:4

Chapter One

The house across the footbridge looked less sinister and sad in the spring.

Josie Fisher sat on the bench near the *grossmammi haus* and wished she could forget the other home that stood stark white, empty and waiting, off in the distance. She'd grown up in that house, and each time she went near it, the memories tore through her like a thunderstorm.

But today, with the spring wind in the air and flowers blooming all around, Josie felt hope in her heart. The early daffodils and dandelions her sister-in-law, Raesha, had planted around the yard lifted their determined heads to the sun. The old oaks and red maples were lush with new leaves. The herb garden behind the main house was coming along nicely. She could almost smell the fresh mint and basil, the dill and oregano. Josie watched as a robin pecked at the grass near the hat shop. She and Naomi had planted sunflowers there. It would take a while for those to grow and bloom.

Turning her head to the sun, Josie remembered Naomi Bawell's sage advice.

"Look at the sunflowers, Josie. See how they lift their faces toward the sky. They seek *Gott*'s love, same as we do."

Josie loved Naomi Bawell and clung to her as if she was indeed Josie's true grandmother. Naomi and Josie lived in the small *grossmammi haus* located behind the main house on the Bawell farm. Lived together and watched out for each other, as a *grossmammi* and *kinder* should. Josie felt safe there inside the solid walls with the tiny kitchen and living room, two bedrooms and a washroom in the back. A breezeway separated their apartment from the rambling main house where her brother, Josiah, lived with his wife, Raesha, and their six-month-old son, Daniel.

And with little Dinah.

Josie's daughter by birth, but their daughter now to raise Amish. After they were married, they'd officially adopted Dinah.

Over two years ago, Josie had left three-month-old Dinah on the Bawell porch. Hard to believe that tiny baby girl was now walking and jabbering, her mischievous smile as bright as the sunshine.

You ran away and left your child. The voice that echoed inside her head made Josie look down at her dark blue tennis shoes.

But she is safe now and healthy and happy, and so are you. That voice made her look up again. Toward the sky.

"I did the right thing."

Yes, she'd done the right thing after being attacked by an *Englisch* boy. She'd felt it necessary to leave her baby with someone who could love her and take care of her. The Bawells had always been kind to Josie when she was little and afraid.

Now she was an adult but still so horribly afraid. She rarely left the property except to attend church and occasionally go to the general store. She'd been ruined by a man who'd later done the same thing to an *Englisch* girl, and because that girl also had a powerful family, Drew Benington had stood trial and had been sent to jail. After that, another girl had come forward to testify. Josie's friend Sarah had written to her about his arrest and the trial since they'd all known him. Sarah had no idea what had happened to Josie, but Josie's relief after reading her friend's letter had been short-lived. What if Drew tried to get in touch with her? How would she handle that?

Would she ever be able to truly rest and give up her guilt?

Drew didn't believe he was the father of a little girl and had denied signing any papers to acknowledge that. He had given up any legal paternal rights.

Josie prayed she'd never see him again, and she thanked *Gott* that Dinah was safe and happy.

But on sweet warm afternoons such as this one, Josie longed for the arms of another man. The boy she'd left behind in her shame and misguided confusion.

Tobias.

"I will walk you home."

He'd told her that the first day they'd met by a rocky stream that flowed down the mountain. By the time their walk home was over, Josie had a huge crush on Tobias Mast. After that, they had managed to find each other at singings and frolics. He had smiled at her the first time she went to a youth gathering after church.

Sitting across the table from each other after they'd sung lively hymns had soon become her favorite part of attending church. She knew she'd see Tobias there.

"I will drive you home."

Drive her home in his buggy? That was a big step but one she cherished. It meant he wanted to court her.

"I will allow that," she told him with a smile, her heart already lost to his beautiful deep blue eyes. His curling light brown hair always needed to be combed, but he smelled fresh and clean, like that mountain stream.

"I cleared it with one of the ministers and with your friend's family," he said. "Then next we will arrange for you to meet my *daed* and my *bruder.*"

Josiah had allowed her to come to Kentucky, hoping she'd find a suitable husband. Maybe she had. But she'd been mad at Josiah for so long she didn't want to prove him right.

Yet she couldn't resist Tobias. "We will?"

"*Ja.* And since you have a *bruder* back in Ohio, I will ask his permission to court you."

"No," she'd said, causing Tobias to frown. "I mean— my brother is not concerned about me. I make my own decisions."

"Are you sure about that?"

"I am when it comes to you," she'd replied, being the flirty girl she thought the world needed. While flirting worked with Tobias, he always respected her. She loved him for being considerate and cautious. She *had* loved him completely.

Now her heart ached with missing him, with remembering his sweet laughs and his kind nature. They had planned a future together in Kentucky. But that future had been shattered the night her whole world had shifted and changed forever.

With the scent of honeysuckle surrounding her and the warm wind moving over the fields and valleys of Campton Creek, Pennsylvania, Josie closed her eyes and wondered where Tobias was at this exact moment.

Tobias Mast paid the taxi driver and turned to stare up at the place where he'd reserved a room for the week. The Campton Center had been recommended to him as a place to stay while he conducted some business here. He'd heard the center, which used to be a private estate, now served as a source of help for the Amish who lived in Campton Creek.

When he'd researched Campton Creek, he'd found the center online at the library back in Orchard Mountain, Kentucky. Tobias had immediately called the Campton Center and explained that he was Amish and he was looking to settle in Campton Creek. A nice lady named Jewel had talked to him.

"If you need a doctor, lawyer, room and board, a safe haven, advice and help on anything, we will find someone for you. That's what we're here for."

"I just need a place to stay for a while," he'd explained. "I plan to buy a home with land in Campton Creek."

"We have several places for sale," the woman had told him. "I'll print out the listings for you and have them ready when you arrive. There are some beautiful properties here."

Now that Tobias had arrived from Kentucky, he wondered at his sanity. He'd come to Campton Creek not only to buy a house and land, but to find the woman who'd broken his heart.

Josie.

Closing his eyes, he remembered Josie's beautiful brown eyes and her golden-brown hair. She'd broken his heart and he needed to find out why. Why had she left him two months before they were to be married?

He could never forget the first moment they'd met.

"Who are you?"

Tobias had turned from where he'd been fishing in a mountain spring that ran through the community. He saw her and smiled. Her dark hair shimmered a deep reddish gold in the spring sunshine. She wore a light blue dress and a white apron, her black cloak open since the spring day had warmed. Her black *kapp* sat squarely over her oval face, its strings dangling against her neck. Freckles danced across her nose.

He went back to his fishing. "Who is asking?"

"I'm Josephine Fisher. I came here from Ohio with my friend. I might stay here."

He thought he heard a challenge in that declaration.

"*Ja?* Well, I'm Tobias Mast and I live here in Orchard Mountain. Why haven't I seen you around?"

She twisted the loose black ribbon of her head cover. "I have only been here for two days. I decided to come on a walk by myself. The woods are so pretty." She lifted her hand. "I love the wildflowers."

Tobias threw out his line and glanced over at her. Mighty spunky to take off into the woods alone. "Don't they have woods and wildflowers in Ohio?"

Her dark eyebrows lifted. "Of course. But I don't like Ohio."

Tobias gave up on the fish since talking to her seemed

so much better. After they had sat on some rocks and chatted a while, he said, "I will walk you back home."

"I didn't ask you to do that."

"I want to. I am headed that way."

"Do you know the way to where I'm staying?"

"Not yet. But I will. *Wilkum*, Josephine Fisher."

She'd given him a big smile that had enveloped his heart. "You can call me Josie. Everyone does."

Josie. He'd fallen for her that day and he still loved her.

Now he'd tracked Josie back to the place where she'd grown up. They had been in love, so why had she left?

He needed answers. He'd stick around until he had them.

After his father's death, Tobias had inherited the family land and home back in Kentucky, but with both his parents dead and his only sibling living in Indiana, he'd decided it was time for him to move on. He sold out and packed a bag the day he deposited the check. After wiring his brother half of the asking price, Tobias had set out for Pennsylvania. Because he was alone and hurting, Tobias only wanted to find Josie and get to the truth, something he'd put off to stay with his ailing father. He couldn't move on with his life until he at least had the opportunity to confront her.

After that, he'd decide how to handle his future. If Josie was here, Tobias aimed to buy a place and settle in Campton Creek with the hope that she'd settle with him.

If she didn't want him, he'd still be near her, and that had to count for something.

Tobias walked toward the big brick home with the impressive columns on each side of the front door. All around, various trees heavy with spring sprouts hung like green veils. Garden trails wound their way around the grounds, annuals and perennials shouting in hues of red, blue and orange. The side yard held a parking lot complete with buggy hitches and horse railings.

That made him smile. Seemed this place did accommodate the Amish. He wondered about this obviously historic house and the Camptons. This town had obviously been named after the family. Tobias loved history and often checked out historical fiction or biographies from the library. Most of his friends frowned on such notions, but he liked to know about things.

His *daed* used to tell him that his curiosity would get him in trouble one day. Maybe so. Right now, he was curious about a clean room and a good meal.

Tobias rang the doorbell and waited.

An older woman with a bright smile on her face opened the door.

"Jewel?" Tobias asked, taking in her white hair and serviceable skirt and blouse.

"No, I'm Bettye," the woman said with a wave of her hand. "Jewel is our new manager, but she had to run some errands. You must be Tobias Mast."

"Yes, ma'am," he said, mindful to speak in *Englisch*.

"C'mon in, then," Bettye said. "I'll get you signed in and show you to your room."

Tobias took in the opulence of the estate house. "I appreciate that. I'm mighty tired."

Bettye checked the register on a small electronic pad, her fingers moving with haste over the keyboard. "Now, Tobias, we serve breakfast to our visitors at seven each morning. And if you ask ahead, we'll leave you some dinner on the stove."

"You must stay busy," he said, liking Bettye's calm

demeanor. "From what Jewel told me, this place is truly a community center."

"Oh, I don't normally do much these days," she replied. "I'm a companion to the owner, Judy Campton. I was her assistant for years after my husband passed. When Admiral Campton died, she and I moved into the apartment over the carriage house. We usually have lots of people moving through here, but it's the end of the day. Jewel will be back soon. She lives here now and keeps watch over Mrs. Campton and me." Chuckling, she whispered, "They all think we're old, you know."

Grinning, Tobias followed her to the stairs while she continued. "The kitchen is located in the back of the house. You'll find snacks and drinks on the sideboard in the dining room. We have one of those newfangled coffee makers that use pods."

Tobias had seen those in his travels and marveled at how the machines made a cup of coffee from a tiny round plastic pod.

"My *daed* frowned on such notions," he admitted. "I think they're amazing, but I'm not supposed to admit that."

"I won't tell," Bettye said. They reached a door on the second floor. "This is your room. It has a small bath and a desk and chair. There is a table where you can eat if you'd like or you're welcome to eat in the kitchen or out on the sunporch."

Bettye turned to smile at him. "We operate from six to six around here, but if you need anything, there is a button on the phone that will ring through to Jewel. She's a light sleeper, and I must warn you—the woman used to be a bouncer at a nightclub."

"*Denke,*" Tobias said, thinking Bettye was one of

the kindest women he'd ever met even when she was warning him to mind his manners. "I think I will fall straight to sleep once I get settled."

"Oh, one more thing," Bettye said as she gave him a key card to his room. "Jewel left you copies of the real-estate listings she mentioned on the phone."

"I'll look those over," Tobias said. "I appreciate her doing that."

Bettye gave him a motherly stare. "Do you plan to buy land here?"

He nodded. "Yes, I do."

He didn't tell Bettye that he also planned to find Josephine Fisher. That was something he had to do in his own way and on his own time.

Once Tobias was in his room and had freshened up, he ate one of the cinnamon cookies along with a bottle of apple juice he'd found on the small wooden table.

Then he sat down in the comfortable chair by the window that looked out over a small side garden full of roses and some pretty shrubs, so he could read the listings he'd found on the desk.

Four different farms for sale. He skimmed the first three pretty quickly. He couldn't afford two of them and the other one looked in bad shape.

But the fourth one caught his attention and had his heart pumping too fast.

The Fisher place. Located next to the Bawell Hat Shop and Farm. The same address Josie's friend had given him. The directions were listed along with the price. Within his budget.

Was this the house Josie had lived in when she was young?

Chapter Two

The next morning, Josie saw her brother, Josiah, approaching the back porch of the *grossmammi haus*. He often stopped by after he made the rounds to tend the animals and take care of the milking.

"*Gut* morning," Josie called, smiling at her brother. Hard to believe she'd treated him so terribly after he'd found her in a local hospital sick with pneumonia just a few weeks after she'd left Dinah on the Bawells' porch. He'd brought her home to recover but it had been a hard road, both spirtually and emotionally.

"*Gut* day to you, sister."

Josiah's smile said it all. Her brother was at last happy and thriving after many years of being a nomad, tormented and in despair. They'd both been scarred by an angry, abusive father who'd treated their mother and them so badly that Josiah had left as soon as he turned eighteen. Josie had blamed him for leaving her there alone.

But he'd never given up on her, and he'd taken her to Ohio with him after their parents died.

He settled on the porch steps and stared out over the

green pastures and the cash crops he'd planted to harvest this fall. Then he turned to her. "Josie, I need to tell you something."

Josie's heart jumped and skidded. She'd always felt that one day, Naomi and Raesha or her brother would tell her it was time for her to leave. Silly, but she couldn't get comfortable even though she felt safe here.

Putting a hand to her heart, she stared at her brother. "What? Is something wrong? Did I do something?"

"Josie," he said, his hand reaching up to touch hers, his dark eyes bright with concern, "you are safe here and you have a home here, always. How many times do I have to tell you that?"

"I try to believe," she said, glancing around. "I know *Gott* brought me home, but I don't want to be a burden."

"You are not a burden," her brother said, shaking his head. "You have been a blessing to Raesha and me, and especially to Naomi."

"I love her." That was true even if at times Josie felt she'd been put with Naomi so the older woman could keep an eye on her. But Naomi had been nothing but loving and kind. They were quite a pair once they got going.

"We all do." He glanced toward the house. "Having you here to be a friend and helper for her means so much to Raesha and me. Naomi loves you as one of her own."

Josie bobbed her head and blinked away tears while she managed to calm herself. "I should not doubt. I will continue to pray and show grace and thankfulness." Wiping at her eyes, she asked, "So what do you need to tell me?"

"I have someone coming to look at the house today."

Josie shifted her gaze to the old homestead that she

saw every day. Her brother had come back to Campton Creek and worked hard to restore it after a terrible fire had killed their parents years ago. A fire she'd felt responsible for starting. "Really?"

"Ja." Her brother paused a moment. "I wanted to make you aware. Will you be all right if they want to buy our old home?"

"I don't mind anyone living there," she said. "I just can't go back there again."

"I understand," Josiah replied, his eyes kind. "But remember, the fire was an accident. You were a child, Josie. A frightened child who'd seen our father abusing our mother over and over again."

Josie closed her eyes, remembering how she'd accidentally dropped a lit lamp when she'd run into the barn to help her mother, to save her mother from their father's brutality. "It still hurts, *bruder.* I dropped the lamp and the hay caught fire and… Mamm screamed for me to run. They didn't make it out. It will always stay with me."

Josiah patted her hand. "But you're safe, and if we do sell, you'll have part of the payment for your future."

"I don't want it," she said on a sharp tone.

Josiah pulled away. "It's okay. We don't know if this man will buy the place."

Raesha came around the corner, carrying Daniel in her arms. Josie had not liked Raesha when she'd first been forced to come and live here. Now she considered her a sister.

"Here you two are," Raesha said, her gray eyes always gentle, her brown hair neat underneath her *kapp.* "Josiah, I'm off to the shop. Daniel will keep me company in the store today since he's fussy."

"Where is Dinah?" Josie asked, always one thought away from worrying.

"She's with Naomi and Katy Carver. Katy will take care of her but you can check on her for me, *ja*?"

Josie gave Raesha a soft smile. "I will do that. I can come and help with Daniel, too. And do whatever you need."

"Denke."

Katy, a couple of years older than Josie and a friend, often sat with Naomi and read to her while Josie helped in the shop. Josie loved Dinah, but she kept her distance, afraid she'd love her too much, so much that she'd want her child back one day. Just being near Dinah brought her happiness, but Dinah clung to Raesha and Josiah, the only parents she'd truly known. Josie could not force them to give Dinah back since she had no means of taking care of her daughter. Dinah would never know the truth.

Josiah stood. "I'm going over the footbridge to meet our potential buyer."

Raesha gave him a quick kiss. "I hope this one will stick." Then she glanced at Josie. "How do you feel about this?"

Josie swallowed her fears. "I hope a *gut* family moves in and puts love back into that house."

Raesha patted her arm, and little Daniel grinned and reached his chubby fingers toward Josie. She grinned back and tickled his soft tummy. He was such a precious child.

Raesha kissed her son and then smiled at Josiah before hurrying to the far side of the big house, where the hat shop and factory covered the other half of the property.

"So do I," Josiah replied after his wife had left. "It will be nice to have that land off our hands and into the care of another family."

He gave Josie a reassuring smile. "We could build a fence."

"No need," she said. "Once it belongs to someone else, I think I'll feel a lot better."

Her brother accepted that as he strolled toward the footbridge. Josie stood to stare after him, hoping she'd spoken the truth. Could she finally let go?

Tobias stood in the yard of the house next to the Bawell place. He knew Josiah had married and he knew the Bawell name. Josie had often mentioned Naomi Bawell, the kind woman who'd been a big help to Josie at times.

He had not seen nor heard from Josie for over three years. She'd left him right after Christmas, in a bitter cold winter.

Then a friend back in Kentucky finally told him Josie had written to her and let her know that she was safe and back home. She'd asked Sarah not to tell anyone, but Tobias had managed to find out the truth when chatty Sarah slipped up and mentioned Josie.

Now he studied the house in front of him. It looked fresh and newly painted, two storied with a long wide front porch and several windows. A smaller house than most, but doable for a bachelor or a couple just starting out.

Josie had never talked about this place much except to say her parents were dead and her brother had left when he was young. She'd often mentioned her brother but she didn't want to talk about the past. She'd missed

Josiah but he'd lived in Ohio back then and Josie didn't reach out to him. How did they both wind up back here?

This looked like a nice farm. But the bigger question was, why they had both left?

A fairly new barn stood behind the house. The property was only a few acres, but he didn't need much. He planned to continue his woodworking and also grow vegetables year-round to sell at market. The *Englisch* loved the farm-to-table trend these days, so they'd buy fresh vegetables in bulk. They called this organic. The Amish called it natural since they'd been living off the land for centuries.

He heard someone behind him and turned to find an Amish man approaching. "Josiah Fisher?" he called.

The man nodded as he came close. "*Ja.* I own this property. I understand you want to look it over."

"I do," Tobias said, shaking Josiah's hand. "I'm Tobias Mast."

Josiah looked surprised, but he quickly hid it behind a steady stare. "Are you from around here?"

"No, I'm from Kentucky," Tobias said, wondering if Josiah already knew who he was. From what he remembered, Josie hadn't told her brother much about him, either. "Orchard Mountain, Kentucky."

"Orchard Mountain." Josiah stood back, his eyes filling with questions. "Did you know my sister, Josie Fisher?"

Tobias couldn't lie. "I did. I knew her well. I was in love with her."

The other man went pale and then turned stern. "That's what I was afraid of. And you came here to buy our place?"

Tobias nodded. "If I like it, *ja.* But you need to know

one other thing. I also came here to find Josie. I need to know why she left me." Seeing Josiah's concern, he added, "I found out from a reliable friend that she's back here and living with you and your new wife."

The other man glanced toward the Bawell property. "She is here, but she won't like this."

"She *is* here?" Tobias asked to be sure he'd heard correctly. Hope hit against despair in his heart. "Is she okay?"

Josiah put a hand on his shoulder. "Let's go inside and talk."

Tobias wondered if Josiah would try to keep him away from Josie. But he'd find a way to see her, sooner or later.

He walked into the house and glanced around, letting his questions stay unasked for now. The small kitchen area and a living room made up most of the first floor. He saw an open door into a big room and figured that would be a bedroom. "You've done a lot of renovations."

"I did," Josiah said. He told Tobias he'd come home a few years ago to sell the house. "Instead, I met the widow next door…and we got married. You seem to have already heard that, though."

Tobias heard the hesitation in Josiah's words. "But?"

"I'm just surprised you're here," Josiah admitted. "I never expected this since so much time has passed."

"Why is Josie here?" Tobias asked, needing to know.

Josiah guided him to the back of the house and stared out the wide window that looked out to the barn. "She'll have to be the one to tell you about *why* she's here. That's all I can say other than she wanted to come home. It is not my place."

"But something happened?" Tobias said. "You know why she left me?"

Josiah whirled to give him a solemn stare. Running a hand down his beard, he said, "I will not talk about my sister with you. If you like the property, you can make an offer. But I warn you, I will have to tell Josie about this. If she does not want to see you, or if she disagrees with you buying this place, then I will not sell it to you. She's been through enough."

Tobias saw the concern in the other man's eyes. "I'll take the place," he said. "Name your price."

"You saw the asking price," Josiah retorted. "Are you listening to me?"

"Then I'll give you that price." Tobias turned to take another look at the new kitchen cabinets and the big worktable. "I hear what you're saying, but I'm not leaving until I see Josie."

"You might be in for a world of hurt," Josiah said. "Josie doesn't get out much. She likes to keep to herself."

"Why? Is she ill?"

Josiah shook his head. "She is healthy and only just now getting back to normal. It's not for me to say."

Tobias backed off. "I understand. But I won't give up."

Josiah shot him a look of admiration. "I can see that clearly. But you might be in for the fight of your life. She could bolt and run again, and I don't want that."

So Josie had been running away? From what? Or maybe from who?

"I don't want that, either," Tobias assured him. "But I do want to buy this property, and one day I hope to get some answers." He shrugged. "Even if Josie never sees me or acknowledges me, I'll be here. Right here, watching over her and waiting for her."

Josiah nodded, appreciation in his eyes. "I pray that she'll see the good in you and accept your presence. She could use a friend, someone she can trust."

"She trusted me once."

"*Gott*'s will, she may again," Josiah said. Then he turned to leave. "I will let you know if I can accept your offer, Tobias. But don't hold your breath."

"I've been holding my breath since she left me," Tobias admitted. "I've got nothing but time."

"You're welcome to look around all you'd like. You can lock the door behind you."

"*Denke,*" Tobias replied.

After Josiah left, Tobias went to the corner window and stared out across the land. Josie was right next door, in that big house. So close, but so out of his reach.

Could he win her back?

Or was she too far gone to see that he still loved her?

Chapter Three

Later that day, Josie waited in the living room with Naomi. She wanted to find out if Josiah had sold the house, but he'd been busy all day long and she'd helped Raesha with the gift shop that served as the storefront for the hat shop. Spring brought in more tourists who wanted to buy homemade breads and jams, goat-milk soaps and lotions, and, of course, hats. So they'd barely had time to grab a sandwich in the back for dinner.

Now she was tired and hungry but also worried. She needed to remember what she'd learned in counseling. *Don't borrow trouble. Live in the moment and try not to project too many worries into the future.*

And trust in God.

"Should we head over to supper?" Naomi asked. "You know it's a treat to eat with the entire family when we can."

"We'll go in a moment, Mammi Naomi," Josie said. "I thought Josiah would come here first to talk to me."

Naomi's eyes had grown weak over the years, but Josie could tell the older woman was staring a hole through her back. "Child, you need to stop fretting.

The house will always be there, even if someone else moves into it."

"But someone else could be happy there," Josie replied, touching a hand to her *kapp*. "That would make me very happy."

"You are so sure about that?"

She whirled to look down at the woman in the chair. "I believe I'm sure, *ja*."

"Sit and let us discuss this," Naomi said, used to Josie's rants and nervousness. "You are troubled by this news?"

"I'm worried," Josie admitted. "What if they aren't happy? What if that house makes them…not happy."

"A house has no power, young one," Naomi replied on a soft note. "A home has the power of love and grace and forgiveness."

"I want those things—in that house," Josie said, pointing a finger toward the window. "I need to know that, but my family didn't have those things."

"Josie," Naomi said, her smile serene, "you are right. You didn't have much grace and forgiveness, but your *mudder* loved you both so much. Now you have your *bruder* back and you have family right here in our home. So you have found love and grace and forgiveness, ain't so?"

"It is so," Josie said, turning back toward the woman who had always loved her. "I'm trying to live each day to the fullest, but today has been a difficult one."

"You are doing your best, child."

Naomi lifted slowly to stand. Josie moved the walker close so they could go to their middle-of-the-week supper with Josiah and Raesha. Usually the *kinder* were already in bed on these nights, probably because Josie couldn't bear to be around Dinah too much. She'd made progress, but it was hard. She appreciated that her brother and Raesha didn't demand she get more involved with Dinah. Holding the child for too long only made Josie sad for the past she'd lost. Would she ever be able to love anyone again?

"The sooner we get to supper, the sooner we can hear what Josiah has to say," Naomi pointed out.

Josie gave Naomi a wry smile. "You are the old, wise one."

Naomi chuckled. This was a joke between them. Old and wise versus young and confused.

"I am that," Naomi said, "but you are becoming more mature and wise by the day. I am proud of you, Josephine."

Josie let the sweetness of Mammi Naomi's words flow over her. "I will try to be worthy of your praise."

"Then help me get to my supper," Naomi retorted with a playful grin.

Josie helped her out the door and across the breezeway, the soft early-evening wind flowing over them with a feather's touch. Josie couldn't stop herself from glancing over at the house that haunted her dreams. The tree line blocked most of the house and barn, but she could see the corner of the front porch where she used to sit and play with the rag dolls her *mamm* had made for her. Josiah should have come to tell her if they had a buyer or not. But he'd busied himself all day with things that seemed suddenly urgent. He hadn't even stopped by the shop to see Daniel and Raesha.

Was he afraid to tell Josie that someone had made an offer?

Or maybe he didn't want to disappoint her if the place had not sold.

When they reached the back door to the main house, Josie turned once again to glance at the Fisher house. She saw a man standing on the porch in the very spot where she used to hide and play all by herself. The man looked toward her.

A man who seemed familiar. Just her imagination, Josie told herself to calm her jittery heart. She'd had Tobias on her mind and in her dreams for a long time, so it stood to reason she was now seeing him when he wasn't the one standing there.

Maybe Josiah had sold the place and he'd already turned the farm over to the buyer. Why else would someone be back there this late? And why did her heart skip and jump from seeing the man standing there?

After they'd made their way to the kitchen of the big house, the smell of chicken potpie wafting toward them, Josie saw the look that passed between her brother and Raesha.

Something was going on. She'd have to find out what exactly. The old dread resurfaced, making all her anxieties and doubts bubble up like boiling water.

Josie got Naomi settled, then went into the *bobbeli* room to check on Daniel and Dinah. She did this when her fears started pulling her back into the dark.

Daniel slept away, his dark curls reminding her of her brother. She went to Dinah's bed and stared at the precious girl. Precious because Josiah and Raesha loved her so much, but hard to look at. Dinah only reminded Josie of the man who'd ruined her life. Her chestnut-haired daughter looked a lot like a Fisher, but Josie could see the markings of the *Englisch* boy who'd attacked her at a party. A boy who'd been Tobias's friend at one time.

I can't think about that now.

Naomi had taught her to pray when she was scared.

Josie stood by her daughter's crib and prayed that Dinah would always be happy and healthy and that she'd never know the truth of her birth.

Then she turned and went back into the kitchen to eat with her family. But now even Naomi seemed secretive and worried, her eyes holding Josie in a warm warning.

"What is going on?" she asked, her hands on her hips. "Josiah, what happened today?"

Her brother motioned to a dining chair. "Sit and let us eat."

Josie sat down and forced her fears away as they each silently said grace. But the silence seemed like an eternity to her.

When her brother lifted his head and opened his eyes, she said, "I can't eat until I know why everyone is looking at me as if I've grown two heads." Josie sank down farther on her chair and glanced from her brother to Naomi. "You know, too. All of you do. Please tell me if something bad has happened."

Naomi put a wrinkled hand over Josie's fingers and brought their clutched hands down against the table. "Your brother will explain and then we'll have our supper."

Josiah sighed and looked at his wife. Raesha nodded and took his hand. When he looked at Josie, his expression changed into a frown, his eyes filling with a dark doubt and then sympathy. "Josie, I showed the house to a man today and he wants to buy the place right away."

Josie let out a sigh of relief. "Is that all? Well, that's

gut. Does he have a family? Is he from here? I saw someone over there as we were coming over. He looked familiar. Who is it?"

Raesha's eyes were wide, her expression quiet and blank. Naomi still held to Josie's hand. But now Josiah would not look her in the eye.

Josiah looked down in a hurry and then lifted his head, his eyes meeting hers. "It's Tobias, Josie. Tobias Mast. He's come to find you and he wants to buy our place."

Josie's heart stopped.

Her mouth fell open as she stared at her brother. "What?"

Raesha got up, came around the table and touched her shoulder. "It's true. He found out you are here and he wants to buy the property. But, Josie, you don't have to ever see him if you do not feel so."

Josiah nodded in agreement. "I told him as much. I also told him I will not sell to him if you disapprove or feel uncertain."

"Feel uncertain?" Josie pushed her chair back and stood. "I feel so much more than uncertain, *bruder.* The man I was supposed to marry is here? It's been over three years since I left Kentucky. Why did you tell him that I am here?"

"I didn't," Josiah said, his eyes dark with regret and sadness. "He already knew. A friend of yours told him."

Josie should have never written to Sarah Yount. But Sarah had been her best friend since the day she'd arrived in Kentucky. They'd shared a lot of secrets, but Josie had not shared her worst shame even with her best friend. Josie had often wondered if Tobias had wound up marrying Sarah. Apparently not. Or worse, what if he'd brought Sarah here with him? But then, if he were married already, he wouldn't be here and demanding to see her.

She shook her head, her hand to her heart. "I cannot see him. I cannot. He shouldn't have come. I do not want him to live next door, Josiah. How could you even think that?"

Josiah rubbed his hand down his beard and looked helpless. "I was caught off guard and surprised. I wasn't sure what to tell him, honestly."

Raesha nudged Josie to sit down. Then her sister-in-law served the meal, the tension in the air as thick as the steam from the chicken potpie. Only Josie couldn't eat.

Josiah tried to eat his food but finally put his fork down. "I told him you wouldn't like this. He only wants to know why you left."

"He can't know that." Josie's eyes watered and she put her head in her hands. "What am I to do? I do not want to leave."

"You will not leave," Naomi said, her voice commanding and firm. "You will not go back out into that world. You need to be here, where we love you and understand you." Then she twisted to give Josie her full attention. "I need you here. We all do. And you need us."

After sighing and sitting silent for a moment, Naomi continued. "We will sleep on this and pray on it, of course. Your *bruder* has been trying to rid himself of that place for years. *Denk* on that. You have to let it go, too, and this might be the best solution, for so many reasons."

"I want to let it go," Josie said, trying to keep her voice calm. "But I don't need to *think* about this or wait until tomorrow. We cannot sell the house. Not to Tobias, of all people. Why would he even want it?"

Josiah looked at Raesha and then back to Josie. "He came for you, Josie. He wants you back."

Josie stood again, her whole body shaking. "Well, we all know I am not fit to be around him, let alone be his wife. That will never happen. He cannot live next to us. That cannot be."

She turned and ran out of the room and out onto the breezeway. The late-day wind lifted at the strings on her *kapp* and cooled her burning cheeks. Then she whirled and watched the setting sun shoot its last rays across the green land. The beams of light hit the house behind the tree line with a creamy-golden glow that hurt her eyes with its beauty.

At that moment, it seemed as if God had just touched his hand to the house that had been her prison and now was part of the yoke of shame she could never shed.

Josie stood watching the house, her mind whirling with a warring dance of both pain and joy. Tobias was here in Campton Creek, and he'd looked straight at her just a few minutes earlier. She *had* seen *him* there on the porch.

Her brother's words came back to her. *He came for you, Josie.*

But she couldn't let the joy from those words take over the pain that fractured her heart.

Tobias Mast might think he wanted her back, but if he knew the truth, he would turn and leave and she'd never see him again.

And if he stays, she thought, wondering what that would be like, *would he even see me then?*

No. She would not give in to the need to rush over

there and call out his name. She would not give in to the love she still held in that secret place in her heart. Love for a man who would be ashamed and embarrassed to be around her.

Josie watched the sun fade away and the dusk settle into muted grays as a hush came over the land. The house next door became a dark, looming shape that made her catch her breath and turn away, tears falling softly down her face.

From inside, she heard Dinah cry out, "Mamm. Mamm."

Heard that sweet voice while her eyes held to that looming shape in the darkness.

Josie sank down on the floor and cried the tears she'd been holding back for so long. The last time she'd cried like this was when her brother had found her inside that empty house with Dinah in her arms. She'd planned to take her baby and leave again, but Josiah had forced her to tell him the truth. She'd always believed she'd caused the deaths of their parents in the barn fire.

But Josie knew in her heart that her mother wanted to run out of the barn with her.

Only their father had held Mamm back.

He'd held her back, and Mamm had cried out, her arms outstretched to her child.

Josie's arms were now wrapped against her stomach as the gut-wrenching pain of hearing her daughter's cries only mirrored her own cries as she saw her mother's tormented face surrounded by fire. How she longed for Tobias at that moment. She'd never told him what had happened that horrible day. Now she would never get that opportunity.

"What am I to do now, Lord?" she called out in desperate prayer. "What am I to do?"

Her whispered prayer lifted up into the night and disappeared into the emerging stars. A crescent moon hung bright and dipping just out of her reach.

Everything was always out of her reach.

Her baby. Tobias. Her mother. She could never have any of them back.

Raesha came out onto the porch. "Josie?"

Josie wiped at her eyes and lowered her head. "I am here."

Raesha sank down beside her and took Josie into her arms. "*Gott*'s will, Josie. *Gott*'s will."

Josie knew she should believe that and let things take their course, but how? How did she do that when the man she'd loved, the man who'd promised her a good life in Kentucky, was now here and he still wanted her?

She lifted up and looked at Raesha. "How do I find my way? Tobias will not accept me once he knows the truth. How am I to survive with him living so close? How?"

Raesha wiped at her own eyes. "We will be here to help you. This could be a *gut* thing. Tobias came all this way to find you, so he must still love you very much. You can take your time in deciding, but...what if you were honest with him?"

"He'll leave again and I will have to live with yet more heartache. I do not think I can bear any more, Raesha. No more."

Raesha stroked Josie's damp cheek. "And yet you'd send him away without knowing what might have been. What plan *Gott* has for you and Tobias."

"I thought my plan was clear. To be content and safe

here with Josiah and you, Naomi and… Dinah. Little Daniel, too."

"You are safe. We will not let anyone hurt you again. You know that is your brother's only wish."

"Tobias could hurt me."

"Or he could heal you, Josie. He could heal you."

Josie lifted her head and glanced at the darkness. "I never imagined I'd see Tobias again."

"God imagined it," Raesha replied. "He knows your pain. He wants you to find the peace you seek. His will always shows the way."

"So Tobias is here for a reason?"

Raesha nodded. "He came to find you, and he's willing to buy that house just to be near you. That's what he told Josiah."

"Just to be near me." She let that cover her like a warm blanket. "That might be all he will get if he lives right there."

"That might be enough," Raesha said. "Enough to see what could happen."

She helped Josie stand. "*Kumm* and try to eat some supper. Naomi is concerned about you."

Josie nodded and wiped at her tears. "I'm not hungry but I will try. This is a big shock."

"I understand."

"Is Dinah all right? I heard her crying out."

Raesha smiled. "She is sound asleep again. A drink of water and a kiss, and she went back to bed."

Josie closed her eyes to the pain that sharpened each time she thought of all the nighttime kisses she'd had to give up in order to give her child a good life.

How much more was she supposed to give?

When they came back inside, Josiah breathed a sigh

of relief. Without a word, he touched a hand to Josie's arm. "I am sorry."

Josie nodded. "I did not mean to upset everyone." She turned to Naomi. "I will take you back. You must be ready for bed."

Naomi shook her head. "Finish your supper and then we will go through."

To appease them, Josie took a few bites of the potpie Raesha had kept warm on the stove. But the food stuck in her throat and she finally pushed her plate away.

Josiah almost said something, but his wife gave him a warning glance and he looked away. Raesha took her plate. "I'll finish up here. Leftovers tomorrow for dinner."

Josie hugged her brother. "I will consider this and we will talk later. I do not know what I will do."

Josiah nodded, his dark brown eyes wide with worry. "Sleep, sister."

Josie doubted sleep would come. How could she shut her eyes without seeing all the images she'd tried so hard to put out of her mind? Her mother's tears and screams. Dinah's cries and needs. Tobias the last time she'd seen him, their last kiss.

He had not known it was their last kiss. He still had hope.

"I cannot wait to marry you," he had whispered, his words breaking her heart as he talked about the new year coming. He went on and on about building a house, having their own land, how he'd continue with his woodwork and how he wanted to grow vegetables for restaurants.

Josie had only smiled and touched his cheek. "I love

you," she'd said. "I love you and I know you will succeed with your dreams."

"I want to take care of you, Josie," he'd told her. "I want you to have the best I can provide for you."

"I want that, too," she'd replied, her mind in turmoil over all she would have to give up.

Then she'd left in the middle of the cold, dark January night, her heart torn apart and a baby growing in her tummy.

A baby who belonged to another man who had assaulted her and used her without any qualms and left her drugged and drowsy without even remembering her name.

How could they ever reconcile with that between them?

Chapter Four

Tobias waited at the property the next day to see if Josiah Fisher would let him buy the place. A dark cloud hovered in the morning sky, threatening a good rain. But Tobias hardly noticed the weather.

The more he'd thought about things, the more Tobias felt God had led him here to this spot for a reason. A reason that went beyond starting new.

He wanted to go back. Back to the past and his life with Josie. They'd been happy and ready to get married. He'd had a solid plan to take over some of his father's land and grow produce to sell to the local restaurants. He'd gotten all the permits and studied up on all the laws regarding homegrown organic foods. He'd sell his wood carvings on the side, too.

Josie had approved all of it, and they'd laughed and planned their future. Until that January, when Josie had become quiet and pale, her moods shifting like the unpredictable winter winds. Something had been bothering her since before Christmas, but she refused to discuss it with Tobias. She kept telling him she loved him, her words almost desperate. What had she been hiding?

The last night he'd seen her, she had been so sweet, but almost sad. "I wish Christmas could have lasted forever."

"We'll have lots of Christmases together when we're married," he told her, his hand holding hers. He remembered how she trembled and stared out into the January sky.

"I would like that."

"You will have that. We will celebrate all the seasons of life, Josie. I will always take care of you. Always."

She nodded, tears in her eyes. "I want that, too. To always be with you, Tobias. Only you."

She'd left him that January without any word of explanation, not even a goodbye note.

For the last few years, Tobias had wondered why she'd left and where she had gone.

Now she was so near but still far away from him. He thought he'd seen her last night with an older woman in a wheelchair. They'd moved along the open breezeway between the main house and the other smaller house behind it. A *grossmammi haus*, probably.

The woman he'd spotted had stopped and stared for a brief moment. Josie?

He stood now in almost the same place on the front porch of the Fisher house and glanced over at the neat, rambling Bawell property. A successful property with thriving livestock and a growing business.

Maybe one day he'd have that, but right now he only wanted to see Josie.

Overhead, lightning hit the sky and then thunder followed off in the distance. He'd get soaking wet trying to get to the taxi booth, but he'd needed to come back today to look this place over once more. He wanted to buy this house and land, and he felt that in an urgent way.

He watched as Josiah Fisher came out of the big two-storied white house next door and began walking toward him. Had Josiah told Josie Tobias had come to buy the land and that he wanted to see her?

Josiah met him on the porch, his expression as dark and grim as the sky behind him.

"She doesn't want me here, does she?" Tobias asked after seeing the sympathy in Josiah's eyes.

A soft blowing rain began and Josiah motioned to the empty house. "Let's go inside before we get soaked."

Tobias followed Josiah into the house, hope washing away with each drop of rain. "Josie did not like my idea, *nee*?"

Josiah paced around the small living area and then went to stare at the kitchen sink and check the stove.

"You don't have to explain," Tobias said. "I understand if she's not ready to see me." Then he held up a hand to stop Josiah's pacing. "Did I do something to hurt her? To make her stop loving me? Is that why she went away?"

Josiah removed his hat and rubbed his head. "I'm sorry, Tobias. But I cannot hurt Josie any more. She's doing so much better now. She's healing and she has a *gut* life here."

Tobias went still with fear and dread, his hands clenching into fists. "Better? Healing? Was she ill?"

Josiah's eyes widened. "I have said too much. I only came to tell you that I can't accept your offer. I am sorry."

Tobias watched as Josiah started toward the door. "Why won't you tell me the truth?"

Josiah shook his head and tucked his hat close. "I can't."

Then he went out the door and ran into the rain.

Tobias stood inside the empty house, the dark skies all around him pouring out the grief he'd felt since Josie had disappeared.

"Why?" he shouted to the heavens. "Why did she leave me?"

When he heard the door slipping open again, he whirled, thinking Josiah had returned.

Instead, he saw a young woman standing there, wet and cold, shaking with a chill, her lightweight cloak and black bonnet soaked. She removed the bonnet and tried to adjust her *kapp*. Then she lifted her head and looked at him.

Tobias gasped, his gaze holding hers. "Josie?"

She stood against the wall, frightened and afraid. She looked different. More mature and world-weary but still beautiful to him. "Josie, you came."

She nodded but never moved from the wall near the door. Clinging to her bonnet with both hands, she kept her gaze leveled on him. "I followed Josiah and hid until he left."

Her words were whispered and choppy. Was she afraid of him?

Tobias moved toward her, but she held out a hand. "Do not."

"I want to hold you, to touch you," he said, unable to stop the words. "I have missed you."

"You must leave," she said. "If you will not listen to my *bruder*, then listen to me. I do not want you here."

Tobias felt the sharp slap of her words so much that his eyes burned. "What did I do to you, Josie?"

"You did nothing," she said, her eyes wide, her stance firm. "You did nothing. I only came to make you see reason."

Tobias moved closer. "All I see is the woman I loved, the woman I still love. I want to buy this place. I *need* to buy this house. *Mei daed* is gone. Died about four months ago. I sold the land and came looking for you. I could not leave him, but now… I have no one left. I came for you, Josie. And whether I live here in this house or not, I am not going to go away until I get some answers. I will not leave you, no matter."

The woman standing before him started to cry. "You must leave, Tobias. It's over. It has to be over."

Then she turned and ran out into the rain.

He ran after her but stopped on the porch. He didn't want to frighten her. "Josie?" he called, the wind taking her name out into the trees. And taking her secrets with it.

Tobias stood there staring after her, his heart breaking all over again while the wind and rain lashed at his soul. Why had he come to this place anyway? Had he been wrong after all?

He watched Josie run across the arched bridge between the properties, watched and wished he could have held her close. She looked so tormented, so lost, her dark eyes misty and full of regret, her hands holding to the wall behind her.

Tobias made sure she made it home and saw her dart into the small house past the main house. So she did live in the *grossmammi haus*.

She'd told him he'd done nothing to cause her to run away from him.

Thinking back over her words, Tobias had a realization. If he'd done nothing, then who had? And what had they done to make her so sad and afraid?

Josie couldn't believe she'd gone to see Tobias. But she had to see him with her own eyes to believe he was actually here. After so many nights when she'd dreamed of their time together and had imagined what their life could have been like if she'd stayed and married him, she had one fleeting moment that maybe her dreams could come true.

But that was not to be.

Now she hurriedly dried herself and put on a clean dress and apron, hoping Naomi had slept through the whole time she'd been out in the rain.

When she came out of her small bedroom, she saw Naomi waiting patiently in her wheelchair. "Oh, you're up," Josie said. "I'll start breakfast."

Naomi held up a wrinkled hand. "*Kumm* and sit here, Josie."

Josie moved to the chair near Naomi. "Are you all right?"

"I'm *gut*," Naomi said. "I am concerned about you. Why did you go out in the storm?"

Josie could not lie to Naomi. "I went for a walk."

Naomi nodded. "Oh, a short walk?"

Josie looked down at her hands. "I went over the bridge."

"Over the bridge toward your old home?"

She looked up at Naomi, tears forming in her eyes. "I had to see, Mammi. I had to know. He is here. Tobias was there in the house. Josiah told him he cannot buy the place. But…he still wants to do so."

"Did you speak with him?"

"Only to tell him he should go."

"What did he say to that?"

"He wanted to know what happened. He wants to stay."

"How do you feel about that?"

Josie let out a shuttered breath. "I don't know how to feel. I've pushed those feelings away and stanched them so tightly I can't open my heart again. Not to Tobias. Not to anyone."

Naomi sat silent for a moment, her head down. Sometimes she did nod off. Josie hoped this was one of those times.

But her beloved *mammi*'s head came up. "I have thought about this situation." Naomi reached for Josie's hand. "*Mei* dear, maybe you should tell Josiah to let Tobias buy the place."

"Why?" Josie asked. "Why would I want that kind of torment?"

"It might not be such a torment," Naomi said, her eyes full of compassion. "Tobias came all this way to find you and he wants your old home so he can be near you. That says a lot about his faithfulness and his mindset."

"He always was stubborn," Josie admitted. "He's set in his ways. When he wants something, he goes after it."

"So he wanted you once," Naomi said on a chuckle. "And he still loves you. That is a *gut* thing."

"It could be, *ja*, but he is still very angry and hurt. I cannot tell him the truth." Josie shook her head. "I do not know what to do, Mammi Naomi."

Naomi nodded. "I have one more question."

"Okay."

"What was the first thing you felt when you saw him there in your old home?"

Unable to deny it, Josie wiped at her eyes. "I felt joy and… I felt peace. A short sweet peace, as if I could finally breathe again."

"And then all the pain came crashing down?"

"Yes."

Josie got up and started breakfast, her hands shaking as she measured oatmeal and poured milk.

Naomi rolled her wheelchair over to the kitchen. "Maybe you could concentrate on that joy and peace, knowing Tobias is nearby."

Josie finished cooking the oatmeal and measured out sugar and cream before adding some fresh berries. "How can I have joy and peace knowing the man I was supposed to marry is living alone in a house that I hate?"

She placed Naomi's food on the table and then sat down with hers. But her stomach recoiled and her heart beat a hurtful tempo. How could she find any peace now?

Naomi said, "Let us have a quiet moment with the Lord."

Josie closed her eyes and thought again about seeing Tobias this morning. He looked the same, only older, stronger and more mature. Beautiful. He was a beautiful, loving, kind man. The kind of man she'd always dreamed of marrying.

Would it be so bad to have him back in her life?

When she heard Naomi's spoon hitting her dish, Josie opened her eyes and saw the truth. She couldn't allow Tobias back in her life. He would not want her if he knew the truth.

* * *

Tobias went into the kitchen at the Campton Center, his mind on breakfast. He'd missed the early breakfast so he could meet with Josiah Fisher this morning, but that had not gone well. He'd been here three days now and he wasn't ready to give up yet.

Especially after seeing Josie. She'd grown even more beautiful since he'd seen her last, but she looked fragile. Like a delicate flower tilted in the rain. Tiny and dainty.

With a shattered shimmer in her pretty eyes.

Tobias stared at the fancy coffee maker, his mind still on Josie. The more he thought about it, the more convinced he'd become that something bad had driven her away from Kentucky. And him. Since they'd loved each other, he knew he couldn't have done anything to make her take such a drastic step. He aimed to find out more.

"That thing ain't gonna start up by itself."

He turned to find Jewel grinning at him behind her black glasses. After stepping forward, she pushed a button on the machine and brought it to life.

Jewel was an interesting woman. She wore her dark hair short and spiky, but she dressed in colorful full-skirted dresses or what she called tunics over bright pants. And her shoes were always a surprise. Flowery tennis shoes or painted boots. He never knew what she'd have on next. She changed during the day since, as she'd told him yesterday, "I wear a lot of hats around this place."

That was true. Sometimes she was the plumber and sometimes she was the cook. Others came and went, helping here and there. Lawyers, doctors, nurses, businesspeople, all willing to help people who needed their help. But Jewel ran the show.

He wanted to ask her who he could find to mend a broken heart.

Jewel nudged him. "See the light? That means it's ready for your pod."

Tobias blushed. "Sorry. I have a lot to think about."

"Did you find any property?" Jewel asked while she handed him a round pod of dark coffee. Then she opened the coffee maker and pointed.

Tobias put the pod in and shut the lid, then found a mug and hit the biggest cup size available. "I found the perfect place," he admitted. "But I can't have it."

Jewel found two muffins and motioned to the kitchen table near a big bay window that looked out over the sloping yard and the creek past the swimming pool.

"Sit, Tobias, and tell me your troubles."

"How do you know I have troubles?" he asked after he brought his steaming coffee over.

"Everybody's got something," Jewel replied in a sage tone, waving her hand in the air.

She wore intricate rings on each finger, so Tobias saw flashes of yellow, deep blue and a shimmer of red.

Tobias didn't know what to say, so he bit into his carrot cake muffin.

"Take me for example," Jewel said. "I went to juvie, had a bad rap sheet, mostly petty crimes, and I hated the world. Plain and simple."

Tobias lifted his eyebrows. "What's juvie?"

Jewel chuckled. "Juvenile detention center. In Amish speak, that'd be *kinder* jail."

"Children's jail?"

"Teenage and underage jail," Jewel said slowly.

"You were in jail?"

"I was. But once I got out, I decided I didn't want to

go back. Thankfully, I met Judy Campton, and she told me I had potential but that I also had a thick noggin. I took her words to heart."

"You've known Judy Campton for a while, then?"

Jewel squinted. "About fifteen years now. Thanks to her, I worked hard and let God take care of the rest. I found employment here and there, waiting tables and taking on odd jobs while I got an education. Now I have me the best job in the world. I landed here and became manager about a year ago—and exactly when she and Bettye needed me, too. And I don't plan on leaving."

"So you like being in Amish country?"

"Love it," Jewel replied. "The Amish don't judge me and I don't judge them. It is a mutual admiration society."

Tobias shook his head. "You are one amazing woman, Jewel."

"And I'm a good listener," she said. "Judy taught me that when I listen, I can hear things."

Tobias wasn't so sure about that, but Jewel's logic couldn't be challenged right now. He needed help and she was willing.

"Don't give me that look now," Jewel said, her big green eyes staring him in the face. "Talk to me."

Tobias polished off the other muffin and took a long sip of coffee. "I want the Fisher house."

"The one near the Bawell place?"

He nodded.

Jewel slapped his arm with a mighty force, causing him to frown. "Sorry. I'm just so tickled for you."

"As long as you don't try to tickle *me*," he retorted.

"Well, that wouldn't be proper. Now, tell me—did you make an offer?"

"I've offered everything, including my heart, but they don't want to sell to me."

"What? They sure do too want to sell that place," Jewel said, one hand grabbing at her short sprouts of hair. "Josiah and his sister left it empty for years. He came back and fixed it up and then got himself married to that precious Raesha. I know for a fact he wants to be done with that property."

"His sister doesn't want him to sell," Tobias said, his heart burning. "I mean, she does not want *me* to buy the property. She doesn't want me here at all."

Chapter Five

"Why not?" Jewel asked, her head lowered but those dark brows jutting up.

"It's a long story."

"I've got a few minutes."

Tobias hesitated, but Jewel gave him an imploring stare. "We're here to help, Tobias. You look like you need a friend."

He did indeed need a friend. So he poured his heart out to this strange, eclectic woman. Then Bettye and Mrs. Campton came down to sit in the sunroom, and soon they'd heard the whole story, too.

"I have worked with Josie," Mrs. Campton said. "She was in bad shape when she returned to us."

"Why?" Tobias asked.

Silence, then measured glances between Bettye and Mrs. Campton.

"Do you all know what happened?"

"I don't," Jewel replied, her eyes bright with curiosity. "Miss Judy keeps her secrets to protect those who are hurting."

"I don't know much," Bettye said, her eyes soft with

concern. "But people talk and I do know that was not a happy house for either of the Fisher children."

"I can't reveal any confidences." Judy Campton grasped her pearls with a shaky hand. "You must understand Josie was lost and now she is found. She's doing much better, but she has a long way to go to be completely well and good."

"Why won't anyone tell me?" Tobias asked. "If I can't buy that place soon, I'm going to have to find somewhere to live or go to Indiana and live with my brother. He and I do not always see things in the same way. He blames me for Josie's leaving and I have no idea why she left."

Judy Campton held up her hand, a diamond solitaire flashing at him like a beacon. "If you want my advice, I'd say try again to buy the house. If that doesn't work, stay here and find work and a place to live. Josie needs you, Tobias."

"She did not seem that way this morning. She told me to leave."

"She also needs time," Judy Campton said. "I'd hate to see you give up when you could be the blessing she needs so she can have the life she deserves. Go back to Josiah and ask again."

Tobias filtered that advice, but he didn't think he'd ever get the answers he needed to win Josie back. "But if he says no, you think I should still stay in Campton Creek."

"Yes, and while you are here, you show Josie in a million little ways that you have staying power."

He looked at Bettye after hearing that tall order. "A million little ways?"

"Little ways can lead to big trust and great reward,"

Judy added to Bettye's advice. "And Josie needs to learn to trust again."

Jewel hit her hand on the table, startling all of them. "I told you, if I listen, I hear things. And I just heard good advice for you, Tobias. Be still and know."

"You heard that?" he asked, smiling.

"I did. Be still but take action while you're in a holding pattern. That's what Mrs. Campton just told you. The trust will come if she sees you ain't going anywhere."

Trust. In a million little ways. Be still and know.

Tobias had never been good at waiting, but he'd do it for Josie. For the life he still wanted with her.

"I will try your suggestions. *Denke*, ladies, for being so kind to me."

"That's our job," Jewel said, almost slapping him again, but thankfully she just chuckled. "And that's our hearts. We love people."

Tobias went to the phone on the wall near a small desk that had been set up for anyone who needed to use it. He called the Bawell Hat Shop and left a message for Josiah. He'd try once again to buy the Fisher property, and if that didn't work, he'd go to plan B. Finding a job and staying in Campton Creek.

Then he would have to start the countdown on a million little ways to make this work.

"You want me to lie to my sister?"

Tobias shook his head, hoping Josiah would see reason. "No. I want you to let me buy your old place as a silent investor for now."

"For now?" Josiah pulled at his beard. "What do you mean?"

Tobias glanced around the bench they had found when he'd called Josiah to meet him near the Hartford General Store. "I want the place and I have the money. Let me buy it but don't tell Josie."

"I cannot hide that from her."

"All she needs to know is—" Tobias stopped and sighed. "It's a bad idea, isn't it?"

"Ja," Josiah said with a smile of relief. "The worst thing you could do is lie to her and withhold information. She doesn't trust anyone these days and that would be a hard blow to her. Especially coming from you."

Tobias let out a sigh and stared at the big creek that ran through town. "I am at a loss."

"We all are at times."

"Could you at least hold the house for me if I make a down payment?"

Josiah sat silent for a moment. "I can do that. I will hold it for one month."

"Two?"

Josiah chuckled. "You do not give up, do you?"

"Not when I want something."

"I hope one day my sister will see the good in you, Tobias."

"I will make her see that I will not give up on her, either."

Josiah's smile held a bittersweet tinge. "I hope so. If you can win her over, the house is yours. If not, I'll refund the down payment in full."

After they'd worked out the details, Josiah left and Tobias walked along the street. Campton Creek was a beautiful town and everyone here had welcomed him with smiles and well wishes. Now he just needed a job and a place to live.

When he spotted a help-wanted sign in a furniture store, Tobias hurried inside. It was an Amish establishment where all the furniture looked handmade. When the bells on the door jingled, a muscular man came out from the back.

"Can I help you?"

"Ja," Tobias said. "I saw the sign. You're hiring?"

"We are," the man said. "I'm Abram Schrock. I opened this store about three months ago and I need experienced woodworkers."

"I have experience," Tobias replied. He explained what he'd done in Kentucky. "I do carvings and I can work with any tool. I've made everything from tables to chairs and cabinets and chests." He took a breath and added, "I also carve things—birds, flowers, butterflies."

Abram grinned. "I can see you are eager."

"I need a job," Tobias admitted. "I want to settle here in Campton Creek." He wouldn't tell Abram anything beyond that, but he sure hoped the man would give him work.

Abram nodded, his dark eyes full of questions. *"Kumm* into the office and we will talk."

Josie sat in the buggy, her *kapp* centered on her head and her eyes straight ahead. She did not like going out, but today she'd had no choice. Naomi was feeling bad and Raesha had to take care of little Daniel. He had a cold and had been fussy all week. Josiah had work to do in the fields, but he and Raesha would take turns checking on Naomi. That left her to do the weekly run to the Hartford General Store. At least Katy had readily agreed to drive her into town.

"It will be a girls' trip," her always chirpy friend had

told her as she pulled her family's buggy up to pick up Josie. "Do not worry. I will take care of you, and if you get uncomfortable, I'll finish the shopping."

"You are a *gut* friend," Josie had told her as they took off. She hadn't told Katy about Tobias showing up. Most of the community knew very little about her past except that she had a baby out of wedlock and her family would raise the child. But no one here held it against her, and they did not speak of it to protect both her and Dinah. The bishop had made sure of that. Or so she hoped. Josie had gone before the church and confessed that she was an unmarried mother and that she'd made some bad choices. She was forgiven. But that didn't mean some might not talk.

What if Tobias heard something? Another reason for her to fret about him being here.

Katy kept reminding her she needed to forgive herself. No one knew the whole truth about her being attacked. She did not want that shame to hang over Dinah's head.

"You are quiet today," Katy said, giving her a sideways glance as they clopped along.

"I am enjoying the nice weather," Josie replied. She'd always loved being outside. Mainly because bad things had happened inside her home when she was young. She'd spent a lot of time outside and in the barn, until the day she'd accidentally set the barn on fire. Blinking, she shuttered those memories.

"It is a beautiful day," Katy said, taking a long breath. "*Gott* brings special days for special reasons."

"It is the season," Josie replied, used to Katy's philosophical side. "Late spring is always special."

"*Ja*, because *Gott* saved this day for us, a day of renewal and rebirth as the land comes back to life. A sign that we need to do the same."

Josie shook her head and decided not to argue with Katy.

They were both laughing when she glanced at the Schrock Furniture Market and saw a sight that shook her to the core.

Tobias, walking out with Abram Schrock. Shaking hands with Abram. Smiling and nodding.

"Who is that?" Katy asked with too much interest.

Josie couldn't speak. Tobias glanced up and into her eyes, his expression as surprised as her beating heart.

"Are you all right?" Katy asked, glancing from Josie to the two men.

"Drive," Josie said. "And watch where you're going."

Katy shot one more look at Tobias.

While he never stopped staring at Josie.

After Katy tied the big draft horse to the hitching rail in front of the general store, she hopped down and waited for Josie. "Who was that?"

"Why would I know?"

"He looked at you, Josie, as if he knew you."

Josie glanced around. The furniture store was down the street from the block-wide general store. But she didn't see Tobias anywhere on the street.

"I will tell you on the way home, when we are alone."

"*Ja*, you will," Katy said, her tone firm. "You know you can trust me with anything, but you seem to have one more secret."

Josie stopped and turned back. "I think I should go home."

"*Nee.*" Katy held her arm. "You can do this. You need to get out more and this is important. Raesha and

Naomi need you to help, and today that means stocking up."

Josie took deep, calming breaths and prayed she wouldn't have a panic attack. She had not suffered one in a long time, months maybe.

"Breathe in, breathe out," Katy kept telling her. "Remember your list. Study it. That will calm you down."

Josie managed to keep walking as she searched the aisles of the big general store to make sure Tobias wasn't waiting for her. When Mr. Hartford greeted them with a smile, she smiled back.

But inside she was shaking and wishing she could go back home. When would Tobias leave? Because she didn't think she could keep handling things with him so close. And she had to wonder what he'd been doing at the furniture market. He had always been talented with wood carving and making beautiful things. She still had a tiny horse he'd carved for her years ago.

Then the unthinkable occurred to her. Abram had been asking around for someone to help out in the store and the workroom out behind the store. Someone who had experience making furniture and carving wood.

Had Tobias taken that job?

Tobias stood in the sunroom the next morning, giving thanks that he'd found a job at least. And that he had two months to do a million little things to make Josie trust him again. And maybe tell him the truth about why she'd left him.

But he hadn't been so great at finding a place to rent or stay. He talked to Bishop King and, ironically, the bishop had suggested the Bawell place.

"They have been known for taking in travelers, relatives and anyone in need. I've seen a lot of folks move through that big house."

Tobias had lowered his head. "I cannot stay there, sir."

"Oh, and why is that?"

Then he had to explain to the bishop, who he knew would not repeat what he'd told him.

Bishop King nodded after Tobias opened up with what he was feeling. "I know of Josie Fisher. She is a kind woman who's been through a lot. The Amish don't talk much of such things, but we are learning that the best of us sometime have emotional issues."

"But you won't reveal what's bothering her to me," Tobias said, making it a statement.

The bishop shook his head, his beard swishing against his dark coat. "I will not. You know where we stand on such things."

"I do and I respect that, but it's frustrating since I'd like to help her."

"*Gott* will see her through, and you showing up here to become part of her life again could be part of that plan." The bishop kept his eyes on Tobias. "If you take your time and do things in a proper way."

"So everyone tells me," Tobias said on a chuckle. He sure hoped so. He prayed so. He'd listen, as Jewel had so sagely suggested, and hope the Lord would show him the way.

Now he wondered what to do about a living arrangement.

He'd checked the Campton Creek newspaper and *The Budget*, but he'd found nothing. He started his new job today, so he'd have to worry about this later. Jewel had told him he could stay in the little room upstairs for another week.

That didn't give him much time, but he couldn't stay here indefinitely.

Tobias drained his coffee and hurried out to get to work before the Campton Center opened for business. People came and went here during official hours and he didn't want to be in the way. At the center he'd met a lot of Amish going about their business.

Nodding to Jewel and the efficient lady lawyer who had an on-site office, Tobias went out the side door and started his walk to work. He took in the quaint town proper and noticed the park across from the creek. This was a nice place. Small but not too small, with a lot of Amish influence but the modern world out on the main highway.

He didn't want to find an apartment away from the village, however. He needed to be near Josie.

The first thing on his list was to buy her a spring plant and have it delivered to the Bawell place. She could nurture the plant and watch it grow. But he went into the flower shop and didn't see the kind of flowers Josie liked.

He'd have to figure something out and soon. When he saw a crop of wildflowers growing near the park fence, he had his answer. After taking the flowers he'd picked back to the Campton Center to put in water until he could have them delivered, he saw Jewel. Together, they picked more flowers from the garden.

"I'll keep 'em fresh and I'll even find someone to deliver them," she told him. "I won't tell who sent them."

"I appreciate that. I think Josie will know."

Just one of the many ways he could show her he cared.

Would she listen?

Would she hear?

He'd do anything to be able to talk to her.

I only want to talk to her, Lord. I pray for understanding and guidance.

Tobias needed *Gott*'s will to also be his will. He could not fail. If for no other reason than that Josie needed someone to love her.

Chapter Six

Tobias entered the furniture market and took in the scent of wood shavings. The smells of cedar and pine had always brought him comfort. If his hands were busy, his mind would follow, and maybe he'd figure something out while he did an honest day's work. And maybe he'd sleep better tonight.

Abram greeted Tobias immediately. The man always had a smile. "Here is my new helper. Are you ready to get to work?"

"I am," Tobias said, smiling. "I have missed having work to do."

"That's the attitude I like," Abram said. "But before we get started, would you mind taking this list over to the general store?" He handed Tobias a small piece of notepaper. "Mr. Hartford ordered some of the special chemical-free adhesive I use, and it should have come in late yesterday but it didn't. Would you mind checking on it?" Abram touched his left knee, rubbing his hand against it. "My gout is hurting something awful this morning."

Tobias had noticed yesterday he walked with a limp.

"I will go and check," he said, familiar with nontoxic and chemical-free adhesive. Then he grew curious. "How do you manage all day on that bad leg?"

Abram tugged at his beard. "I don't, most times. That's why I need a good helper. My last two did not work out. I have good employees out in the work barn, but I need to train someone up, since I only have three girls and they are all married and have duties to their families. They each have *gut* husbands who prefer to farm instead of work with their hands. I need someone who sees furniture the way I do. Our furniture has always been an art form, made with pride here in the country we live in."

"Do you think I could be that someone?" Tobias asked, hopeful. He liked nothing more than cutting, sanding and priming wood. He worked with the wood, not against it. The wood had integrity. He hoped his work would, too.

"We shall see," Abram replied with a knowing grin. "Depends on how fast you can get to the store and back."

"I am on my way," Tobias said, laughing.

He hurried across the street, his heart lifting to know that he might have a chance to create beautiful, sustainable objects out of wood. He'd had so many plans for the home he and Josie would have shared if they'd married. Tables, rocking chairs, dressers and hutches, cabinets and wardrobes. Maybe a cradle one day, too.

Those plans would happen if he could win her over and they could finally get married. A big goal but one he was willing to work on.

He walked briskly, eager to get back and begin his training. When he reached the general store, he quickly pushed at the door and entered.

Only to find Josie standing at the counter with a paper bag in her hand. When she looked up and saw him, her face went pale.

She did not look happy to see him.

Mr. Hartford spoke to Josie again.

"Josie, you said you needed to return something that you bought yesterday?"

"Ja," she managed to say barely above a whisper, wishing with all of her heart she hadn't needed to come back here today. "I got the wrong yarn." She swallowed, tried to breathe. "Raesha needs light blue. This is too dark."

"Then we'd better remedy that," Mr. Hartford said with a chuckle. Seeing Tobias standing there, he said, "I'll be with you in a minute." Then he went to find the yarn she needed.

Tobias lifted his chin in acknowledgment and took one step forward, his eyes wide with surprise. "It is good to see you, Josie."

Josie looked down at the counter, unable to speak, her whole system shutting down. What should she do? Josiah had come with her today since he needed to pick up some feed out behind the store. This was only supposed to be a quick exchange.

Why had she gotten the wrong yarn? Probably because her mind was on the man now staring at her.

Josie looked everywhere but at Tobias. Her mind would never work the way others did. She'd been damaged, traumatized, shattered. Would she ever be put back together?

"You cannot even look at me?"

She lifted her head at those soft words. Tobias had

moved closer. Close enough for her to see the pain in his eyes.

Swallowing, she closed her eyes. "I need to go. Would you tell Mr. Hartford I'll *kumm* back later?"

She rushed past him even as he reached out a hand to her.

Josie needed air and sunshine. She hurried around the building and searched for her brother.

"Josie?"

Whirling, she saw Tobias behind her.

He held out a bag to her. "Here is the yarn you wanted. Mr. Hartford said it was an even swap."

Josie took the bag, her hand briefly brushing Tobias's. *"Denke."* A shiver went down her spine. He smelled clean and fresh, and he looked healthy and muscular. "You seem well," she managed to croak.

"I am *gut*," he said, his eyes telling her he wanted to say more.

Before he could speak, Josiah hurried to them. "Josie?"

Josie spun toward her brother. "I have the yarn. I am ready."

Josiah shot Tobias a long stare, but said nothing. "Then we should head home."

Josie didn't know what to say to Tobias, so she turned and headed toward the buggy.

But she heard her brother's words. "Everything all right, Tobias?"

"Ja."

She looked back and saw him turn toward the front of the building. He looked over his shoulder, his gaze holding hers, his smile soft and reassuring.

Her heart couldn't be sure of anything except how

much she missed him. When she got into the open buggy, Josie sank against the seat.

"Did you talk?" Josiah said, his tone hopeful.

"Briefly." She wiped at her eyes. "Why is he still here?"

Josiah clicked the reins and started the docile horse toward home. "I heard he found work at the furniture market."

Josie glanced toward the market. "Abram needs a strong worker."

"So you are all right with that?"

"I don't know," she admitted. "If he is not buying our home, why is he still here?"

Her brother sent her a quick glance and then watched the road. "I think he came here for more than a house, Josephine."

Josie gulped in air. Tobias wasn't going away. Could there be some hope for them after all?

Josie couldn't stop shaking.

After Josiah dropped her off, Josie hurried inside the *grossmammi haus* and dropped the bag of yarn onto the dining table. Then she rushed to her room and sat down in the rocking chair to stare out the window.

"Josie?" Naomi called from her room.

Naomi had been asleep when Josiah had come by to ask Josie if she wanted to ride with him so she could return the yarn. She should have let him do that deed, but he'd been preoccupied with Daniel being sick and trying to get his chores done. Her brother was acting odd these days. He barely spoke on the way home, his eyes straight ahead and his expression bordering on a frown.

Probably because he wanted to sell the house next

door and she'd asked him not to sell to Tobias. Seeing Tobias had upset both of them, no doubt.

Josiah had given her a worried glance, then taken off toward the barn to finish out the day's work. Maybe he felt bad about her running into Tobias. It wasn't her brother's fault that Tobias had shown up out of the blue. No, all of this was her fault. She should have left her husband-to-be a note, explaining that she had to leave. But she'd been so distraught she'd left Kentucky as soon as she could.

Josie got up and touched a hand to her *kapp*. Her hair had gotten long again. She'd cut it when she'd been hiding out, so no one would recognize her. Now it was coiled in a tight bun on top of her head. She wanted to tear at the cover and pull at her hair.

But she had to stay calm and try to get through this.

"I'm coming," she called to Naomi.

Gathering her strength, she hoped Naomi wouldn't notice how frazzled she was. "Are you all right, Mammi Naomi?"

When the older woman didn't call back, panic set in. Josie rushed into Naomi's room and hurried to the bed. "Naomi? Naomi?"

"Was der schinner is letz?"

"That's what I'm asking," Josie said on a sigh of relief. "I thought something was wrong with you, but instead you are asking me that question."

"I was worried when you had to go back to town," Naomi said. "How long did I nap?"

"About an hour," Josie replied while she straightened the covers and helped Naomi sit up. "Are you sure you're fine?"

"I've never been better," Naomi said. "Why do you fuss so?"

Josie sank down on the rocking chair that matched the one in her room, the soft cushions comforting her. "I'm sorry. I… I saw Tobias in town, at the store."

Naomi's squint widened. "I might need a cup of tea before I hear this."

Josie tried to stay patient. "Would you like me to bring it to you?"

"*Neh.* We will go into the kitchen."

Josie helped Naomi up and into her wheelchair, then pushed her into the kitchen. After making two cups of tea and bringing the cookie jar over so Naomi could have a snickerdoodle, she finally settled down beside Naomi.

"He came into the general store and…talked to me."

Naomi stirred sugar and cream into her tea. "Did you respond?"

"I tried. But I got flustered and ran out without the yarn."

"Oh, dear. Josiah won't like having to go back."

"No, I mean, I have the yarn. Tobias followed me and brought it out to me."

"He does sound like a kind soul."

"He looked *gut*," Josie said before she could take it back. "He always had a soft drawl to his voice."

"That's the Kentucky in him," Naomi said, now wide-awake and intent. "Was he born there?"

"*Ja.*" Josie allowed the memories to roll over her while she nibbled at a cookie. "His parents were so kind. His mother died a few months after I got there. I think I helped him through that and that's what bonded us.

He had an older brother who moved to Indiana. They used to fight a lot."

"Most *bruders* do," Naomi said on a soft chuckle. "Tell me more."

Josie needed to tell someone the things she'd held so tightly to her heart. "His *daed* was a sweet man. He welcomed me and allowed Tobias and me to walk out together. He was happy that his younger son had found someone."

"I'm sure he saw what a wonderful person Tobias had found."

Josie stopped and put a hand to her mouth. "We were happy once, Mammi Naomi. We truly were."

Naomi nodded and reached for her hand. "I can see that in your eyes. You still love him."

Josie pulled away and stood. "I can't love him. And he can't love me."

"But it sounds to me as if you both still care about each other. You've never talked about Kentucky much— or Tobias, either, for that matter. Your voice softens when you're remembering him."

"He was the love of my life," Josie admitted, tears burning her eyes. "But…it can never be now."

"You need to be patient and you need to be kind to him, in the same way you were when he lost his *mamm*. After all, he has done you no harm."

Josie lifted her head and stopped her pacing. "You're right. Tobias has done nothing wrong. I shouldn't be angry with him."

"Not one bit. But your anger toward this other boy has caused you a lot of pain. You can't hold that against the man who has come here to find you."

Josie realized she'd been holding on to that anger

and it had turned her from kind to bitter. Why should Tobias bear the brunt of all her woes? She glanced at Naomi. "You've done it again."

Naomi took a big bite of her cookie and lifted her eyebrows. "Done what?"

"Tricked me into seeing the light."

"I only listened and commented as needed," Naomi said with the innocence of a lamb. "You figured it all out on your own."

Josie sat back down, a tremendous lightness making her smile for the first time in days. "I did, didn't I? I will be civil to Tobias when I see him. But… I will not love him again. That is over."

"Of course. Whatever you decide."

Josie started clearing away their dishes. "I've decided. I won't change on that."

"As long as you're considerate of Tobias and his feelings, too, I think you've made the right choice."

Josie took Naomi out on the porch to enjoy the nice breeze and the sunshine. While Naomi read the large-print Bible Josie had given her at Christmas, Josie sat on the steps and stared at the house across the way. Maybe she should tell Josiah it was okay for Tobias to buy it.

But no. She might have to tolerate him staying here and finding work, but she could not tolerate him living so close to her, in a house that had brought her only pain and terrible memories. While she watered the daylily bulbs she and Naomi had planted around the breezeway, Josie thought about Tobias again. Having him near did bring her joy, but her secrets shattered that joy with a piercing clarity. She couldn't change the past. But maybe she could learn better in the future.

Raesha came around the corner, carrying Daniel on

her left hip while holding a bundle of fresh flowers in her free hand.

"There you are," she said, out of breath. "I came home with the *kinder*. He's even fussier today." Then she handed Josie the cut flowers. "Someone delivered these to the shop."

Josie took the beautiful flowers and sniffed at them. "Oh. Do you need me to put them in water?"

Raesha laughed. "They need water, but they aren't for me, Josie. The note had your name on it."

Josie looked down at the flowers in her hand, the paper covering part of the bundle. Lifting the stiff wrapping away, she smiled. "Dandelions, asters and trout lilies."

"Chickweed and daffodils, too," Naomi noted. "All so pretty with the yellow tones mixed in with the pinks."

"Who sent me flowers?" Josie asked. "They seem to be fresh picked."

Raesha and Naomi exchanged motherly glances. "There was no name on the note," Raesha said. "The delivery person wouldn't say who, either."

Josie sniffed the fresh flowers and then looked over at the house that seemed to watch her all the time. "My favorites," she said on a soft whisper. "I love yellow flowers the best."

And she knew of only one person who would go into the woods and find wildflowers for her.

Tobias.

She knew it had to be him.

And so did the two women watching her so closely.

Chapter Seven

Tobias loved the smell of fresh-cut lumber. A fresh piece of solid wood was always a challenge for him. Each piece held a certain forest scent. His *daed* and older brother didn't mind him making furniture, but they'd frowned on him whittling tiny replicas such as animals to sell as toys. They also frowned on decorative stencils, but the *Englisch* loved that kind of thing, as well as distressed furniture.

He'd finished his first week of working for Abram, and while he'd enjoyed working with Abram, he still hadn't found an affordable place to live. Abram came out of the workshop and waved to him just as he was about to clock out. He intended to retrieve his suitcase from the Campton Center and move to the hotel at the edge of town.

"Tobias, could I speak to you?"

Tobias turned back up the main aisle that showcased gleaming walnut and oak headboards and nightstands along with rocking chairs and cradles. He'd made his first oak headboard this week and hoped it would sell. Oak was a strong, sturdy wood that would last a lifetime. Had he done something wrong? Forgotten to clean and put away his hammer and chisel? Overstepped by meticulously explaining the different woods to the other workers? Abram looked so serious.

"Yes, Abram?"

Abram tugged at his beard, a habit Tobias was beginning to get used to. "I hear from Jewel that you still need a place to stay."

Tobias nodded, thinking the worst. Abram had been willing to hire him even if he didn't have a permanent address yet. "I am looking. She said she'd ask around, but I didn't know she'd told you. I hope that is not a problem."

Abram checked the sale receipts and tidied the long counter where the clerks worked the cash register at the back of the shop. "She asked me because my wife and I have a big house and all of our children are grown and in their own homes. We have a bedroom on the far left side of the house that's near the back porch. It's big enough for a sitting area—my *mamm* stayed there when she'd come visit. But she passed about a year ago. You would have privacy there and you can come and go out the back as you like, and we won't bother you."

Tobias blinked. Abram lived on the other side of the community, away from the Bawell house. "You mean you'd rent the room to me?"

Abram's gaze showed sympathy and understanding. "Jewel told me about your need right after I hired you, but I wanted to get to know you before I asked. You're a *gut* man, Tobias. And I kind of enjoy that Southern accent of yours."

Tobias couldn't hide his smile. "I am glad to hear that."

Abram went on. "Rent would include breakfast every

morning and dinner every night unless you have other plans. We'll feed you all you want."

"No. If I'm paying for room and board, then add a little more extra for meals," Tobias replied. "That's the only way I can accept."

Abram grinned and shook his head. "You drive a hard bargain by offering to give part of my money right back to me and add extra, but I think Beth will agree to that."

Abram named his price, which sounded reasonable. "I added a few dollars extra for meals, but if you start putting on weight, I might have to add more."

Tobias liked Abram, and this would keep him from wanting to go to the Fisher place when he had nothing else to occupy his time.

"Okay, I accept your kind offer." Tobias breathed a sigh of relief. "*Denke*, Abram, for everything."

Abram slapped him gently on the back. "We can swing by the Campton Center on the way home. And since today's Friday, you're in for a treat. Beth makes peach cobbler almost every Friday so I can have some for breakfast on Saturday. That'll include you now, too."

"That will be *gut*," Tobias replied, his stomach growling. He'd packed a lunch from leftovers at the Campton Center, but that had been gone hours ago. "It will be nice to have some good home cooking."

"Beth will feed you—don't worry about that. And you'll bring her joy, eating her food. She loves to bake, and she misses our daughters." Abram took off his leather apron and hung it on a hook behind the counter. "She loves when they bring the *kinder* to visit. Bakes cookies for days. Especially at Christmas, when they bring their husbands, too."

Tobias missed his mother's cooking. He and his father had made do with what they could scrounge up and with the few casseroles and desserts neighbors brought by. He'd had many a young woman try to ply him with food, but while he appreciated the meals, he couldn't take things with any of them further than friendship. Which meant the homemade food that had started on a regular basis had trickled down to not much.

Nodding at Abram, he said, "I'll make sure and let her know how much I'll enjoy the meals, then."

Together they cleaned up and locked down the shop and the workshop. Tobias liked working here with Abram and the two other men who did everything from sawing and cutting to sanding and loading. But those two didn't have an inkling about creating something from wood, although they worked as hard as anyone. Tobias, on the other hand, had shown Abram some of his designs. Abram had immediately liked all of them. The slow pace of creating something by hand had always fascinated Tobias. Thankfully, Abram understood that need to create beautiful things.

Now, if Tobias could just get on with the other business of being here. He wanted to see Josie and talk to her, try to get her to open up to him. Would she allow that?

He wondered if she'd liked the flowers he'd sent. He had meant to send store-bought, but they looked so obvious and were way too expensive. Not that he minded the cost, but he knew Josie loved flowers straight from the earth. She'd planted herbs and sunflowers back in Kentucky. He could still see her running through a meadow of wildflowers, barefoot and free.

A lot different from the shell of her he'd seen recently.

Glad he'd picked flowers from the meadow near the park fence and that Jewel had helped him clip some of the beautiful blooms surrounding the Campton Center, he felt sure Josie would know they were from him. A perfect batch of fresh flowers.

Would his first gift please her? Or would it backfire on him?

He'd find out from Josiah.

And maybe he'd see her in church on Sunday. Abram had invited him, but he'd almost said no. Until he thought about seeing Josie across the way, sitting with the other women.

That, and getting back on track with God, made him decide it was time for him to get serious about the things that mattered in life—a home and a family.

He only hoped Josie would get serious about getting to know him again. He'd have to start from scratch and court her in a proper and considerate way. As impatient as he was, Tobias knew he'd have to take things slow this time around. Or he'd lose her all over again.

With that in mind, he went with Abram to pick up his suitcase and other possessions.

Jewel greeted him with a big smile when he came down from his room. "Are you going to stay with Abram and Beth?"

"*Ja*, thanks to you," Tobias replied with a gentle admonishment. "I am glad to have a place to sleep. Not that my room wasn't comfortable, but it's time for me to move on."

Jewel held her arms open. "Bring it in. Right here."

Tobias laughed as she hugged him tight. The woman had a grip. But it felt good to be cared for and hugged.

Jewel stood back, her floral top making her look

like a flower garden had exploded all over her. "You remember, now—we're here to help. You need to talk, you come on in and grab some of that fancy coffee and a cookie and have a seat. Your friend Jewel here will listen and get you on the right path."

"I will do that," Tobias told her. "And, Jewel, once I'm on my feet and have some extra money, I'll be in here with a donation every week."

"Ah, that is so sweet. I'm gonna pray for you and your girl, Tobias."

Tobias thanked her, and after telling Mrs. Campton and Bettye goodbye, he got back in the buggy. "Here, Abram. The women wanted you to send Beth some spice mix they made."

"Oh, she'll appreciate that," Abram replied after he set the small bag between them on the seat. "She uses fresh spice in everything she cooks."

As they rode along, Abram's white-and-gray Percheron trotting in a graceful fashion, Abram carried on small talk and pointed out some of the farms and landmarks along the way.

"See that bridge?" he said, pointing to the red beams of a wide covered bridge. "That goes over the deepest part of the creek, but it brought the Amish side of town together with the *Englisch* side. The early Camptons wanted it that way since they allowed the Amish to start a community here."

Tobias could see that. "Judy Campton is an amazing woman and so is Bettye Willis. Jewel seems to love both of them."

"You mean Jewel who apparently has no last name," Abram said, nodding. "An odd woman but a loyal one. She does love those two. They saved her, I believe."

"Yes, that Jewel," Tobias said, understanding why Jewel went by only one name. "She's been kind to me."

"We have a lot of great people around here and we all get along, thankfully. I hope you continue to meet everyone."

"I hope that, too," Tobias said. Then he decided to be honest. "Abram, I came here to buy a farm, and I have my eye on the Fisher place."

"Well, now," Abram said, shooting Tobias a quizzical glance, "have you made an offer?"

"I did and I've put up good-faith money, but I'd rather you didn't mention that to others, in case it falls through."

"I won't repeat anything we discuss," Abram replied, his expression solemn. "I will say it would be good to see that place up and running again. It's sat empty for so long now. Since the fire that killed Josiah's parents."

Tobias tried to hide his shock, but Abram caught it. "You didn't know. Of course, you wouldn't. A barn fire. A horrible accident."

Tobias let that soak in. "But Josiah is their son."

"*Ja*, he returned to fix the place up to sell, but *Gott* had other plans. Josiah fell in love with Raesha Bawell and they have two children. A sweet girl named Dinah and a son named Daniel."

Two children. Tobias wanted children. He and Josie had talked about having several. But Josie was living with her brother and his wife, alone and still single.

At least he could be thankful for that.

But was she still single because she loved him? Or was she alone because she didn't want to be with anyone?

He wanted to know more. "I hear Josiah's sister lives there with them, too."

"She does," Abram said, looking away. "She is a

companion to Raesha's mother-in-law, Naomi. Both Raesha's and Naomi's husbands died—years apart— and the two women clung to each other. Josiah fell for Raesha." He paused, gave Tobias a strange glimpse. "Josiah found Josie and brought her home. She has been back now for about two years or so."

Tobias didn't ask anything else. Abram might become suspicious. But he had to wonder where Josie had been the year after she'd left Kentucky. Somehow, he'd have to find that out to understand what had happened to make her leave him in the first place.

Because sending her flowers was one thing, but trying to win her trust enough that she would tell him the truth would be a big challenge.

As the bishop had said, the Amish didn't discuss such things. But how many people in this community knew Josie's secrets?

Josie couldn't stop staring at the flowers.

She'd found a vase and placed them on the small dining table where she and Naomi ate most of their meals. Josie liked to cook and Naomi enjoyed coaching her. Sometimes Raesha would join in and they'd take the meal over to the big house so Josiah could test the food. Those times made Josie smile because she felt loved and a part of something, a part of a strong family.

She thought about Tobias. Did he have any family left? Josiah hadn't mentioned much about him beyond Tobias wanting to buy their old home. Why would he leave Kentucky and everyone he knew to come here?

Because you are here.

That voice in her head gave her hope, but Josie banished that hope before it could take hold of her heart.

These beautiful, colorful flowers also gave her hope, and yet she remembered when she and Josiah were growing up. No flowers around the house and no cut flowers inside the house. Stark, sterile, plain. That was how their father had expected things to stay. No books other than the Bible, no magazines or even newspapers. Her *mamm* heard news only when she went to church, and even then, her *daed* frowned on idle chatter.

After Josiah had taken her to Ohio, Josie had delighted in the wildflowers that sprouted out of the earth in a field beyond their uncle's house. She had been afraid to pick any until Josiah told her it was okay to do so.

She always kept a small vase of flowers in her room there, and when she'd gone with friends to Kentucky, she'd done the same after she'd decided she didn't want to return to Ohio. Tobias learned of her love for flowers and he'd often supplied her with colorful blooming plants or fresh-cut flowers.

The same way he'd done today.

"Are you expecting those blossoms to jump out of the water?" Naomi asked as she rolled her wheelchair to the table.

Josie whirled away from staring at the flowers, remembering their chicken-noodle casserole should be ready by now. "*Neh*, just trying to figure out who sent them."

"I believe you know the answer to that question."

"I think I do," Josie admitted. "But I can't be sure."

Naomi fussed with the white napkins on the table. "This man seems determined to win you back, Josephine. He's found work, according to what you heard and saw in town, which means he's staying here indefinitely. I don't think he'll give up on that house next door or on you, especially not on you."

Josie checked on the small casserole and took it out of the oven. "He can't have either."

Naomi waited, her hands in her lap, as Josie set the steaming casserole on the blue floral pot holder she'd placed on the table earlier. "So you won't consider asking him if he made this kind gesture?"

"I do not want to talk to him."

"You could send him a note."

"Are you trying to get Tobias and me back together?"

"I'm only telling you to mind your manners. We thank people for kind deeds. I know you love flowers. Apparently, so does Tobias."

"What if he didn't send the flowers? Wouldn't that make thanking him a problem?"

"I believe Tobias sent the flowers," Naomi said on a firm note.

Josie poured tea and sat down. Naomi lowered her head and said her quiet prayer. Josie tried to do the same. But how did she pray for two different outcomes? She wanted Tobias to go away. She prayed he'd stay.

Because one thing stood out for her. She'd resented Josiah for leaving her and her mother alone with their father. He'd come back for her only after their parents had died. But Josie had not been kind to her brother and she'd defiantly refused to return from Kentucky during her *rumspringa*.

She'd stayed there to make the point with her brother that she didn't need him, and because she'd fallen in love with Tobias.

But another thing shouted at her now: Tobias had been the only person she'd ever known who had become her champion, her protector, the one person in the world she could trust to never leave her behind. Tobias had planned a life with her, a life where they followed the tenets of their faith together.

But one night had changed all of that.

"Always," she'd told him.

"Always," he'd repeated.

And in turn, she'd had to leave him behind. She'd left, heartbroken and full of shame, but she knew she'd broken his heart, too, in doing so. And yet he'd found her and he'd come to her hoping they could reconcile. After all she'd done to him.

"Child?"

Josie lifted her head, her eyes open. "Sorry, Mammi Naomi."

"Do not apologize for spending quiet time in your prayers," Naomi said. "You have a lot to pray about."

Josie nodded and lifted the creamy noodles and chunky chicken to her lips. Naomi was right, as usual. She needed to pray about all of this and consider her ways. *Gott* had guided her back home, despite her sins and her mistakes. Maybe He'd guided Tobias back to her, too.

Now she just needed to figure out how to handle that without revealing her terrible secret. Because she couldn't tell the man she'd always love that one of his *Englisch* friends had drugged her and abused her in the worst kind of way.

Chapter Eight

Tobias sat by the window in the cozy room Abram and Beth had rented to him. The big window looked out on the pastures and valleys. He could see the peaks of Green Mountain off in the distance. Josie had often talked about Green Mountain and how her big brother would take her up the trails to the top.

Why hadn't she told him about her parents dying in a barn fire? Maybe the trauma of that had somehow caught up with her, since she'd returned here to heal.

He wanted to know what kind of healing she'd needed.

But he'd only hear that from Josie since this community was tight-lipped about gossip.

Sooner or later, he'd meet someone who didn't mind explaining things. But he prayed Josie would tell him the truth without anyone else passing false rumors.

Right now, he had to get to church. Abram and Beth had offered to let him ride with them. He needed church, and he held out hope he'd see Josie there, too. Would she smile across the aisle at him? Or would she run away again?

"Tobias, are you ready?"

"*Ja*, Abram. Coming."

Tobias headed out the side door and met them on the back porch. "It is a good day to worship."

"You seem in a good mood," Beth noted.

Tobias liked Beth Schrock. She was bubbly and jolly and never seemed to have a bad day. But she noticed things other people never saw. Such as how he'd been moping around all weekend.

"I am feeling hopeful," he admitted. "I like it here. Pennsylvania is a beautiful state and this is a good community."

Beth adjusted her bonnet. "Then church is a good place to start."

He offered to drive the buggy and the happy couple immediately agreed.

"You are spoiling us," Abram said from behind him in the open buggy. "First, you walk into my shop and show me the kind of talent a furniture maker only dreams of. Now you help me with the milking and get up before I do to feed my chickens and goats. And Percy there—" he pointed to the high-spirited Percheron "—seems to think you're his baby *bruder* or something."

"He has indeed taken a shine to you, Tobias," Beth said in agreement.

Tobias laughed over his shoulder, then turned to watch the narrow paved lane ahead. "Percy and I reached an understanding after we had a long talk in the barn the other day." Laughing, he asked, "Now, where is church being held today?"

"Oh, did I forget to tell you?" Abram asked, shrugging. "We're going to the Bawell place. They have a large backyard."

* * *

Josie tugged at her *kapp* and stared straight ahead. Katy sat down beside her and straightened her deep blue dress. "You look pretty, Josie."

Josie glanced at her friend, wishing she had Katy's silky blond hair. "I feel drab next to you and all those curls."

Katy snorted. "I hate these curls, but we are not to be vain about that."

"I don't have a vain bone in my body," Josie admitted. "But I do have drab hair."

"Right now, with the sun coming through those big doors," Katy said, motioning toward the back of the benches lined up underneath the shade of several mushrooming oaks, "the sun makes your hair look like dark gold. You need to know that you are beautiful in God's eyes."

Josie smiled at her friend and then looked back since she loved seeing the sunshine shooting across the worship area. A group of men walked up and headed for the benches lining the other side, where the men sat separately from the women.

"Tobias," she said, before she could take it back.

Katy's blue eyes went wide. She turned to stare behind them. "The one you mentioned after you saw him in town?"

Josie managed to nod, but she felt dizzy, her heart racing.

"I should leave."

Katy's hand on hers stopped her. "That would only make things worse." Giving Josie a soft smile, she said, "I understand you don't want to be around him, but if you run out of here, everyone will notice. People will talk, Josie."

Josie huddled against her friend, tears pricking her eyes. "About me? About Tobias?"

She'd told Katy the whole truth on the buggy ride home—that she and Tobias had been engaged, but she'd left after another man had ruined her.

Katy had looked shocked at first, and then she'd nodded and hugged Josie close. "No wonder you got so upset when you saw him. I will keep your secret, Josie. But you'll have to deal with him being here."

Now her friend gave her a questioning stare. "They might get the wrong impression," Katy said, her eyes filling with a meaningful warning. "That he might be the one."

"The baby's…" She stopped and put a hand to her mouth. "I never thought about that. I told you the other day—he is not. That's why I can't be around him. What should I do?"

Katy still held her hand. "You do what you need to do. You smile and stay kind. Being kind to a man you once loved is not a crime. In fact, it is the best thing you can do right now."

"And why is that?"

"If you treat him like you do all the other men who've tried to court you, he'll soon get the same message as they did."

Josie winced at that accurate description. "You have a good point."

"I always do," Katy said, her pert nose in the air. "Now take a deep breath and try to listen to the service."

Josie inhaled, taking in the scents of fresh air and clean clothes, the spring air flowing over the long rows of benches cool on her warm cheeks. She took in whiffs of pot roast and baked rolls, familiar smells that came with eating dinner after church. "You're right. If I act out, everyone will notice. I don't want anyone to think badly of Tobias."

Katy sighed and gave her a knowing smile. "Because you still care about him, don't you?"

Josie couldn't answer that question. But her friend bobbed her head. "That's what I thought."

"How are you?"

Josie whirled from clearing the table where she'd sat with some of the other women during dinner.

Tobias stood with a small bench balanced against his leg.

"I am fine," she responded, glad Raesha had taken the *kinder* inside to wash up. She did not want Tobias to see Dinah.

"You look better today," he said as he held the bench straight up next to him and watched her rake scraps off the table.

Josie tried to catch her breath. "Did I look that awful the other day?"

His gaze moved over her, warming her and chilling her at the same time. "You've always looked beautiful to me, Josie, but you were distraught and, honestly, you didn't make sense. You know you can talk to me, right?"

Josie stopped what she was doing and remembered none of this was his fault. "Did you send me flowers?"

"If I say yes, will you be angry?"

She studied him, taking her time to see him as a grown man now with broad, strong shoulders and a chiseled look that showed he was used to manual labor and hard work. "*Neh*, I would not be angry. But if you did send them, you should not do that again."

"Isn't sending flowers a part of the courting ritual?"

Josie's stomach tightened, memories cutting through her. "We are not courting. I shouldn't be talking to you, Tobias."

"Your brother told me it would be all right to say hello."

"My brother needs to mind his own business."

Tobias looked confused, but he didn't leave. Instead, he glanced around the rolling acreage and then back at the house where several buggies were still parked while their owners went to tend to their horses and harness them to leave. "This is a nice place. I hope you're happy here."

"I am."

She was as content as she could be, considering. Josie steeled herself against needing him, but having him so close made him hard to resist. So she focused on the sweet wind of late spring and tried to take soothing breaths.

"I understand you don't want me to buy your old home, but I don't understand why."

"It would be difficult, Tobias."

"Why? You're here, and now I'm here. I found you and I'd like us to get to know each other again."

"I already know you," she said, remembering their time together, her heart pierced with the sweet memories. Before she could stop herself, she added, "I could never forget you."

"I can never forget you, either," he said, his eyes bright with hope. "That is why I came to find you."

Josie felt panic rising in her stomach. "You shouldn't have come here. I told you, we cannot be together."

He stepped closer. "Josie, if you could just tell me what happened. What went wrong?"

"Josie?"

She pivoted to see Katy waving to her. Inhaling to find her next breath, she said, "I have to go inside and help with the dishes. *Denke* for the flowers. They are very pretty."

Then she turned and hurried into the Bawell house as fast as she could. When she reached Katy, she grabbed her friend's arm. "*Denke*. I was so afraid I'd say the wrong thing."

Katy shifted and slanted her head to one side while she stared at Tobias and then looked back to give Josie a sympathetic glance. "I don't think you could say anything that would make that man go away, Josie. The way he looks at you is the way we all want a man to look at us—with love and longing, and respect."

"I do not deserve any of those things. And he deserves better."

Katy looped her arm in Josie's as they headed inside the house. "I do not agree with that. You could be doing a great dishonor to a man who is trying to show you he wants to make amends."

"He didn't do anything wrong," Josie replied, her tone sounding defensive. She would defend Tobias even while she refused to hope for any future with him.

Katy had other ideas. "Then you need to tell him that."

Josie heard her friend's suggestion. "Why does everyone seem to want to push Tobias and me together?"

Katy gave her another quiet stare. "Because maybe you two should be together?"

Josie considered that and everything else that held her and Tobias apart. What would he do if he found out her secret?

What if he went away forever?

She didn't think she could bear watching him walk away.

But he'd had to bear her doing that very thing.

"You're right," she told Katy after they'd tidied up the big kitchen while Raesha and some of the others went out for a stroll with the *kinder.* "I should at least apologize to Tobias for what I did."

"Is he still here?" Katy asked, looking outside.

"I don't know," Josie said. "But I will go and look for him."

She dried her hands on a white towel, straightened her clothing and pushed at her hair. Right now, this very moment, she wanted nothing more than to be near Tobias again.

Just to be near him.

Maybe they would both have to accept that as the only way they could coexist in the same community. But would Tobias accept that as the final solution?

Or would he give up on her and finally leave?

Josie walked out to the barn and searched the area. All of the church benches had been loaded up and put in a storage room here, or taken back to various homes around the community where they'd be stored in other barns.

When she didn't see Tobias anywhere, her heart sank. Maybe it was for the best that she didn't try to talk to him anyway. Would he accept her apology without her having to tell him anything more?

Then she turned back to the house and saw Tobias standing with Abram Schrock and her brother. They were talking low and looked serious.

What were they discussing?

Tobias listened as Josiah explained how the hat shop worked. Raesha ran the shop and took care of her home, while Josiah worked the land and tended the milking and the livestock. Josiah had some knowledge of growing cash crops, so Tobias had been asking for his advice. Abram had joined them.

"So you not only have a talent with wood, but you want to grow farm-fresh crops for fancy restaurants?" Abram asked, shaking his head. "This young one is a hard worker, Josiah. If you sell him that place of yours, I am thinking you two could team up and have a nice setup here."

Josiah gave Tobias a sharp glance. "That all depends, Abram. I haven't decided if I'm ready to sell or not."

Abram looked confused. "I see. Well, I hope you make up your mind soon enough. I don't want to see Tobias leave. He has a true talent and he brags on my wife's cooking, both of which make my life a lot easier."

Josiah shot Tobias another glance as he smiled at Abram's wit. "I am glad to hear that, Abram."

Tobias was about to change the subject when he looked up and saw Josie watching him. "Excuse me," he said, not caring what anyone thought. He walked over to where she stood by the breezeway between the two houses.

"Josie? What is wrong?"

Josie held on to her apron, her fingers twisting the heavy cotton. "I need to say something to you."

His heart lifted like the wings of a dove. "Okay."

"I'm sorry, Tobias. Sorry that I left you when we had such plans for the future. I know I hurt you. I need you to forgive me."

Confused, he looked into her eyes and saw the regret there. "I do forgive you. I would not be here if I wasn't able to do that. But I need answers, Josie."

She lowered her gaze, then lifted her chin, her eyes meeting his. "I cannot give you answers, Tobias. We can be friends but nothing more. You must accept that."

He shook his head. "I *cannot* accept that. I can forgive, but it is hard to think that you don't love me anymore."

"I didn't say that," she blurted, tears in her eyes.

He took a small step and stopped, but his eyes brightened. "So you might still have feelings for me?"

"No." She twisted the apron corners against her clenched fists, her knuckles white. "I feel friendship for you and I have our memories, but nothing beyond that. I want you to know I'm sorry."

Frustration filled his heart. "I'm trying, Josie. But it's hard to see you and not be able to understand."

He turned to leave but Raesha came out, a little girl holding her hand. He looked at her and then back at Josie.

Josie went pale, her eyes moving over the little girl.

"JoJo," the child said, running to her.

Raesha hurried to the child. "Dinah, your aunt JoJo is busy right now. *Kumm.*"

"JoJo," Dinah said, giggling as she held up her hand for Josie to take, her smile shining with love.

Josie's tormented gaze moved from Raesha back to Tobias.

Then she lifted Dinah in her arms. "I need to tend to Raesha's daughter, Tobias. It was nice to talk to you."

She took the little girl back into the house, leaving Tobias standing there staring behind her.

"Give her time," Raesha said. "She has come a long way to get back home, Tobias."

"*Ja*, and I have come a long way to find her," he replied. Then he turned to leave, knowing in his heart they were all keeping something from him.

He had a feeling the "something" might involve that beautiful little girl. The little girl who had such a familiar face, but a face he couldn't bring to his memory. Maybe the child just reminded him of Josie. There was a striking resemblance.

Dejected, he turned and walked back toward where Abram now stood at their buggy, Beth waiting inside.

"Is everything all right, Tobias?" Abram asked, his voice drenched with concern.

"*Ja*, just meeting some of Josiah's family."

Abram nodded. "Josie is available, you know."

Tobias shook his head. "Not from what I can tell," he replied. Then he hopped up on the buggy and started back toward the Schrock home.

He wished with all of his heart he could make Josie see reason, so they could have their own home. Just as they'd planned so long ago.

Chapter Nine

Josie clipped back the mint, weeding the tiny herb garden, the scents of lavender and basil wafting through the air. A storm had passed through the night and left the garden green and freshly washed. She loved tending to this little herb crop since it was close to the house and out of sight from the tourists who came to the hat shop in droves during the high season.

Why were the *Englisch* so fascinated with the plain life, when they carried fancy purses and backpacks and always had their noses glued to their cell phones? She had an inkling of life outside this peaceful valley, and at first she'd enjoyed the freedom of making her own decisions. But being alone and pregnant soon changed her mind. There was a certain peace in knowing your boundaries and abiding by God's grace and law.

She never wanted to stray back into that world, and since she'd confessed and been baptized, she'd be shunned if she ever left again.

But now she had one more reason to stay.

Tobias.

He truly was trying to court her. Since the Sunday

they'd talked right here near the house, he'd sent her a drawing of a horse that looked similar to the miniature he'd carved for her out of black oak wood. The little horse sat on a dresser in her bedroom. Naomi had asked her about it once, when she'd found Josie holding the horse in her hand.

"A friend back in Kentucky carved this for me," she'd told Naomi. "I cannot give it away."

"You don't need to give it away," Naomi had replied. "We all have little treasures we cherish."

Then Naomi had shown Josie a beautiful brooch her late husband had given her one Christmas. "He told me an *Englisch* man had given it to him after he'd helped him plant his garden. His wife had died and he wanted someone else to enjoy it."

The brooch had been small and crusted with pearls. Josie understood why Naomi never wore it. Jewelry did not fit the plain ways. "It's a treasure for you?"

"Yes, because my husband made another person happy by giving it to me. Just as that little bonnet you placed on Dinah's head when you left her on our doorstep was a treasure to you. Treasures hold memories, so you hold tight to your little horse. Just remember *Gott* has given us the greatest treasure. He has given us His love and our Christ."

Josie sat back now and pushed at her hair, the basket of mint next to her filling her senses with its sweetness. She closed her eyes and imagined what her life might have been like if she could have stayed in Kentucky and married Tobias.

"Josie?"

She opened her eyes and saw him coming toward her. Josie couldn't move, couldn't speak. Was she dreaming?

"Josie, Raesha told me you were back here."

Why did everyone try to mess in her life?

Her heart rushing too fast, she said, "I don't need any company."

Tobias came closer, his dark hair curling around his ears. "She also told me you'd say that."

Josie tried to rise up off the low porch and almost toppled back. Tobias dropped the bag he'd been carrying. He was there to catch her, his strong hands on her arms sending shock waves throughout her system.

After he righted her, he held to her arms. "I brought you something."

Josie couldn't breathe. He was so close, she could reach out and touch his face, sink her fingers into his hair, hold him close. "What did you bring?"

He let her go, his gaze warm on her face. Then he reached down and picked up the bag. "Beth Schrock made some fried pies and sent them with Abram this morning. He gave me several, and I remembered how you love a good fried pie—especially peach."

He pulled a wrapped pie out of the bag. "I have apple, too. Beth is a great cook."

Josie took the offering, wondering what she should do. Tobias had always been a thoughtful man, but he remembered things she'd tried to forget. *"Denke."*

He stood watching her. "Aren't you going to eat it?"

Josie's heart opened a little tiny bit. *"Ja.* I'm terribly hungry." She motioned to the porch steps. "Why don't you join me?"

Tobias bobbed his head. "I am on a break, so I cannot stay long. But I've been hankering for the apple one all morning."

Josie took little bites of the sweet folded dough that

enclosed the juicy peaches. "Beth must have some left-over preserves since our peaches will not be ripe until July."

"I believe so," Tobias replied, his smile so beautiful it brought tears to her eyes. "I didn't ask. I just wanted to taste these. With you."

Josie smiled, the feel of smiling at Tobias foreign and unfamiliar but easy at this moment. "It was kind of you to think of me. You came all the way from town?"

He looked sheepish, his cheeks reddening and his eyes downcast. "I had a delivery nearby and I planned to eat all of these on the way. But… I thought of you, so I am willing to share."

They sat in silence, munching away on the flaky crust and the sweet, syrupy fruit inside. Josie glanced over at her old home. "My *mamm* used to make these."

Tobias stopped eating, glanced at the house and then back at her. "Do you want to talk about your *mamm*?"

Josie turned to him, fear clutching at her throat. Quickly wrapping the rest of her fried pie back into the cloth that had covered it, she stood. "*Neh.* I… I have to go inside and take care of these herbs."

Then she grabbed her basket and hurried up the steps. But she turned at the door. "I enjoyed sitting with you, Tobias."

After hurrying inside, she slammed the door and leaned against it, the rich pie she'd eaten settling like a splintered log inside her roiling stomach.

She could not let this happen. She wouldn't do this again.

Because the more Tobias came around, the more she'd want to be with him. And she could never be with him. She knew that, and if she told him the truth, then he'd know that, too.

Maybe it was time she did just that. Tell him the truth—the one thing that would make him leave Campton Creek for good.

A week later, Josie still hadn't found the courage to approach Tobias. She'd managed to avoid him since seeing him at church, yet she had to wonder what he'd thought about Dinah. Had he recognized his former friend's resemblance in her face and eyes? Or did he only see that she looked a lot like Josie?

Living like this was torment, but she had work to do today. She also now had a plan that would test her strength as much as seeing Tobias again had.

"So you want to go to the Spring Festival tomorrow?"

Josie nodded, her hands held together over her apron, hoping Katy wouldn't question her too much. "*Ja.* I need to get out more, and now that summer is coming, I feel better about being around people my own age. I did promise Raesha I'd help in the Bawell booth. We'll be selling quilts and hats along with our jams and baked goods, of course." Then she lifted her hand. "Not to mention the goat-milk soaps and lotions. They are favorites with the *Englisch.*"

"It's good for you to get out and help," Katy said. "Do you hope to see Tobias there?" Katy held one hand on her hip and her lips twisted to hide her smile.

"Tobias might not attend. He's not a part of this community."

Katy frowned at that. "But Abram and Beth have been including him in everything that goes on around here. Trying to find him a perfect match, I believe." She added, "Surely, he'll help Abram with the furniture booth."

Josie's stomach dropped at that innocently spoken notion. Or from the smug look in her friend's eyes, maybe not so innocently. "He needs to get to know people, so it makes sense they'd try to introduce him to others who are young and…single."

"He is young and he is single," Katy replied. "But he only searches for you in the crowds."

"I'm going to get out of the house and make more friends," Josie retorted. "Because the friend standing beside me now can be annoying at times."

Katy playfully took her arm. "I do not care why you've decided to go, but I'm glad you're going. I'll be busy looking for Samson Miller, so you will be on your own part of the time."

Katy had a crush on Samson and Josie was her only confidante regarding that. Samson didn't have a clue. Or pretended not to have a clue.

"I'll be busy working at our booth." Josie moved around the hat shop, packing the bonnets and men's summer straw hats they'd take to the annual festival. They made all sorts of hats, many of them fitted to size and to the district's specifications. They also made some fancier hats and bonnets that appealed to the *Englisch*. "Did you come here to help me pack things or to tease me?"

"I am marking the bags and boxes as you requested," Katy said, holding up a marker as proof.

Josie thought about being around other young adults, girls and boys becoming women and men who were looking for someone to marry and start a life with.

Then finding homes and planting gardens, growing a family and making plans. The festival would be full of Amish families, and most of the folks her age would migrate to the food booths and find quiet places to get to know each other.

How she longed for that kind of life, but she feared she'd be single and alone forever, especially if something ever happened to Naomi. So she'd decided the best thing she could do was find someone to marry. Anyone. Anyone but the man she longed to be with. She wanted to tell him the truth, but each time she envisioned that, it brought her only pain and shame.

If Tobias heard she'd moved on, maybe he would, too. She hadn't decided how to handle telling another man her horrible secret, but she'd worry about that once Tobias was gone. If she got a marriage proposal, she could call off the wedding once Tobias had left. Because she'd rather be alone than marry someone she didn't love. She'd either leave or stay away from everyone so no one would bother her again.

Katy had a point. What if Tobias showed up this afternoon?

He had been seen around town a lot by many people, single women who would like to get to know him better. He was young and strong, and he made furniture that would last a lifetime. She hadn't thought about him being at the festival.

That made her heart pierce with an agonizing pain that cut her breath away. She adjusted her shoulders and breathed in. She had to pretend she didn't care.

"I don't mind being on my own," she replied to Katy's earlier warning. "I have learned to accept that." Then she added, "I need to find someone to court me."

Katy gave her a hard stare, her grimace almost comical. "Courting? You're going courting? Is this what you truly want, or is this plan to scare off Tobias?"

"Both."

Katy shook her head and gave Josie a quick hug. "I hope Tobias is there and I hope you will talk to *him*. Talking never hurt anyone, but using another man to avoid Tobias is wrong. It's unkind."

Katy was smart and wise, but words could hurt and Josie knew that better than others. How could she deceive a man who'd done nothing wrong? "I will be kind if I see Tobias," she said. "Being kind does not hurt anyone, either."

"That is so true." Katy grinned. "I'm glad you are going."

Josie wasn't glad, but she would put on a good front. She'd learned a lot about deception over the last few years. She prayed every night for forgiveness, but she was caught up in a web that only stretched and grew with each day. The weight of that delicate web tugged at her shoulders like a yoke.

That yoke would grow even heavier when she deceived everyone yet again. But what other choice did she have?

Chapter Ten

Tobias inhaled a deep breath. The day was full of sunshine and the scents of good food cooking over grills and fires. Chicken and roast beef for sandwiches, casseroles and cakes to take home for dinner, cookies and other sweets to sell to both Amish and *Englisch* alike. Tobias had *Englisch* friends back in Kentucky who liked to sample Amish food and sometimes help with the hard work around the farm. He'd partied with some of them during his *rumspringa*. But he got over that pretty quickly when he realized they could get rowdy at times.

After he met Josie, he took her to a few *Englisch* get-togethers. But she didn't seem to enjoy them much. She liked staying close to home, with chaperones nearby. Still, Tobias had managed to sweet-talk her into attending some of the big parties his *Englisch* friends liked to throw.

Campton Creek wasn't any more isolated than the Kentucky community he'd left, but it was much bigger and more spread out. Tobias had to admit this community had a lot going on. Cars and buggies stretched as far as he could see in the clear field just outside of town where the festivals and mud sales apparently were held several months out of each year. He marveled at the many colorful booths that held so many commodities. Maybe next year he'd set up his own booth selling fresh produce like several others along the way.

"What do you think of our little festival?" Abram asked as he handed Tobias a footstool they'd created out of thick grapevines a driftwood gatherer had sold to Abram.

The legs and feet were twisted but sturdy and varnished a deep brown, the oval stool bottom covered with a padded navy twill cushion surrounded by small twisted and varnished vines. It would make someone happy to have this little stool to rest their tired feet upon.

"I am impressed," Tobias admitted. "This is a lot bigger than the mud sales and bazaars we had back in Kentucky."

He'd sold a lot of fresh vegetables at the farmers' market in Orchard Mountain. That had given him the idea of the farm-to-table "side hustle," as his *Englisch* friends had called it.

"I could get used to this," he admitted to Abram.

"We aim to please," Abram retorted with a wry grin. "I'm extremely pleased with the extra pieces you made, Tobias. Those little wooden toys will be a hit."

Tobias beamed with pride as he set out the horses, dogs, baby goats and kittens he'd carved in several sizes, sometimes late at night when he couldn't sleep. He carved when he was worried or nervous, and he'd surely been both of those things over the last few weeks. He'd also brought some from Kentucky, which he hoped to sell today.

Thinking of Josie, he searched the long alleyways

to see if she'd arrived. The Bawell Hat Shop tent was a large one with rows and rows of straw hats with black bands around them, all made by hand with a team of experts. Something all Amish men would need for summer. He noticed prayer *kapps* in both black and white, aprons and women's heavier winter bonnets, too. Theirs was a true, thriving business that attracted a lot of people in both cars and buggies, from what he'd noticed in passing.

Would Josie be here to help inside the booth?

He hoped so. He had prayed to find a way to reach her, but he was losing hope each day. He hadn't sent her anything since the day he'd offered her a fruit pie. She'd ended their sweet time together there on the breezeway in an abrupt manner.

Questions he'd held long inside his soul resurfaced each time he was around her, but he refused to give up.

"Where's your head?" Abram asked, giving him a worried glance.

"Sorry, I was just lost in thought," Tobias admitted. "I want a home, Abram. And a wife and children."

"Well, I want those things for you, too," Abram replied, his hands on his hips. "Any word about the Fisher place?"

"No. Not yet. I have a few more weeks."

"A few more weeks for what?" Abram asked.

Realizing he'd slipped up, Tobias said, "To convince Josiah I'll take *gut* care of the place."

"Oh, that. He'll see that in your actions and your attitude. And meantime, I think my Beth is seriously working on finding you the perfect wife."

Tobias already knew who would be the perfect wife. He would have to tell Abram and Beth the truth, but not today. They had too much to do today, and he didn't want to mar their plans to sell lots of furniture. He'd explain everything to them next time they sat down to a meal together at home.

Home.

Campton Creek was beginning to feel that way.

He looked up and saw Josie walking toward the Bawell booth, her back to him. She carried a woven basket and wore a blue dress and a white *kapp* and apron, but he could find her slim form no matter how many people or things separated them.

No matter how much she refused to admit that she still cared about him. Tobias would find a way, somehow, to make her see that they still belonged together. No matter what.

Maybe he should tell her that so she'd see that, together and with *Gott*'s guidance, they could get through anything.

"Have you seen him yet?"

Josie nodded at Katy's impatient question. "*Ja*, so stop asking me that."

They were sitting behind the Bawell tent, eating a lunch of chicken-salad sandwiches and sliced apples. Josie had grabbed two oatmeal cookies for their dessert.

"Well?" Katy's blue eyes got even bigger. "I would like details."

"There are no details," Josie said. "He's still a very handsome man."

"You should go and visit with him."

"You should mind your own business. Where is Samson Miller, by the way?"

Katy threw a potato chip at her. "He is in his family's booth, selling fresh eggs and goat cheese."

"Sounds exciting."

Katy giggled. "Samson is a single-minded person. He can't be bothered to eat lunch when he's got eggs to sell."

Josie glanced up and thought about how earlier she'd spotted Tobias in the Schrock booth. She didn't dare venture over to that side of the alley, but she could make out his form as he lifted a chair off a parked wagon, his arms strong and sure, his hair always curling underneath his hat. He had the bluest eyes, so like the sky today. His smile had always made her feel special, but now that smile only brought her pain and regret.

Glad they had been busy, she tried not to think of him walking on the same soil as her. Tried not to notice the bevy of young Amish women who seemed to suddenly have a keen interest in furniture and wood carvings.

When she saw Mary Zook walking by with a carved kitten, she knew instantly Tobias had created the work. Her gasp caught Katy's attention.

Katy made an eye roll. "Mary, such a flirt. I guess she had a long discussion with Tobias about wood shavings."

Josie spun to look back at the furniture tent. She didn't see Tobias there. "Maybe he's left already."

"Or maybe he's searching for Mary, Mary, quite ready to marry."

"Stop it," Josie retorted, her words sharp.

"Just as I thought," Katy said. "You are jealous."

Josie dropped her half-eaten cookie. "I am not jealous. I want Tobias to be happy."

"Without you?"

"He cannot be with me."

"He could if you'd just talk to him."

Josie had talked to him, and each time only made things more painful. "He understands."

"Really?" Katy looked beyond her. "Maybe you can ask him if he truly understands, because he's coming toward our booth right now."

Josie stood and went back inside the booth. She saw Tobias walking the alleyway between the merchants, people all around him, his gaze on the Bawell booth.

Mary Zook walked back by and waved to Tobias, her dimples shining. He nodded, his gaze straight ahead. Mary looked discouraged and kept walking.

"I'm taking a stroll," Katy said before she darted away. Raesha had gone to their buggy to feed Daniel, and Dinah was home with Naomi and a neighbor who was watching them both.

Josie was alone in the booth.

Tobias walked right up to where she stood and leaned over the small wooden counter Josiah and some others had set up earlier. "Good afternoon," he said, his smile soft and reassuring.

"Hello." She didn't know what to say, so she sat back on the tall stool and stared at him. "Are you enjoying the festival?"

"Very much." He didn't take his eyes away from her. "A lot of people around."

"Is Abram pleased? Are you selling a lot?"

"We've been steady busy, *ja*."

Josie was running out of small talk. "*Denke* again for the peach pie. I enjoyed it." Glancing at the people milling about, she asked, "Shouldn't you get back?"

"I'm on break," he replied, his eyes full of that mischief she remembered so well. "I wanted to spend it with my best girl."

Josie's throat caught. He'd always called her that. "I'm not that girl anymore, Tobias."

"Josie," he said, his eyes serious now, "whatever happened, whatever you're afraid of, I will handle it—for both of us. I will carry your burdens."

Tears burned but she held tightly to her control. "It is my burden only, Tobias."

Before she knew what was happening, Tobias came around, slipped inside the booth and sat down on the stool beside her without saying a word.

"You shouldn't," she said, her voice shaky now. "You need to go."

"I'm going in a few minutes," he said. He took her hand in his, careful that no one would notice. "I made you something."

He slipped the warm piece of wood into her palm and held it there between their laced fingers. "I will carry your burdens, Josie."

Josie couldn't speak, couldn't move. What if Raesha or Josiah came back? What if she had a customer?

But the world around her seemed to recede as Tobias held her hand in his, the carving warm between them, the world away from them. The touch of his skin ricocheted through her system like a ray of warm sunshine, bringing a peace she hadn't felt in years. She lifted her hand away and saw the delicate butterfly he'd shaped out of what looked like an exotic wood.

"Tobias," she whispered, ready to pour out her heart.

Tobias stood, his expression full of love and understanding. And hope.

"Excuse me."

They both looked up to find an *Englisch* man standing there, his world-weary gaze reading them with a sharp clarity.

Josie stood up, the small carving still in her hand. She recognized Nathan Craig, the private investigator who helped the Amish with missing people or legal problems. He'd helped her brother find her. "Nathan, it is *gut* to see you."

"Nice to see you, Josie," Nathan said. Then he turned to Tobias and introduced himself, giving Tobias a handshake. "Actually, Mr. Mast, I've been looking for you. I didn't want to do this here, but it's a timely matter and I had to locate you today."

Tobias looked surprised. "Me? Why?"

Josie didn't know what to say. Why was a private investigator looking for Tobias?

"Maybe we should speak in private," Nathan suggested, his tone determined.

Tobias glanced at Josie. "I don't mind Josie hearing. I trust her."

Josie felt the volt of appreciation from that comment, only to be followed by a sharp pang of regret. "I cannot leave the booth anyway. What's going on, Nathan?"

Nathan said, "I got a call from an associate in Kentucky. He says an English couple is trying to track Tobias down because you were once friends with their son."

Tobias looked perplexed. "*Ja,* I knew a lot of *Englisch* during my *rumspringa*. Who is this couple?"

"Theodore and Pamela Benington," Nathan said, his shrewd gaze sweeping over both of them. "They have a son named Drew. Do you remember him?"

Josie grabbed the stool and sank down on it, her heart on fire, her pulse pounding like a hammer to nails.

Drew Benington?

Tobias glanced at Josie, concern in his eyes. "I did know him. But I heard he got into some trouble and is now in prison."

"He is," Nathan said. "They only want to ask you some questions and I'm not at liberty to say what they are looking for. My associate only asked me to alert you so you can plan accordingly. The Beningtons are flying up here and they should arrive late tomorrow afternoon. They'd like to meet with you at the Campton Center on Monday if possible."

Tobias nodded. "I have no idea why they'd want to see me," he said. "I haven't talked to Drew in years."

Nathan shot Josie a look that could have been a warning. "As I said, I don't have the details, but can you be there around two o'clock?"

Tobias nodded. "I'll be there. I have to get back to my booth now." He turned to Josie. "We will talk later."

She couldn't speak. She only nodded, the wooden butterfly carving clutched in her hand.

After Tobias hurried back to the furniture booth, Nathan looked at Josie. "Are you okay?"

She shot up off the stool, her hands holding on to the counter with a painful grip. "You know everything, don't you?"

Nathan rubbed a hand over his chin. "I know enough, but I had to find Tobias and give him the message. Josie, do you also know Drew Benington?"

She moved her head, tears pricking at her eyes. "I did."

Nathan didn't ask any more questions. He only

nodded. "Josie, if Drew was your attacker and Tobias doesn't know the truth, you need to tell him. The Beningtons are here to make amends for what their son has done. I can't be sure what they already know and it's not my place to ask. But Tobias needs to hear the truth from you before they tell him. If you need me or Alisha, let us know, all right?"

"Why would I need a lawyer?" she asked, knowing his wife did legal work for the Amish.

"You might not, but if their son told them what he did to you, they might want some answers and they might ask to see you, too. I couldn't tell you that in front of Tobias, since I wasn't sure. Always a good idea to have counsel in the room since this is a delicate and difficult situation."

Josie gasped and put her hand to her mouth. "I went to them early on and tried to tell them, but they refused to listen to me. They didn't believe me when I told them I was pregnant, but, Nathan, I tried to explain. They told me to go away."

Nathan glanced around to make sure they were alone. "If they've somehow verified your pregnancy, the Beningtons might be coming here to talk to you, too. Just be aware. They'll want to speak to you if they have all the facts and they'll want definitive proof."

Josie's stomach roiled. "You mean about Dinah. You don't think they'd try to take her?"

Nathan's expression turned grim. "I don't know and I shouldn't be speculating with you. But they're coming, regardless of why. Even though Alisha helped Josiah and Raesha with all the legalities of the adoption, you still need to warn your family."

Alisha Braxton, the lawyer who'd guided them

through making sure Dinah could stay with Josiah while Josie was still missing. And now Nathan's wife. She'd assured them everything had been by the book. What if she'd missed something?

Nathan looked her over. "Do you want me to call someone for you?"

"Neh." She straightened some crocheted doilies. "Raesha would worry. I'll explain all of this to them when we get home, not here."

"I'm sorry I had to be the one to alert you, but Tobias was here with you, so I didn't know how to handle it. Let me know if you need anything."

She nodded again, grateful that Nathan and Alisha had helped Josiah find her and figure out what had happened to her and Dinah. Along with Judy Campton, they had helped her family in many ways. Nathan had no choice but to tell his associate the truth—that Tobias was here now.

She only wished Nathan had warned her earlier, but he'd found her and Tobias together and had to move fast. Why did Drew's parents want to see Tobias? Would they try to turn Tobias against her? Or would they try to take Dinah away?

She couldn't let that happen. It would destroy her whole family. They all loved Dinah.

Nathan wouldn't repeat anything to anyone not involved. But her friend Sarah back in Kentucky knew everything. Had Sarah been forced to tell Drew's parents the truth? Or did they remember how, in a fit of desperation, Josie had blurted out the facts? Facts they'd refused to believe.

Raesha came back to the booth, smiling down at little Daniel as he bounced in her arms. "Was that Nathan

Craig?" she asked, her keen gaze sweeping over Josie and then back to the departing man.

Josie nodded while Raesha settled the babe inside his portable crib. "He was just passing by."

She'd have to tell her family about this, but right now she felt a panic attack about to overtake her.

Her world, which just moments ago had seemed to right itself when Tobias was holding her hand, had come crumbling down once again.

The parents of the boy who'd assaulted her would soon be in Campton Creek. And they needed to talk to Tobias.

She had no choice but to tell him the truth. But when and how could she do that?

Chapter Eleven

The hours seemed to drag as heavily as the weight on her shoulders. Josie watched the Schrock booth and saw Tobias talking to customers and helping people load furniture. He had to be wondering what was going on.

Josie tried to engage with customers and friends, but finally she told Raesha she wasn't feeling well. Tobias had left the furniture booth and she had no idea where he'd gone.

"Do you want to go home?" Raesha asked, concern in her eyes. "I can get someone from one of the other booths or from the youth group to help."

Josie nodded. "I can walk home. That might do me good."

Raesha smiled at some lookers and then turned back to Josie. "Are you sure? You look pale."

Josie pushed at her sleeves. "I think it's all the people. I thought I could do this, but I'm sorry, Raesha. I just need to be alone and I don't mind walking."

Raesha smiled as she handed a bag of bread and homemade strawberry jam to an Amish woman and took the payment. Then she pivoted around to face Josie. "A walk might do you good. Just be careful."

"I'll be fine. The road is very open. I'll take the shortcut."

Josie glanced down the way at the furniture booth. She hadn't seen Tobias since he'd left an hour ago. Maybe she'd get word to him before he talked to the Beningtons.

"I'm going to tell Katy I'm leaving," she said, giving Daniel a kiss and nodding to Raesha.

Making her way along the alley filled with people, she went to the Schrock Furniture booth. Abram saw her and waved.

"Hi," she said, glancing around. "I was looking for Tobias."

Abram gave her a knowing smile. "He went to lunch and then he had a delivery to make. I doubt he'll be back until time to load up and clear out."

Disappointment warred with relief in Josie's head. She had to do this, but maybe she could find Tobias along the route home. "I'll talk to him later, then. *Denke.*"

Abram smiled. "Tobias is a good man, Josie. I hope you find him."

Like so many, Abram wanted her and Tobias to be together. That could never happen, especially now when her whole world was falling apart.

She left the big field and followed the path past all the cars and buggies, trying to stay away from anyone who might stop and talk with her. After looking everywhere, she didn't find Tobias at any of the lunch booths. Maybe he'd gone on home to the Schrock place after his delivery. That was too far in the other direction to get to and back before dark, and people would notice if she went there alone.

She'd send word somehow to let him know she needed to see him. She just hoped she wouldn't be too late.

Monday morning, Tobias explained to Bettye and Jewel that he was to meet the Beningtons at Campton Center at two o'clock. "I'm sorry for the short notice but they were firm on the day and time."

With no church yesterday, he'd managed to stay busy in the barn while Abram and Beth went visiting. But he'd thought about going to see Josie. Her reaction to hearing about Drew had puzzled him.

"We live for short notice," Jewel said, bringing him out of his worries. "I'll pull out some cookies and brew a big pot of coffee. Sounds like you've got some business to tend to."

"I have no idea what they want," Tobias replied, worry scorching his insides. "I did hear Drew went to prison, but I'm not sure why."

"Maybe he's getting out and he wants to make amends," Bettye suggested, her gaze meeting Jewel's.

"Could be," Jewel replied.

Tobias figured they knew something but weren't talking. He'd just have to wait and see. He couldn't stop thinking of how Josie had sunk down on her stool, shock draining the color from her face. She'd never liked Drew and had stopped going to the *Englisch* house parties a few weeks before she'd left. Was she upset that he might still be Drew's friend?

He'd have to explain that he hadn't seen Drew in a long time. Tobias had been so distraught after Josie disappeared, he didn't go to many social gatherings, *Eng-*

lisch or Amish. Then he had to take care of his *daed*, which meant he barely left the farm unless it was to take Daed to doctor appointments and to pick up supplies. Curiosity was making him antsy and on edge.

As the time to meet drew near, he left work and walked back over to the Campton Center. Jewel met him in the hallway and then placed a thermal coffeepot and water on the big table where the pro bono counselors and lawyers met with people. When they heard a knock at the door, Jewel hurried to open it.

Tobias sat, white-knuckled and worried, Bettye with him.

"I'm praying," Bettye said. "No matter what, Tobias, we're here when you need us."

Jewel walked back in, followed by Nathan Craig with a woman dressed in a dark suit and an older man and woman.

Jewel said, "Tobias, you've met Nathan. This is his wife, Alisha, who is a lawyer. And this is Mr. and Mrs. Theodore Benington."

Tobias stood and nodded. "Hello." Why had they brought a lawyer?

The woman with golden-brown shoulder-length hair answered his unasked question, her tone all business. "I'm here as a mediator, nothing more."

Now he needed a mediator?

Jewel and Bettye discreetly left, shutting the door behind them.

Tobias sat back down after everyone had found a place. "What is this about?"

The older woman's eyes teared up. "I'm Pamela, Drew's mother. We're here because he asked us to find you."

"He wants you to forgive him," Mr. Benington said, his voice shaky.

"Forgive him?" Tobias shook his head. "For what?"

The older couple looked at Alisha. She nodded.

Pamela leaned across the table. "He's ill, Tobias. Liver cancer. He's in prison, but he's dying, so he insisted we come here to find you. He needs forgiveness."

Tobias lowered his head. "I am sorry to hear of this, but Drew owes me nothing. We were friends for a season and then we went our separate ways. You didn't need to come all this way to tell me that."

Alisha cleared her throat. "Tobias, the Beningtons are here today because their son begged them to find you. But he wanted them to find another person, too."

"Who?" Tobias asked, more perplexed than ever.

"Josie Fisher," Alisha said, her gaze moving from him to her husband.

Josie's frantic worry had mounted by the hour. Yesterday she'd begged Katy to drive her to the Schrock place so she could talk to Tobias, but no one had answered the door. Worried that he'd found out the worst and left before she could explain, she'd told Josiah and Raesha about the Beningtons. She couldn't put it off any longer.

"I don't know what they want," she said after they'd all had the midday dinner. "But I have to find Tobias before they talk to him. I tried yesterday, but he was nowhere to be found. If they know about me, they'll tell him. And then they'll want to see Dinah."

Naomi's gaze held hers. "But how would they possibly know about Dinah?"

Josie wiped at her eyes. "I went to them one night

when I became desperate and…told them I might be pregnant. They refused to believe me and told me to get out of their house. After that, I ran away."

"You never told us that," Raesha said.

"It didn't seem to matter," Josie admitted. "They did not believe me and their son wanted nothing to do with me. They only thought I was trying to trick their son into marriage, which I never wanted."

Raesha gasped and grabbed Josiah's arm. "They can't take her, can they? They won't take Dinah away?"

Josiah paled, reaching for his wife. "I do not know. They might not even realize a child is involved." He let go of Raesha and tugged Josie close. "We cannot say what they know or why they are here."

"We should call Alisha," Raesha said, wiping her eyes. "She can advise us same as she did when Dinah first arrived. She handled the adoption and told us we were clear to raise Dinah. We have all of the paper-work."

Naomi moved her wheelchair closer and reached for Raesha's hand. "Do not fret. Don't go borrowing worry."

Josie cried against her brother's fresh-smelling shirt. "I have to find Tobias. Now."

"I'll take you into town," Josiah said, nodding to Raesha and Naomi. "We'll find him and I'll be there, nearby, when you tell him."

Naomi nodded and held tightly to Raesha's hand. "We will pray while we wait for your return."

Now Josie sat in the buggy beside her brother, re-membering when she'd first returned to Campton

Creek. Back then, she had been numb and afraid and ashamed. Today she was stronger but still afraid. If Drew's parents took Dinah, her family would never get over losing their little girl.

She would never get over losing her own child.

"They have money, *bruder*. They can hire lawyers and make things hard for us."

Josiah hushed her. "We have love and we know a good lawyer. We did everything right, Josie. Alisha made sure of that."

When they reached town, Josie's nerves scattered and scurried. She couldn't breathe, couldn't think about what she'd say to Tobias.

"He should be at work," she told Josiah. "I'll go in and find him. We can go somewhere private to talk."

She hurried toward the store, her heart racing. Somehow she had to find the words and the courage to tell Tobias her secret. At long last.

Praying with all of her heart, Josie rushed into the market, the scents of cedar and pine only reminding her of Tobias.

"Well, where's the fire?" Abram asked from behind the counter. "Are you all right, Josie?"

"I need to talk to Tobias," she said, out of breath.

Abram's expression changed from jolly to dour. "He's not here. He had to meet with some people over at the Campton Center. Want me to give him a message?"

Shock caused Josie to go limp against the counter. "I'm too late."

Abram came around and sat her down on a chair. "What is wrong, Josie?"

"I need to tell him something important," she said, tears misting in her eyes.

Abram patted her shoulder. "Does it have to do with the people he's talking to? He told me about that."

She nodded, unable to speak.

"Then go and find him. You might be of some help to him."

Josie doubted that, but she didn't have a choice. Maybe she could get to him before the Beningtons did. "*Denke*, Abram."

She stood and steadied herself. "I have to go."

Abram watched her hurry away, but she didn't care anymore what anyone thought. Except for Tobias. She wished now she'd told him the truth right away. But she'd been foolish and prideful. Thinking of the beautiful, delicate butterfly he'd carved for her, Josie found her strength.

She had to do the right thing. Tobias deserved that much at least.

Tobias stared at the couple across from him. "Did you say Josie?"

Pamela nodded. "Drew especially wanted us to find Josie. He's unable to come and tell her himself, but he wants her to know he's sorry."

Tobias leaned against the table. "Sorry for what?"

The front door burst open, causing all of them to glance toward the hallway. Tobias heard Jewel talking to someone and then footsteps approaching.

Jewel knocked on the partially open door. "I'm sorry to interrupt, but, Tobias, someone is here to see you."

"I can't... Can they wait?"

"No." Jewel's eyes went wide, her brows lifting like two dark wings, while she tried to communicate with him. "It's urgent."

Still reeling from what they'd said to him about Josie, Tobias stood and glanced at Nathan and Alisha. "I'm sorry. I'll be right back."

They nodded and turned to continue talking to the Beningtons. Probably to keep them occupied until they could give Tobias more information.

Tobias hurried out into the hallway. "What is going on, Jewel?"

"She's out in the sunroom," Jewel said, giving him a gentle shove. "Go on now."

Tobias walked to the back of the house and stopped at the door to the sunroom.

Josie sat on a wicker chair with her head down and her hands twisted against her apron.

"Josie?" He hurried into the room and knelt in front of her. "What are you doing here?"

Josie lifted her head, tears streaming down her face. "I have to talk to you and tell you what happened. Before they do."

Tobias touched his hand to her tears. "You mean Drew's parents? They said Drew had a message for you." A sense of dread settled over him. "Drew did something to hurt you, didn't he?"

Her eyes filled with more tears, fear and dread darkening her gaze. "What…what was the message from Drew?"

Leaving his hand on her warm cheek, Tobias said, "He wanted you to know he's sorry." Then he dropped his hand and looked into her eyes. "Why would he need to apologize to you, Josie?"

Chapter Twelve

Josie's worst nightmare had come true. Now Tobias would know her dark secret and her great shame. Would she have to leave again and never see her family? Give up on seeing Dinah grow up? Or, worse, would Drew's parents take Dinah and never let her return to them?

"Josie?"

She looked up and into Tobias's eyes. He deserved the truth. She would hurt him again, but at least he could move on knowing he had done nothing wrong.

Tobias pulled up a chair and took her hands into his. "You have to tell me everything."

"I do not want to, but, yes, now I have no choice."

"What did he do?" Tobias asked, the tone of his voice edged with anger.

Josie took in a shuddering breath. "It was at that big party at his house a few weeks before Christmas. He always flirted with me and said vile things about you and me and how we were so square and not cool."

Tobias's hands squeezed hers. "I told him not to tease you in that way. What else did he do?"

When she tried to look away, Tobias touched a finger to her chin so she had to look into his eyes. "Tell me."

She took in another gulp of air, her lungs burning with the need to scream, her heartbeat throbbing through her pulse. "He gave me a glass of punch then told me you were looking for me." She stopped, the memories as bright as the red geraniums blooming in a huge pot by the pool. "He pointed to the back of the house, so I went to find you. He followed me."

Tobias let go of her hands and stood, his elbows bent, his hands on his hips. "What did he do, Josie?"

"The drink had something in it. I only took one or two sips, but it made me dizzy and I felt sick. He pushed me into a room and… I couldn't get away, Tobias. I couldn't get away."

Tobias stared at her as if he hadn't heard correctly. But realization covered him in a rush of bright anger that darkened his cheeks and changed his expression into a hard-edged, grisly acceptance. He backed away and went to the glass door leading out onto the terrace.

Leaning his forehead against the glass, he shuddered. "No," he said, his voice rising. "No."

Josie held her hands to her face, her head falling as she tried to hide her shame and the horror of what had happened. The vivid memories she'd tried so hard to bury came back in full-forced clarity. "I'm sorry. I did not want you to know. I couldn't tell you."

"So you left me?" he said, his voice rising as he turned to face her. "You left me and let me believe the worst—that you didn't love me, that I had failed you?"

"I had no choice," she said, her body numb with pain and grief. "I had no choice. I didn't think you'd love *me* anymore if you knew."

He stood pressed against the door in the same way she'd stood when she'd gone to see him in her old home. "You didn't trust me enough to tell me? You know I would have done anything to protect you, to make this up to you."

"I was afraid of that, afraid you might confront him and he'd lie to you. I barely remember it happening because he drugged me and he was drunk, Tobias. So drunk that he didn't even remember my name or that we'd been in that room."

Tobias paced in front of her. "You found me that night, told me you weren't feeling well. Why didn't you tell me what had happened?"

"I was in shock and terrified," she said, each word dropping like a pebble against glass. "Afraid of his power and money, his friends who made fun of me, of how you'd react and what you might do to him."

"So you decided you'd just run away. We could have worked this out and we could have still gotten married. I… I would have listened and understood."

"Think long and hard on that," she said, standing to face him as she found her courage. "Would you have been able to get past it and still marry me?"

Tobias stopped and stared at her, his eyes misty and red rimmed, his expression grim and defeated. "I would have done anything, anything, Josie, to keep you with me."

She nodded and then she put a hand to her stomach. "Even accept another man's child as your own?"

Tobias felt a rushing roar inside his head. He'd been angry in his life, but nothing like this. This was a rage that made him want to break every window in this room, made him want to find Drew Benington and tear him apart.

But that was not the Amish way.

How did he deal with this now? How did he keep moving, working, living, trying to have the life he'd been denied? How, when a man he considered his friend had betrayed him and Josie in such a callous, horrible way? Why had Tobias forced her to go to that party, knowing she felt uncomfortable among those rich *Englisch* teenagers?

This was on him. All those years he'd wondered, and it was his fault, after all, that she'd left.

"You wanted the truth," she said on a raw whisper, taking his silence as a condemnation. "Now you have it. Dinah is my child and that is why I had to leave. I would not shame you into marrying me out of a sense of duty. I had to leave, and when I came back to this area, things got bad, and out of desperation, I left my baby on Raesha and Naomi's porch."

Tobias couldn't speak. The thought of her out there alone in the cold of winter, pregnant and afraid, made him want to rush to her and hold her tight. But the thought of her not trusting him to help her or still love her held him away.

Why had God brought him here to find her only to have this happen? The Beningtons showing up so she was forced to admit what she'd kept from him? Was that *Gott*'s plan?

Maybe it had to be this way so they both were forced to see the real truth.

"I do not understand why you went to such extremes."

"I left my child with two women I'd trusted before,

and then I became ill with grief and longing and lone-liness. I caught pneumonia and almost died, but *Gott* had other plans for me. My brother came back here to sell our place, and he went to the neighbors' to let them know he'd be over there renovating the house and barn."

Tobias wiped at his eyes and nodded. "What else happened?"

Josie wrapped her arms around her stomach in a pro-tective stance. "Josiah noticed the pink hat Dinah was wearing and knew immediately it had to be mine." She paused and swallowed away the grief. "I carried that little bonnet with me everywhere. It was the only thing I had left from my *mamm*. But I wanted Dinah to have it, to keep her warm."

Tobias closed his eyes and then blinked. "How did Josiah find you?"

"He'd been searching for me—hired Nathan Craig to find me once he lost touch with me after I left Ken-tucky. But I was still out there trying to hide, sick and hoping I'd die."

Tobias closed his eyes again, thanked God she had not died. "I'm glad he found you."

"It took a while," she said, nodding. "But, yes, Na-than located me in a nearby hospital and Josiah brought me to the Bawell place. But I was so dead inside, I wouldn't tell anyone the truth." She took a long breath. "I was mean to everyone and caused a lot of trouble, but Naomi and Judy Campton helped me find my way again."

Judy Campton. So she had to have known all of this, but she couldn't blurt it out to him. And here he stood in what used to be her home. Ironic that he was back here with Josie.

"You told Josiah that Dinah was your child?"

"Yes, but they had already found proof," she said. "DNA from Josiah and Dinah showed he was related to Dinah. That's why he was able to keep her with him even before he found me. But I didn't want anything to do with her after I came back. She reminded me too much of… Drew."

Tobias sank down on a padded floral stool, exhaustion and shock overcoming him. "So here we are. You have a child and you left me because of what Drew did. I'd say he owes you a lot more than an apology."

Josie lowered her head. "I am shocked that he asked his parents to do this. He can't come but sending them is harsh. He's even more of a coward than I thought and I hope he never gets out of prison."

Tobias only now remembered people were waiting in the other room. "They were about to tell me everything."

"I had to find you," she said. "You needed to hear this from me."

Anger stiffened his spine. "You were forced or I would have never known."

"I'm sorry. I wanted to tell you," she said, her tone quiet and defeated. "I was about to the other day at the festival, but then Nathan showed up. Either way, I've hurt you. I will always regret that."

Tobias let things settle in his head. Then he looked back at Josie and motioned toward the front of the big house. "Do they know about the child?"

Josie put a hand to her mouth, her eyes burning with a solid fear. "I don't know, but…they might have figured it out since I went to them before I ran away. They didn't believe me then, but what if they came to find out?

That's the other reason I had to tell you. They might try to take Dinah away from us. I will not let that happen."

Tobias stood. "You need to know something, Josie. They told me Drew is dying of liver cancer. That is the reason he sent them to find both of us."

Josie gasped and seemed to shrink away. "He wants atonement before he dies."

"*Ja*, so it seems. I am glad he didn't show up here. I am not sure how I would have handled that."

Tobias reached out his hand. "I need to get back in there. Will you *kumm*?"

"I… I don't think that is such a *gut* idea."

Before he could convince her, Jewel came out into the sunroom, her gaze apologetic. "Josie, your brother came to check on you. Now Alisha is asking that you all come into the conference room."

"Josie?" Tobias reached out to her again. "I'm with you now. We have to stand together."

Josie didn't look so sure. "You are not angry at me?"

"I am angry," he admitted, "at you, at Drew for what he did, at myself for being so naive and for the time we've wasted when we could have worked this out somehow."

Josie's expression showed her torment, her cheeks flushed, her eyes downcast. "I am so sorry, Tobias. So sorry."

"We will talk about sorry later," he said. "Right now we need to go into that room and face Drew's parents. Together."

She took his hand in a tentative silence and Tobias breathed a sigh of relief, only to be followed by a deep sense of dread. His world had shifted, his faith had been sorely tested, and the enraged anger he felt clutched him so tightly he thought he might suffocate.

But now he knew what she'd tried so hard to hide, and somehow he had to accept what had happened and reconcile that with what might have been.

Or what could come now that the healing would begin.

I need strength. I need to talk to someone. I need Gott's help.

The woman he had loved from the moment he'd met her had not trusted that love enough to share the worst time of her life with him. Now he had to accept that a man he'd befriended in his running-around time had ruined Josie and ruined their plans for a future together. She had a child by another man and she'd given that child to her brother. He knew she'd made that sacrifice for the sake of the child. Josie had put Dinah on the Bawell porch for a reason. Josiah had told Tobias that the Bawells had helped her as a child, when she was living in fear. She must have felt they would give Dinah a good, safe life. But he had to grasp the question burning inside his head. Did she love Dinah or was she just tolerating the *kinder*?

Because he now knew who little Dinah had reminded him of the one time he'd seen her.

Drew. Dinah reminded him of Drew.

How would either of them get past that?

Chapter Thirteen

Josie did not want to go into that room, but Tobias held her hand, obviously not caring about rules or decorum at this point.

Josiah came out of the office near the conference room. "Josie, I was growing concerned."

Jewel stood between them. "I explained what's going on to Josiah. Let Josiah go in with you, Josie. He is your brother, after all, and he knows what needs to be said."

Josiah gave Josie a questioning glance.

"Tobias knows the truth now, *bruder*," she said, her throat raw and her head pounding. "All of it."

Josiah glanced from her to Tobias. "I will go in if you both agree. But Dinah is my child now."

Tobias indicated a nod. "I think that would be in Josie's best interest. After all, you are Dinah's legal father, *ja*?"

"I am," Josiah said, appreciation and regret in his eyes.

Josie could see Tobias had become a man overnight and now he'd grown even stronger. Then again, the news he'd just learned could do that to a person.

He'd held her hand, but could he truly forgive her? She'd seen the hurt in his eyes when he'd finally realized the truth. That also meant he realized she'd kept this a secret for well over three years. Years of lost time between them. Too long for secrets between them. What if they couldn't repair the damage she'd done?

No more secrets, she decided. Here and now, she would face the truth and try to be strong, as Naomi had taught her.

Giving Tobias a glimpse that she hoped showed that courage, she indicated she was ready.

He opened the door and guided her into the room. Josiah followed behind.

Josie stood just inside the door, her gaze moving over Nathan's sympathetic face and Alisha's concerned frown. They had worked so hard to make sure Dinah was safe and protected.

Then she glanced over at Drew's parents. His mother's eyes were as red and swollen as Josie's had to be. His dad looked haggard and beaten by the world.

Her heart went out to them. They had no way of knowing what Drew had done to her, and they'd refused to believe her the one time she'd tried to talk to them. But someone had stepped forward to make him pay. Now he had a horrible disease that couldn't be hushed or hidden away. A disease that no amount of power could overcome.

She should feel some type of vindication. Instead, Josie felt sad and full of pain and regret. She'd have to forgive him—not so much for his sake, but because that was the Amish way and she needed the peace of mind that forgiveness brought.

"Josie," Alisha said, rising to take her arm. "I'm glad

you came." Then she looked at Tobias. "Are you both okay?"

Tobias nodded, but didn't look okay. "*Ja*. Josie told me everything."

"And what is everything?" Drew's father asked as he stood.

Nathan motioned him back in his seat. "I think Josie is ready to talk to you two. Is that why you came, Josie?"

Josie shook her head. "*Neh*, I came to find Tobias." Then she faced the Beningtons. "Tobias told me about Drew. I am sorry. I understand he had a message for me."

Drew's mother wiped at her eyes while Alisha guided Josie and Tobias to their chairs. Josiah found a seat off to the side.

"Drew did some horrible things and now he's in prison," his mother said, her gaze on Josie. "He's trying to make amends before…before he dies. We hope to bring him home soon, if the parole board will agree to an early release."

Josie wondered if Drew was truly sorry or if he only wanted to get out of prison and die at home. She brushed that doubt aside and took the high road. "I hope you can do that."

Tobias still looked shell-shocked. "Josie told me what Drew did to her and why she was forced to leave Orchard Mountain. I had no idea. She did not want me to know, but she felt she had to tell me the truth."

Mr. Benington let out an angry huff of breath, his expression hardening. His wife grasped his hand. "Theodore, we came here for a purpose. Don't chide her now. Drew made it clear he wanted Josephine to know that he is sorry. So very sorry."

Tobias stared them down. "Chide her? She did nothing wrong. It seems to me Drew is the culprit here, and apologizing won't change that."

"He made mistakes," Drew's mother said. "He *is* serving his time. We are so sorry, Josephine. You came to us and tried to make us see, but we didn't want to believe the worst of our only child."

Josie couldn't speak. They did remember her coming to see them. Did they remember what she had told them?

"Look," Nathan said. "Now that we're all here, and we have Alisha's law expertise to guide us, let's put it all on the table." He narrowed his gaze on the couple. "You've delivered the messages from Drew. Josie and Tobias at least know now that he regrets what he did. His actions hurt both of them. What more do you need to say?"

Drew's father cleared his throat and stared at Josie. Then he said the words she'd dreaded since Nathan had come to the festival booth. "Did you have Drew's child, Josie? If you did, we'd like to see our grandchild."

Tobias watched Josie's face for a reaction. Her gaze landed first on him and then her brother. "I… I don't know how to answer that question."

"A simple yes or no will suffice," Mr. Benington replied, his tone quiet but firm. "You blurted that out to us and then you ran out the door."

Josiah moved forward and put a hand on Josie's shoulder. Josie took in a calming breath. She looked pale and distraught. Tobias wanted to help her, to protect her, but he had to let her tell this story.

Josie lifted her shoulders and looked over at Drew's parents. "I did have Drew's child. A little girl."

Pamela Benington began to sob. "Oh, my. Oh, I can't believe this. Josie, I'm so sorry, but…we have a grand-daughter."

"No, *I* had a child," Josie replied. "A child I had to give up."

"What?" Theodore Benington glared across at Josie. "You gave her up for adoption?"

"I had no choice," Josie said, her voice growing stronger with each word. "But I put her in the best home I could find."

"Where is she?" Pamela said, still crying. "We have to see her."

Josiah held up his hand, palm up. "Dinah is with my wife and me. We adopted her. Raesha and I fell in love a few months after Dinah and Josie came to us. I saw Dinah first and recognized the pink baby bonnet she was wearing. It had Josie's initials stitched inside. I questioned Raesha and Naomi, and they admitted the child had been left on their porch."

He explained who the Bawell women were and how they'd watched after Dinah until he could prove he was her *onkel*.

"They became instant nannies to little Dinah, and Raesha and I fell in love. After we married, we officially adopted her."

Theodore hit his hand on the table and then pointed at Josie. "You left our granddaughter on someone's porch?"

"Not just anyone's porch," Josiah continued while Tobias fisted his hands to keep from lashing out at Drew's irrational father. "The Bawell porch. Two good women who had plenty of love to give a child."

When Theodore tried to speak, Tobias responded. "Let him explain."

Josiah took a breath and continued. "When I found out through a DNA test the child Raesha and Naomi were taking care of was related to me, I searched for Josie. My sister was very ill in a nearby hospital. Nathan helped me locate her and bring her home." He stopped and looked at Josie. "Josie came to live with us, but she gave up her rights as a mother. Dinah is our daughter now—mine and Raesha's."

Alisha leaned forward, her shoulder-length hair falling around her face. "I went exactly by the book in helping them to adopt Dinah." Then she crossed her hands on the table. "But the Amish have their own way of taking in children. They don't ask questions, and they make sure the child is safe and well cared for."

"Our son didn't agree to that kind of dubious law," Theodore said.

"He never signed the birth certificate," Josie replied. "Your son didn't even remember what happened."

"He wasn't given the chance to sign," Drew's father retorted.

"But he has a child," Pamela said. "We're related to her, too. We should have been informed."

Alisha jotted notes. "After Josiah and Raesha were married, I contacted your son at his college, Mr. Bennington. They wanted to formally adopt Dinah, and Josie had agreed. But Drew refused to believe the truth, so he said he didn't care and wanted no part of this. He wouldn't sign a VAP—Voluntary Acknowledgment of Paternity. I think by then two other girls had come forward, but he was still in denial and refused to sign any paperwork that could implicate him in a crime." She stopped for a pause, then added, "Later, of course, he went on trial for those two attacks."

"He never told us about this situation and it didn't come out at the trial," Drew's father said. "But he could still claim rights."

Alisha nodded. "Yes, *he* could, but we'd have to go through a lot of paperwork and legalese. As you told us, we're running out of time."

Josiah cleared his throat. "My wife and I love Dinah. She is happy and healthy. Josie helps out with her and our son, Daniel. We'd hate to lose our daughter."

"Our granddaughter," Pamela reminded them. "I'd like to see her."

Her husband took her hand. "Honey, we'll talk to our own legal team and see what can be done, but Drew won't be able to raise her and he might not even get to see her before he dies."

"We could raise her," Pamela said. "We can give her anything she needs or wants."

"She has everything she needs," Josie said. "You can't do that to my family."

Tobias took her hand. "You've said what you came to say. Josie is tired and I have a job to get back to." He looked toward Nathan. "Are we finished?"

Nathan gave the Beningtons a long stare. "For now, I think."

"I'd like to see my granddaughter," Pamela insisted. "I promise I won't say or do anything to frighten her. I just need to see her. Just this once until…until we can decide how to handle this."

Josiah almost spoke, but Alisha shot both him and Tobias a warning glance.

"We'll be in touch," she said to the Beningtons.

"Thank you both for coming. Meantime, I'll go back over the law and check all the steps we took again. For now, Dinah is legally adopted by the Fishers. It will be up to them if you can see Dinah before you go."

After they all moved outside, Josiah motioned to Josie. "We should go and tell Raesha what's happened."

Josie nodded, too shocked and confused to argue with her brother.

Tobias stopped him. "I need to talk to Josie. If you don't mind, I'll borrow Abram's buggy and drive her home."

Josiah's frown indicated he didn't like that. "Josie?"

Josie looked from her brother to Tobias. "It's all right, Josiah. I'll be all right."

Reluctantly Josiah headed to the buggy. Her brother probably wished he'd never found her at all. They could be raising Dinah without all of this drama she'd brought with her.

Tobias touched her shoulder. "*Kumm* with me. I'll explain to Abram. It's a slow day anyway, so he'll understand."

"What will you tell him?" she asked, hoping word wouldn't spread about the Beningtons being here.

"That I need a couple of hours with my best girl," he said. Then he stalked away, the joy that endearment used to hold no longer in his voice.

Chapter Fourteen

"Take as long as you want," Abram had told Tobias earlier. "Tobias, are you all right? I am here to help with whatever you need."

"Just your horse and buggy. After Josie and I talk, I'll need to take her home."

Abram nodded. "Later, if you want to unload what's really going on, I am a *gut* listener and I do not repeat what is said to me in confidence."

"I do owe you an explanation and I will give one, later."

Now Tobias sat in the park with Josie, hidden from the street by a big hedge and a mushrooming oak tree. The sky, so blue and perfect, didn't know of the turmoil in his heart. *Gott* had to know, but right now, the world seemed surreal and like a dream. Josie—his Josie—had a child. She was a mother, though she did not actually mother this child. So she was more of an aunt to Dinah?

"This is confusing," he finally said. "A lot to take in."

Josie sat with her hands clutched in her lap. "I have caused a lot of people so much heartache," she said. "I acted out because I was angry that Josiah had left me in that house. But I had no idea what that had cost him. He went to Ohio, seeking help from my *mamm*'s family. At first, they believed he had just run away and wanted to be free. But Josiah stayed Amish. Barely had a *rumspringa*. But they treated him, and later me, very badly. After the barn fire, he came back and took me with him, and for a while life was better. But they blamed us for not telling them about how cruel our *daed* had become."

Tobias tried to imagine what she'd been through. "So your *daed* was mean?"

"Ja," she said. Then she sat silent for a moment. "He would pick fights about anything. Our *mamm* shielded us from his wrath, but…he took it out on her. So many times." She looked up and to the east, where her old home was located. "I used to show up at the Bawells', making excuses. We needed sugar or flour or I fell and scratched my knee and I didn't want to wake my mom."

Tobias couldn't imagine a little girl living like that. "You were brave, Josie. You've always been brave."

She turned and stared over at him, her eyes brimming with pain and dark memories. "I am not so brave, Tobias. It is my fault that my parents died."

Tobias didn't think this day could get any worse. "What do you mean?"

She kept her gaze on him. "They were fighting out in the barn. My *mamm* went out there to tell him supper was ready. He wanted supper on the table at a certain time. I don't know what happened, but he became angry and started shouting at her." Josie took a long breath and clutched her hands tighter together. "I grabbed a lamp since it was getting dark and ran out to the barn, but when I saw him grabbing her, I tripped and dropped the lamp. The hay caught on fire and then my mother screamed for me to run. I stood and called for her. 'Mamm, Mamm!'"

Tobias took her hand. "Josie, you don't need to tell me."

"No, I do. I have to. No more secrets, Tobias. No more."

He held her hand, his eyes following the panic rising up in her like a dark cloud. "Josie—tell me, then."

"I called for her and she tried to run to me, but he held her there. He held her with fire all around them. I ran for help, but when I got back it was too late. Too late to save either of them."

Tobias pulled her close. "You never told me. I am so sorry."

"It is hard to see it all again. But in my mind, late at night, I see it and then I dream that horrible dream of hearing my own screams, of watching that fire surround my mother." She sobbed against his shirt. "I ran to the Bawell house, and Mr. Bawell and his son went over to help. But it was too late. I stayed there until Josiah could come and get me."

Tobias held her, his heart beating along with hers. "You have suffered enough, Josie. Enough."

She pulled away and wiped her eyes. "Now you know my secrets. Josiah didn't even know about me dropping the lamp. I came home after Josiah found me in the hospital, but I couldn't take being back in Campton Creek and seeing Dinah being raised by someone else. I tried to take Dinah and run again, but I wound up hiding upstairs at the old place. Josiah found me and that's when I told him the truth. I blamed myself for the deaths of my parents."

"But he did not send you away. He understands it was not your fault."

"He got me help," she said. "Judy Campton helped me understand that I cannot carry that blame for the rest of my life. But after Drew, my blame and the shame of what he'd done to me almost did me in forever."

She touched a hand to Tobias's jaw. "I stare at that house every evening when I'm sitting on the side porch. Stare and remember things I've tried to forget. And one night a few weeks ago, I thought I saw you standing there on the porch and now I know it was you."

Tobias could see how that had caused her to have a setback of massive proportions. "That is part of why you don't want me living next door. That and... Dinah. You knew I'd see Drew in her features."

"I did not want you living there because I did not want you to know all of the awful things I've done."

"Things that were done to you, Josie. People who were cruel to you. How can I blame you for that?"

She dropped her hand. "But you do blame me for not being honest with you, don't you?"

Tobias couldn't deny that. "It's not blame. It's regret. Regret that you could not trust me enough to tell me what had happened. We could have worked through this together, for our purpose, for *Gott*'s purpose."

A blush moved over her face. "Could have? But not now. Now it's over for us, isn't it, Tobias?"

Tobias couldn't answer that question. "I have much to think about, Josie," he admitted. "I came here with *one* purpose, to find you and hear what had happened."

Her eyelashes fluttered as she blinked away tears. "And now that you've accomplished that?"

Tobias stood and paced underneath the sheltering oak. "Now I want to buy that house and...be near you. That is what I want right now."

Josie stood and gazed into his eyes. "I won't stop you buying the house if that is truly what you want. Why you'd want to stay after all of this, I cannot understand."

"I'm staying because I have no one waiting for me back in Kentucky, and I have nowhere else to go."

"I hope you won't regret that."

The disappointment and despair in her eyes ripped through his heart. "I regret that I wasn't able to protect you. I will be here, waiting, whenever you feel that you can trust me and love me again."

"What if that never happens, Tobias? I am damaged, scared, afraid to leave the house most days. I don't know how I could be a wife to any man."

"Then I will still be near you. And that has to count for something, ain't so?"

Josie bobbed her head and didn't speak.

"I will take you home now," he said. "You must be tired."

"I am," she said. "And I want to talk to Josiah and Raesha. They cannot lose Dinah. None of us want to lose Dinah."

Tobias could see that Josie loved the little girl.

But that would always be between them. The reminder of the boy he'd considered a friend doing such a vile thing to the woman Tobias loved.

They might not ever get past that, but with *Gott*'s grace, Tobias planned to try.

Exhaustion tugged at Josie as she went to open the back door to the main house. Knowing her family would be waiting for her, she almost turned to go back to the *grossmammi haus*. The old Josie would have done that, but today she'd become a new person. A person who'd been through the worst and was still standing. Tobias knew all of her secrets, and he'd seen all of her flaws. Maybe he'd decide he needed to move on.

She'd stood up to Drew's parents, the people who'd scorned her and accused her of only wanting their son's prestige and money. Now they'd been forced to see him for what he was, the same way she'd seen him from the first time she'd met him.

She'd never dreamed his ways would ruin her life with such terrible destruction. But now she had family to protect her. Maybe she'd be able to forgive him and let her faith carry her through. Stopping, her hand on the doorknob, she couldn't help looking over toward the old place. When she saw a horse and buggy in the winding drive, she knew Tobias was there. He walked up onto the porch.

And waved at her.

So close she could run over there and hold him in her arms.

So far away she couldn't touch that place inside his heart that she had pierced and shattered with her fears and deceit.

"I will find a way to win you back," she whispered, thinking she'd been foolish to fight this. "No matter what."

Then she went inside to face her family.

They were waiting, a plate of uneaten sandwiches on the table, a pitcher of fresh lemonade on the sideboard.

"I'm not hungry," Josie said.

"Neither are we," Naomi replied. "Your brother told us what happened in town. How are you dealing with this, Josie?"

Josie poured some lemonade into a glass, her hands

trembling. "I've had to relive all of the worst times of my life, so I'm not great."

She sank down on the high-backed chair next to Josiah. He hadn't spoken a word to her. "I am so sorry that I brought this on all of you."

Naomi held up a finger. "You did not bring anything on anyone. You were betrayed and wronged, your life ruined. Maybe you didn't make wise choices, but *Gott* always knows the outcome. He brought you home, Josie. Home, where you need to be."

Josiah nodded, his dark eyes full of pain. "He also brought Dinah to us and, now, Tobias. This is something we should consider."

Josie glanced at their faces. "You have been discussing this, *ja*?"

Raesha glanced at her husband. "We have enough to worry about right now. These people could take Dinah away."

Naomi shot Josie a warning glance. "We will not fret about that. She belongs here with us and we will pray on that."

"Isn't that what you've been discussing?" Josie asked, confused and weary. "I don't want Dinah to go away. You all must know that."

"We do," Raesha replied. "We all love her."

Josiah stood up. "I talked to Tobias briefly after he dropped you off earlier. He still wants to buy the house, Josie. How do you feel about that?"

"We talked about it," she said, "and I told him I would not stop him. But he has accepted that he and I can never be more than friends."

"Accepted?" Naomi looked skeptical.

Josie set down the half-finished glass of lemonade,

the syrupy, honeyed sweetness of the drink making her feel ill. "I think I've lost Tobias. I knew this would happen and now it has. I should be glad that he finally sees me for what I am. He might still want the house, *bruder*. But he does not want me anymore."

He wanted this house and he wanted Josie here with him. Hopeful after he'd talked to Josiah in the driveway of the Bawell property, half an hour later Tobias found himself at the Fisher house and wondered if he truly still wanted the same things he'd come here to find.

A home to call his own? Yes, he still wanted that.

A family of his own? No doubt about that.

Josie?

He'd stopped there on the porch when he caught a movement on the breezeway across from the footbridge.

Josie, headed to the main house. How did his heart always sense her presence before his head caught up?

She stopped and stood so still she could have been a dream only.

But she was real and she had been through the kind of trauma that most did not return from.

Gott's will, he reminded himself.

In an instant, she had gone inside. Tobias stood there in the sweet wind and wished he could go back in time and change all the things that had brought him here.

But he couldn't erase becoming Drew's friend or falling in love with Josephine Fisher. And he couldn't erase the awful consequences of talking her into going to that fancy Christmas party when she had not wanted to do so.

He had caused this turn of events, maybe because

he had turned away from his faith in the blink of an eye and, just like that, bad things had begun to happen.

Gott's will or his own selfish pride?

Tobias watched the Bawell house, the afternoon sun radiating through the trees like a beacon, the hot wind moving over his skin while he remembered that chilly winter when he'd lost the woman he loved.

When he saw Josie running out of the main house, her head down, his first instinct was to go to her and comfort her.

But he held back, remembering the revelations this day had brought. Did she blame him for everything that had transpired since the last time he'd seen her? Was that why she'd told him to leave when she'd found him here in the house?

Tobias watched as she went straight into the *gross-mammi haus*, and then he reluctantly got back into Abram's buggy and headed toward town. By the time he got back, the day would be almost done. And he might be out of a job.

Defeated, Tobias had a feeling he'd be moving on soon enough anyway. He couldn't make Josie love him if she could never forgive him for taking her to that party. If her family lost little Dinah, none of them would ever get over it.

Chapter Fifteen

❧

"So now you know the whole story."

Tobias waited for Beth's and Abram's reactions as they both sat quietly in their favorite chairs, Beth knitting and Abram tugging at his beard.

Tobias sat across from them, wondering how he'd managed to mess things up so badly. He should have stayed in Kentucky, unknowing and lonely. That which he'd believed to be hurt could not compare to the jagged, sharp pain of despair he now held in his heart. The blame of his part in Josie's tragedy held him like a prison, causing him to stare at a piece of wood for ten minutes and then not be able to create anything out of it.

What right did he have to create anything meaningful in this world? He'd failed the woman he planned to have a life with. He should have protected her and kept her safe.

Beth put down her knitting and glanced at her husband. "Are you going to speak or should I?"

Abram's eyebrows formed a V over his nose. "What would you have me say?"

Tobias braced himself. Was he about to be kicked out of their home and be out of a job again?

Beth made a clucking noise. "Tobias, we had heard things about the babe that was found on the Bawell porch and how Josie came to be here. But the *blabbermauls* soon quieted down once Josie confessed all and asked for forgiveness. Forgiveness that she didn't actually need since this happened against her will. But she wanted a fresh start, and so she confessed to taking a wayward path. We refused to spread any rumors since she has returned to the fold and she seems to be putting her life back together." Beth worked her knitting needles. "Dinah is a beautiful little girl."

Tobias saw the sincerity in Beth's gray eyes. *"Denke,"* he said. "Josie has been shamed enough. She has been hiding away at the Bawell place, and then I showed up and scared her back into hiding even more." Shrugging, he dropped his head. "She'd finally begun to attend gatherings more, but this latest might set her back. I feel like I'm to blame for that."

He wanted to add he was to blame for all of Josie's troubles.

"You came for all the right reasons," Abram pointed out. "Everything has brought you to this moment. So don't go blaming yourself for anything."

Tobias shook his head, wondering if Abram could see his guilt. *"Ja,* but look at me. I'm a for-sure mess and I messed up things for Josie when I made her mingle in the *Englisch* world."

"Josie has a mind of her own," Beth said. "She didn't have to go to that party."

"She is strong now, but back then she was searching for something, and she was innocent and naive. I tried to change her and I made a big mistake. We would be married today if I had not tried so hard to blend in with the *Englisch*."

Abram removed his reading glasses. "I believe you have both learned a hard lesson, but you are also both more mature now."

Tobias tried not to let his frustrations show, but he must have made a horrible frown. Beth sent her husband a worried glance. "State your point, Abram."

Abram took his time while seconds ticked by. "Josie is here and single. You are here and single. I'd say *Gott* worked to bring you both together again, because now you're both done with running-around time, and you are mature and wise beyond your years."

"Wise but not together, Abram. I doubt we will ever be together again."

Abram shook his head. "You are together—you are both together here. If you buy the Fisher place, you'll be almost as together as two people can be."

"But not really together," Beth cautioned, "although I do see your point, husband."

Tobias stood and shook his head. "I'm confused."

Beth gave him a sympathetic glance. "Life is confusing at times, but you have everything you want right here. Do not waste any more time filled with regrets and doubts, Tobias. Fight the good fight. Make Josie love you again, despite the guilt you both carry. Why come all this way just to give up now?"

"*Ja*, that is what I was trying to say," Abram agreed, proud of himself. "You two belong together."

Tobias went to his room and thought about how Beth and Abram had taken him in and fed him. They'd also nurtured that empty spot in his soul. He could never repay them, but he thanked *Gott* he'd found them.

Keeping thanking Gott.

The voice in his head told him he might be moving in the right direction even if everything felt wrong. How could he be sure? He wondered if the Beningtons would make trouble for them. Tobias didn't see any way out of that.

Chalking up Beth's and Abram's determined suggestions as just wishful thinking, he decided he'd bide his time and see what happened next. Josie would have to make the next move, but with all of this going on, he was afraid she'd shut down again. She had shut him out completely and now he understood why.

Her memories of their time together were tangled up with the pain of how her life had turned out. How could they ever find their way back to each other?

Two days had passed and no one had heard a word from the Beningtons. Josie wanted to take a breath of relief, but she feared this was the quiet before the storm.

She wondered about Tobias. She had not talked to him since that awful morning in the sunroom. Should she reach out to him?

No. He knew the truth now. She'd seen the doubt and disappointment on his face. He wouldn't be able to get past this and forgive her since she'd left him without an explanation.

And refused to tell him the truth until she'd been forced.

Josie stood on the breezeway and studied the dark clouds on the horizon, but she had to go to the main house and help Raesha with food and cleaning.

Raesha had already planned a quilt frolic this afternoon, and Josie felt she should be there since they'd already invited everyone. No one here felt like quilting, but Naomi had told them they could not cancel it since they'd planned it weeks ago.

"It will take our minds off the things we cannot change nor predict," Naomi had announced, making it hard for Raesha and Josie to sit idle. "We must continue on and set people straight if they bring it up."

Someone would manage to ask pointed questions. Josie only had one question. She wondered if Drew's parents were still in Campton Creek. They'd been insistent about seeing Dinah.

But when she'd voiced her worries last night at dinner, her brother had frowned and left the house.

Naomi told her Josiah acted as most men did in times of trouble. He took refuge out in the fields and in the barn. But Josie had to wonder if her brother was tired of the drama and scandal she'd brought into his life.

Josiah used to tell Josie that because of her he'd found the woman meant to be his wife. Why had something so wonderful *gut* had to happen because of something so horribly wrong?

She couldn't get anyone to talk to her about this, so they all went about their lives as usual.

The frolic was still on, and while they worried they also worked. That was how things were done around here. And on days when they had quilting frolics, Raesha left the hat shop early and her assistants took over.

Josie enjoyed the timeless art of stitching patterns and colors into something tangible and useful. She could see life in their handmade quilts, all patterns and squares and bright colors, coming together to form something beautiful.

Gott's work in every stitch. That was what Naomi always said. And although Mammi's eyes couldn't see to stitch, she sat with them when they did and regaled them with her wisdom and wit. She always encouraged when someone messed up a stitch.

"It doesn't have to be perfect," she'd say. "We are not perfect. Only *Gott* is."

Perfection. Josie had always dreamed of the perfect family, the perfect home with perfect children.

Naomi was right. There was no such thing.

Life didn't need to be all wonderful to be life, she decided. She'd been forgiven by her community and by *Gott*. What more did she need?

She wanted Tobias to forgive her for not turning to him.

Josie needed the distraction of stitching and laughing, that was what she needed. She had not been sleeping well, and each time she finally fell asleep, she had dreams of someone ripping Dinah out of her arms.

That nightmare could come true at any time now if the Beningtons found a way around the law.

Tobias held the chisel against the wood, determined to make another leg so the stool he had in mind would be balanced and precise. The tall, heavy stool wouldn't stand on just three legs, after all. He'd measured and shaped, using an air compressor to run the band saw. After making the cut, he'd started gouging the line into the wood so he could form a tenon to meet the mortise. The tenon and mortise would hold the corner of the stool's seat to all four legs. He'd take an awl to mark and make the spot where he'd add the special glue Abram used to secure the tenon joints.

This particular stool—called an Amish folding step stool—would serve well in any kitchen. He could almost picture an Amish woman sitting on the high stool, peeling potatoes or snapping beans and then turning to use it as a stepladder by pulling out the small retractable steps hinged underneath the seat. This one was made from solid oak that would be sanded and varnished to a dark burnished golden-brown sheen.

Josie came to mind, as she did most of the day and night. Why couldn't he let her go?

Maybe because he'd traveled hundreds of miles to find her, and now that he had he was too stubborn to give up? Most men would have by now, and especially after all the things he'd heard during the last few days.

Two days since his world had crumbled with each new revelation. Two days ago, he'd only wanted to love Josie and know why she'd left him.

Now he knew the truth and it stuck in his throat like a brittle bone. What she'd been through no woman should have to endure. Tobias didn't know how to get around everything that now stood between them. So he kept whittling and shaving, using the wood to keep his thoughts centered and precise.

"Do not gouge that leg to the bone, Tobias," Abram cautioned as he hurried by carrying a two-by-four cut from pine. "Else that stool will look kind of funny and tilt to the left a bit too much."

Tobias stopped and stared at the wood he had braced on the saw table. "You stopped me just in time."

"You were not focusing on the carving," Abram replied, his tone soft. "But once you get it together, that will be a mighty fine step stool that anyone should be proud to have in their kitchen."

Why did he get the feeling Abram wasn't just encouraging him about his talent? The man wanted what was best for Tobias and he would forever be grateful for that.

But he'd need a lot of tools to figure out the next step in his life. He loved Josie. That would never change. But could they work things out between them? A marriage shouldn't start this way—with sad, tragic memories hovering between the bride and groom.

How could he fix this?

In a million little ways.

That was what Jewel, Judy and Bettye had suggested. He didn't have much time left to win over Josie. The house was waiting, but would she ever want to live there again? Would it be fair to her to make her live in a house that had brought her only fear and pain and nightmare memories?

He had to put this out of his mind for now.

Tobias worked on the stool the rest of the afternoon. The work did help his mind to settle. Maybe he'd carve some more trinkets. Those had sold well at the festival and now Abram had made a shelf in the showroom for what he called Tobias's toys.

"I could use more carved horses and maybe a couple buggies," he'd told Tobias this morning. "The flowers and wooden dolls go over well with the women, of course." Then he'd chuckled. "Your whittling fingers are going to be tired, for sure."

Tired would be good to Tobias. Maybe he'd sleep so deeply he wouldn't dream of things he could not have.

He and Abram were closing up for the day, the other workers waving as they left for home, some on foot and some picked up by cars or buggies. Tobias always stayed back to help since he rode home with Abram every day anyway.

When they heard the front doorbell jingle, Tobias turned from tallying receipts to find Jewel hurrying toward him, her eyes bright.

"Oh, good, you're still here," she said, eyeing Tobias.

"Jewel, what's wrong?"

"The Beningtons, that's what's wrong," Jewel said under her breath.

"It's all right," Tobias said. "Abram knows all about what is going on."

Abram nodded. "*Ja*, I do, but I'll give you two some privacy."

He shuffled toward the workroom.

Jewel stared over at Tobias. "They want to see Dinah. They've talked to a local lawyer and one back home. That's all I know. We need to get word to the Bawells and Josie."

"When do they want to meet Dinah?"

"This weekend," Jewel said. "Can you let them know? I tried to call the hat shop, but her assistant said she had taken the afternoon off. I didn't want to send this in a message from someone else."

Tobias glanced back to the workroom. "I usually ride home with Abram."

"I can drive you to the Bawell place," Jewel said. "And give you a ride back to Abram's house after."

"That is kind, but you might have to wait."

"I can do that. We're done for the day, and the ladies can handle being upstairs alone without me for a little while. I'll alert one of our on-call volunteers, too.

Alisha Braxton might not mind coming to sit with her grandmother."

Tobias agreed and went to report to Abram. "I will be home soon. Don't wait supper."

"Beth will leave you a plate on the stove," Abram said. "I hope things get worked out for all of you, Tobias."

"I pray so," Tobias said.

Somehow, he'd become the go-between with the Beningtons and the Bawells. While this made him uncomfortable, how could he refuse?

Josie would need him if…if the couple took little Dinah away.

When he saw Jewel's economy car pulling up outside the furniture market, he waved to Abram. Then he hurried out and hopped inside the automobile.

"Let's go," he told Jewel.

His friend didn't waste time pulling out onto the street.

Chapter Sixteen

The ladies were leaving for the day. Chattering and hugging each other, they gathered onto buggies or headed out on foot, waving as they left the Bawell property.

Josie let out a sigh. "I'm glad everyone came, but it's hard to keep smiling and stitching when I can't focus."

Raesha nodded, unable to speak for a moment. "I was determined to keep going on with life but, honestly, the hours seemed to drag by."

"You two need to be thankful that your friends didn't ask nosy questions," Naomi retorted. "They were kind and willing to ignore the tension we all feel. If they have heard anything, they had the *gut* sense and sweet grace to remain silent on things."

"You're right, of course," Raesha replied as she busied herself with a quick supper of sliced ham and fresh vegetables from the garden. "Josiah will be home soon and I don't want to burden him with all this worry."

Josie figured her brother had burdened himself all day, worrying about what might happen next. He'd barely talked to her over the last few days. He seemed to carry a lot of guilt, too. Or maybe he wished he'd never found her and brought her here.

Gott's will, she reminded herself. The Lord God had brought them this far. He'd see them through.

When they heard a loud knock at the front door a few minutes later, Raesha's gaze met Josie's, fear evident in the frown that marred her face.

"I'll get it," Josie said, to save Raesha from having to leave the food simmering on the stove.

She hurried to the door and opened it, thinking maybe someone forgot something from the frolic.

Tobias stood there, his eyes bright with the same shock she'd experienced all week. "Josie, I need to speak to all of you."

Josie's heart burned with fear and dread. "Drew's parents?"

He nodded, then glanced back at the car parked underneath the shade of a big oak. Jewel sat at the wheel, the windows down so she could have some air. She gave Josie a quick wave.

Dread in her soul, Josie nodded and said, "*Kumm* inside."

When Raesha saw him, she sank down onto a chair and put her hands to her face. Naomi wheeled her chair close. "*Wilkum*, Tobias. Would you like something to drink?"

"No, thank you, Naomi. Is Josiah nearby?"

They heard the back door opening. Josiah walked in. "I'm here. I saw Jewel's car out front."

"She gave me a ride," Tobias explained. "I have news from the Beningtons."

Josiah quickly washed up and then sat down beside

Raesha. She grabbed his hand like a lifeline. "What news, Tobias?"

"They are still here and they've talked to lawyers here and back in Kentucky. They want to see Dinah this weekend."

The room went silent. Josie looked up at Tobias. His gaze held hers and her world seemed to tilt. "This is my fault," she said. "I should have kept away. Dinah would be mine, free and clear. No one would have found her."

Tobias shook his head. "Drew had someone locate me, Josie. And they happened to find both of us." Giving her a regretful stare, he added, "I'm the one to blame."

"Stop that nonsense," Naomi said on a gentle admonishment. "*Gott* brought you both here for a reason. Dinah needed you, Josie, and she needs us. Tobias wanted to find you and he has. This is not over until *Gott*'s will shall prevail."

Raesha stood, her hands pressing against the heavy wood of the dining table. "Does *Gott* want us to suffer when we watch them take her away from us? They are strangers who had a horrible son. He's dying now, so they want a replacement for him."

Naomi looked surprised, but her expression filled with compassion. "They also want our forgiveness."

Josiah stood and took his wife into his arms. "It will be all right. I'll make it right, somehow."

Josie couldn't look away from Tobias. His discomfort bristled off every pore. He did not want to be here. Maybe he didn't want to be around her at all. She was damaged, ruined, a shame to her family and friends.

"You don't have to do this," she said to him. "You have no part in this. Tell the Beningtons they can speak to me directly if they want to see our Dinah."

Tobias looked shocked, his cheeks reddening as if she'd slapped him. "I do not mind, Josie. I know the truth now, and that is all I ever wanted."

Josie advanced, her frustrations boiling over. "Now you know, Tobias. Now you see what happens when I'm involved. I tried to hide this from everyone and I almost lost Dinah and myself. I was better, healing, growing. But Drew had to do one last deed to destroy me. He might say he's sorry, but he had to know what his parents coming here would do to all of us. Especially you. He wanted you to know and he wanted this to happen."

She froze, her hands going to her mouth. The hurt she saw in Tobias's eyes almost did her in. But she couldn't be the one to bring him comfort.

"Josie?" he said, his plea a whisper. "Listen to me, please."

"Neh," she replied, lifting a hand toward him. "I have to get out of here. I can't breathe. I can't go through this again."

She turned and ran out of the room, tears brimming over. She'd hurt him yet again, and that was the last thing she'd wanted to do.

She needed air, needed to calm the nerves that jangled like chains across her body.

Why did her shame always win out? Why couldn't she just forgive herself and fight for the child she had to admit she loved? The child she had come to love too late.

Tobias couldn't move. He stared at the door that had just slammed behind Josie. Then he looked at Naomi. "What should I do?"

Naomi sat silent for a moment. "You should go and

find her. Don't question her. Just stay with her, Tobias. She needs to know someone will stay with her."

He didn't question that.

He took off through the house and went out into the growing dusk, the sunset drenching the coming night in a rich burnished red streaked with shades of pink.

Where had she gone?

He looked toward the old place and saw a slight figure running across the footbridge. Tobias took off after her, thinking Jewel would be worried. But Jewel would understand.

He tore through the meadow, the scents of spring wafting out in sweet floral winds. The world looked etched in beauty and the woman running away from him seemed like someone in a dream.

His dream. His Josie, running from what she couldn't accept.

He had to make her see that this was not her fault. Back then, he had acted out and shown off, tried to impress her with his *Englisch* friends. And he had failed her.

How will I ever make her see?

He stopped to catch his breath and spotted her on the front porch of her old home. She seemed to always run back here when she was afraid.

Running back to the one place that had always scared her in the worst kind of way.

Josiah had found her at the Fisher place the last time she'd run away. She'd come and found Tobias at her old home when she'd first confronted him. Now she'd gone back to the house that stood like a constant reminder of her sins and her guilt. Did she think she was unworthy of running toward anyone or anything, that she had to come back to the place that tormented her to absolve herself?

Maybe if he stayed with her and sat silent, she'd see that he had enough forgiveness and strength to cover both of their sins.

With *Gott*'s grace and will, they had to find a way back to each other.

Josie sat huddled against the corner of the porch, her breathing shallower now. This had always been her safe spot on the bad days. She'd hide here and then scoot underneath the wide railings to run away into the yard and hide in the barn or inside her favorite cluster of trees and saplings.

Now she sat, her knees pulled up and her arms wrapped tightly against her legs, the memories that had hovered like vultures circling now, returning with a force that left her stunned and speechless.

When she heard footsteps on the old planks, the panic almost returned. But she knew the person coming to find her would not physically harm her.

No, he just held her heart captive in a sweet, torturous way that brought a piercing joy and a cruel, even more piercing pain.

Tobias came around the corner in a slow stroll and stopped when he spotted her there. Without saying a word, he sat down beside her. Without saying a word, he breathed along with her as the night settled over them like a warm cloak while the sun slipped away to be replaced with a thousand stars and a half-moon that shimmer like a beacon.

After a while, he reached out his hand and wiped at

her tears. Then he touched his hand to hers. He didn't force her to move or to let go of herself.

Tobias leaned against the wall, inches from her. His knees folded up like hers, his hand warm over hers. His fingers settled against her own in a way that offered protection and peace and a safe place.

Josie sat still and quiet, her tears a silent stream of overflowing agony.

She ached to be held, to be touched, to be loved. Ached to hold Dinah again and to see her brother and Raesha smiling and laughing with their *kinder*.

The unbearable pain crested inside her, and when she thought she would drown in it, Tobias moved closer and gently pried her hands away, his fingers wrapping around hers in a soft, strong grip.

"Josie," he said. "Josie."

She let go and turned toward him, falling into his arms and holding tight as he surrounded her, his arms pulling her close, his broad shoulders offering her a place to lay her head, his presence covering her in such a safe comfort she thought she might die from the sheer beauty of it.

"It will be all right," he whispered. "I am here and I will not let anyone hurt you ever again."

Josie heard his promise, so she held to him with all her might, thinking this was the first time she'd felt safe since the night Drew had ruined her life.

She didn't speak. There was no need. Tobias provided the quiet comfort and security she remembered so well. She loved the scent of him—the smell of pine and cedar and soap. She loved the way his steady breath calmed her and settled her.

She loved this.

But she didn't know how long this could last.

So even though this felt right, Josie couldn't let go completely. Something else would come along and destroy her all over again. It always did, didn't it?

Tobias finally spoke again after a quiet silence. "I am so sorry, Josie. So sorry for what I caused."

She lifted up to stare at him. "Why would you be sorry?"

"It is my fault," he said. "I took you to Drew's house that night, and I wandered off and left you alone. He took advantage of that and he…took advantage of you in a way that can never be forgotten. Or forgiven."

He held her away, his eyes full of grief and regret.

"I understand why you didn't want me back in your life. I remind you of that night when I wasn't there to stop Drew. I understand why you can't love me anymore. I will respect that and leave you be, but I'm not going anywhere, Josie. I'll be right here waiting, if you can ever forgive me."

Then he stood and helped her up.

Shocked and confused, she shook her head. "Tobias, I—"

"*Neh*, don't explain. I get it now." He glanced over at the Bawell house. The lamps had been lit and shimmered through the windows, the glow of a family reaching out into the dark night.

"I should get you home. I'm sure Jewel is wondering what happened to me."

Josie couldn't speak. He thought she didn't want him because this was his fault? How wrong could a man be?

How could she show him differently when she'd pushed him away and ignored the truth and the lies between them? She'd also ignored what had been glaring at her the whole time. Tobias was a good man and she loved him. She'd fought so hard against loving him that she'd almost forgotten she was allowed to feel what her heart couldn't hide. Now it might be too late for them.

But this was Tobias. He'd absorb the blame to take the weight off of her even when he hadn't been to blame. He had been nearby and unaware that night, true. But that didn't make this his fault. Had she secretly been harboring blame for him because he'd stepped away from her?

Neh. Drew had made her believe Tobias was looking for her that night.

Tobias had had no way of knowing that.

And yet now he blamed himself.

Josie didn't argue with him. Instead, she said a silent prayer for guidance and help. And she promised herself she'd win him back and make him see that he had done nothing wrong.

Tobias had done everything right. Somehow she had to convince him of that. But with everything between them, she had no idea how she could possibly make him see reason.

Chapter Seventeen

When they got back to the house, Tobias found Jewel eating supper with Josiah, Raesha and Naomi. Dinah was sitting in Jewel's lap, tugging at the elaborate charms on Jewel's heavy necklace. Baby Daniel cooed from his high chair.

Jewel looked up with a smile when he guided Josie back through the door. Josie had remained quiet on the short walk back, so he took that to mean she'd accepted what he'd told her.

He took full blame and now he understood that she blamed him, too. Deep down inside, she had to feel that way or she would have disputed him. When he'd held her there on the porch, he'd hoped they had broken through to each other. But not yet, he feared.

Her unspoken anger shouted at him in a loud and clear message.

"Hi," Jewel said in her upbeat way. "Dinah and I are discussing jewelry. I told her that's how I got my name. My mama loved her jewels, so when she finally had a girl after four boys, that's what she named me. Clever, huh?"

Dinah giggled with glee as Jewel bounced her and tickled her. "I know you Amish gals don't wear jewelry, but I have to confess I have a thing for it."

Josie stood off to the side, a slight smile on her face. But her eyes were misty and burning with tears.

Tobias looked around. "I'm sorry. Jewel, we should go. You'll have to drive across town in the dark."

Jewel waved a hand in dismissal. "Nope. Not yet. Dinah and I are going into her room to read a book. She gets to pick which one. But you are to sit and eat and…talk."

Giving Tobias one of her mock-stern glares, she said, "Besides, I drove all over Chicago and Philly, young man. I think I can get you across the big bridge to Abram and Beth's place."

Raesha motioned to two chairs. "You need to eat and we need to finish talking."

Josie nodded and went to wash her hands. Tobias did the same. He didn't have much of an appetite, but at least he'd be in the same room with Josie.

That brought him some comfort.

After Jewel had made a production of taking Dinah away so they could have some privacy, Josiah let Raesha get Daniel settled in his crib while he sat and watched them nibble their ham and vegetables.

When Raesha came back and sat down, he leaned forward. "We will let Drew's parents see Dinah on Sunday afternoon, with Alisha present as our lawyer. But we will fight to the finish to keep her with us. Always."

Josie finally spoke. "I am her mother. I didn't give her up. I gave her to you to raise Amish so I could be close to her."

Tobias grew hopeful. "That should be enough to convince any judge since Drew refused to sign any papers."

"Unless that judge is friends with powerful people," Josiah pointed out. "But let's hope that nothing can change for Dinah. We adopted her, and from what Alisha tells us, if Drew refused to acknowledge the child, then his parents have no legal right to raise her."

"But what if he now wants to acknowledge her as his, before he dies?" Tobias asked.

"Would he do that?" Raesha's hope deflated as she put her elbows on the table. "For sure he wouldn't do that."

Naomi lifted her hand. "We can only be sure of one thing. That the Lord God will see us through, no matter."

Tobias wondered about that, but he knew he had to keep the faith. He prayed that this had been the plan all along, and he hoped the Lord would give them the outcome they so desired. Why should Dinah be snatched away from a family that obviously loved and provided for the child?

How could that happen, especially now that he and Josie had found each other again? Somehow they had to keep Dinah here.

Because if the child had to go away, Josie would never recover and he'd never have the opportunity to show her how much he loved her.

A little while later Jewel came out of the big bedroom on the main floor. "Dinah is fast asleep. I tell you, that is the sweetest child ever." When she saw their drooping expressions, she gently clapped her hands. "Now, we are not having any of this. You all know how this works—the Lord provides. God is good, all the time.

We pray without ceasing." Winking at Josie, she said, "Did I leave anything out?"

Josiah actually smiled. "Jewel, for sure you could quote the whole Bible, ain't so?"

"So very so," Jewel replied, grinning. "Now I thank you for the food and I'm gonna take Tobias home 'cause he looks pure bushed." Putting her hands on her ample hips, she added, "We got all day tomorrow to worry ourselves."

Tobias had to agree with the woman. They wouldn't stop worrying, but they had to bide their time.

He had to bide his time and hope *Gott*'s plan would also be the plan Tobias had himself. He wanted to marry Josie. But he had to start all over proving he was worthy of that.

She'd need someone to hold her if Dinah had to go away.

Josie sat with Katy on the breezeway steps that Sunday afternoon, her hands twisting the material of her apron. "I don't think I can do this."

Katy touched a hand to her arm. "That is why I'm here. To be with you when they arrive. Nothing to be afraid of. They only want to see their granddaughter. Maybe they'll visit and then leave."

Glad she had someone to confide in, Josie stared at the sunflower fence where tender buds were popping out of the ground. "Or maybe they'll be even more determined to take Dinah away from us."

"You have the law on your side," Katy reminded her. "The law and the Lord. All the fancy lawyers in the world can't change that."

"But Alisha says they could turn the tables, make

me look like a bad mother for abandoning my child."
She tugged at her bonnet strings. "I am a bad mother.
I am. I didn't love her enough to fight for her, but now
I'd do anything to keep her near me."

"You made a huge sacrifice, Josie. You let your
bruder and Raesha take her. It is for the best. You get
to watch her grow up, and maybe one day you can explain all of this."

Josie would never be able to explain to Dinah what
she'd done. "I will not break her heart," she whispered.
"I will keep her close and watch her and pray she has
the best life—a happy home, a *gut* husband, many children and people to love her."

"Just as you have now that you're home," Katy replied. "If you add Tobias to that, you could almost be
happy."

Almost happy. "Is that as close as I'll get?"

"If you let yourself, you could be completely happy,"
her friend said with a soft smile. "Stop fighting that."

Josie wiped at her eyes. "I want to tell Tobias that I
still love him, but now he is blaming himself for what
happened. He thinks he should have been there to protect me. I can't find the words to tell him that he is
wrong."

Katy shook her head, causing one of her golden curls
to fall across her face. "You two need to find a spot and
talk to each other, Josie. Honesty always wins out. Confession is good for that very reason."

Josie glanced over at the house where she'd sat with
Tobias the other night. "We can't seem to take the next
step. He was so kind to me the night we heard that
Drew's parents wanted to visit Dinah. He held me and
let me cry. He didn't ask a lot of questions."

"I give him high marks for that," Katy replied. "He is willing to forgive you. You have to forgive yourself."

"It is very hard," Josie admitted. "Maybe I should go for a walk while the Beningtons visit with Dinah."

"Be strong," Katy said. "Face them."

"When did you get so smart?" Josie asked, standing to stretch. The warmth of the sun shone brightly on her sunflower buds. Lifting her face, she reveled in the warmth of the afternoon. "I must go in."

"I'll take Daniel over to the *grossmammi haus*," Katy said. "If you need to leave, *kumm* and find us, *ja*?"

"I will." Josie gave her friend a quick hug. "*Denke*, Katy."

When they heard two vehicles moving up the long drive, Katy hurried to take Daniel. Josie followed, nerves making her breathing shallow. When she entered the living room, she was surprised to see Tobias coming in with Alisha.

He nodded to her and kept his gaze down. Josie could see the hurt and tension twisting his expression, the anxiety in the way he tugged at his suspenders. He stood with Alisha, waiting.

Then Theodore and Pamela Benington entered the house, causing Tobias to gaze at Josie, an unspoken message in his eyes.

Raesha pointed to the sofa while Josiah stood silent. "Please *kumm*."

"Thank you," Alisha said. Today she wore her hair up and had on a long floral skirt and a lightweight cotton blouse. Since her grandmother and her husband had both once been Amish, Alisha always respected the Amish ways. "We won't stay long."

Pamela looked uncomfortable. She sat straight up,

her summer sweater a dark navy that matched her plaid pants. She clutched a triple strand of pearls. "This is very difficult," she finally said, her voice low. "Where is Dinah?"

"I'll go and get her," Raesha said. "She should be up from her nap by now."

Theodore studied the sparse room, then let his gaze settle on Josie. "I'm sorry we didn't believe you the night you came to us for help. We should have listened and we could have easily had a paternity test done once the child was born. If you'd stayed."

Josiah held up a hand. "We agreed to let you see Dinah. I did not agree to let you remind my sister of what has transpired. No changing that now. This is where we are today. Dinah has to be our first consideration."

Alisha nodded, indicating she agreed. "So, Mr. and Mrs. Benington, you can visit with Dinah today. But Josiah and Raesha followed the Pennsylvania adoption laws to the letter. The Amish take in their own, so they didn't have to officially adopt Dinah, but they wanted the protection of abiding by the state law. Josie knew what she wanted for Dinah. She wanted her to be raised Amish."

Pamela looked around. "But why? We have so much more to offer her. She'd have everything she needs—a complete education, college later and a home that is comfortable and safe."

"Our home is comfortable and safe," Josiah replied, his tone soft. "And our scholars are educated. Dinah will be happy here. Happy and Amish, as her mother wants."

"You mean, the mother who gave her up," Theodore said, glaring at Josie.

Alisha shook her head. "That will not help the situation."

Tobias stood. "Stop this. I will not allow you to judge Josie when your son is the one to blame. Him and...me. I am to blame for not watching after her."

Raesha came back in with Dinah then, so he sat down. Josie glanced over at him and saw the anger and shame in his expression. His skin blushed a burning red and his eyes flashed fire. He looked up at her and held her gaze for a moment, anguish dark in his eyes before he looked away.

Raesha must have sensed the tension. She sat down beside Josiah and forced a cheery smile. "Here is our Dinah. She is a little over two years old now."

Dinah giggled and held up two fingers and made a sound. "Tuw."

"Yes, you are learning your numbers already," Raesha replied, her smile serene while she gave the couple sitting there a stern glare.

The Beningtons completely missed the pointed remark. They were captivated by Dinah. As they glanced from her to each other, Josie saw the pain and joy merging on their startled faces. Dinah smiled at them, her dimples running deep, her blue-green eyes wide and full of innocence.

Josie wanted to run, but Tobias somehow managed to move closer to her, finding a chair to pull up beside her. She could almost feel the heat radiating from the rage she saw in his eyes. Who was he angry with? The Beningtons and Drew? Himself? Or her?

She supposed all of the above.

Chapter Eighteen

Dinah took over, pushing out of Raesha's lap to be let down. She toddled here and there, her curious gaze moving over everyone in the room. She had their rapt attention, so she took her time staring at each of them and making adorable faces, jabbering away before rushing up to Josie, her little arms reaching. "JoJo, take."

Josie inhaled a shaky breath and lifted the child up. "Hello, you," she managed to mumble. Touching a hand to Dinah's soft chestnut curls, she sat silent, too overcome to speak.

Tobias poked at Dinah's tummy, causing her to laugh and squirm. Then he reached inside his pocket and brought out a little wooden toy—a small birdhouse with a tiny bird perched in the opening. "Here you go," he said, his voice soft now.

Josie smiled at the carved birdhouse, her heart blossoming with thankfulness. It was big enough that Dinah couldn't put any small parts in her mouth, and it looked as if he'd carved it from one piece of wood.

"That's very kind of you," she said to Tobias.

Dinah laughed and held up her prize. "Birdie."

Josiah looked as if he might burst into tears. Raesha wiped at her eyes. Naomi rolled her chair up close, her quiet strength filling the room. "Dinah, what have you? *Kumm* and show Mammi."

Dinah pushed off Josie's lap, her light green dress billowing out around her chubby legs while her bare feet hit the floor. Her light *kapp* barely contained her thick curls, but she hurried toward where Naomi had stopped her chair near Theodore and Pamela.

That put Dinah between Naomi and the couple. Naomi lifted her arm and turned Dinah around. "Dinah, this is Theodore and Pamela. They came to visit you. Why don't you show them the gift Tobias brought to you?"

Dinah giggled and pointed to where Tobias sat near Josie. "ToTo and JoJo."

Everyone laughed at that. "You are so smart," Naomi said, smiling at the *kinder*. "'ToTo and JoJo' has a nice ring, ain't so?"

Dinah bobbed her head, her curls bouncing.

Tobias gave Josie a quick glance and looked down at his hands. Josie thought that did have a nice ring, but would it ever happen?

Pamela wiped at her eyes. "Dinah, hi. I'm…so glad to meet you. I'm Pamela. Pam."

Dinah offered her prize to Pamela to look at, then twisted around, her bare feet pressed together on the wooden floor while she turned shy.

"That's so pretty," Pamela said, glancing at Tobias before she handed the carving back to Dinah. "Did you carve this?"

"Ja," he said, looking sheepish.

Pamela's smile was bittersweet. "I still have the little car you carved for Drew. He kept it on a shelf in his bedroom."

Tobias only nodded and then shot Josie an apologetic glimpse. He was caught between the friend he'd once had and the woman who'd left him. Her heart couldn't deny empathy for him.

Theodore cleared his throat. "She looks like—"

He stopped and rubbed a hand down his face. "This is harder than I thought it would be." Glancing toward his wife, he said in a low voice, "So like him."

Pamela could only nod. "So precious and beautiful." She sniffed and touched a hand to Dinah's curls. "I can't thank you enough for letting us visit. I understand now how you must feel, thinking we'd…do anything to upset her." Leaning down, she reached out her hands. "Dinah, would you like to sit in my lap?"

Dinah glanced at Josiah and Raesha, as if unsure.

Josiah swallowed and sighed. "It's all right, *bobbeli*. Go ahead and sit with the nice lady."

Raesha stood. "I have iced tea and cinnamon crumb cake. I'll get it ready."

Glad for something to do, Alisha did the same. "I'll pass out the tea."

"I'll help," Josie offered, but Tobias tugged at her arm, shaking his head slightly. "I'll do it."

She didn't argue with him or Alisha. He might need to move about to purge some of his anger and regret. He was usually calm when she was a mess, but today he had jumped to her defense, his own emotions spilling over.

In spite of her flaws, Tobias saw her heart. Josie could keep that realization close, at least.

She saw his heart, too, in the little carving he'd made for Dinah. The child was at no fault. Tobias knew that and accepted Dinah the way they all had. The way she now did. Had she accepted the child too late to keep her close?

Tobias had stayed close to Josie once he'd found her again. Was that how *Gott* did it? Did He remain close even when someone couldn't accept His love? Josie wished she'd been more devout in knowing the Lord watched out for His lost sheep. She could see that now. Tobias was a strong example of such a stance.

Tobias would always be the kind of man who put *Gott* and his faith first. Who looked after others with an unyielding sacrifice and stood up for what was right. She didn't deserve him and yet he was here, and he was standing by her and the child who had come between them. That same child who now held a room full of tense, worried people in the palm of her little hand.

Why had Josie held back from truly loving her daughter? She had always loved Dinah, and she'd resented her, too. Josie had brought Dinah here out of sheer desperation and she'd returned here for the same reason—they had nowhere else to go.

Glancing around while Dinah made these sad people smile and laugh, Josie remembered Katy's words about being almost happy.

She could be completely happy if she only looked at the blessings here right in front of her.

Now she had to show Tobias he could do the same. Could they be happy here together again? No matter what?

Tobias helped Raesha serve the tea and cake while Dinah made everyone laugh with her toddler antics. She chirped like a bird, galloped like a horse and lifted her arms like a butterfly. All the noise woke Daniel, and now he was laughing and crawling behind her. Dinah had never been a fussy baby unless she was sick, but today she seemed to have picked up on the stress in the adults and had decided she'd make them feel better.

Smart child. It had worked to break the ice that gripped all of them.

After about an hour where Dinah moved from lap to lap, Alisha came up to where Josie stood by the kitchen sink. Placing her empty glass down, she turned to Josie. "Josie, you've handled yourself well today. I can only imagine how hard this has been for you."

Josie kept washing dishes, her gaze on the green fields and valleys beyond the house. "I've been through a lot, but I know this is where I belong now."

"And what about Tobias?"

Josie looked at her *Englisch* friend. Alisha had almost gotten killed over a year ago at Christmas. But Nathan had helped save her and they'd found each other again after many years apart.

Instead of answering the question, she asked one of her own. "Are you and Nathan happy now that you're back in Campton Creek and married?" she asked, curious.

Alisha's soft smile said it all. "Yes, we are. We're going to build a new house not far from our cabin, and we already have our offices set up around the corner from Campton House."

Shrugging, she said, "I never dreamed I would come back here to practice law. But Nathan loves his work, and now I love mine even more. We like the simple life here." She touched her stomach. "And…we're expanding."

"Expanding?" Confused, Josie looked down and then back at Alisha. "You're *ime familye weg*? Pregnant?"

Alisha bobbed her head, her eyes misting. "Only Nathan and a few other people know, but I'm telling you to give you hope, Josie. Nathan and I found each other again, against all the odds." She glanced at where Tobias was playing on the floor with Daniel and Dinah. "I hope you and Tobias can do the same."

Josie gave Alisha a quick hug and turned to watch Tobias with the *kinder*. "He would be a *gut daed*."

"And you are a good mother," Alisha said. "Now, I need to get them back. They're leaving tonight to go back to Drew. He's toward the last days now."

Josie thought she should feel something for Drew, some sympathy or regret. But she only felt pity for the man who had abused several young girls like her. Her only prayer for now was that his parents wouldn't take Dinah from them.

Walking over to where the Beningtons walked toward the door with Josiah and Raesha, Josie stood next to Tobias, who now held Dinah in his arms. He saw Josie and gave her a soft smile.

"Thank you again," Pamela said, her expression more serene now. "We have to get back to our son. I know the Amish don't allow for pictures, but—"

Alisha looked at Josie and then at Raesha. "Drew would like to see a picture of her."

Josie gulped in air, wishing she could make them all go away, but Tobias took her hand, grounding her.

Josiah glanced at Raesha and then Naomi. Naomi nodded. "We all have little treasures that carry us through the day. I believe one picture should be allowed."

Alisha turned to the Beningtons. "This is not to be

shared with anyone except Drew. I know you'll respect that because we all want to protect Dinah's privacy."

"We will," Theodore said, his tone humble now. "We will cherish a picture of Dinah forever."

Josie felt hope stirring in her soul. That statement sounded so final and full of resolve. Had they seen that this was the right place for Dinah?

Raesha sat Dinah in her little rocking chair and chatted with her, out of the way of the phone camera, while Alisha took two quick pictures with Pamela's phone and then handed it back.

Pamela pulled up the pictures. "Perfect." She turned to Josie. "I know you don't think Drew is sorry, but he is and he really did send us here. He wants you and Tobias to be happy." She looked at the picture of Dinah. "And this will make him happy."

Tobias never let go of Josie's hand, even when she wanted to scream and wail in pain for her child and her family. She didn't do that and she didn't run away.

Instead, she straightened her spine and said, "Dinah is dear to all of us. We love her. I hope you will consider that when you talk to Drew."

Alisha gave the Beningtons a moment to speak. When they said nothing, she glanced at Josiah and Raesha. "I'll be in touch."

Pamela turned one last time. "Thank you again for letting us see Dinah." She touched a hand to Dinah's. "You are precious."

Dinah grinned and then dropped her head against Josiah's shirt. Obviously, the child was tired. Josie rushed to take her.

"I'll get her tidied up."

Josie and Tobias held back with Naomi and Dinah

when the others walked outside. After they were alone with Mammi, and Dinah was down on the floor with Daniel again, Josie put a hand to her mouth and turned to Tobias. He tugged her into his arms.

"I've got you. Always," he said, his arms holding her close. "I've got you."

Dinah looked up from her toys and pointed. "ToTo and JoJo. *Ja.*"

"Ja," Naomi echoed, clapping her hands. "You are a wise one, my little Dinah."

Tobias helped Josie finish up, and together they got Daniel and Dinah washed up and ready for dinner. Dinah was a sweet child with an open heart. Daniel gurgled and cooed, his smile as bright as his *mamm*'s. Tobias wondered what it would be like to hold a child of his own. A bitterness grabbed at his chest. Drew had forced himself on Josie. She'd had a child—without Tobias.

Because Tobias had been too addled to see the truth in front of him. Drew was no friend of his.

When Tobias caught Josie watching him while he admired the *kinder*, he straightened up and mentally shook himself. He shouldn't be daydreaming about children, and he had to let go of the piercing bitterness that clouded his vision.

"I should go," he said, glancing at the sun. "It will be dark soon."

Naomi heard him. "Tobias, why don't you stay for supper? You've been so kind in helping us through this. Surely we can feed you."

Tobias couldn't be sure how to answer, so he deferred to Josie. Telling himself he should get out of here, he heard the words come out of his mouth. "Would you mind?"

Josie sent Naomi a firm glance. But she turned back to him. "You are *wilkum* to stay, of course. We're having sandwiches and potato salad. Not much, but none of us has much of an appetite anyway."

Tobias had been too nervous to eat much at breakfast and his stomach was protesting. "Sounds like a feast to me."

Josiah and Raesha came back inside. "That was difficult," her brother said, running a hand down his beard. "Josie, how are you holding up?"

Josie glanced at her brother. Dark circles lined his eyes and he looked as exhausted as she felt. "I'm all right, *bruder*. I made it through, at least."

Raesha sank down on a chair. "I'll get the sandwiches out after I catch my breath. That was the hardest two hours I've ever sat through."

"We all need a little rest," Naomi said. "What do you think, Josiah? Did we convince them to leave Dinah be?"

Josiah shook his head. "I do not know. I pray so." He glanced about and said, "I'm going to check on the animals and close up the barn for the night."

He walked out before anyone could comment. Raesha sent Naomi a concerned frown, her eyes full of torment. "I don't like seeing him in this way. What should I do?"

Naomi adjusted her chair. "Let him go. Men tend to hold things inside, but he knows you will listen when he needs you."

She gave Tobias a pointed nod. "Tobias, what about you?"

Surprised, Tobias blushed under that matronly scrutiny. "I am here because...because I hold the guilt for all of this."

He couldn't finish. He turned and went out the door, too. But instead of heading to the barn, Tobias took off toward the footbridge and then stalked to the Fisher house.

Naomi was right. Men did hold things inside, and right now he was about to explode with anger and grief for what might have been. He didn't know if he had the heart to get past any of this.

Chapter Nineteen

Josie didn't stop to think. She dropped what she'd been about to do and took off after Tobias. Knowing where he'd probably gone, she squinted in the late-afternoon sun and saw a lone figure over on the porch of the Fisher house.

Why did he always go back to that place?

Why had she been doing the same lately?

Were their memories so tied up in tangles that they both needed to go to that house for different reasons?

She made her way slowly through the tall grasses and skinny saplings that lined the old arched bridge. People around here loved bridges of all sizes and shapes. The solid structures brought everyone together and made winters lovely and summers pleasant. This small one had worked to bring her and Tobias together several times.

Was God leading her toward the path home?

Tobias lifted his head when he heard her coming, though he didn't wave or invite her up onto the porch. Well, it wasn't his house now, was it?

"Tobias," she said, her sneakers hitting the old planked porch floor. He barely looked around.

Josie decided she'd had enough of missing out on her dreams. She'd win him back, completely. Somehow. It wasn't lost on her that she'd fought him with every fiber of her being, and even still she didn't feel worthy of him. But her heart skipped right over those important details. Having him near today had helped her through dealing with Drew's parents.

But, right now, Tobias didn't want to hear her words of encouragement and appreciation.

So she didn't speak again. She scooted up beside him and stood staring out at the view. This was the best spot on the property to see the fields and valleys and the bridges that took people back and forth to Campton Creek.

Crops waved green and shiny new across the fields. The clean lines of earth formed a sweet symmetry that lifted and shifted over the valley, the highs and the lows merging against the golden shots of sunshine. Off in the distance, wildflowers popped here and there, lending color amid the fresh green and the brown earth.

"This is a beautiful spot," Tobias finally said. "I'd planned to talk to Josiah again about buying it, but now I don't know. Maybe it is a bad idea, considering."

She didn't speak for a moment. She had to adjust her mindset with the image of him previously wanting to live here and now suddenly wondering if he shouldn't.

Her heart burning, she asked, "Have you changed your mind, then? Because of all that you now know about me?"

He turned to her, his eyes going dark with understanding. "Josie, no, no. I didn't mean because of you.

You are not at fault. I feel responsible for what happened to you, so I can now see why you pushed me away."

Did he think that? All this time he'd been here, she had pushed him away, but not because she blamed him. Although if she'd been honest, she did feel angry at him for taking her to Drew's house that night. Had she been subconsciously holding that against Tobias?

He glanced over at her, apprehension in his eyes. His expression went to stone. "You do blame me. You still don't want me to stay in Campton Creek, do you?"

They stood looking into each other's eyes, so many unspoken words between them. Everything went quiet and still, the trees calming. Even the birds seemed to settle and wait.

Finally, Josie gave in to what her heart already knew. "I think buying this farm is a fine idea, Tobias. You should stay here. You have a job and you have found a place to make your own. I don't have any right to stop you."

He finally pivoted to face her, the agony etched on his face now turning to relief and hope. "Are you certain sure?"

Josie wasn't sure of anything right now, but her heart seemed to know better than her mind. "I am certain sure."

He let out a breath. "*Gut*, because I gave your *bruder* a good-faith payment to hold it for me, and time is running out."

"You did what?" she asked, her head fuzzy with confusion. "You mean, all this time, Josiah and you cooked up a deal, thinking I'd finally cave?"

Tobias had the good grace to blush. "No. It's not like that."

"It sounds like that," she retorted, trying to decide if she should be extremely mad or very glad. The old, misguided Josie would have lashed out. Today, after everything they'd had to deal with, she couldn't muster up any anger toward her brother or this man. But she was a bit confused. "My own kin, lying to me."

"He did not lie. He withheld a business transaction."

Josie finally smiled, able to accept that she wasn't all that mad after all. "I will deal with Josiah when I get back home. Are you still staying for supper?"

"Am I still invited for supper?"

"Ja," she said, liking this new easiness surrounding them. But she knew the underlying problems were still there. "*Ja*, I think we should all stick together right now. Josiah will need a friend and…we all need you."

His expression changed and softened with relief. "Josie, do *you* need me?"

She wouldn't lie to him ever again. "I think I do, but I'm afraid. I need you to be patient with me, Tobias. I know it's asking a lot because you've already been through a lot. I left you, I wasn't honest with you, I pushed you away, and now you know the worst there is to know about me. And yet you're still here. I just need you to be patient."

"Josie," he said, taking her into his arms. "I am a very patient man. I'll talk to Josiah and get this house sale settled. Then I'm going to fill this place, piece by piece, with beautiful things so that if you do decide to move in here one day, you won't have any bad memories at all. I only want you to have good memories."

Josie's heart beat too fast. "What if I can't let go of those horrible memories? I have not had the best life and a lot of that was my doing."

"No, most of that was others doing things to hurt you. I am not one of those others. I'm Tobias. Your ToTo. The man who never forgot you. I'll be here, no matter what."

He tugged her into his arms and held her close. "I have missed you, Josie."

Josie allowed this small comfort. Tobias wouldn't leave her and he would never hurt her. He would wait for her. She had to cling to that.

Then she lifted up to stare at him. "You are not to blame, so don't go thinking that about yourself. I came out here to tell you that. I want you to understand."

Tobias looked bashful and unsure again. "I feel responsible, Josie. I was trying to be someone I could never be, and I left you while I trudged around that big house with Drew's friends. When I look back on it, I'm ashamed that they probably knew what was going on and lured me away. And I fell for that because my pride wanted to believe I was somebody important to them."

Seeing the raw torment in his eyes, Josie touched a hand to his face. "We have both changed and now we see the clear path. But we don't have to rush anymore, Tobias. We start over, in a million little ways."

His torment changed to mirth. "Now you sound like Bettye. She told me that is how I should win you back—with a million little ways."

Amazed, Josie took his hand and tugged him toward supper. "So you sent flowers and carved me the butterfly, and then our worlds fell apart again when Drew's parents showed up."

"*Ja*, but I have a lot of little things left to make you forgive me and…come back to me."

Josie shook her head. "That could take a while."

Then she amended, "There is nothing to forgive, Tobias. But I have to be sure. I've been hiding here so long, isolated and in fear, I'm not sure I can be the girl you fell in love with, ever again."

"As you said, we don't have to rush," he replied. "Except to supper. I am for sure starving."

Josie smiled at him. "This was a hard day. The worst. But you made it tolerable."

"That's why I'm here," he said, his tone and his expression turning serious. "To make up for everything that has come before."

When they got back to the house, Josiah had returned and washed up. He glanced toward them when they came in the back door. "Supper," he said, his tone almost angry.

Josie's mind whirled with a shaky anticipation mixed with a tentative contentment. She and Tobias had reached a crossroad of sorts, although there was still so much between them. Dinah had to come first. Josie would not lose her yet again.

Raesha and Naomi gathered them around the table and Raesha passed out roast-beef sandwiches on fresh sliced bread, as well as pickles and fresh tomatoes. Naomi served the potato salad from her wheelchair. Then she poured fresh cold tea into their glasses.

"Denke," Tobias said. "For letting me stay today and for supper tonight."

"You are *wilkum* anytime," Naomi replied. "Now let us pray."

Everyone bowed their heads in silence.

Josie knew what her prayers held. She wanted Dinah here and safe, and she told the Lord she'd show more love than she already had to her child. She also prayed that, somehow, Drew's parents would not press the issue of taking Dinah away. Then she asked the Lord to show her the way back to Tobias, with no guilt or regrets between them, so they could have the life they'd always planned, but here, together.

And then she prayed with all of her might that she'd be able to live in the house that had shaped her and changed her and still to this day frightened her.

How could she ever make that happen?

Tobias followed Abram into the workshop the next morning, his heart lighter now that he and Josie had gotten closer. It would be a long haul to bring her completely around, but at least she was willing to allow him back into her life.

"So how did it go yesterday?" Abram asked after he'd examined a cabinet they'd been sanding. Finding a rough spot, he picked up a sanding cloth and worked on the dark wood. "It was late when we heard you return. You must have gone to bed right after."

Tobias picked up a polish rag and started going over the wood so he could stain it and bring out the beautiful grain that reminded him of a tiger's stripes.

He nodded. "It was a hard day, watching Drew's parents with little Dinah. She is a precious child, and Josiah and Raesha have done a wonderful good job of taking care of her."

"But?"

Tobias dropped his rag. "But I see Drew in her and... I resent that."

"You resent what your friend did, or you resent the child?" Abram asked, his hand stilling on the wood.

"I resent and regret all of it. I was supposed to protect Josie from such awful things and I failed."

"Let's get some of that fresh coffee I smell," Abram suggested. "At least our craftsmen know how to make *gut* coffee, ain't so?"

Tobias followed him to the corner break room and took a cup of the hot brew. He wished he'd never mentioned his feelings, but he needed to vent to someone and Abram was a wise listener and counselor.

Abram wasn't about to let up, either. "You have much on your shoulders," he said, his voice low while the other workers laughed and went about their duties. "Too much. You need to remember *Gott* has a plan for each of us."

"I tell myself that," Tobias replied. "But I get impatient with whatever the good Lord has cooked up for me. Josie and I have lost a lot of time together already."

Abram stared into his coffee as if trying to see answers there. "I do not think He's cooked up anything. His timing is perfect, even when we veer off the path. If we stay the course in our faith, He will bring us back around again."

Tobias gave him a smile. "Josie and I did reach a truce of sorts. She has agreed to me buying the Fisher place."

"Well, there you go," Abram said before draining his coffee. "See, that's a good step in the right direction."

"It is," Tobias agreed. He took a couple of sips and then rose to get back to work. "I'm going to meet with Josiah today to get all the paperwork straight. But we are moving along."

"And Josie is okay with that, you said. So there is hope."

Tobias nodded. "She is okay with me buying the property, but we have a long way to go to get back where we were."

"If you marry, will she live in that house?"

"That's the part I'm not sure about," Tobias said, his gaze moving over the cabinet he needed to finish. The wood had started out rough and edged with splinters. Humans could be much the same. "I have to keep working on things with Josie, I think. We're polishing out the rough spots, and I hope one day, together, we'll both be healed."

"Now, that's the kind of attitude I like to hear," Abram said, slapping him gently on the back. "It will all work out for the *gut*, Tobias."

Tobias wanted to see that day. "I'd best get this polished and stained so it can dry properly before Nancy Henderson comes back wanting to load it on her truck."

"She is persistent and she has green money," Abram said, chuckling. "The *Englisch* do have their bright spots."

After they'd both settled into their routines, Tobias thought about all the changes in his life. He was so close to having what he wanted at last—a new home and being back with Josie.

But he feared she might not ever want to live in the house he was buying. She'd asked him to be patient and he would be, but had he pushed her too much, insisting he must live in the one place she'd tried to escape? Would it be a mistake to ask her to live there with him?

In *Gott*'s time, he reminded himself.

Meantime, he'd start courting her properly again, and he'd plan out next spring's crops so he could get his farmers' market up and running. Between work here and doing that on the side, he'd be a busy man. Josie might enjoy helping with the farmers' market. He'd build a strong shed out by the road and make it comfortable enough so they could both sit there and sell fresh produce. That would be nice.

Staying busy and saving up money between now and then would be his next goal. He wanted to make sure Josie had everything she'd need to start their new home together.

But he would never be too busy to forget how much he had missed Josie and how his insides boiled with anger each time he thought of how Drew had treated her.

He'd have to send up a lot of prayers to get past that image. Before he could even form a prayer, the furniture market's front door opened and Mary Zook peeked inside.

"Tobias, you're here. I'm so glad."

Chapter Twenty

Josie finished snapping the beans she'd gathered from the garden. She and Naomi would have beans and ham with fresh sliced tomatoes tonight for their dinner. They needed some quiet time.

It had been a week since the Beningtons had visited and, while the whole family had calmed down, Josie couldn't rest. She checked on Dinah all day long and took her for walks around the property, pointing out trees and flowers along the way.

Dinah loved to chatter and she absorbed new words easily. "Tree. Pine?"

"Pine is correct," Josie proudly told her this afternoon.

"Bidge," Dinah said, her hand waving toward the arched footbridge to the Fisher place.

"Bridge," Josie replied. "Bridge."

"Bidge. Go."

They'd walked across the footbridge over and over until finally Dinah had turned toward home because she wanted a drink of water.

Home. What if Dinah lost her home and had to go to

a new home far away? The thought of Dinah growing up in that huge, cold house where she'd been conceived in such a horrible way made Josie feel ill.

She didn't like having these disturbing flashbacks.

"What is wrong with you tonight?" Naomi asked. "I know you are concerned, as we all are, but I thought things were better with you and Tobias."

"Things are better," Josie said, heading to the sink to wash the beans and get them boiling in the pot. "Or at least I thought they were."

Rumors showed a different picture, however. Another thing for Josie to fret about.

"Child, come and tell me," Naomi said from her comfortable chair in the small living area.

Josie watched the water begin to boil. Then she dropped in the beans and seasoning, making sure the bits of ham she'd broken to flavor the beans covered the top.

After lowering the heat, she sat down across from Naomi. "Katy told me Mary Zook is bragging about how Tobias helped her design a side table for her mother. Apparently, she spent most of this week in and out of the shop, checking on the progress of the piece."

"I see," Naomi said with a soft smile. "Well, he is talented and he has to make money, so why does this bother you so?"

Josie stared across at Mammi, wondering what was going through her mind. "I don't mind him making furniture or money, but I do mind Mary Zook spending a lot of time with him. She's been after a husband since before I came back home."

"Oh, I see. So you don't want her to have the man who should be your husband, ain't so?"

Josie blinked and frowned at Naomi. "I didn't say that."

Naomi went back to her knitting. "No, you didn't say that at all. But your expression and the jealousy in your words told me that."

Josie got up to check the beans and slice the ham. "You are imagining things."

"I might be old and I can barely see what I'm knitting, but I know you still care deeply about Tobias."

"I will always care about him."

"So why are you worried about Mary Zook?"

Josie whirled, shame coloring her face. "Because she told Tobias she'd heard he was seeing a lot of me and then she asked him if he knew about me."

Naomi's teasing expression turned sour. "That young woman needs a good talking-to. She knows not to spread gossip."

"But it's true," Josie said. "It's true, and since I haven't heard from Tobias all week, I'm wondering if he sees how horrible it would be if he's with me."

Naomi tried to stand. "Bring me my chair."

"Neh," Josie said, thinking Naomi would make her hitch the buggy so they could go confront Mary. "I am okay. Tobias is free to talk to other people. It's just that I'll never be completely forgiven and this community will never completely forget."

Naomi settled back, her frown remaining. "You need to know that the people who count have accepted you back and you do not have anything to be ashamed of. You confessed before the church, and the bishop himself approved you living within our community. Mary Zook is just trying to stir up trouble because she is the jealous one. She knows you are loved and she knows what she's doing."

Josie was about to tell Naomi to calm herself when they heard a knock at the back door.

"That is probably my brother wondering if we're arguing. I've already had a talk with him about keeping it secret that Tobias had made a down payment on our old place."

"We never argue," Naomi said on a soft huff. "We heavily discuss. And besides, Josiah knows tonight is our alone dinner here at home. He's probably embarrassed that we found out about what he's done and he's come to apologize for keeping all of us, including his wife, in the dark."

"I'll just go and see." Josie hurried to the breezeway door and opened it wide, expecting to see Josiah or Raesha waiting.

Tobias stood there, looking uncomfortable and unsure.

Had he come to tell her he didn't want to be with her after all? His gaze shifted everywhere but on her.

"May I come in?" he asked when he finally did look at her, his eyes full of a mysterious light.

Josie glanced back at Naomi. "We're about to have supper."

"Let the man in," Naomi said with a wave of her hand. "And invite him to eat with us."

Josie moved aside, hoping Naomi wouldn't keep chattering. "Have you eaten?"

"I came straight here from work," Tobias replied. "I have my own buggy now. Abram helped me fix up an old one, and he loaned me a buggy horse he keeps in town to make deliveries."

"We are about to eat," Naomi said, hearing him. "Josie, turn down the beans and we'll fry up the ham after Tobias washes up. Take him out to the pump on the porch."

Josie took the hint and turned back toward the porch. "She can be bossy sometimes."

Tobias tried to hide the grin tugging at his mouth. "She wants us to have alone time, which is what I need right now."

Forgetting the pump and water, Josie whirled. "You came to tell me that you've changed your mind about everything, haven't you? You've come to your senses and you don't really want me in your life anymore?"

Tobias stepped back, drawing his head away so he could see her clearly. "Whatever gave you that idea?"

"Mary Zook," she said before she could stop herself. "She's telling everyone that she and you have been spending a lot of time together. And that you should stay away from me."

Tobias started laughing.

"You think that is funny?" Josie asked, an image of him laughing with Mary making her want to run away and get out of his sight. Or maybe throw cold water on him.

"I'm laughing because I've never seen you so worked up, not since I've been here. And I've seen you a lot of ways, Josie. Sad and upset, embarrassed and afraid, but not like this. You do care about me certain sure."

"I only care that you'll fall into Mary's trap. She wants a man, Tobias. Any man."

"Oh, so she's just flirting with me because she'll take any man who comes along?"

"That's not what I meant and you know it."

He tugged her close, his hands holding hers, his

eyes full of confidence and hope now. "So what do you mean?"

Josie tried to pull away. "Nothing. It's just she's gossiping about me, telling people you shouldn't be with me." Shrugging, she added, "Hearing that brings up all of the bad memories I've tried so hard to push away."

Tobias touched a hand to her cheek, his fingers rough from work but soft to the touch. His jaw muscles went tight, his eyes no longer full of teasing mirth. "This is why I came to see you. I heard what she'd said and, Josie, I set her straight about all of it."

Josie's heart went from hurting to rejoicing. "What did you tell her?"

"I told Mary Zook that I'd finished the little table she had to have for her *mamm*'s birthday and then I loaded it on her buggy for her. She gave me some freshly baked oatmeal cookies and I ate one while she smiled at me. Then I explained that I did not like people gossiping about you and that I came here because of you."

Josie took in a breath and put her hand over his on her cheek. "You said that to her?"

"*Ja*, and more." He grabbed her hand and brought it between them, putting it close to his heart. "I told her I know all about what you've been through and that I admire you even more than I did before. And then I said that one day I plan to marry you."

Josie felt his heart beating against her palm, her own pulse matching the steady rhythm. "You said all of that with a mouthful of oatmeal cookie?"

"I waited until I'd chewed that one, and I ate the second one after I'd explained things to her." He grinned, his nose touching Josie's. "She left in such a rush she almost slung that pretty little cabinet off into the gravel."

"She did not."

"She did," he said, leaning close. "I told you the truth. Mary Zook is not the woman for me, and I'm pretty sure she won't be gossiping about you ever again."

"Tobias," she said, pulling him close. "I do not deserve you."

"You're right," he replied as he leaned close. "You deserve way better than me."

She gave him a quick, shy kiss and then turned, taking him by the hand. His gaze on her told her he wanted the kiss to last longer, but someone might see them here. "Get cleaned up. I have to fry the ham."

"I'll set the table and help you," he replied. "Then your brother and I have some important business to take care of."

She whirled, her fingers on the doorknob. "You are buying the house."

He nodded. "Are you sure you want me to do that?"

"I am," she replied, her hidden fears tamped down for now. "I did give Josiah a hard time about keeping secrets from me, but he made a good point. If I'd known, I would have fought against both of you."

Tobias hurried to wash his hands and face, and grabbed a towel hanging on the hook next to the pump. "You don't have to fight anyone anymore, Josie. Remember that."

Josie wanted to remember that, but they might have one more big fight before they could finally work their way back to each other.

The Beningtons could return any day now. She was fiercely afraid of what they would demand from her family.

Chapter Twenty-One

Josiah smiled over at Tobias. "Looks like the Fisher farm belongs to you now, Tobias. I'll get this paperwork to Alisha Craig, and I'll take your check to the bank first thing tomorrow."

Tobias reached across the dining table to give Josiah a handshake. "A fourth up front, then monthly payments, and so on and so on, until I'll have you paid in full."

They'd discussed the plan and Josiah had agreed. Since no Realtor was involved, they could make their own rules, but Alisha had drawn up a simple contract that stated the terms of the transaction.

Now it was done.

"I know where you'll be living," Josiah replied after shaking his hand. "I'll come looking for my money if you miss a payment. But you're wise to pay on the installment plan rather than handing me the rest of your savings. Might need that for another day."

Josiah had to be referring to Josie. If they got married, Tobias wanted to have some money in the bank to get them going.

"A rainy day," Tobias replied, thinking of furniture and gardens and children. Would he and Josie have children? He hoped so.

Josiah nodded and gave Tobias a solemn glance. "Do you think Josie will live there with you?"

That was the one thing Tobias couldn't predict. "I do not know. I'd like to believe our love can overcome even the memories of that house, but I have wondered if I'm doing the right thing." Looking toward the door, he added, "She told me she wanted me to do this, but she did not say if *she* wanted this, too."

Josiah tugged at his beard. "It could be *gut* for her to start fresh there with new, happy memories. But I warn you—things need to go slow with Josie."

Tobias stared down at the typed words on the simple contract they'd agreed upon. "Or she might bolt and I'll lose her all over again."

"Ja," Josiah replied. "She did not want to return here, but…we are so glad she did."

They were alone in the kitchen of the main house. Raesha had taken Dinah and Daniel over to see Naomi and Josie while the men conducted business.

The quiet centered Tobias even as he was anxious to get on with his new life. "All I can do is hope that my love will see her through."

"Your love and the Lord's grace," Josiah replied. "Raesha and I had a lot to work through when I first returned here. Even before we realized we wanted to be together, she was willing to take Josie into her home. She did it for me and because she believed it was the right thing to do. It wasn't easy, loving Dinah and knowing her real mother would be close by. We've all worked hard to be a family, and we were doing fine."

Tobias looked down at the table. "Until I showed up, and then the Beningtons after that."

Josiah's smile was bittersweet. "You did throw a wrench into things, but I believe you are helping Josie to see that she is worthy of love. Her moods have improved now that she's accepted you being here."

"But?"

"But we always knew there was the possibility that the boy who did this might show up or try to make trouble one day. When we heard Drew had gone to prison, we all breathed a sigh of relief and Alisha did the right thing by getting in touch with him in prison on our behalf. As Alisha explained to the Beningtons in that first meeting, he immediately refused any claims on Dinah because he knew it would prove him guilty of what he'd done." Josiah shook his head. "Sometimes, I wish I'd never agreed to finding him and telling him he had a child. If we'd kept her a secret, we'd all be going on with our business and raising Dinah as we'd planned."

Tobias could see the apprehension in Josiah's eyes. "I understand that feeling. Drew committed a crime, the worst kind of assault on a woman, but now he wants to make restitution before he dies. So that means even though the law is on our side, his parents could make demands simply because they have the means and they want their grandchild with them."

"Just another wrinkle to get through," Josiah said. "So if you truly love my sister, you'll need to be strong for her. If something happens and we have to give Dinah to them, we will all be devastated, but Josie will not recover. And then we'll lose her forever."

"I'm not going anywhere," Tobias said, waving the

paper. "This should prove that. If Josie can't marry me, I will still be here, waiting for her to change her mind."

Josiah studied Tobias for a moment. "Then I wish you well with your new home, Tobias."

They shook hands again, then walked over to the *grossmammi haus* together. Josiah turned to Tobias when they reached the door. "Are you coming in to share the news?"

Tobias nodded. "I want to talk to Josie before I head back to Abram's house."

He needed to know how she really felt about this.

Josie glanced up when the men entered. While Daniel and Dinah had played with some wooden blocks, Raesha and Naomi had grilled her about Tobias buying the farm.

"I'm fine with it," she'd told them earlier. "He needs a place to live and he wants to grow produce to sell up on the road. That and working with Abram will keep him busy."

They'd chatted a while about the merits of hard work. Tobias had never been afraid of doing what needed to be done. He went after what he wanted in life, his plans solid and thought-out. Not like Josie, with just dreams and nothing solid to count on.

"And where do you fit in?" Raesha had asked, her smile serene while she kept one eye on the *kinder*.

"I don't know yet," Josie had admitted. "I am glad that Tobias knows the truth now, but we have so much to work through and many decisions to make."

The door had opened before they could continue, leaving Raesha and Naomi giving her concerned glances.

"The paperwork is complete," Tobias said with a smile, his gaze moving over Josie. "I now own the land across the footbridge."

Josie's heart did that quick jump of fear that always happened when she thought about her old home. She'd gone after Tobias the other day, but she'd been so intent on soothing him that her heart had steadied before she even realized where they were.

Then she remembered him finding her there on the porch a few days ago and holding her while she cried. Remembered how she'd run over there when Josiah had first gone to talk to Tobias about buying the place. What a broken mess she'd been that day, drenched from the rain and terrified of seeing Tobias up close.

But, looking back, she could see the pattern that linked her to the Fisher house.

After she'd been released from the hospital and had been back here for a while, afraid that she'd lose Dinah again, she'd taken Dinah to the old place to hide out. Josiah had found her in an upstairs bedroom. So much had changed since the night Josiah had found her inside the house, holding her baby close.

Sometimes she truly believed *Gott* had led her to leave Dinah with the Bawell women. This was where Dinah belonged. Josie belonged here now, too. Moving across the way would be like taking an ocean voyage.

No. The place could not be a threat to her anymore. She had to overcome her memories and her fears. Maybe she'd be able to handle all of it, after all, with Tobias by her side.

"Josie?"

She looked up to find her brother and Tobias staring at her. "What?"

"I asked if you are sure about this," Josiah said, his gaze tender.

"I will be fine," she said. "The worst is over. Tobias knows my secrets and he's still here. It will be nice having him next door."

Tobias shifted on his brogans. "Josie, can we take a walk and talk?"

She stood and looked toward Raesha and Naomi. They both inclined their heads.

Dinah had been playing with blocks in the corner, but she jumped up, teetering. "Go walk."

"Neh," Raesha said, grabbing her up to tickle her tummy. "Go bathe."

"Walk with ToTo," Dinah retorted, pointing a chubby finger at Tobias.

"Go get bath," Josiah replied with a big grin. "Like a fish." He began to make bubble sounds and pretend he was swimming.

Distracted by his antics, Dinah stopped fretting long enough for Tobias and Josie to slip out onto the porch.

The air was fresh with the gloaming, but the sun hadn't gone all the way down. A hint of coolness filled the warm dusk, its gentle wind flowing across Josie's face.

"Will you walk with me over to the house?" Tobias asked, his tone full of hope.

Josie glanced at the home she'd once lived in. This was it, then. Time for her to see if she could do this.

"Josie?"

She glanced from Tobias to the property he had just bought. The house glowed white, with a shimmering sheen of creamy sunshine covering it in the same way it had the night she'd first seen Tobias there. Looking at it now, she thought it looked new and shiny and ready for someone to make it a real home.

"Who would ever dream you'd come here and own this house," she said. "Who would ever dream we'd be standing here together."

"I dreamed it," he said, taking her hand. "I dreamed it night and day from the time you left me until now. But the dream isn't complete, is it?"

Josie's gaze moved from him to the house. Now that this was real and he was here to stay, planning to live over there, her world shifted yet again and settled back, her heart thudding and jumping. *Help me, Lord.*

Would she be able to do this? Why did the thing she'd longed for the most still seem just aside of her grasp. Could she find the strength to start a new life here with Tobias, finally?

Tobias waited her out. He'd do that. He'd wait. But would that be fair to him? To have to wait on her to decide? To have to wait on her to change? To wait on whether they'd lose Dinah or not?

"How long are you willing to do this, Tobias?"

He looked confused and defeated. "Do what?"

"Wait on me. You waited back in Kentucky and I never returned. Now you've bought this house and you'll wait for me even longer? Even if I can't set foot back inside that house? Even if we lose Dinah?"

Tobias tugged her close, his eyes washing her with the same warmth that had settled over the house. "Walk with me, Josie."

How could she resist him? He'd always been the one. She loved him with a deep, abiding love, but a love she'd held close like a secret, in the same way she held the wooden treasures he'd carved for her close to her heart each night before she went to sleep. The little horse and the beautiful butterfly. Her treasures from this man, the wood warming from her touch in the same way she felt safe and warm whenever he touched her.

He must have sensed the conflict warring in her soul. "You have to know that from now on, I will protect you, I will cover you, I will take care of you," he said, his tone soft and husky. "I wasn't there before when you needed me the most, but I am here now and I will make sure no one ever hurts you again."

She stopped him when they reached the footbridge. "And what about you, Tobias? Who will hold you and protect you? I wasn't there when you needed me, either, but I hope I can make that up to you now." Shaking her head, she looked down at her sneakers. "I do not want to hurt you again, ever."

"I hope that, too, but having you with me now makes up for you having to go away before," he said. "Look, Josie. Look at us. Here we are on the bridge between your world and mine. I want you in mine and I'm willing to wait for that to happen."

Then he leaned toward her and kissed her, a soft touch of his lips to hers. Josie's heart sighed as she held to him, the memory of their time together coming back in a sweet flow of love and need. For a moment, the old doubts crowded in and the tormented memories tried to take over. Her shame, her pain and the realization that she'd convinced herself that she could never marry him almost stopped her in her tracks. She wanted to turn and go, but she had to stop running, didn't she?

When he pulled away, she stared into his eyes and mustered up her courage. "Why don't we go and look at the house before it gets too dark."

Tobias smiled and took her hand.

Josie held her breath, said her prayers and promised herself she would never let this man down again. Crossing this bridge with Tobias was all she'd ever wanted, and maybe it was fitting that they should want to make a home together here in this place.

Did *Gott* want this to be their home? Or were they trying to change a past that would never leave them alone or let them forget?

She stopped in the yard, the shadows coming toward her like creeping memories, her hand tight inside of Tobias's. Josie took deep breaths, smelled the scents of honeysuckle and fresh grass, of water and earth, of hope and peace, felt the last of the sun shining on her face.

She closed her eyes and breathed it all in. This moment, if she could just keep this moment.

"Josie?"

She opened her eyes and saw Tobias there. "I'll be all right. I have you back and we'll take the rest as it comes."

"You don't have to go inside tonight," he replied. "You're right. For now, this is enough."

Then he tugged her close and told her about his dreams for this place.

And for once, Josie didn't even notice the darkness.

Chapter Twenty-Two

Josie could almost relax now.

It was easy to see her future. While Tobias had not officially asked her to marry him, they were becoming closer every day. He'd been by several times to move things into the Fisher house. Now that he had a serviceable buggy, he'd bought a strong quarter horse to get him around and to help him clear the land behind the house.

Today she watched from her perch on the breezeway as Tobias and several men from the community, including her brother and Abram, helped him to haul logs from some trees they'd cut down on the back corner of the property. Abram wanted to pick the best of the hardwood, of course. The rest would be used for firewood or shredded into mulch that Mr. Hartford would sell at the general store.

Josie took a sip of her lemonade and watched as the sun began its descent toward the west. She'd worked in the hat shop most of yesterday and today. Long days, but she always enjoyed learning how to steam and press the rims and ribbons to make the straw summer hats that the Amish men wore to work. Raesha had started the seamstresses to making prayer *kapps*, too. They now made them in both white and black sturdy silk or lightweight organdy and muslin, and shipped them out on a daily basis.

If she and Tobias did marry, she hoped Raesha would let her work part-time to earn some household money. *If.*

Such a tiny word for so many things in life. Raesha had sent her home while she finished up some paperwork. When Dinah had begged to come with her, Josie had put her down for a nap inside the main house and left the back door open so she could hear her. Daniel was sleeping in the tiny office behind the front desk of the hat shop.

That gave Josie a few moments to watch the men at work, their figures tiny since they were far from the Fisher house.

When she heard a car roaring up the dirt-and-gravel lane, her heart stilled, frozen against her ribs. Josie hopped up and saw the Beningtons getting out of a fancy taxi.

They were coming toward the house.

She ran inside the *grossmammi haus* to alert Naomi.

"They're back," she said, out of breath.

"Who?" Naomi asked from where she sat reading the local paper.

"Drew's parents," Josie said. "Raesha is still at the hat shop. I'll go and check on Dinah."

Naomi nodded. "Bring her here with us."

"I have to warn Raesha," Josie said, her mind reeling. They were back for a reason. They wanted Dinah.

"Where is Josiah?"

"With Tobias and the others, clearing the land out beyond the house."

Naomi glanced at the door. "He should be here."

"I'll take Dinah and try to let Raesha know they are here."

She rushed into the room where Dinah sat playing in the crib. "JoJo."

Josie picked up the child and kissed her cheek. "JoJo is here."

Then she hurried to the hat shop, surprising the seamstresses and the men working the steam machines when she entered through the back door. When she reached the door between the workroom and the front shop, she saw Pamela and Theodore through the partially opened door, already talking to Raesha.

Carefully opening the swinging door an inch, she listened.

"We just want her to see her father," Pamela was saying, tears in her eyes. "Drew would like to see her before it's too late. Please, let us have some time with her and our son together."

"You're asking me to hand over my child?" Raesha said, shaking her head. "Did your lawyers tell you to do this?"

"No," Theodore replied. "Drew asked us. We're trying to avoid lawyers."

They wanted to take Dinah to see Drew. No, that would put trauma in Dinah's mind and confuse her. No.

Raesha glanced back, probably concerned about Daniel. Josie and Dinah were hidden from sight and the hum of the work machines drowned out Dinah's chatters.

Josie didn't stop to think. She whirled and went back

out the way she'd come and then took off walking as fast as she could.

She went past the *grossmammi haus* and hurried to the main house. After gathering food and clothing, she left by the front door, careful to stay out of sight, Dinah giggling as if they were on a grand adventure.

She had to keep Dinah away from Drew's parents. If they took Dinah all the way to Kentucky, she might not ever see her daughter again.

"Go walk," Dinah said, squirming to get down.

"It's all right," Josie said on a winded whisper. "I have to hold you, sweetheart."

"Walk," Dinah said on a stern demand.

They made it to the road, but she stayed near the tree line, darting from tree to tree so no one would notice them. When she reached the drive to the Fisher place, Josie stopped.

Where should she take Dinah?

The men were finishing for the day when Tobias heard someone shouting.

He turned to find Raesha rushing across the footbridge, her arms waving in the air.

"Josiah," he called, pointing.

All of the men stopped what they were doing and hurried from the copse of trees they'd been harvesting to run back toward the Fisher house.

"What's wrong?" Josiah asked as he grabbed Raesha by her arms.

"The Beningtons came again. They want to take Dinah to Kentucky to be with Drew until…until he passes. I told them I'd have to talk to you and I was worried about Josie."

"Where is she?"

Raesha gulped a breath. "I don't know. Drew's parents came around to the hat shop and we talked for a while. Then Daniel woke, and I brought him home and went to check on Josie. Naomi said she had gone to get Dinah up and had not returned."

Josiah's eyes filled with fear and concern. "What do you mean?"

"I can't find Josie and Dinah," Raesha said. "They are gone."

Tobias glanced around. They'd all been so occupied with getting these trees down they hadn't noticed anything unusual going on at the Bawell place or back at the house here. But his instincts kicked in.

Looking toward his house off in the distance, he turned to Raesha. "Gone?"

Raesha's eyes watered, tears streaming down her face. "I don't know. The Beningtons finally left, but they said they'd be back. Do you think they had someone take Dinah while they were talking to me? Maybe Josie went after them somehow?"

Josiah took Raesha into his arms. "We will find them."

Tobias tugged at his hat and searched the countryside. "Surely they wouldn't do that. Did they have a court order to take Dinah?"

Raesha shook her head. "They only wanted to know if we'd allow it and I said no. But I did tell them we would discuss this. We can't let them take her without one of us with her, if we agree to this at all."

"We won't let that happen," Josiah said. "Go back and stay with Daniel and Naomi. We will search for Dinah and Josie. I'll call Nathan, too. He'll get to the bottom of this."

Tobias turned to the other men. "We need to call it a day."

Abram nodded. "We'll help you look for the *bobbeli*. But we should hurry. The sun will go down soon."

"And Josie," Tobias replied. "I'm going to find her. I have a feeling that wherever Josie is, Dinah will be with her."

"Walk," Dinah said, her bare feet pattering on the wooden floor.

"We did walk," Josie replied, wishing she'd thought this through a little better. "But we need to get out of here, don't we?"

She'd panicked, no doubt. The first panic attack she'd had in a long time. But the thought of those people taking Dinah away had made all of Josie's rational thoughts go right out of her frazzled mind. She'd done what she had to do.

She'd removed Dinah from the situation.

Only once she had Dinah, they didn't have time to grab anything much to travel with. So she'd come here, where she'd wait until dark, and then they'd sneak out. She'd only had time to grab some snack food and a change of clothes for Dinah.

Josie sank down against the wall. "Dinah, I've made a big mistake."

Dinah turned and slanted her head. Then she ran into Josie's arms. "Walk?"

"No more walk," Josie said. "We have to wait until dark. We have to stay here and then we walk—somewhere."

"Go," Dinah said, heading toward the closed door. "Go home."

Josie's eyes filled with tears. "I don't know where home is anymore."

She looked around her and let the tears flow. Dinah saw her crying and toddled back to her.

Her big eyes wide, the little girl's chubby fingers wiped Josie's face. "Boo-boo."

"A big boo-boo," Josie said, the tears falling freely now. Taking Dinah into her arms, she said, "You know I love you. So much."

"So muk," Dinah echoed, her fingers warm against Josie's face. Then Dinah kissed her with a big smack. "No boo-boo."

Josie wrapped her arms around her daughter, every fiber of her mother's heart wanting to protect this child from all the ugliness of the world out there. "Safe, Dinah," she whispered. "I have to keep you safe."

And the only way to do that was to take Dinah back home, where she had people to protect her.

Wiping her eyes, Josie heaved a breath and stood. Then she heard footsteps coming up the stairs.

Someone had figured out where they were.

Josie held Dinah and realized there was no way out anyway.

Tobias opened the door to the room that used to be Josie's bedroom, the same room where she'd brought her baby once before.

"I had a feeling," he said, a tired smile moving over his face. "Everyone scattered, searching for you two, but I just knew you'd come here first."

Josie tried to speak. Dinah looked at her and then at Tobias. "JoJo cry."

Tobias rushed across the room and held them both close, his own eyes wet with tears. "JoJo is safe now, Dinah. And so are you."

* * *

Two days later, Josie and Tobias sat with the Beningtons at their home in Kentucky. Josie remembered the large paneled den with the big fireplace. Today the room was cool with air-conditioning, and a big square swimming pool shimmered blue just beyond the floor-to-ceiling windows and doors covering one wall.

A hospital bed had been placed in the corner, near a full bathroom. And in that bed lay Drew Benington.

She looked back from the beautiful gardens and stared at Drew. "You've seen her," she said, referring to Dinah. "We have to go back home tomorrow."

Drew nodded, barely able to speak, his eyes on the little girl sitting on a plush floral rug, playing with a teddy bear her grandparents had given her.

"She is so beautiful, Josie."

Tobias stared at his friend and then gave Josie a reassuring look. "She is in good hands, Drew. She is well loved."

Drew nodded, his once thick blond hair gone, his once healthy physique now shriveled. "I need you both to forgive me. I am so sorry. So very sorry. I'm not asking because I'm dying. I'm telling you this for Dinah's sake. Take care of her, and… I want you both to be happy."

Josie swallowed all the pain and hatred she'd felt for this man, her emotions pouring over her with a soothing release. She had to forgive. That was the Amish way. She and Tobias had talked about this on the long ride here in Nathan's SUV. He'd insisted on driving them to Kentucky, because his job was to protect his clients.

They had decided they could tolerate this visit only by forgiving Drew. He had confessed, he had asked for forgiveness and he was dying. What more could he suffer?

Facing the man who had assaulted her had been the most difficult thing Josie had ever done, but with Tobias by her side, she was at peace. At last.

They sat for a while longer, and then, after leaving Drew sleeping, they moved to the front hallway with his parents.

"We can never thank you enough," Pamela said. "We understand how difficult this has been, but once he saw her picture, he wanted to see her."

Josie refrained from what she wanted to say. "Dinah won't remember much about this, but this was the only way I could find peace, the same peace Drew is seeking. I forgive your son for what he did. I love my child, and my brother and Raesha love her dearly, too."

Tobias held Dinah and stood with Josie. "I love this one, too," he said, smiling at Dinah. "And I pray you will respect the terms Alisha came up with for us."

"We will abide by the terms," Theodore said. "We promised Drew we would."

They would get to visit Dinah several times a year, but Dinah would never know they were her paternal grandparents.

They'd offered money to help, which Josiah and Raesha had turned down.

"If you ever need anything," Theodore said again.

"*Denke*," Josie replied, "but you have given us the only thing we need. Dinah is ours and that now includes both of you. We are thankful that we were able to work things out."

Pamela kissed Dinah and then hugged Josie. "We will never forget what you've given to us, either."

They hurried to the sleek SUV and got Dinah tucked into the car seat between them in the back. As the vehicle pulled out of the circular driveway of the big brick house, Josie took one last look before she turned and smiled at Tobias.

"It's over," he said, his eyes full of love and hope. "Now we can start our new life together."

Drew died a week later.

Tobias came and told them on Sunday.

"Walk with me," he said to Josie after they'd all sat silent with their prayers.

She didn't hesitate. He guided her toward the house. Already it had changed. He'd built two rocking chairs and placed them on the front porch. Then he'd added a swing in her favorite corner spot with the view. Jewel had helped him pick out colorful potted plants for the porch.

He took Josie to the swing. "Will you sit with me?"

She laughed. "*Ja,* of course."

Tobias took her hand. "Josie, I love you and I want to marry you. Before you answer, I need to know one thing."

Her heart couldn't take much more. Had she done something wrong again? "What?"

"Will you be able to live here with me? Because if you cannot, I will sell this place and find us another house. Abram says there is a big farm for sale near his place."

Josie put a finger to his lips, her heart full of love.

"Tobias, I spent about four hours in this house last week with Dinah. She prattled and played while I worried. But I prayed, too. I prayed so hard, and I thought of you and me and how long it's taken us to find each other again." Heaving a deep breath, she said, "I could see it all so clearly sitting in the room I used to sleep in. The soul of a house is only as good as the people who live there. I lived in this house and grew up in this house, but I lost my soul when my parents died."

"So you don't want to be here?"

She looked at the man she loved and held back tears. "I didn't want to be here back then, but wherever you are, that is my home. I will marry you and I will make this our home. It will be full of love and children, and we have Dinah right across the way. It is enough. More than enough. This will be a fine home, and… I think my *mamm* will know I am safe here now. With you."

"Will I be enough?" he asked, his arms pulling her close.

"Always," she whispered, kissing his face with feathery little smacks. "More than enough. I love you. I'll always love you."

Tobias kissed her, and then he guided her to the front door. After opening it, he lifted her in his arms and took her inside.

"*Wilkum* home, Josie."

Josie smiled and kissed him again. Then she looked around and saw clusters of sunflowers in various vases all over the big living room. "How?"

Tobias laughed. "Jewel knows a lot of people who know how to get sunflowers shipped out early."

Josie touched her hand to his jaw. "I love Jewel. And I love you."

Tobias kissed her, and then together they lit the lamps and toured their new home while the setting sun shot rays of creamy-golden light through the windows, the kind of light that banished the darkness forever and washed their newfound love in the sweet grace of God.

* * * * *

"Are you okay?" Stone asked, tightening his hold around
her waist and gripping one of her hands.

"I— Yes." She didn't have time to explain to Stone
why this had nothing to do with her sore ankle, nor why
avalanches were her worst nightmare and that was the
real reason why she'd suddenly swayed in his arms.

Not when there was work to be done. There were
people in Holden Springs who needed help, and she knew
she should be there.

Tugger whined and pressed against her leg as he'd
been taught to do as a therapy dog. He could tell her heart
rate had increased and her pulse was pounding in her ears,
even if she didn't show it in her expression, although
there was probably that, too. The dog was responding to
cues most humans couldn't see, and Felicity reached out
and absently ran a hand between Tugger's ears to steady
her insides.

"Have they set up a temporary disaster shelter yet?"
she asked.

"Yes. At Holden High School," her sister said.
"They're using the cafeteria and the gym, I think. I'd go
myself except I have clients in the middle of service dog

training back at the center. Do you mind taking Tugger and heading out there?"

Felicity did mind. More than anyone would ever know, because she never talked about it, not even to her siblings. But now was not the time to give in to those feelings. She could cry into her pillow later when she was alone and the people of Holden Springs were safe.

"I'll take Tugger." She nodded. "And Dandy, too," she said, referring to a young black Labrador retriever who was part of the therapy dog program.

"I can tag along, if there's anything I can do to assist," Stone said. "That way you'll have an extra person for the dogs."

Felicity was going to decline, but Ruby spoke up first. "Thank you, Stone. They need all the help they can get. From what I hear, there are a lot of families who were suddenly evacuated from their homes."

"It's settled, then," Stone said. "I'm going with you."

Felicity didn't feel settled. The last thing she needed was Stone alongside her. It would distract her from her real work.

She sighed deeply.

A bruised ankle.

Stone's unnerving presence.

And now an avalanche.

Could things get any worse?

Don't miss
Their Unbreakable Bond by Deb Kastner,
available January 2022 wherever
Love Inspired books and ebooks are sold.

LoveInspired.com

IF YOU ENJOYED THIS BOOK, DON'T MISS NEW EXTENDED-LENGTH NOVELS FROM LOVE INSPIRED!

In addition to the Love Inspired books you know and love, we're excited to introduce even more uplifting stories in a longer format, with more inspiring fresh starts and page-turning thrills!

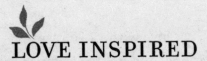

LOVE INSPIRED

Stories to uplift and inspire.

Fall in love with Love Inspired—inspirational and uplifting stories of faith and hope. Find strength and comfort in the bonds of friendship and community. Revel in the warmth of possibility, and the promise of new beginnings.

LOOK FOR THESE LOVE INSPIRED TITLES ONLINE AND IN THE BOOK DEPARTMENT OF YOUR FAVORITE RETAILER!

LITRADE1221

LOVE INSPIRED

Stories to uplift and inspire

Fall in love with Love Inspired—
inspirational and uplifting stories of faith
and hope. Find strength and comfort in
the bonds of friendship and community.
Revel in the warmth of possibility and the
promise of new beginnings.

Sign up for the Love Inspired newsletter
at **LoveInspired.com** to be the first
to find out about upcoming titles,
special promotions and exclusive content.
